The Night of Morningstar

Peter O'Donnell

THE MYSTERIOUS PRESS • New York

The Mysterious Press, 129 West 56th Street, New York, N.Y. 10019

This Mysterious Press Edition is published by arrangement with
Souvenir Press Ltd, 43 Great Russell Street, London WC1B 3PA

Printed in the United States of America

First Printing: June 1987

10 9 8 7 6 5 4 3 2 1

Library of Congress Cataloging-in-Publication Data

O'Donnell, Peter.
  The night of morningstar.

  I. Title.
PR6029.D55N5   1987   823'.914   86-62782
ISBN 0-89296-222-4

Also by
Peter O'Donnell

MODESTY BLAISE
SABRE TOOTH
I, LUCIFER
A TASTE FOR DEATH
THE IMPOSSIBLE VIRGIN
THE SILVER MISTRESS
LAST DAY IN LIMBO
XANADU TALISMAN
DRAGON'S CLAW
DEAD MAN'S HANDLE
PIECES OF MODESTY

One

GARCIA was adjusting his tie when he heard the expected peep of the Mercedes horn. He put on the jacket of his pale grey suit, set the alarms, locked his flat, and went down into the street that ran north to Boulevard Mohammed-Cinq. Willie Garvin leaned across, opened the passenger door of the grey 450SL, and said, "Morning, Rafael."

"Thanks, Willie." Garcia climbed in and leaned back with a gentle sigh. "Am I getting old, do you think?"

Willie looked at him. "How old d'you feel?"

"I am not sure. But in the apartment next to mine lives a beautiful girl and a wealthy young lawyer."

"I know. We vetted them, and they're legitimate. So?"

"I saw them going in last night. You know. Laughing, eager for each other, he with his arm about her. But I was not envious of him. I did not even speculate as to what they would soon be doing together."

Willie wagged his head.

> ". . . What that is, 'oo can tell?
> But I believe it was no more
> Than thou and I 'ave done before
> With Bridget and with Nell."

Garcia frowned. "I don't remember them. Nell, you say?"

"It's the last lines of a poem, Rafa, you dope." Willie switched on the engine.

"Ah." Garcia thought about it. "Yes, I see now."

"And don't worry about failing to speculate on the couple next door. It just means you're not becoming a dirty old man."

"At my age, the idea has its attraction."

Willie smiled. The car moved off, shortly turning left to join the traffic moving west towards the centre of Tangier. After a few moments Garcia said, "When did Mam'selle tell you she was planning to wind up *The Network*?"

"About a month ago." There was a hint of apology in Willie Garvin's voice.

Garcia made a small dismissive gesture with a well kept hand. "It's all right, I don't mind."

"I just thought . . . well, you've been with 'er longer than anyone."

"Yes, by God, that is something. But I am glad she did not tell me till yesterday. With the Amsterdam negotiations to complete, I would not have wanted such a distraction on my mind, and she knew that. Look, Willie. Anything she does, any time, is good with me. That is how it has always been."

"Sure." Willie halted for traffic lights and glanced with affection at the man beside him, a man with a square brown face, thick greying hair, and a body now putting on a little fat.

Garcia said, "Ten years ago, what am I? I am number three in a smalltime mob here. Now I am top man with you in *The Network* and I have enough money to last me three lifetimes." He was silent for a moment, remembering. "Do you know how it was in those beginning days?"

Willie eased the car forward, crawling in the heavy morning traffic. "She doesn't talk much about the past, but I've picked up bits 'ere and there. I know she came out of the desert when she was about seventeen, as near as she can guess, and she got a job working in a casino run by the Louche gang."

Garcia nodded. "It was a time of gang war. They shot Louche and his number two. It was finish for us all, we thought, if we did not scatter and disappear. But then this young girl, with black hair and eyes as old as the eyes of God, she spoke words of fire, whipping us with them, calling us spineless sheep." He chuckled suddenly. "She was not yet fully grown then, and quite skinny. La Roche got mad and tried to slap her down, but she was quick as a snake. Dropped him with a kick in the balls."

Willie grinned. They were in Place de France now and traffic was picking up speed, but he kept a leisurely pace. They would be in plenty of time for the meeting she had called that morning in the big office suite above the Banque Populaire de Malaurak. He said, "That must've been before she was combat trained, but she's got natural speed."

"It was well before," Garcia agreed. "She did not go to Cambodia to train under Saragam until almost two years later." He chuckled again. "That was just before she bought a certain Englishman out of jail in an adjoining country, and put him to the test before taking him into *The Network*."

"I know that bit," said Willie.

"Of course. Well, like I was telling you, she picked up the pieces of the Louche mob, and she put some courage into us. When the hit-men came to clean up, we were ready with the tricks she had devised." Garcia rolled his eyes upward. "My God, when I think of all her tricks over the years. So there are five men, and when they come to the casino they find only a young girl, very frightened. She tells them we are holed up in one of the rooms above, and we are bad people, and she hates us, so she tells them they can come to the room by two ways, a staircase at the front and a smaller one at the back, which is true."

Garcia nodded solemnly. "It is perfectly true, and she takes two of the men to show them the back way, but when they are on the stairs she turns and – *pam! pam!* They finish at the bottom, one with a broken arm, and she has both their guns. She tells Krolli to watch them while she runs back to the front to warn the three men there to be careful that nobody fires down at them through a skylight in the landing passage. This means they must crouch together in a very short piece of passage while their two friends at the back are checking the roof, so they believe."

Garcia began to shake with silent laughter. When he could continue he said, "But we have worked five hours to her orders, cutting away the floorboards and the joists and the ceiling below, then replacing the boards in one piece, like the trap of a gallows. You get it, Willie?"

"Resting on a ledge at one end, and a vertical prop the other end?"

"So." Garcia beamed. "I knocked the prop away myself with a sledgehammer, and down they came with five of us waiting for them in the passage below." He leaned back with a little sigh. "That was the beginning. Then for half a year was fought the war of the four gangs. It was not easy, Willie. Somehow, after that first day, I knew she would win, but it was not easy. Some of the men quit. Two were killed. But at the end there was only one gang, and from this came *The Network*. In two years we controlled eight areas covering the whole Mediterranean shore. Then she established links in the Americas and the Far East, and always, from the beginning, I was her number two."

"You earned it." Willie slowed for the turn at the end of Rue de Belgique. "You backed 'er when it looked like suicide. You and Krolli and Nedic. She's told me that."

Garcia lifted his shoulders slightly. "I could see the . . ." He groped for a word. "The force. I could see the force in her, Willie. Strange to say, it is something we did not speak about among ourselves, but I think the others saw what I saw."

"I can imagine." Willie's voice was soft. "When I got back from Hong Kong after running that test mission she sent me on, I was scared stiff she might not accept me for *The Network*." He glanced at his friend. "And scared you might speak against me."

Garcia shook his head. "I could see you were troubled about what I would say, but she always picked her own people."

"I didn't know that then. Anyway, you're a decent old sod, Rafa, so thanks. The way she moved me up the ladder, you could easily 'ave turned nasty with me."

"Willie, Willie my friend, I am fifty-seven years old. When she found you and gave you your chance I was already fifty-one. Too old for the job, and afraid that soon I would fail her in some important operation. From the beginning I thought you might be the one I was hoping for, and after six months I knew it. I knew that you would become her right arm in a way that I could never be, and I was glad as hell, Willie. You know something? I had already spoken to Mam'selle about retirement, but when she put you to run in tandem with me I was glad to stay on. It was good to have a younger man take over as ramrod in the field operations.

Just what she needed. Just what *I* needed, by God."

"Well . . . it worked out all right." Willie scratched his cheek speculatively. "It's going to feel weird when we all split up."

"She tells me it will take three months," said Garcia. "There is much to be made tidy. Area heads will be permitted to take over their own areas if they wish." He grimaced and shook his head. "Without her they will lose *The Network* style, and things will quickly go wrong. Better to retire."

"That's what you'll do?"

"Of course. I will go home to Uruguay, to San Tremino where I was born. I left there without a peso and I will go back with a million dollars. Not bad, Willie."

"Crime pays all right."

"You also will retire?"

Willie nodded. "The criminal classes aren't what they used to be. Villains 'aven't got the same discrimination these days. They've turned vicious. Time I left the profession."

"What you say is right. I am thankful Mam'selle has decided to make an end of it. This last year we have spent more time dealing with such people than in our own operations."

"We usually come out with a profit when we break up a vice mob."

'True. But that is not our job. Inspector Hassan has mentioned to me that he does not approve of a private police force."

Willie laughed. "We're not within a mile of that. And even if he doesn't like the principle, he's more than 'appy with the results."

Garcia looked at his watch. After a moment he said, "Before she spoke to me yesterday about the close-down I was going to ask your opinion of The Graduate now he has completed his three months of training, but it hardly matters now."

"It might. The Princess aims to run one or two cleaning-up operations."

Garcia smiled to himself. Willie Garvin alone had the sanction to address Modesty Blaise as Princess. It was unthinkable for anyone else to do so, but Willie was very special indeed, more than a trusted lieutenant, more than a friend or courtier; certainly not a lover, yet closer to that unfathomable young woman who ruled

The Network than most husbands to their wives. A strange relationship, almost impossible to comprehend, yet one which Garcia found peculiarly pleasing.

He said, "So what is your opinion of The Graduate?"

Willie turned into the car park at the rear of the bank, ran the car into his reserved space, and switched off. Garcia was speaking of Hugh Oberon, who had been recommended for recruitment by the head of the Riviera area. Oberon was of good family, Anglo Irish, and had graduated from Oxford with a degree in Modern Languages. His dossier stated that he claimed to have acquired a large contempt for academics during his years at University. A long sabbatical when he came down, during which he travelled widely, persuaded him that crime was the only business likely to provide him with sufficient material reward plus the excitement for which he had developed a craving. Theft was his main field of endeavour. He had worked both solo and with a gang, and had once put together a small organisation of his own. This had failed in its second operation, and Hugh Oberon had been lucky to serve only a year in a French gaol. After his release he had worked freelance for whoever could use him until being picked out as a possible recruit for *The Network* and sent to Tangier.

Willie said, "He's the best man we've ever 'ad, according to the test results. That rare thing, the brilliant all-rounder. I took 'im through the combat tests meself, and I was a bit relieved to come out of it with me 'ead facing the right way."

"I think like you that he is something special," Garcia agreed. "He could perhaps be another Willie Garvin."

Willie sighed. "Maybe that's why I can't stand 'im."

Garcia shook his head. "No. I spoke wrongly just now. He could have been another Garvin, but it is too late. He has gone the wrong way." Garcia lifted a hand and wobbled it with spread fingers in a balancing movement. "It is too late. Where you had confidence, he has conceit. Where you had judgment, he has arrogance. Where you had respect for Mam'selle, he has envy. I think he is one of the new kind of criminal you spoke of just now, Willie. He is eager to use the gun and the knife, the bomb too, perhaps. He is vicious, that one, behind the smiling eyes and the warm manner."

"He won't fit our style, then."

"Not at all. The quiet operation, the long-runners that make no news, they are not for his kind."

"From what the Princess said, we'll just be cleaning up from now on. The Graduate might be useful for that, I suppose."

"Even cleaning up must be done in our own style, Willie."

"I'm not arguing. It's your pigeon, my old mate. You'll be telling Mam'selle what you think?"

"I have already done so. She wishes to have another look at him before deciding whether to send him away now or let him work out his time in a job where he can cause no harm. That is why he has been told to come to the meeting this morning."

"Right." Willie looked at his watch. "Time we went up." They got out of the car and moved towards the private door of the bank, a well guarded door. Willie Garvin felt his heart lift a little. For some six years now he had seen Modesty Blaise almost every day, sometimes briefly, sometimes for long spells; and occasionally, during an operation, for days and nights on end. Yet whenever he was about to see her again there was always that quick lift of happy anticipation.

It would be different once *The Network* had been wound up, he reflected with a touch of unease. It would be very different. He hoped to God he'd be able to cope.

✻   ✻   ✻   ✻   ✻

The air-conditioned office was large, and lay on the top floor of the block which rose above the Banque Populaire de Malaurak. The tall window occupying one wall looked north over the town to the sea beyond. On the other walls hung a Cocteau, two Chagalls and a Matisse landscape.

Seven men were seated around the room in comfortable modern armchairs. Six sat at ease. The youngest, a man with an athlete's build, dark curly hair and green eyes, sat forward in his chair, a little tense, or perhaps eager, or perhaps impatient. This was Hugh Oberon, also known as The Graduate.

A large desk stood across one corner of the office. It carried three telephones, a small panel of press-buttons, a gold pen in a rack, and two manila folders. A dark-haired girl in her middle twenties sat behind the desk, occasionally turning a page in the open folder before her, and speaking unhurriedly in a quiet, mellow voice. She wore a white blouse with short sleeves, and a wine red skirt. Her only jewellery was an antique amethyst pendant, not very large, which hung at her throat.

Oberon studied her with profound interest. He had seen her briefly when he had been brought to her for interview a few weeks ago. Now, his induction and basic training completed, he had been summoned to this meeting of the legendary Modesty Blaise and her lieutenants. Oberon was intrigued but in no way awed, for he found it difficult to accept that these quiet, relaxed men and this quiet, impassive girl could have controlled an organisation like *The Network* for so long.

Perhaps they had been hard men once, but they had gone soft now. There was no fire in their bellies. They were yesterday's men. Even Garvin was past thirty, placid, devoid of the good raw lust for dominance that you had to have if you were going to make it big. Oberon was quite certain he would have won that combat session two days ago if Garvin had not managed a lucky counter to the *shotei* strike. As for the rest . . .

Oberon looked casually round the room. There was Garcia, well over fifty by the look of him and running to fat. He was responsible for general administration and for disposal of precious metals and precious stones. Beside him sat Krolli, the swarthy Greek leader of the task force whose main job was to protect the organisation from rivals. Lensk, thickset of body and with sleepy brown eyes, ran the section concerned with international intelligence and industrial espionage.

The man nearest to The Graduate sat with feet barely touching the floor. This was Wee Jock Miller, product of a Glasgow slum, so Oberon had gathered. Miller was just five feet tall and looked almost as broad. His face bore a long thin scar, as if from a razor, and one eye was false. He was in charge of all transport used by the organisation, whether road, sea, or air. The man on his right was

Braun, the ash blond German responsible for all *Network* communications, technical equipment, and small arms. Both he and Miller were knocking forty, Oberon decided. They were all too old, too tired. This was a young man's world.

The girl herself, about his own age he judged, was something of an enigma. She must have been a real hell-cat once, if half the stories told of her were true, but he could see no hint of it in her now. She had become spongy like the others, he concluded. Little wonder she was talking about winding up *The Network*.

Modesty Blaise turned over a typed sheet and looked at the next. "Now regarding pay-offs," she said. "Area chiefs will be responsible for their own people, whether they remain operating or close down. I shall be responsible for all staff here in Tangier and in the North African ports from Casablanca to Tripoli. You can tell your respective staffs that the minimum pay-off will be two thousand dollars and the maximum fifteen thousand, depending on length and quality of service. I'm the sole judge of quality."

Hugh Oberon flicked a glance at the other men. No reaction, no protests, just polite interest. She was continuing, "As regards yourselves, I've made it policy to award bonuses twice a year, but there will be a substantial final bonus, and also I shall be putting Jock Miller on the list of pensioners since he lost an eye in service."

The chunky Scot scowled and made a grunting sound of acknowledgment. Modesty Blaise said, "There are ample funds for all this. Over the past two years I've been laundering our revenue, and almost all assets held by our various companies are now legitimate. This bank and this office building were never anything but legitimate, and negotiations for the sale of them have almost been completed." She turned the last page, then glanced to her left. "Have I forgotten anything, Willie?"

He shook his head. "Can't think of anything, Princess."

"Good. Does anyone have a question?"

Braun said, "I would like instructions for the disposal of weapons and explosives, Mam'selle."

"Yes. That comes later, after we've finished tidying up one or two matters. But in principle no weapons will be sold. I shall probably have them sunk."

Lensk spoke. His true name was not Lensk. He had defected from the KGB five years ago, and *The Network* had sent him to a plastic surgeon for a new face, but his English was still heavily accented. He said, "I have agents in many countries, Mam'selle. Do I bring them out or sell them to a national intelligence organisation?"

"Bring them out if they wish, let them stay if they wish. Don't sell them."

"Ahmed Hamza is in prison in Baghdad."

"I haven't forgotten. Getting him out will be part of our tidying up programme. Is there anything else?"

After a moment Braun said, "It is not important, but I am curious to know if any of us here intend to continue independently."

A half smile touched her lips briefly as she said, "Krolli wants to take over the Aegean area. The rest of you have told me you intend to retire." There was a murmur of amusement, and one or two glanced quizzically at Krolli, who grinned and spread a deprecating hand.

Modesty Blaise closed the folder. "Anything further before we run through the programme of what I want done before final close-down?"

Hugh Oberon glanced about him. None of her lieutenants spoke. One or two heads were shaken. He felt excitement flare suddenly within him, and his mind was illumined by a strange clarity as it came to him that this was a crucial moment, a moment on which immense matters hinged. She had brought him to this meeting for a purpose, and he now saw what that purpose must be. *The Network* was up for grabs, the whole goddam *Network*, but none of her top men wanted it. Even Krolli wanted only an area. Yet its value as a going concern was incalculable, especially if drugs and vice were incorporated in future operations. Nobody could buy *The Network* outright, but if the right man took it over he could negotiate payment of a fair percentage to her annually, say for a ten year term . . .

She was looking at him now, looking at him directly for the first time, and he said in a cool voice, "I have something to say."

She studied him with unreadable eyes, and he met her gaze with knowing amusement. After a brief silence she said, "I was about to tell you to leave us now, Oberon. Do it."

He smiled. "But I have something to say, Princess."

None of the other men exchanged glances or gave any physical sign of increased tension, but the atmosphere in the room became even quieter than before. Modesty Blaise said, "You address me as Mam'selle, or Mam'selle Blaise. Never in any other way. Now leave this office. Garcia will speak to you later."

Oberon stood up, green eyes sparkling, poised on the balls of his feet. "I think you would be disappointed if I did leave," he said. "I think this is a test. I think you're surrounded by dead-beats, and I think you know it. So let's talk, you and I."

Watching her, Garcia saw the midnight-blue eyes become almost black. He winced inwardly, but allowed nothing to show in his face or demeanour. She said slowly, "If you look about you, Oberon, you'll notice that I employ quiet people. There are no big-mouths, no cowboys. We want no dramas, no muscle flexing. Now get out, and wait in the downstairs annex till Garcia comes for you."

A quiver of doubt rippled through Oberon's confidence, but he stilled it quickly. Surely it was impossible that she could simply throw away a prize like *The Network*, impossible that she could have had him attend this meeting except for the purpose of proving himself to be the man she wanted. He continued to smile, and said, "I'll stay till somebody puts me out."

They would not all come at him, he knew that. A brawl here was unthinkable. He hoped and expected that it would be Garvin who got the job, for he was utterly certain that he could take Garvin this time. Perhaps Garvin himself feared as much, for at the moment he seemed to be opting out of the situation, leaning back in his chair and gazing absently at the wall above Oberon's head.

Modesty Blaise pressed one of the buttons on her desk, drew the second folder towards her, opened it and began reading to herself. Oberon eased his feet apart into a good combat stance, ready for instant action. She had probably summoned the two bank guards from below as chopping blocks on which he could demonstrate his ability. A pity. But perhaps Garvin would come next. It was a little creepy, though, the way Garvin and the rest sat placidly waiting. Not even waiting, really. He could detect no hint of expectancy in any of them.

There came the sound of the outer door to the ante-room opening then closing. Without looking up Modesty Blaise said, "Did you bring that Hilton letter with you, Willie?"

"Sure, Princess." Willie roused himself and reached for his inside pocket. At the same moment there was a tap on the door. She called, "Entrez." Oberon's head half turned to watch the door as it opened. Something black and silver flashed across the fifteen foot gap between Willie and Oberon, a knife with the Bowie style of blade and a metal alloy hilt with a sharkskin finish. He carried two such knives in twin sheaths tailored into the inside left breast of his jacket. They were made with his own hands and balanced to make one revolution in twelve feet. His skill with them was of so high an order that his accuracy could only be measured in millimetres and his speed in microseconds.

He had thrown from a sitting position, and without losing speed by transferring his grip from hilt to blade. The play of the wrist retarded the natural revolution of the knife, and the end of the hilt struck Oberon solidly above the ear in the instant that his head turned. There was not enough weight to stun, but ample velocity to cause pain, shock and a long moment of distraction. In that moment Modesty Blaise said, "Miller."

The squat Glaswegian bounced from his chair like a rubber ball, turning on one foot, the other lifted high in a pivot kick, body leaning away for balance. Willie's knife had barely dropped to the floor when the toe of the viciously swinging foot hit Hugh Oberon's solar plexus. Nerve-shock wiped out consciousness before the brain could register the blow. For a second the body remained upright, rigid, eyes fixed and unseeing, then it began to fold forward, the knees crumpling.

Wee Jock Miller ducked and caught the man across his broad

shoulders, then turned, a look of dour satisfaction on his scarred face. "What'll ye have done wi' him, Mam'selle?"

"Take him into the ante-room, please." She picked up a telephone and said, "Sick-room." The Moroccan boy in the white jacket who now stood in the open doorway moved aside and watched with round eyes as the unconscious figure was carried out. Modesty Blaise said into the phone, "Dr. Aquilina, please come up at once with two men and an invalid chair. Take charge of the man you'll find outside my office, and put him under sedation." A pause. "Yes, that's right. Thank you." She put down the phone and said to the boy, "Coffee for everybody please, Mahmoud."

"Mam'selle." He backed slowly, unwilling to tear his eyes from the sight of Willie Garvin strolling across the room to pick up a knife and slip it back in its sheath.

When the door closed, Garcia said, "My apologies, Mam'selle."

"No fault of yours, old friend." A small gesture brushed the idea aside. She looked down at the second folder. "Now I'd like to run through the list of tidying up operations, but we won't deal with anything affecting transport until Jock Miller's back in the office. Let's start with the computer rigging operation in Zurich. How many weeks do you think your technicians will need to complete, Braun?"

Thirty seconds went by. Nobody was surprised. Braun, of the handsome young face that belied his age, always checked and cross-checked mentally before making a commitment, but when he made it you could be sure it would be met. He said, "Six days from the time Lensk secures access for them to the maintenance company."

Lensk said, "Between two and three weeks from now. I cannot be more precise at present."

Modesty Blaise nodded. "That's satisfactory . . ."

The discussion continued. Jock Miller returned and took his seat. Coffee was brought on a trolley. Modesty Blaise poured. The men left their chairs and mingled, sipping coffee, talking quietly. Garcia watched her as she stood speaking with Krolli by the big window. Almost ten years now, he thought with a curious pang. He was thankful that it would all be over soon, but by God he would miss her. Just now, for the first time ever, she had called him 'old friend', and he had stared down at the floor to hide the tears he could feel pricking his eyes. He remembered the men who had mocked him for serving under a woman, the men who had thought it would be easy to destroy her and take what she held. They were long dead now, or in the gutter. When men came to kill her she had neither asked nor given quarter, and it was years now since any man had mocked Garcia.

After ten minutes she returned to the desk and her lieutenants took their seats. Nobody had discussed Hugh Oberon. He was of no interest. For the next hour the tidying up operations were discussed. At last she closed the folder and sat back in her chair. "When we've cleared all this," she said rather slowly, "there's one thing more I intend to do. It's not *Network* business and there's no profit in it, so it wasn't included in the programme, but I want to put Bora out of business before I go."

There was an almost imperceptible stirring from the listening men. After a few moments Lensk said reflectively, "He does not intrude on our affairs, Mam'selle."

"No. But he runs three or four thousand kilos of base morphine from Turkey to Marseilles every year, and he pushes cut heroin all round the Mediterranean."

Jock Miller said, "An' then there's the wee girls." Those who knew Bora's operations knew he sold girls to wealthy customers in the Middle East. Some were bought, some kidnapped, and Bora specialised in very young girls since they were much in demand. Jock Miller was a man with few scruples, but when he thought about Bora selling small girls to jaded clients his fingers itched for the razor he had once carried.

Modesty Blaise said, "Yes. I don't know how many he sells in a year, but I intend to stop him."

Krolli shook his head doubtfully. "It will cost, Mam'selle. Bora has men and guns. Good protection. If we go to war, lives will be lost."

"We're not going to war, Krolli. I'm going to take Bora off the scene. He holds that organisation together, and when he disappears it will disintegrate."

Lensk smiled sleepily. "Another will come into being, Mam'selle."

She inclined her head in acknowledgment, and gave a wry half-smile. "I know, but it will take time, and anyway that's for somebody else to worry about. I'm simply concerned with breaking the Bora mob. This is a personal matter, and I don't propose to use any *Network* people except those who care to volunteer. There will be bonuses for those who do."

Krolli glanced across the room and said, "Is Willie in?"

Willie Garvin lifted his head and gave him a pained look. Krolli grinned and made a gesture of apology. "I just asked, Willie. Okay, I am in also, Mam'selle. How many men will you need?"

"About a dozen. They won't be at high risk." She looked at Jock Miller. "I'll need a motor fishing vessel and two motor launches. Are you in or out?"

"In, Mam'selle." Lensk and Braun murmured agreement.

She said, "Thank you. What about people to man the ships?"

Miller shrugged. "Easy".

Lensk said, "We have very good intelligence regarding Bora. I have a man inside his organisation, and we get advance notice of all his schedules. One thing of interest is that Bora suspects the Americans are trying to penetrate his operations. The BNDD are behind this."

Braun said, "Who are they?"

Lensk sighed. "You should lift your nose from circuitry occasionally, Hans. The Americans have a Federal Bureau of Narcotics and Dangerous Drugs."

Modesty Blaise said, "If they put Bora out of business first, well and good, but it's unlikely because they can't work as freely as we can, so we'll ignore that possibility. Lensk, does Mifsud in Malta still sell a few girls to Bora from that brothel of his in Strait Street?"

"He does, Mam'selle. Bora takes them aboard the *Isparta* off Malta by night, en route for Marseilles. But not small girls, for Mifsud is a man of conscience, you understand. He just sells three or four prostitutes whose disappearance will not bring inquiries, and Bora takes them back with the rest to Mersin for distribution."

She looked at Garcia. "Our dealings with Mifsud have been confined to smuggling and gold manipulation, but I shall want him under full control for two or three days when the time comes."

Garcia spread a hand. "I can ensure that he will do as he is told, but he is not a man of action, Mam'selle."

"He won't have to do anything but keep his mouth shut when you provide him with an extra girl to sell to Bora."

Garcia stiffened a little in his chair. "An extra girl?"

"Me." She looked at her wristwatch. "We'll discuss details nearer the time, but you all know the shape of what I have in mind now, so you can think about it. Thank you for your support in the matter of Bora, and if there are no further questions I'll say good morning to you."

She stood up. The men rose with her. Garcia said, "Regarding Oberon?"

"Ah, yes. He could be a danger to us over the next few weeks. We have the *Abosso* sailing for Perth today, haven't we?"

Miller said, "At eighteen hundred hours, Mam'selle."

"Have him taken aboard and kept under sedation until the ship sails. Tell Captain Gambetta to put him to work for the voyage, and to give him a thousand Australian dollars before letting him go in Perth."

Garcia smiled. "Very well, Mam'selle. That is most satisfactory."

There was a general movement towards the door, and she said, "Stay behind for a word please, Willie."

When the rest of her lieutenants had gone, Willie Garvin moved to where she was standing by the big window, looking out over the city, arms crossed in front of her, lightly holding her elbows, relaxed. She had been relaxed all through the meeting, but there was a difference now. The touch of aloofness, the distancing of herself from the others by a small but positive degree, had now gone, and her eyes smiled with an easy warmth when she turned her head to Willie as he joined her.

"They're very good," she said. "They must be thinking I'm out of my mind, but they don't show a hint of it."

"About the Bora caper?"

"Yes."

"They just think it's eccentric, Princess, and they expect that from you. They like it. We all do. It makes us feel we're different." He paused, frowning a little. "It won't stay different though, once you quit. It'll all go sour. I wish Krolli 'adn't asked for the Aegean."

"So do I, but it has to be his own choice. I can't refuse him."

"No." Willie watched a thin white feather of vapour mark an aircraft's path out over the sea. "Do you 'ave to do the Bora job yourself, Princess?"

She looked at him with a touch of surprise. "Ah, come on now, Willie. Who else?"

There was nobody, of course. *The Network* had some girl couriers who were skilled and gutsy, but playing a white slave role to get aboard the *Isparta* and then doing whatever would have to be done there was far outside their field of competence. It would be a high risk job demanding combat skills and exceptional gifts for improvisation. Willie shook his head and said, "Sorry. That was a daft question."

She studied him curiously. "Is there something about the Bora format that worries you?"

He shrugged. "Not a thing. You've put yourself into much dicier situations before. I suppose it's just last-lap nerves."

Her eyes narrowed a little, and there was a touch of sharpness in her voice as she said, "Get rid of them, Willie. If we let that affect our mental balance we're in trouble."

He smiled and lifted his hands in a placating gesture. "I know, Princess, I know. Don't worry, I'll spend a few hours doing the Sivaji exercises tonight."

She relaxed. "I've been using them myself. Tell you the truth, I'm more anxious about what comes *after* the last lap."

"The new life?" He grinned uneasily. "Me too."

"You? But you're going to have a lovely little pub somewhere in the country. You'll be able to play mine host and entertain girls galore. It'll be a dream come true for you, Willie."

"Let's 'ope so. You got any ideas for yourself yet?"

She grimaced. "Like what? I'm not starting a business career, I've had one of those. I can't see myself opening a tea shop or a hat shop, and I'm not much good at good works."

"Stables, maybe?"

"God knows. I think I'll just get settled in England, then see how I feel."

"You decided whereabouts you'll be?"

"I'm not sure. There's a penthouse that looks out over Hyde Park. Perfect for me, according to Blakeson. Or an equally ideal cottage somewhere in Wiltshire."

Willie said, "Why not take both?"

Her eyes sparkled. "You're a great problem solver, Willie love."

He looked down, then said casually, "When it's all over, will it be okay if I . . . you know, keep in touch?"

She punched his arm gently. "You won't be allowed any choice."

He ran a hand through his thatch of rather untidy fair hair. "I've never really got around to saying thanks for all these years."

"You've said it a dozen ways." Memories flickered through her mind. Times of action, times of waiting, times when death had seemed certain, even a time when he had nursed her back from the brink after a near mortal wound. He had never failed her. And the fact that she had done as much for him in no way diminished her appreciation. She said, "Are you busy next weekend?"

"Nothing special, Princess. Anything you want done?"

"I'd like a slow, wide-ranging talk about remaining operations. Would you be free to come up to Pendragon for the weekend?" This was the splendid villa in Moorish style she had built on The Mountain, west of Tangier.

Willie said, "I'd love to." He meant it. This would not be the first weekend he had spent there, and he always revelled in the pleasure of idling the hours away with her, talking, reflecting, never discussing operations directly, letting the subconscious work on problems, taking the hour long swim in the pool with her, fifty-two lengths to the mile, relaxing, perhaps having a light combat workout, playing a game of chess or backgammon, listening to some music, talking, watching her move about the kitchen as she prepared a meal . . .

"Come Saturday morning," she said. "I'll make a paiella for dinner."

"Smashing."

When he had gone she remained by the window for a while, eyes on the horizon where sea and sky met. It would be just as well, she thought, to continue her daily practice of the Sivaji yoga exercises through the coming weeks. There could be no change of plan, but the thought of the totally new life she would soon have to lead was giving her more apprehension than she had known for years.

✲   ✲   ✲   ✲   ✲

Willie Garvin went down in the lift and met Garcia coming from the sick room. Garcia said, "I have arranged about Oberon."

"Oberon? Oh. Sure."

"Are you busy this evening, Willie?"

"I'm taking Pauline to dinner, but I'll be free after I've seen 'er home." Pauline was one of their couriers, a typically chic and attractive Parisienne. She would have been more than glad to have Willie Garvin stay for breakfast, but he was strict in avoiding any entanglement with a *Network* girl.

Garcia said, "Could you take her to *La Nymphe d'Argent* for dinner? Lisette says two men have demanded protection money from her, and they will call this evening. Just beginners, she thinks, but she would like them stopped at once."

"Pauline's going to love that."

"Ah, it won't take you a minute, Willie, and Pauline will understand."

"All right, Rafa. Leave it with me."

Willie went on out to the car park, got into the Mercedes and sat looking at the wall without seeing it. Another three or four months and . . . then what? The life of a very rich man with a country pub. What could be more pleasant? The pub would be in the English countryside, on the Thames perhaps. Not too far from London. There would be the companionable customers, the growing circle of friends. London an hour away, with its theatres, concerts, and infinite variety of entertainment. What could be more pleasant for a man who had lived with raw danger at his shoulder for so long? What could be more . . . more bland?

Willie Garvin sighed and started the car. It was going to be pretty weird, he decided.

Two

THERE were twenty-three females in the poorly lit hold, and ten of them were not yet in their teens. One was a child of nine. Each had bed-space for an inflatable mattress, and a bag or case for toiletries and small belongings. Two cubicles with chemical lavatories had been built in a corner of the hold, and two plumbed-in basins provided the means of washing.

They were not well groomed and did not look their best, these women and children, but they were perishable merchandise to be kept in good condition until the *Isparta* returned to Mersin. Then they would be expertly groomed in readiness for the buyers who would attend the sale at the house a few miles along the coast. Final delivery was by negotiation and arrangement, according to destination.

This was the after hold. Its forward bulkhead had been pierced to receive a door frame and a door with a mortice lock. Beyond the door was a short but wide alley, and from the end of this a companion ladder led down to the engine room catwalk. A guard, with an automatic in a shoulder holster and a riding crop looped on his wrist, dozed on a folding canvas chair in the alley. In the engine room, the second engineer sat at a small table below his gauges and browsed through a girlie magazine.

It was two in the morning. The ship had hove to briefly off St. Paul's Bay soon after midnight to take the four Maltese girls aboard, three of them moving like sleepwalkers from the effect of a soporific drug, and the fourth appearing to be in the same condition. Malta and Gozo lay twenty-five miles to the south-east now.

The other women and children had been aboard longer. There were Turks and Greeks, Cypriots, Cretans and Sicilians. It was

Bora's policy to collect them from his agents on the outward trip to Marseilles rather than on the return, because the longer confinement made them submissive and apathetic. The youngest child was crying, and a Sicilian girl was trying to comfort her in a language the child did not understand. Most of the others were sleeping. The *Isparta* ploughed steadily on at nine knots over a calm sea and under a thin crescent of new moon.

At fifteen minutes to three, one of the girls who had been taken aboard off Malta roused from sleep, sat up, pushed back her blanket, and lifted the patchwork shopping bag from between her legs, where she had kept it for safety. She was a tall girl, olive skinned, with a fat face and a fringe of black hair almost obscuring her eyes. When she pushed back the fringe and spat out the rubber pads in her cheeks she looked very different, even in the dim light of the twenty-five watt lamp that lit the hold.

The Sicilian girl watched curiously as the tall girl in the thin black tunic and skirt started moving towards the door. The child stopped crying and asked a question in the heavily accented Greek of one of the small islands. Modesty Blaise stopped, looked towards the Sicilian, who sat with her arm about the child, and said softly in Italian, "Keep the little one quiet and don't wake the others. All things will be better soon."

The Sicilian girl looked frightened and crossed herself. Modesty Blaise knelt by the door. Her bag held many things beneath the bundle of clothes and impedimenta. She took out a pencil torch and a tiny leather wallet with three lockpicks. The key was in the lock from the other side, which made the probes useless, but with a pair of long-nosed pliers she was able to grip the tip of the key and turn it. This was a satisfactory beginning, for it meant there would now be no need to blow the lock with a pellet of plastic explosive, alerting the guard and possibly the duty engineer.

She closed the door behind her and turned the key to lock it. The guard dozed in his chair. The kongo was in her right hand, an inch-thick spindle of hardwood which mushroomed at each end. With it she could strike from any angle, her knowledge of the nerve centres enabling her to numb a limb, to stun, or to render unconscious. Her left hand held a tube like a lipstick case. She twisted the end between finger and thumb and held it a few inches below the nose of the dozing guard. The gentle emission of ether made barely a sound, but perhaps instinct roused the man. His eyes opened, his head came up, and she clipped him smartly behind the ear with the kongo. He slumped, and she turned to her bag for the hypodermic and the ampoules of phenobarbitone.

When she had given him a three-grain injection she moved to the end of the short alley. From this point the layout of the engine room was visible to her. Everything she had seen of the ship so far was in accord with the plan provided by Lensk's man inside the Bora organisation, and the engine room proved no exception. There was the companion ladder, the catwalk, then another ladder down to the engine room deck, with the duty engineer sitting at the far end. No certain way she could reach him unobserved, she decided. If his wide-angle vision was average, he would glimpse movement as she went along the catwalk, and the telephone to the bridge was at his elbow. It was not likely that there would be more than one man on the bridge, not on this ship and at this time of night. There might be nobody there. If so, this would not be the only ship in the Mediterranean running on autopilot and with an empty bridge. But it was a risk she could not take.

She went back to collect the bottle of wine and glass that stood beside the chair of the unconscious guard, and to rummage in her bag for a red blouse.

Two minutes later the Second Engineer caught a hint of movement as he turned a page of the girlie magazine. When he looked up he saw a girl on the catwalk, leaning over slightly, looking down with a smile, and holding up a bottle and glass invitingly. She was a girl of quite striking beauty, in a black skirt and red blouse with two top buttons undone. From where he sat he could see quite a lot of her legs, and the sight of them started an ache in the pit of his stomach. She was calling something to him, but he could not hear above the noise of the engines. Her appearance surprised him, not because she was on board, for he knew that Bora travelled nowhere without a girl or two for his pleasure, but that she was here now, in the engine room at this hour.

The Second Engineer was a Libyan, and not a man to reject good fortune when it came. As long as he did not tread on Bora's corns, all would be well, and he could easily check the situation first. He stood up and beckoned. The girl advanced to the end of the catwalk and came rather awkwardly down the ladder, clutching the bottle under one arm, the glass in her hand, and showing a lot of excellent thigh.

As she came near enough to be heard she gave him a rather nervous smile and said in Arabic, "Bora sent me down."

"Bora?" He stared. "To me?"

"He had a reason. I will show you."

The Second Engineer watched curiously as she set down the bottle and the glass on his table. From an almost invisible pocket in the side seam of her skirt she took a wooden object and held it up for him to see. A shaft, a little wooden shaft some three inches long with a big knob at each end. The Second Engineer put the matter to his imagination. The shaft was quite short, and in any event it swelled out into this knob at both ends, so it was hard to see how it might be used for . . .

The girl laid the shaft across her right palm and folded her fingers round it to make a fist. She held it up to show how the knobs now projected at each side of her fist. The Second Engineer stared, baffled. "So?" he demanded.

This was the last he remembered of the incident.

Modesty Blaise went back to fetch her bag and gave him an injection before putting on her black tunic again and making her way up to the main deck. The night was dark, and all was quiet. It took her five minutes of careful surveillance to discover that there was a duty officer on the bridge but no helmsman. The wheel was on autopilot. She came in from the port wing, choosing her moment, and dropped the duty officer from behind.

A mile to the southwest of the *Isparta* a motor fishing vessel kept station, as it had done since the Malta rendezvous, showing no lights. It carried two launches, ready to be lowered simultaneously to port and starboard. Ten men in black, with black headmasks to hand, waited in silence by the boats. Five plus two crewmen would go in one boat with Willie Garvin, five plus two crewmen in the other with Krolli. It was an hour since the men had been stood to, and none had spoken in that time. Krolli ruled his heavies with an iron hand, for he had Willie Garvin to answer to. These two stood by the rail with Wee Jock Miller, watching the distant lights of the *Isparta* to starboard with practised patience.

The time was three o'clock, and they knew that the signal might come at any moment, but they did not voice this to each other. Seven minutes went by. Abruptly a pinpoint of red appeared, just behind the port light. It moved in a small fast circle, then stopped and vanished. Jock Miller said, "Boats awa', lads," and as his crewmen began to move he answered the signal briefly with a green flashlight, receiving a quick on-off acknowledgment.

Krolli sighed gently and murmured, "It is criminal that she is retiring." Willie Garvin chuckled, slapped him on the shoulder, and turned to follow his men into the launch.

Down in the engine room of the *Isparta* again, Modesty Blaise brought the speed down gradually until the engines were at dead slow, then climbed to the main deck once more. It was unlikely that the change of revolutions would wake anybody, except perhaps the First Engineer. She positioned herself by the officers' quarters to keep watch for him. Her own gun, a Colt .32, was holstered at her waist now, and she also held the guard's automatic, a Browning. The two launches would be coming in fast, but if the alarm was raised she would have to hold the deck while *The Network* men closed with the *Isparta* and boarded her.

Soon she saw the cream of their wakes as they swept out and round to come alongside to port and starboard. They had almost closed before she heard the sound of their muffled engines, then came the thud-thud of padded grappling hooks and the squeak of fenders. A dark figure came over the rail, and she saw the glint of a knife blade. Willie Garvin. She flicked the flashlight and he moved towards her.

"All right, Princess?" His voice was a whisper.

"So far."

More dark figures were swarming over both rails now, spreading out, making for the foc's'le, the bridge, the engine room.

Krolli's men had studied the plan of the ship for two hours the day
before, and each man knew his task. Krolli himself loomed out of
the darkness, teeth white against the black mask in a smile of
acknowledgment as he moved on with two men to the after door
of the officers' quarters. Modesty and Willie followed them into
the passage that ran between the cabins. Doors were being
opened, lights switched on, and soft-spoken warning commands
given to startled men rousing from sleep.

The stateroom Bora occupied lay midway along the passage,
and the door was bolted. Willie Garvin located the bolt with a fine
wire, pressed a thimble sized lump of plastic explosive against the
point where it lay, set a tiny detonator for a ten second delay,
stuck it in the p.e. and moved aside. The door shivered to the small
explosion. Willie kicked it open and switched on the light.

The girl screamed. Bora, eyes wide, lips drawn back in shock,
lunged for the drawer of the locker beside the double bed. His
hand was on the gun when iron fingers clamped on both with
shocking force. A blade glittered before his eyes, then vanished,
and something pricked his neck in warning. Chill blue eyes looked
down at him from the eyeholes of a black headmask. He froze,
and felt the revolver plucked from nerveless fingers. His eyes
twitched to focus on the figure at the foot of the bed, and he caught
his breath as new fear exploded within him.

The girl beside him was still screaming, clutching bed clothes to
her. Modesty Blaise moved round, took her wrist, jerked her out
of bed, threw her under the shower and turned on the cold water.
Bora struggled to force words from his dry throat. "Let us talk,"
he croaked, "let us talk. We can reach an accommodation. Listen,
I have five hundred kilos of base morphine aboard. You know
what that will fetch in Marseilles? Half a million dollars!"

She said, "I know." There was a hypodermic in her hand and
she was filling it from an ampoule. "And when they've refined it
to pure heroin it will fetch two million, and when it reaches the
States, ten. And when it's cut ready for fixes it will sell on the
streets for around a quarter of a billion. I've been hoping you'd
come after me so I could kill you, Bora, but I've decided to make
do with second best now. All right, Willie."

A finger and thumb pressed on the carotids. Bora struggled briefly, then was still. She slid the needle into his limp arm. The girl had crawled out of the shower and now crouched with a blanket hugged about her, whimpering. Modesty said, "Put her in the after hold with the other women, and send a man to carry Bora to the launch."

The girl shrank away as he took her arm and hauled her to her feet. "No!" she said with the throaty Syrian accent. "They will beat me!"

"*Insh' Allah,*" Willie said philosophically, and marched her out of the cabin. There had been much coming and going in the passage, voices raised in protest or command, and the sound of at least one more female voice. A man appeared in the doorway. Modesty motioned to the unconscious figure of Bora. The man picked him up and carried him away over one shoulder. Modesty followed them out on deck.

To the southwest the motor fishing vessel *Almarza* was showing her lights now and closing a little. On the *Isparta*, beams had been lifted from the forward hatch and the ship's crew were being sent down into the hold by rope ladder, with Krolli supervising. Modesty went up on to the bridge. Jock Miller was there with Delorme, the First Officer from the *Almarza*, neither wearing a mask. Delorme was busy at the chart table. The unconscious duty officer had been taken away.

She said, "Any problems?"

Miller shook his head. "We'll have the new course in a moment an' we'll be coming round a point or two, just."

The new course would be the first part of a dogleg. Destination was the island of Pantelleria, ten hours away at a speed of ten knots, but Delorme would plot a dogleg and keep the speed down to ensure that they would not reach the island until an hour or two before dawn next day. During that time Willie would work shifts with Jock Miller in the engine room, and she intended to relieve Delorme for bridge duty herself.

She went down to the main deck again as Willie emerged from a companionway. He said, "I told the girls they'd 'ave to stay locked up for another day but they'd be all right in the end, and I said they'd better not kill Bora's bird because it might make things complicated." A man approached, carrying a quilted jacket, and Willie went on, "I 'ad your coat brought across with us, Princess. It's a bit nippy when you stop moving about."

"Thanks, Willie."

He took the jacket and held it for her. As she slipped her arms into the sleeves he said, "Oh, and O'Leary found the smack. It's split up into about twenty waterproof parcels, all with floats and strung together, so it looks like they were going to slip it overboard off Marseilles for a waiting boat."

"Yes. Don't jettison this lot. I want it left aboard for evidence."

"That's what I've told 'em, Princess."

Sammy Wan, the half Chinese who was Krolli's second in command, appeared from forrard and said, "We have found something in the paint locker you should see, Mam'selle."

"I'll come now. Take over up here, Willie."

On the deck below, the door of the paint locker stood open. In the passage a *Network* man with a Sten gun crouched by a figure sprawled limply on the deck beside a crumpled canvas sack. The light was dim here, and Sammy Wan lifted a hand lamp to throw a circle of brightness. The man lying on the deck was well built but looked shrunken at this moment. His skin was pale brown, his hair black, his features lean and regular. Above one ear the hair was thickly matted with blood, and his breathing was barely discernible.

"He was in the sack," said Sammy Wan, "with heavy weights."

She squatted, and gently lifted the matted hair to feel the broken flesh and crushed bone. "If he was for dropping over the side, why keep him?" she said absently, eyes closed as she tried to feel the extent of damage to the skull.

"Don't know, Mam'selle."

"Rig a stretcher and carry him up to the wardroom. Has Krolli kept the captain separate from the rest of the crew?"

"Yes, Mam'selle."

"All right. Be as quick as you can."

Ten minutes later the man lay on the wardroom table with a pillow under his head. The pulse was feeble, but his breathing was very slightly better now with the improved intake of oxygen after the near suffocation he had suffered in the sack.

She was cleaning the wound when Krolli brought in Riza, captain of the *Isparta*, a plump wary man whose mouth twitched with spasms of fear. Modesty Blaise glanced up and said, "You've worked for Bora for over seven years, so don't pretend you don't know any answers. Who is this man?"

Riza licked his lips. He knew that Modesty Blaise had taken over the ship, but he did not know exactly what the situation was, and his fear of Bora ran very deep. He spread his hands and said, "I would be glad to tell you if I knew, but Bora does not confide in me."

She began to tape a sterile dressing in place and said, "Take him out and throw him overboard, then bring the First Officer to me."

"At once, Mam'selle." After ten years, Krolli did not need briefing in what she wanted him to do.

Riza began a cry of protest, but Krolli cut it short with an elbow jab to the solar plexus, then frog-marched the man out of the wardroom. It was thirty seconds before Riza could get his breath, and another minute before Krolli brought him back to the wardroom with apparent reluctance and said, "He claims to have remembered what you wish to know, Mam'selle, but if you think he is lying I will set fire to him for a little while before throwing him in the sea."

Riza shuddered and cried huskily, "No, no, I will not lie! It is the American spy, this one. He came to us three-four months ago, with a good history, but Bora is careful and made some checks. It was a false history, and so Bora let the man make this journey on the *Isparta*, but then he was made to talk, first by much beating, and when he kept silent Bora used the needle and pentothal. Still he resisted, and his words were much confused and not to make sense, but we learned that there was no back-up and that this voyage was secure. These things were all that Bora was caring about."

"Who hit him?"

"That was Bora himself, with an iron bar, for he was very angry."

"Why keep him in the paint locker before throwing him overboard?"

"Because Bora thought he will perhaps live till morning, and perhaps will be in his senses to know what is happening when he is put in the sea. This would give more pleasure to Bora, you understand."

She lifted her eyes from her work, and Riza shuddered again, for it seemed to him that they were as cold and black as the emptiness of outer space, yet lit with a small flame of loathing. "I understand," she said. "Did you get the man's name?"

"Ah, that. Yes. It came out with the pentothal, when there were some moments he believed he was being how-do-you-call? . . . yes, debriefed after a mission. His name is Ben Christie."

She said, "All right, Krolli. Take him away and send Willie to me."

Three minutes later she was completing the dressing when Willie Garvin came in and said, "Krolli told me. Looks like this is the BNDD man Lensk told us about."

"Or CIA." She wiped the man's face with a swab of damp cottonwool. "I don't think the Narcotics Bureau people would run a penetration mission. He was probably seconded from the Company for this job. Get on the radio and talk to Doc on the *Almarza* in speech code. Tell him we're sending across a man with a fractured skull, and he's to do the best he can for him. See to the transport arrangements yourself, Willie. I want to save this one if possible."

Willie lifted an eyebrow. "Something worrying you, Princess?"

"A little. If Lensk knew this agent was in the field, maybe others knew too, so it's not surprising his cover was blown with Bora. If I'd thought about it, I could have warned McGovern and got him pulled out." McGovern was the CIA man in Rabat.

Willie said, "Mac would listen all right, but I doubt if he could've got H.Q. at Langley to listen, and that's where the orders come from. I don't reckon there was any way you could've changed things, Princess."

She looked down at the shrunken grey face and made a small grimace. "I expect you're right."

The sky in the east was beginning to show a hint of first light when she stood on the main deck and watched the blanket-wrapped figure on the stretcher being lowered to one of the launches. She had considered saving the unconscious man the strain of the short journey by bringing Doc Howie across, but against this the *Almarza* had a small surgery fully equipped with adequate facilities for an emergency operation if one was called for.

The forward hatch was closed now except for the gap left by a single beam. The prisoners would have rather more than twenty-four hours to spend below. They could go without food for that time, but she intended to have water lowered to them. Bora had already been taken across to the *Almarza* on the other launch, and would be kept under sedation until the job was over.

An hour later, after she had made a careful inspection of the *Isparta* to satisfy herself that all was secure and there was no chance of a breakout by the prisoners, the launches returned to pick up most of the *Network* boarding party. With them they brought food in vacuum containers for the skeleton crew and the women. Those remaining aboard Bora's ship, apart from Modesty and Willie, were reduced to Jock Miller and Delorme, Krolli and Sammy Wan. A mile apart, the two ships trudged slowly on their way, with the launches hoisted aboard the *Almarza* once more.

Shortly before noon, when he was due to take over from Miller in the engine room, Willie Garvin climbed to the bridge. Modesty Blaise was there, handing over to Delorme, who, like Willie, had slept for four hours in one of the cabins. On the foredeck, Sammy Wan was taking over from Krolli as hatch guard.

The morning mist had long since cleared, and the day was fine, the sea calm. When she had finished handing over, Modesty moved to the port wing with Willie and stood looking across at the *Almarza*. "I talked to Doc Howie an hour ago," she said. "He doesn't think an op will be necessary. Concussion is severe and damage impossible to assess at present, but he'll make exhaustive tests as soon as we get Ben Christie to Les Genévriers." This was *The Network's* own small ten-bed hospital.

Willie nodded absently. He was thinking how marvellous it was to be standing here beside her, looking out over the quiet sea, towards the end of another operation. There had been many times like this over the years. Quickly he crushed the pang of unease that touched him as he recalled that this was the last time. "It's a good one to sign off with, Princess," he said pensively. "I mean, as a caper it's got a nice shape and a very pleasant texture. On top of that, it's unique. I can't remember a time when there wasn't a single 'itch. Never. There's always something that goes wrong so you 'ave to improvise, and often enough it's one thing after another. I think God must 'ave suspended Murphy's Law for this one."

She laughed, and looked at him sideways, and put her hand over his as it rested on the rail. He saw the tiny lines that laughter brought to the corners of her eyes, and a wave of pleasure touched him. When he had first come to her, to be remade almost as totally as the caterpillar is remade a butterfly, she had never laughed, rarely smiled. He thought that perhaps laughter was his gift to her, his one small gift in return for all she had given him.

"I'll go and relieve Wee Jock," he said.

She followed him down from the bridge, then went to the stateroom, took off her shoes and stretched out on the bed. It was a little worrying about Willie, she thought. Running a country pub would never be sufficient occupation for that remarkable intelligence or for the exercise of his many skills. Perhaps her most satisfying achievement in the ten-year story of *The Network* had been to provide Willie Garvin with the chance to realise his immense potential. He had repaid her tenfold, though he would never believe it, both in ways that were plain and in ways that ran deep. She was thankful these times were ending now, so she would never again lead or send him into tasks that might so easily destroy him.

And yet, and yet . . . with his retirement he would surely need a greater challenge and stimulus than a country pub could offer. Her eyes were half closed, but they opened wide as a new thought struck her. Was it possible that these worries concerning Willie Garvin's retirement might also apply to her own? In all her remembered life she had never known a time without struggle and danger. How would it feel to be entirely free of it; safe, unthreatened, with no operations to plan, no opposition to be outwitted or outfought?

It would feel fine, she told herself firmly. Just fine. There were hundreds of ways for a rich woman to enjoy herself without having people try to shoot her or knife her or snap her neck. She took a deep breath, ran a command to relax through the nerve network of her body, and began mental feedback to augment the brain rhythms that would bring sleep.

*   *   *   *   *

"Good morning. It's nice to have you back with us."

He stared until he could bring the girl into focus. She was short and dark, with a cheerful smile, and wore a dress and apron like a nurse' s uniform, but no headdress. He felt that for a long time now he had been going through a hot dark tunnel, sometimes hearing voices, sometimes seeing blurred pictures. There had been much dull pain in his head, but that was gone now. He had a shapeless recollection of being moved several times, in darkness and in light.

His mouth was dry, and he drank thankfully when the girl brought him water to drink through a thin plastic tube. When he had taken enough he concentrated on forming words, and said in a weak rusty voice, "Who are you?"

"You can call me Leah." She touched a hand to his brow, then took his wrist. "I am your nurse.'

"What . . . this place?"

She chuckled. "Most often people say, *'Where am I?'*."

He tried to smile, then memory flooded his mind, not complete memory, but enough to make him go rigid and choke back a cry of fear. Bora . . . the *Isparta* . . . the questions . . . the things the grinning ape with the earring had done to him before they gave up and started on the pentothal.

The girl was holding his shoulders now, soothing him. "It's all right, you're safe now, quite safe. The doctor has mended your hurts and everything is well. Please rest, Mr. Christie. Don't be troubled about anything. You are in good hands."

So she knew his name. When he had stopped shivering he said with an effort, "All right. Where am I?"

"That's better." She smiled down at him over her substantial bosom. "You are in a house on The Mountain, near Tangier. It belongs to Mam'selle Modesty Blaise."

He lay limply, eyes closed, trying to think. At last he said, "How in God's name did I get here?"

"Ah, that is not my business, Mr. Christie." Her English was accented but very good, and her voice echoed the cheerfulness of her smile. "Mam'selle will tell you all things. I only know that you were on a ship, and she took you from it to her own ship, then brought you to the small hospital which is for her own people. But then, when Dr. Howie was satisfied, she had you moved here to her house, and I came with you to nurse you here."

He wondered if this was real, and muttered, "Modesty Blaise?"

"Yes, Mr. Christie. Now no more questions. I am going to feed you with a little soup, then the doctor will come to see you. After that you will sleep again, and if you are very good I will ask Mam'selle to come and talk to you this evening."

He looked up into the dark smiling eyes, and felt a surge of wondering joy at the solid realisation that he was alive. It was a miracle, unbelievable . . . and yet it was true. He managed a spectral smile and croaked, "I'll be good, Leah. Very good."

*　　*　　*　　*　　*

When he woke again that evening he felt hungry, and knew that his body must be mending. Leah helped him to the adjoining bathroom and made him sit on a stool in the shower while she soaped and rinsed him. When she had towelled him dry she brought him pyjamas, settled him in bed, and plugged in a shaver to clean the heavy stubble of beard from his face. Finally she combed his hair and held a mirror for him to study the result.

With the memory of those hours on the *Isparta*, he would not have been surprised to find himself looking at a gaunt old man with white hair, but apart from a hollowness of cheeks and eyes he seemed little changed. The hair had been shaved along one side of his head where a healing gash was surrounded by a great blue-black mottled bruise.

"Not bad?" she said with a grin.

"Could be a lot worse. Thanks, honey."

For dinner she brought him oxtail soup, grilled swordfish with courgettes, asparagus spears and creamed potato, followed by a fresh fruit platter and coffee. The food was beautifully cooked and served, the portions small, ideally suited to a patient whose appetite would quickly be appeased.

When he had eaten she took the trolley away, leaving him propped up in bed with his second cup of coffee, and as she wheeled the trolley from the room a tall girl came in, a girl with black hair, a lightly tanned face, and eyes of deep midnight blue. Her hair was piled in a chignon to show a long smooth neck rising from wide shoulders. She wore a shirtwaister dress of pale green cotton, her legs were bare, her feet sandalled. Her only jewellery was a pendant in gold filigree lying against the slope that rose from firm breasts to the hollow of her throat.

Her height, thought Ben Christie, was about five feet six or seven; not small, but seemingly so when compared with the legend surrounding her name. She carried a round silver tray with a half bottle of champagne and two glasses, and she moved with the grace of a dancer as she came round the foot of the bed.

"Hallo, Ben," she said, and put the tray down on the bedside cabinet. "I'm Modesty Blaise."

He said, "I know. What I don't know is how to say thank you — " His throat closed suddenly, and to his horror he found that his chest was heaving and tears were streaming down his cheeks.

"This is medicinal," she said, and began to untwist the wire of the cork. "Doc Howie tells me it will do you neither harm nor good. Willie Garvin, on the other hand, insists that it always *feels* as if it's doing you good, so I thought you and I might split half a bottle and try to make a judgment on an empirical basis. Doc Howie says there's no brain damage, and in fact your skull wasn't fractured. Also those two missing toe-nails will grow again, and your ribs should heal nicely because you're very fit and the musculature is excellent."

She twisted the cork free and quickly caught the burst of foam in a glass, still talking. "Don't worry about the hiccups, Ben, it's a

reassuringly natural reaction, so just let it all out. Oh, and don't
worry about making a report, there's no rush. I've spoken to Jim
McGovern, your man at the Rabat embassy, and told him you're
safe. In fact I allowed him to visit you at our little private hospital
before we moved you here. He wanted to have you flown home in
a hospital plane right away, but I told him to get lost. He couldn't
make trouble without giving a lot of exposure to the CIA here, so
there was no problem."

The spasm passed and he sat breathing deeply, wiping his face
with tissues from the box she held for him. "Christ," he said,
"what an exhibition."

"I didn't think so." She rested a hand briefly on his shoulder.
"I'm more inclined to think about Bora having to use pentothal
because he failed with the toenails and the rib-cracking etcetera."

His laugh was shaky but his voice firm as he said, "Thank you,
ma'am. Thanks for everything, then and now. I'm glad you told
McGovern to get lost, but I'm not clear why."

She looked at him with a touch of surprise. "There was no
option. I'd taken you under my protection, and as long as you
were having good medical care I couldn't hand you over to anyone
while you were still unconscious."

He looked at her curiously. "The obligation isn't that
obvious," he said slowly.

She shrugged. "It's up to you now. Doc Howie says you'll be fit
to travel in two or three days, meantime I'll arrange whatever you
want."

"I'd be grateful to stay, if it's not too much trouble."

"You're welcome. You'd probably like to talk to Jim
McGovern, so I'll get him along here tomorrow." She smiled, and
it warmed him strangely. "The room won't be bugged, I promise.
You'll be fully secure."

"You're an extremely kind lady, ma'am. Do I get to know what
happened since Bora stuck a needle in me aboard the *Isparta?*"

"Why not?" She gave him a glass, picked up one for herself,
lifted it to him, and said, "The CIA?"

He lifted his own. "The Network?"

She smiled again. "To both." They drank, and she sat sideways on the edge of the bed. "It was just luck, Ben. I decided to smash Bora because I hate his rackets, so I was one of four girls they took aboard off Malta. I broke out a few hours later, took care of the duty engineer and the officer on watch, then signalled an m.f.v. of ours that had been shadowing the *Isparta*. Willie Garvin brought a boarding party across in two launches, and we had no problem securing the ship." She shook her head. "I think it was the easiest thing we've ever done. So free of snags I began to worry. The only surprise was when one of my men found you in a sack in the paint locker, ready for drowning."

She paused to sip her champagne, and Christie said, "You knew who I was?"

"We'd known earlier that the BNDD was trying to penetrate Bora's organisation, but we didn't know who the near-corpse in the sack was until I questioned Captain Riza. Then it made sense. I imagine you were seconded from the Company?"

He nodded. "My mother comes from the Lebanon, so I speak the language and I'm dark enough to look the part. Do you know how I got blown?"

"Not specifically, only that your cover story didn't stand up. I got your name from Riza. It came out under the pentothal, but that's about all they got from you."

After a little silence he said, "So you found me, and then what?"

"I had you taken across to our m.f.v. It's well equipped for casualties, and one of our *Network* doctors was aboard. He patched you up and looked after you in the sick bay until we finished the operation and came back here to Tangier."

He drank some champagne, watching her openly, profoundly intrigued by this extraordinary young woman. His head felt clear, and though he could now feel a pleasant tiredness beginning to touch him, he did not want her to go. "Is it okay to ask how you finished the operation?" he said.

She grinned suddenly, wickedly, looking at him over her glass. "We reduced to a skeleton crew," she said, "until we were a mile or so off Pantelleria an hour before first light. Then I sent everyone across to the m.f.v except Willie, and we took the *Isparta* in at about two knots and ran her solidly aground just north of the harbour. All the crew were battened down in the forward hold, together with five hundred kilos of base morphine we found. It was still not quite first light when Willie and I took off in a rubber dinghy with an outboard for the *Almarza*. That's the m.f.v. There's a penal colony on Pantelleria, so we knew there'd be armed guards around to take care of Riza and his crew."

She reached for the half bottle to top up their glasses and went on, "Then I got a radio signal through to my section chief in Rome, and he tipped off Vinezzi of Interpol, which more or less wrapped it up." Again the gamine grin touched her mouth. "Willie let the women loose as soon as we grounded. They were a pretty docile lot, but he felt they might give the *Isparta* mob a bit of well deserved stick once they realised the men couldn't climb out of the hold. We heard later that they threw a load of smouldering rags and sacks down, so Riza and Co. were damn near suffocated by the time the police and guards arrived."

Ben Christie closed his eyes. "That's beautiful," he said. "My God, that's truly beautiful." He drank, savouring the champagne, savouring the images her tale had conjured up for him, savouring the quiet pleasure of her presence and of this moment. After a while he said, "So Bora's in an Italian slammer now?"

She shook her head. "We took him with us. Bora was too rich and had too many lawyers to stay long in gaol."

"Was?"

"I didn't kill him. He left here by private plane in a life-support crate, and he's now in the Sheikdom of Malaurak, a very feudal piece of desert with a lot of oil underneath it, ruled by Sheik Abu-Tahir, a very old friend of mine. There are still plenty of genuine slaves between the Red Sea and the Persian Gulf — you know that if you've worked undercover in the Middle East. Bora's one of them now, Ben, and not a palace slave, either. He's got hard labour for life."

"Good." The word came harshly from Christie's throat. He sat thinking, remembering, wondering, and at last he said, "Where's your percentage?"

"There isn't one." She drained her glass and set it down with a look of self mockery. "I'm retiring, and I thought I'd do a good deed to mark the occasion."

"Retiring?"

"That's right." She stood up. "There comes a time, and right now it's time you went to sleep. I'll send Leah in to settle you for the night and give you a sleeping pill if you need one."

He was loath to have her leave, and as she made to pick up the tray he put a hand gently on her wrist. "Wait, just for a moment. I'm back to my first question. How do I say thank you?"

"Well, maybe by not spreading this story around," she said with mock gravity. "I don't want my wicked reputation ruined, even if I am retiring."

"Whatever you say." He felt a little baffled, a little annoyed with himself for being unable to see in her the Modesty Blaise whose lengthy dossier he had once studied two years ago before his first North African assignment. "Will you come and talk to me again tomorrow, please?"

"Maybe, but I have a lot to do. I'll arrange for Willie Garvin to bring Jim McGovern here, and you can have a talk with Willie after McGovern's left, if you like."

He nodded, smiling. "I'd enjoy that for second best. Look, you've been kind enough to call me Ben, but I guess that was partly medicinal and I won't presume on it. Okay if I call you Mam'selle? Miss Blaise sounds kind of starchy, and every time I say ma'am I feel like a character in an old western movie."

She looked down at him, amused. "Mam'selle is my name among *Network* people."

"I know. So let me be an honorary member until you wind the organisation up. Is it really true you're retiring?"

"You can bet on it. I've run our last operation, and there's just a complicated load of straight business matters to clear up. From now on it's the safe life for me."

He pressed her wrist, then took his hand away. "I hope it works for you, Mam'selle," he said soberly. "I sure hope it works for you."

Three

IF she had been given to looking back she would have done so with amusement at her expectation of a peaceful new life, for the turning of a dozen seasons had shown that this could never be, and she had long been wryly aware that she might not have wished it so.

On a spring night in London, moving across the poorly lit carpark beside the Thames with her friends, she felt the touch of adrenalin in her blood as subliminal awareness gave warning, and when the small unidentified sound came from the darkness she twisted sharply to one side by instinctive reaction. The short steel shaft, travelling like a bullet, only grazed her upper rib before burying itself to the feathered butt in the side of a Commer Caravanette.

She had been walking a little ahead of the other three, key in hand ready to unlock the Rolls, which stood near the end of the line, but now she swung about, whipping an arm round the blind girl's waist and lifting her bodily behind the shelter of the van, jostling the two men and snapping urgently, "Quick! Stay close!"

They obeyed, huddling against the offside rear wing. Professor Stephen Collier said, "What the hell was that?"

She had only glimpsed the butt jutting from the Commer, but had recognised it, helped by the association of its flight sound. "Crossbow bolt," she whispered.

Sir Gerald Tarrant said softly, "You or me?"

"Me, I think. Quiet, please." She pressed the blind girl's arm and murmured, "Can you hear him, Dinah?"

Collier's wife stood holding her breath. Blind from childhood, she had immensely acute hearing. After a moment she whispered, "If I'm facing twelve, he's at one o'clock and about fifteen paces away. I heard a weird creaking. Could that be the bending of the bow to reload?"

"Yes."

Collier muttered, "Jesus!" and slid an arm round his wife's shoulders. It was nine o'clock of a pleasant May evening and they were alone in the carpark because they had left the concert during the interval, after the Beethoven piano concerto, being agreed beforehand that they preferred to miss the Mahler symphony and dine at a reasonable hour.

Modesty Blaise gave her jacket to Tarrant, reached behind her back for the zip, slid out of the wool jersey dress that would hamper movement, and kicked off her shoes. The bulk of the Festival Hall loomed behind them. Beyond the van that gave them cover were two ranks of cars, then the lower walkway and the lamps of the Thames's southern embankment. Dinah whispered in her soft Canadian drawl, "He's moving round to eleven o'clock, Modesty."

"I'll angle out from here at five. Can you keep track of him?"

"Sure, honey, Up to about forty paces on this gritty ground."

"Just call a number for me every few seconds, and 'in' for if he's closer to you, 'out' for farther away."

"Right. Ten o'clock now, moving slowly. Out a little."

She was gone, a paleness of back and shoulders above the barely visible black tights and pants. Tarrant and Collier stood breathing with infinite care, making no sound, standing close to shield Dinah. Five seconds later she said in a flat voice, "Nine. Out." She turned her head fractionally. Collier held her hand, squeezing it gently, loving her for the cool and steady way she had withstood shock and so quickly picked up her cue from Modesty. His own nerves were feeling horribly taut.

Christ, he thought. A bloody crossbow. You never knew what it would be next with Modesty. He wished to God that Willie Garvin had been at the concert with them. A potent fellow, Willie, and when it came to this sort of thing he and Modesty worked as if sharing a brain. Still, nothing to be too uneasy about even with Willie absent, Collier told himself. He had had the doubtful privilege of seeing Modesty Blaise at work more than once, on his behalf and on Dinah's. It wasn't relaxing, but it was certainly impressive.

Dinah said, "Eight. In."

Collier remembered the rapier death-duel with Wenczel, the fencing master, in the desert arena, and the hideous moments in the ancient Mayan temple in Guatemala, when Dinah had lain under a sacrificial knife, and —

"Seven. In."

Tarrant would be recalling his own particular memories of her, thought Collier, memories of lying half-crippled by torture and watching her fight for both their lives in the icy Caves of Lancieux. And now . . .

Unease touched Collier. Seven o'clock? That would bring the crossbow bastard round on their flank, with an unobstructed view. His spine crept. Dinah had cupped hands behind her ears now, facing towards the row of vehicles just south of them. Tarrant was looking in the same direction. Collier turned his head, and in that instant there was sudden movement in the gap between two cars twenty paces away. She flashed into view against the light of a lamp, and he saw the straight bare arm and shoulder acting as a fulcrum as she vaulted the roof of the low-slung Capri, one long leg tucked beneath her, the other darting out as she cleared the car, ball of the foot striking hard to something solid in the shadows of a Volvo estate wagon.

A dark figure staggered off-balance into the lamplight, but did not fall. Something clattered to the ground, something with the sound of steel. A grunt. Quick movement. The man wore a black tracksuit and was tearing a stocking mask from his face for clearer vision. He came at her with swift ferocity, feinting, then spinning with practised skill to deliver a high reverse roundhouse kick that might well have broken her neck had it landed.

She seemed to lean quietly away from it with ample time, and Collier saw once again that strange phenomenon by which her anticipation, the mark of the true combat master, gave the impression that she was moving more slowly than her opponent. As his boot passed only the necessary inch from her head, she twisted and struck low with her heel to his exposed crotch. He made a wordless whimpering sound and toppled against the side of the Volvo, doubling up. Her knee hit him just above the bridge of the nose, and as his head came up she struck with a short back-elbow jab to a point behind his ear. He dropped like a half empty sack and lay still.

Collier exhaled, cleared his throat and said conversationally, "I was talking to a chap the other day, and he always uses that carpark under the National Theatre next door. He says you get a better class of toxophilite there."

Dinah said anxiously, "Is it over? Is Modesty all right?"

"Fine, sweetheart. The chap she just kicked in the knackers seems a bit pensive but that's hardly surprising."

Dinah heard Modesty's approach and reached out a hand. "Are you really okay, honey? I'm sure I can smell blood on you."

"I think the crossbow bolt split the skin over the upper rib, just beside my left tit. Yes, I'm a bit gory there but it's only a scratch, truly Dinah."

Tarrant came round from the side of the van. "I haven't touched it," he said, "but it's a crossbow bolt all right. A killer at that range."

Collier had made a pad of his handkerchief and was holding it pressed over the cut in her side. "We want something to tie it on with till you start clotting," he said. "In films women always wear petticoats to tear up for such purposes. You two should be ashamed of yourselves. Let's have your tights, Dinah."

Modesty said, "No, use mine, the feet are in ribbons now." Then, to Tarrant, "Can you hush this up? I don't want my name in the papers as an intended murder victim."

"My dear, we can't just walk away. It's a police matter, and in any event you surely want to find out who the man is and why he tried to kill you."

"I don't recognise him, but he's a pro. Combat trained. A hired hit-man I'd guess. The police won't find out who sent him because there'll be a cut-out. Look, we're only assuming he was after me. As head of an intelligence department you're a much more likely target for some terrorist mob, and if you let the police make the natural assumption they'll hush it up and investigate under wraps."

Tarrant rubbed his chin dubiously. "You're suggesting I give false information to the police."

Dinah said, "Ah, come on now. You owe the girl plenty."

Tarrant sighed. "True. Very well, I'll go and find a telephone."

"Hang on." Modesty pulled on her dress and turned for Collier to zip it up, then slid bare feet into her shoes. "There's a phone in the Rolls," she said. "Here's the key, you can call the police from there." She twisted a long strand torn from her tights. "I'll go and thumb-tie the toxophilite."

Tarrant took the key and moved off along the line of cars. He remembered about the phone in the Rolls now. According to Modesty it was Weng, her houseboy-chauffeur and self-confessed snob of the seventh dan, who had insisted on the car telephone and who was virtually the sole user of it. Weng was not on chauffeur duty tonight because he was busy cooking the Chinese meal to which they had planned to return. Willie Garvin and his girlfriend would be arriving at the penthouse soon from Willie's pub near Maidenhead, to join them for dinner. Tarrant decided that he would have to make more than one call. Dinner would be a little late tonight.

Beside the Volvo, holding her husband's arm, Dinah was saying, "You have to excuse Steve coming out with the dopey bits, Modesty honey."

Collier said, "My sweet, nobody knows better than this female knacker-kicker that coming out with the dopey bits is my own particular alternative to sticking my thumbs in my ears, waggling my fingers, crossing my eyes, and running round in a screaming panic."

"Don't call her names," said Dinah. "And that reminds me, what's a toxophilite?"

"*Reminds* you? What reminds you? No, don't tell me, your logic destroys me. It's an archer, a bow and arrow chap. Oh God, now you've made me uncertain. Perhaps it's a chap who clips hedges in the shape of peacocks."

Dinah shook her head. "I don't know how anyone as nutty as you got to be a professor, and in mathematics yet. It's a good job I love you, buster."

Modesty rose from tying the unconscious man's thumbs together behind his back with the twist of nylon. "I've always liked Steve's dopey bits," she said, and came towards them, hands in the pockets of her jacket. "Thanks, Dinah. Our bowman friend was all set to shoot another bolt, and I had to get a fix on him without him seeing me."

"I don't know what they'd do without us girls."

Collier moved to lean against the car, not looking at the slumped black figure on the ground, trying to cool the fierce hatred that burned within him, trying to forget that this bastard, this vicious, loathsome, coldblooded bastard, had tried to shoot a bolt of steel into the heart of the girl whose friendship he and Dinah treasured above all others. Strange that what Dinah had once been to Willie, and what Collier himself had once been to Modesty, troubled none of them to the smallest degree. He knew there were few women Modesty could count as friends, and this did not surprise him, but he was also aware of the deep empathy that existed between her and the wife he adored.

They were standing side by side now, the dark head two or three inches higher than the honey coloured head, arms loosely linked, waiting with that patient abstraction he knew was common to both. Dinah had been taught it by her blindness, Modesty by the childhood years of fighting to survive.

Moonlight touched their faces, and he saw that Modesty was frowning a little, as if at some growing anxiety. After a while she said uneasily, "Weng's going to be furious about us being late for dinner."

Dinah nodded. "I was just thinking the same thing."

Collier began to laugh.

✳   ✳   ✳   ✳   ✳

"He's a rock hound."

"A what?" Tarrant turned the small object gently in his hands. The green gemstone measured an inch across. It was carved in the shape of a tiger's head, and mounted on a small sphere of black Perspex with a flat base.

"A rock hound," Lady Janet Gillam repeated. The long 'o' of her Scottish accent gave the sound of 'rawk hound'.

"Is he one of the millionaires she and Willie rescued from Limbo?" Tarrant inquired.

"Och, no. Ben Christie was long before that. He was that American narcotics man she got out of trouble just when she was winding up *The Network*. D'you not know that story?"

Tarrant glanced round the sitting room. Modesty and Collier were standing by the big floor-to-ceiling window, looking out over the light-bejewelled blackness of Hyde Park. Willie and Dinah were on the chesterfield, he listening with attention while she spoke. Tarrant surmised that he was now being given a more detailed account of the crossbow incident earlier that evening. By the time Modesty and her party reached the penthouse, well after ten, Willie had already arrived with Lady Janet, who farmed not far from his Thames-side pub in Berkshire and was his steady girlfriend. It was Steve Collier who told the story of the carpark attack, with a strong flavour of his particular brand of humour, making light of the incident. Tarrant suspected that Modesty had primed him to do so for Janet's benefit.

Weng had been mollified. Dinner had been served, and it was now half past midnight. The Colliers were to stay the night. Willie would take Janet back to *The Treadmill* or to her farm, dropping Tarrant at his London flat on the way. Lady Janet was the daughter of a Scottish earl, but it was not for this that Tarrant held her in high regard. She had been with him as a prisoner in Chateau Lancieux during the final days of his torture, and he well remembered how she had borne herself under pain and seemingly certain death.

She was sitting on the broad leather arm of his chair at this moment, to show him the carved peridot, and he said, "No, I don't know the Ben Christie story. They're reluctant story tellers."

"I know." She shook her head of short auburn curls. "I'd not have heard it myself if it hadn't been that I met the man when he was in London for a week or two last summer, and he told me."

Over by the window Collier stood holding a brandy glass and

saying quietly, "It's no use your making reassuring noises at me, darling. I've been up the sharp end with you, accidentally and uselessly, but nevertheless there. So has Dinah, and we've learned a thing or two. Assassination is pretty easy, even if the victim is you, because the assassin can choose time and place and method. That Robin Hood this evening only just failed. A sniper with a telescopic sight could knock you off three times a day with no trouble unless you start living like a prisoner, and you won't do that."

"No. But I'll be careful, Steve, I promise."

"You bloody well better had. Worrying makes my hair fall out. Were you telling the truth when you said you didn't know the crossbow chap?"

She smiled. "Yes. So you've worked out that if he wasn't acting for himself he was probably hired, and whoever hired him might now hire someone else."

"Of course I've worked it out. I'm not a statistician for nothing, you know."

"It doesn't follow that there'll be a new attempt, but I really will be careful, and I'll put my head together with Willie's to figure who might want me put down. It can only be a revenge thing, and I'd have thought anyone with a grudge going back to the *Network* days would have come at me long before this. Perhaps Sir Gerald was the target after all."

Collier sighed. "Perhaps. I just hope the bugger talks under police questioning, so you're not left in the dark. God knows why you're always getting mixed up with such nasty goings-on." He swirled his brandy moodily. "If you ask me, you ought to have a bit more regard for your friends. Dammit, you and Willie are the only rich friends we've got, Dinah and I, and if you go bimbling off into the Great Hereafter we'll have to mix exclusively with poor people for the rest of our lives. What's that sinister thing Janet's showing Sir Gerald? A sex aid for the ill-equipped?"

"You've been looking at rude catalogues." She took his glass. "A touch more, to cheer you up."

"I'd love to, but no. When we get to bed I shall need all my wits about me to convince Dinah you're quite safe and there's not a thing to worry about."

On the chesterfield Dinah said, "I know very well there's nothing to be done, Willie. You can't cover her twenty-four hours a day and she wouldn't allow it anyway. She'll just carry on as usual and hope to beat the strike if and when it comes." Dinah sighed. "Oh, I'll worry all right, but Modesty always inspires me with optimism, the way she does you, so deep down I'll believe that if they come at her again she'll make out somehow, like tonight. But Steve's different, he's afraid to be an optimist, so can you give me a line to feed him, Willie?" She felt for his hand. "Something plausible to stop him fraying round the edges?"

Willie said softly, "Tell him Tarrant'll pinpoint the opposition through the bloke Modesty clobbered tonight. Failing that, I'll talk 'er into doing a vanishing trick for a few weeks. The opposition can't 'unt for her without coming in close to ask questions, and I'll be waiting. Weng's the likeliest channel for 'em, and he plays a lovely stake-out. Once I get a line on who's paying, I'll sign 'im off, no messing. Will that stop Steve going around with 'is hair clenched?"

"Willie, it's just what I needed."

She felt his fingers tighten a little on hers, and noted the slight metallic quality in his voice as he murmured, "You can be convincing with it, love. It's all true."

Lady Janet was saying, ". . . so each year, round about the anniversary of the time she took him half dead from that awful ship with the drugs and the women, Ben Christie sends her a wee gift of some stone he's dug up and carved. He told me there's no great intrinsic value, and the carving isn't exactly Fabergé, but at least it's a personal way of saying thank you for another year of life. D'you not think that a very touching thing for him to have said?"

Tarrant took his eyes from the peridot to smile at her. "It's something I've felt myself but wouldn't be able to say."

"You have my sympathy. We British are the most easily embarrassed race in the world. With each stone he sends a card saying, *I hope it works, Mam'selle,*"

"Works?"

"He explained to me that this is what he said to her then, when she told him she was retiring." Lady Janet made a small grimace. "But it didn't work, of course, either with her or with Willie."

Behind her Collier said, "Of course it didn't work, and who's to blame? None other than this seemingly benign and avuncular Edwardian gentleman upon whom you're wasting your beauty and personality, and whose exterior hides a black and stony heart."

Tarrant nodded regretfully. "It's true about the heart," he acknowledged, "but those two are well able to get into trouble without my intervention. I've only once actually asked anything of them, you know. Other occasions have just, as it were, arisen."

Lady Janet nodded. Collier said, "Other occasions meaning occasions when people shoot bits out of them?"

"I'm not the only one of us three to have involved them in such occasions," Tarrant observed mildly.

"Christ, no," Collier said in a low voice, remembering. Then he shrugged and gave a half laugh. "But let's not start arguing about who caused which scar. As you say, they don't need our help. Modesty tells me this green and black thing you're studying is a sex aid, Sir Gerald. Why don't you go and distract my wife with words of comfort and reassurance while Lady Janet shows me how it works?"

"I need no urging to talk to Dinah," said Tarrant gallantly. The telephone rang as he got to his feet, and a few moments later Weng appeared. "Sir Gerald's office wishes to speak with him, Miss Blaise," he said.

She was pouring a glass of port for Dinah, and did not look up as she said, "I expect you'd prefer to take it in the breakfast room. You'll be quite private there."

"Thank you, my dear. I do apologise." He crossed the ceramic tiled floor with its scattered Isfahan rugs and went into the breakfast room. Two minutes later he returned. Janet sat with Dinah on the chesterfield now, Modesty kneeling beside them, talking as the blind girl held the carved peridot set in the Perspex base, sensing it with perceptive fingers. Willie stood by the fireplace chatting quietly with Collier.

Tarrant decided there was no point in seeking a private word

with Modesty and Willie. Everybody here knew who and what he
was. He cleared his throat, and as the murmur of conversation
faded and heads turned towards him he said, "The inspector at
Waterloo has just rung my duty officer. It appears that the man
with the crossbow was murdered in an interview room at the
police station about half an hour ago."

There was a silence. Modesty stood up, glanced at Willie then at
Tarrant, and said, "Willie suggested a special guard, but I didn't
think the police would accept the idea."

Tarrant said, "I'm sure they wouldn't have. Why the hunch,
Willie?"

"Just a long shot." Willie was watching Modesty, who had sat
down beside Dinah now and taken her hand. "If it was a hit job,
whoever set it up might 'ave an eye watching, and when the
hit-man was picked up they might try to stop 'im talking. Looks
like they did."

"They?"

Willie shrugged.

Collier said in a thin angry voice, "How in God's name did the
police let the man get murdered in their own station?"

"A man arrived purporting to have come from Special Branch at
the request of my department," said Tarrant. "He showed an
apparently authentic warrant card, and required the prisoner to be
brought to the interview room for questioning. A uniformed
constable remained in the room. Almost as soon as questioning
began, the prisoner appeared to have some sort of seizure and
became unconscious. A doctor was sent for. He arrived ten
minutes later and pronounced the man dead. The apparent cause
was some form of poison introduced by a very small dart found
embedded in the prisoner's neck. The Special Branch man quietly
disappeared at some time during the doctor's examination. The
inspector rang my duty officer, and of course was told that we had
requested no Special Branch intervention."

Modesty said, "It's very professional. They must have been all
set to write him off if he was picked up."

"A dart?" said Collier incredulously. "Some thirty-inch pigmy
in a loin cloth walks in with big boots, a bowler hat and a

forty-inch blowpipe saying he's from Special Branch, and our guardians of the law all jump up and salute? It couldn't happen in a Disney cartoon."

Modesty only half suppressed a snort of laughter, and he rounded upon her. "It's all very well for you to sit there and guffaw, darling, but it's bloody frightening for those of us who haven't had our nerves cauterised. There's Willie just cheering me up by telling me how the Robin Hood of the South Bank can be used to identify the miscreants who sent him, so they'll be brought to book, and next moment Sir Gerald pops in and starts collecting for a wreath for the sod. Where does that leave *you*?"

She got up and went to him, patted his arm, kissed him on the cheek, and said, "He's lovely when he rants and raves, isn't he, Dinah? But he exaggerates a bit."

The blind girl said, "I hope that's what he's doing. I'm worried too, honey."

Tarrant moved to pick up the brandy he had left beside his chair. "For what it's worth," he said, "we have an identification of the crossbow man."

Modesty looked at him in surprise. "So soon?"

"A lucky break. I requested earlier that a photograph be sent to my duty officer urgently. It reached Whitehall by messenger at eleven-thirty, the D.O. passed it on to Records," he looked at Modesty, "where Finch was on shift."

"The magic memory man."

"Yes. It seems Finch blinked rapidly, as he always does, then went straight to the Q-List files. The man was Hugo Gezelle, a Belgian aged thirty-eight with a record of criminal violence, known to have fought as a mercenary in at least two black African countries, suspected of terrorist connections, suspected of two paid killings in the last fifteen months, one in Italy, one in Turkey, both by crossbow. I imagine it was the crossbow m.o. that triggered Finch's memory as much as the photograph."

Lady Janet said, "Will it help, knowing who he was?"

"It's bound to offer lines of inquiry." Tarrant looked down into his glass. "Whether they'll lead anywhere is another matter."

Modesty said a little tersely, "Look, I'm getting a bit sick of the encircling gloom that seems to be closing in, so here's an announcement from your hostess. I have a date in San Francisco next month with Kim Crozier, and I haven't mentioned it to anyone till now. But I won't wait till then to fly out. I'll disappear during the next two days, and I'll lose myself somewhere in the States, maybe go walkabout down through the canyon country for two or three weeks till I'm due in San Francisco."

She stopped speaking, and after a moment Collier said, "So what?"

"So I'll be safe, dum-dum, that's what. An indistinguishable human molecule in the vastness of the U.S. of A. Safe. That's what you're all worried about, isn't it?"

"You'll have to wear a false nose," said Collier with authority, "and an assumed name is mandatory. Now let's see. How about Petal as a forename? Yes, Petal would do very nicely for you I think. The late toxophilite, whose family jewels you tenderised so splendidly, would have liked Petal. Then there's the surname. How about McBoot? Petal McBoot. Has anyone got a better idea?"

Nice work, thought Willie Garvin. Professor Stephen Collier had picked up the message that Modesty wanted the tension eased and was setting himself to the task, which he was better equipped than anyone to perform. There was a murmur of laughter, indignation from Dinah, a leisurely regrouping as new conversations were started, and within a few minutes the atmosphere was relaxed once more.

At one o'clock Dinah said, "Modesty, can I take Janet through to the guest room? She hasn't seen the Ben Christie piece of Wyoming jade he sent last year, it's the one on our dressing table, isn't it?"

"That's right. Yes, of course, carry on."

Collier said, "I'd better come too. I might have left my sock suspenders lying around the boudoir, and I wouldn't want to send the girl into a frenzy of excitement."

"Och, it's a thoughtful man you are, Stephen," said Lady Janet. "If they're red ones God knows what I might have done."

When the door had closed after them Tarrant said, "They managed that well. Do you have any private words for me?"

Both shook their heads. Willie said to Modesty, "You meant it about vanishing, Princess?"

"Unless you've a better idea."

"No, it's as good a way to play it as any. You disappear and I watch out for anyone asking questions. Maybe I'll move in 'ere in case they try getting at Weng."

"Whatever you think best, Willie." She looked at Tarrant. "Do you have any private words for us?"

"A few." Tarrant smoothed his moustache with thumb and forefinger. "Your crossbow man was also suspected of having contacts with The Watchmen. I didn't mention that in front of the others, it would only increase their concern. Can you think of any reason why The Watchmen might want to kill you?"

Again she shook her head. "No. Perhaps you were the target after all. We've never asked you about The Watchmen because we find ourselves in enough trouble without asking questions, so we only know what we've read in the papers." She began to pace slowly, arms crossed, hands loosely holding her elbows. "And we rather doubted that The Watchmen existed."

"So did most intelligence services," Tarrant said ruefully. "A firing squad assassination of the Turkish Embassy staff in Madrid. The wrecking of the nuclear plant in the Haute Savoie. The blowing up of that dam in Utah. The kidnapping and hanging of the Russian general visiting Krakow. Nothing they do is consistent, and nobody can understand what The Watchmen are against. Or for. One operation is clearly right wing, the next clearly left wing. You get a highly skilled military action apparently inspired by ecological fanatics, another that's clearly anti apartheid, another that's equally clearly as anti black as the Ku Klux Klan, and so it goes on."

Willie said, "That's why we didn't think The Watchmen existed. How d'you know it's not different terrorist mobs doing all these things?"

"That was the first theory," said Tarrant, "and certainly it's normal for responsibility to be claimed by more than one group, or persons purporting to represent groups. But then we found that in every case The Watchmen made their claims not to the press or

police but to one or other of the national intelligence agencies –
and did so virtually at the same time that the event took place.
Liaison among the intelligence services of different countries
tends to be cautious, so it's taken some time for us to accept that
The Watchmen set up all these operations."

Modesty said, "Could they be strictly mercenary? I mean, like
Salamander Four in their own field of industrial espionage and the
multinational war games? Salamander Four will agree a contract
with anyone, if you meet their price. They take no sides. Maybe
The Watchmen are the same."

"That was the second theory," said Tarrant, "but it won't
work. If you have a service to offer you have to be available to
your customers – to the Greek Cypriots who want a bunch of
Turks rubbed out, or the Polish patriots who want a Russian
general strung up. Well, we've tried to engage their services. I put
Josh Flint on the job of making contact, with a very acceptable and
plausible offer."

Willie said, "Josh is good. Lot of experience be'ind 'im and very
inventive."

"They killed him," Tarrant said bleakly. "The last report we
had from him came through our Lisbon signals. Then he was
found garotted in the Tagus."

"Ah, bugger it," Willie said with morose anger, and wandered
aimlessly away, hands deep in pockets.

"In France," said Tarrant, "Vaubois put in one of his best
SDECE operatives. He hasn't reported for ten days now, and is
presumed dead. We've even had a rather weird meeting with
representatives of Russian and Polish security services to exchange
information about The Watchmen. They didn't admit to having
made any attempt at penetration, but I'd be surprised if they
haven't, and I'm quite sure they wouldn't have wanted an
exchange of information if they'd had any success."

Modesty stood gazing absently out of the window and said, "If
there's no way to hire The Watchmen then they must be acting for
themselves, but with what aim? Shooting a few Turks might please
Greek extremists. Hanging a Russian general might please Polish
dissidents. But there's no relevance between the two things, no

common denominator. What's the third theory, Sir Gerald?"

"There isn't one, my dear. When The Watchmen carry out an operation they make no threats or demands beforehand. They simply do whatever it is, with an immediate announcement to one national security service only, saying they have acted in the cause of justice on behalf of —— then fill in any extreme group you fancy, known or unknown, and of any conceivable complexion."

Willie said, "Eccentric idealists? I'm not buying it. Some of those operations would cost a fortune. You'd need a permanent task force of 'ighly trained people with an operating base plus full communications and transport back-up. I can't see some eccentric idealist multi-billionaire financing a caper like that."

Modesty turned from the window and said, "He's right. You're being conned, Sir Gerald."

"Conned? In what way? And by whom?"

She smiled. "I don't know. It's your problem. The thing is, it doesn't seem likely that tonight's effort was organised by The Watchmen, whichever of us was the target. A simple killing just isn't their style."

The door to the main passage opened and Collier followed his wife and Lady Janet in. "May we rejoin you?" he asked hopefully. "We've exhausted all possible comment on the jade alligator, and played a couple of games on my travelling Scrabble set, and had a nice chat about my back trouble and those dizzy spells I keep getting, but then Dinah kept saying she was fed up and wanted to get back to some steady drinking —"

"God, he's such a liar, isn't he, Jan? We were perfectly happy to go on talking if he hadn't been fidgeting about, demanding to know why we hadn't brought a bottle with us, and how much longer we were going to wait."

Lady Janet said with a small smile, "Aye, he's an outrageous man, but I've maybe known worse husbands." She looked at Modesty. "I'd best be getting along home now. It was a lovely dinner, and I'm only sorry if things have been spoiled a wee bit by what happened before. If you need Willie to stay here tonight, I can drop Sir Gerald off and drive myself home. It's no problem."

Modesty shook her head. "I'd take you up on it if there was any point, but there isn't, Jan. That's the truth." She pressed a bell beside the fireplace. "I'll have Weng fetch your coat, and Sir Gerald's hat and umbrella."

      *   *   *   *   *

Ten minutes later, sitting in the back of a Volvo parked on the slip road fifty yards from the main entrance of the penthouse block, watching through a small clear area of glass in the tinted window, Hugh Oberon, who had once been known as The Graduate, saw the Jaguar emerge from the underground carpark and turn right. It passed within a few feet of him at no more than fifteen miles an hour, and in the light of the overhead fluorescent lamp he saw Garvin at the wheel, the girl with short auburn hair beside him, and the older man in the back, who would be Tarrant.

He saw the car pause, then turn out into the main road. Acid was in his throat from the surge of hatred that swept him, triggered by the glimpse of Willie Garvin. He had only to think of Modesty Blaise to know that same sick burning in his gullet, even after so long.

He sat breathing deeply, consciously taking control of his mental processes. She might have been dead now, the blood stilled, the eyes sightless, the limbs stiffening. But the Belgian crossbow specialist had failed his test, and in a way Oberon was glad. Perhaps, one day, there would come the chance to take her himself, but it would not be by striking anonymously from the dark. He would make sure that she knew him, and he would wipe that cool aloofness from her face with crushing humiliation before he finished her.

He looked at his watch. There had been no need to drive here from the police station after killing the Belgian, but something had drawn him to the place where she lived, perhaps a need to feed his hatred by being close to the object of it, and to taste the strong pleasure of contemplating revenge. Not that he would be required to account for his movements. The Watchmen had given him sole responsibility for supervising the test and covering any failure.

He started the car, drove to the phone box near Clarendon Gate, and dialled a number. He let the ringing tone sound twice, depressed the cradle and dialled again. A curiously penetrating male voice said, "Yes?"

"He blew it. The target took him out."

"Terminally?"

"No. Tranquillised. Then Boy Blue took over."

"And?"

"Preventive measures were taken. No song was sung. The matter is closed."

"Very well. Ten hundred hours tomorrow. Here. Goodnight."

"Goodnight."

Four

THE arrow was twenty-eight inches long, a two-bladed broad-head designed for hunting. Oberon watched Major the Earl St. Maur nock it on the linen bowstring and raise the centre-shot bow, drawing it with the same movement, left arm straight, right forefinger just touching the chin. He hung on his aim for no more than a second, then loosed.

The three turkey feathers, set spirally, imparted spin and thereby counteracted the tendency of the broadhead to sail off course. Oberon heard the small sound of the string touching the bracer and watched the red feathers marking the arrow's flight. It struck the tall beech a hundred yards away, just above the white disc painted on the trunk. Major the Earl St. Maur lowered his bow and moved off across the pasture, the quiver at his belt bobbing in rhythm with his pace.

Moving beside him, Oberon said, "Have you ever used a crossbow?"

"Great Scott, no. A toy."

Oberon wondered if there was anyone else in the world today who exclaimed Great Scott. "Easier to conceal though, Major," he suggested. "Hugo Gezelle could disassemble his and get it into a briefcase."

"More important to shoot straight." St. Maur's beaky nose lifted slightly in contempt. He was a tall man with thick sandy hair, pale blue eyes and a thin aristocratic face. Very much stronger than his musculature suggested, he possessed the physical condition of a world class athlete. Now thirty-four, he had once held a commission in a Marine Commando battalion. Complaints that his rigorous and realistic training had killed three of his men in a year had brought his methods under the scrutiny of a Court of Enquiry. Its members had been sufficiently shocked by their findings to decide that the Army did not wish to keep Major the Earl St. Maur, even in the most deadly of its special forces. They had invited him to resign his commission. The alternative was dimissal from the service, for which there were more than ample grounds.

"It's a pity this Belgian chap failed his final test," St. Maur said in his nasal and penetrating voice. "He was rather promising. Why do you think he missed this Blaise woman?"

"That's impossible to say. I was watching from the bridge with night glasses, and it seemed to me she moved at the last moment. Instinct, perhaps."

"Rubbish. He made a noise and she reacted."

"Whichever it was, I think you set him too hard a test for his finals. She's a pro."

"She used to be."

"Still is, when it comes to combat qualities. I'd place her among the six people in the world you'd find hardest to kill."

"But you want a chance at her yourself."

Oberon smiled. "One day, Major, one day. After we've completed Morningstar."

"She didn't see you last night?"

"No. She wouldn't have known me anyway. I don't think she saw me for more than a few minutes during the time I was in *The Network*, and last night I was wearing a beard ready for emergency action to take the Belgian out if the need arose, as it did."

"What did you use?"

"A Special Branch warrant card and one of Golitsyn's gimmicks. Hollow cigarette, spring-loaded with a gland dart. The gland's squeezed on entry, forcing the poison in."

"Curare?"

"No. The boffins who supply Golitsyn have found some way of extracting a cardiotoxin from the sea wasp, so he tells me."

St. Maur turned his head to look coldly at Oberon. "Sea wasp? The bloody man's pulling your leg."

Oberon grinned. "For once he wasn't indulging his peculiar sense of humour. I looked it up. The sea wasp isn't an insect, it's a

jellyfish that floats around off north-east Australia, and it can
sting an adult to death in one minute flat."

They reached the beech tree which stood where two hedgerows
met at the corner of the field. The trunk was heavily pitted and
splintered in and around the white circle. St. Maur worked the
arrow out of the wood, examined the shaft and the fletching, then
looked away up the slope to the edge of the copse where a bale of
straw stood on end against a low embankment.

This was not the first time Oberon had walked round the
eighteen-target archery golf course set out in the private sector of
the St. Maur estates. He kept still and silent while his companion
again nocked the arrow on the bowstring, aimed, and loosed. As
they began to walk up the long grassy slope St. Maur said, "We
were testing Blaise, too. Golitsyn says she would make a first class
recruit."

Oberon felt rage sweep him, but kept it down and walked on in
silence until he was sure of his voice. Then he said, "I disagree, but
not because she's a woman or because I hope one day to kill her.
How much does he know about her?"

"A good bit. His people built up substantial files on her when
she was operational, and Golitsyn once had dealings with *The
Network,* when she acted as intermediary between him and
Tarrant arranging a spy swap."

Oberon shook his head. "I know her better than Golitsyn. I
worked for her and I know the pattern of thinking she imposed on
The Network. There's not a hope in hell of recruiting her. She'd be
against everything The Watchmen stand for. Even if she wasn't, it
would be a bad move. The point is, Major, she's soft-centred. I
know that's hard to believe, but it's true. Her skills and
intelligence are selective. In some ways she's remarkably able, in
others she's a bloody fool."

"She's controlled some very hard men, Hugh. And destroyed
others."

"Certainly she has. I don't question her performance, but her
motivations would make you sick. It would be foolish even to
approach her on recruitment, because she just might decide she
ought to put us out of business, like she did Bora and one or two

others. We'd kill her, of course, but she might cause a lot of disruption before we managed it."

The two men walked on in silence. As they reached the bale of straw with the arrow buried in it St. Maur said, "Very well. I'll tell Golitsyn it's no go."

Oberon said carefully, "He could be insistent."

Pale blue eyes looked through him without emotion, yet he felt the familiar frisson of alarm that the gaze of Major the Earl St. Maur could always trigger in him. "Golitsyn can't insist," said St. Maur. "He's finance, admin, and policy. Von Krankin and I have exclusive responsibility for recruitment, training and ops."

Oberon wondered how to suggest tactfully that Golitsyn was perhaps first among equals in the triumvirate governing The Watchmen, but decided not to try. He said, "I've supervised the Gezelle test and covered his failure. Is there anything else before I return to base?"

St. Maur did not answer for a few moments, then he said, "Under the circumstances, and in view of what you've just told me about Modesty Blaise, it might be good strategy to deter her from nosing around."

"I'm not sure I follow you."

"Someone tried to kill her. Police investigation is one thing, but I wouldn't like her to make a serious attempt at personal investigation, not at this stage. She can't be sure that she was the intended victim, and if somebody killed Tarrant during the next few days it would seem that the earlier attempt was against his life rather than hers. Do you follow me now?"

Oberon said, "Yes. But I think it might — " He broke off as St. Maur took up his stance and drew the thirty-five pound bow. There came the twang of the loose, and they watched the red feathers lift and drop in a shallow arc, dwindling in perspective to end as a red dot against a white-painted stump beyond the stream. "Tarrant's killing might encourage her to investigate rather than make her lose interest," Oberon finished.

"I disagree," said St. Maur, and shouldered his bow. "But I won't issue an order until I've discussed it with Golitsyn this morning."

"He's here?"

"Arriving today."

Golitsyn would be travelling on a Portuguese passport that gave his occupation as a director of a reputable company of wine exporters. Oberon said, "If he agrees, do you wish me to do the job?"

"No. I don't want it done by a Watchman. Hire a suitable person if we decide to go ahead."

"You've said 'under the circumstances' and 'at this stage'. Is there some particular significance?"

St. Maur looked straight ahead as he walked, yet Oberon could still see the sudden glow that came to the stony blue eyes, and for once the penetrating voice was almost soft as he said, "Very much so, Hugh. Operation Morningstar is on programme now. September."

Oberon stopped dead, and the earl stopped with him, turning, showing his teeth in that rare crocodile grin of his. "It's been announced?" said Oberon. "A western summit meeting in September?"

"It won't be announced until Friday, but it's agreed. Golitsyn has confirmation from his people in Washington, Paris and Bonn, as well as here."

"And it's to be at Funchal, as predicted a year ago?"

"Not quite. It will be on Porto Santo, which is even better for us. Golitsyn didn't merely rely on what the computers made of the factors fed into them. He made sure that his colleagues put their tame opinion-shapers in the west to work, pushing the idea of Madeira as a venue."

That would certainly be true. Oberon recalled a morning when he and Golitsyn had stood on a rocky hill watching two six-man patrols in the valley below manoeuvring for advantage in a First Blood exercise with knives. The small eyes in the heavy face had been twinkling with humour as Golitsyn spoke in that deep, chesty voice. "Certainly it has cost five or six millions to establish cover for a base here, soldier boy, but the gamble is not so great. The next summit must surely be in Europe, so that the President can pretend respect for his miserable allies and try to persuade them not to go to bed and pull the blanket over their heads. But it will not be in a major country, because other major countries would be offended, and also because a little flattery might well tip the scales in persuading Portugal to do more for NATO. But Lisbon is very difficult for security. An island is far better. And Madeira has a superb climate. So all Intelligence indicated Funchal, and the computers agreed, and our agents of influence in the foreign media and foreign governments made suggestive little noises . . ."

The bowstring thrummed again. Oberon drew in a long breath of sheer joy. The prediction had been close enough. Porto Santo was the small island twenty-five miles from Funchal. So in only four months The Watchmen would make their first genuine strike, as planned. And he, Hugh Oberon, who had been brushed contemptuously aside by Modesty Blaise, was now into something bigger than she had ever dreamt of, for he was the right arm of the triumvirate that governed The Watchmen, a stronger and more deadly right arm than Garvin had ever been.

They were crossing a rustic bridge now, and Oberon said, "Will you cancel the San Francisco job and concentrate on specific training for Morningstar now?"

"Definitely not. A month is sufficient for that, I don't want the men to get stale. You're to carry out Operation Baystrike as arranged. A draft plan is being drawn up by von Krankin now, and we'll examine it when we're both back at base next week. As an additional duty I shall want you to vet a possible recruit while you're in the States. We'll arrange a rendezvous in San Francisco, and if you think he's good material you can run him through a first degree Mohs test."

Oberon nodded. The Mohs scale was for measuring the hardness of abrasives. The Watchmen used the term for measuring one aspect of potential members. Tests for skill and ability would come later.

"Have him kill a woman," said St. Maur. "Or a child."

"What's his background?" Oberon asked.

"He was a sergeant in the U.S. Army. Taken prisoner in Vietnam. Eighteen months in a prison camp. Indoctrination.

Killed two guards escaping, and took six weeks to reach his own lines. Could have been a hero, but the prison experience had embittered him. Why the hell didn't his stinking rotten country use the bomb on those gooks and finish it? Because America's turned into a load of pap, that's why. And so forth. He's been in trouble with the law twice, once for assault, once for armed robbery. Then he got smart and became an enforcer and hit-man for a Los Angeles organisation, but that only lasted two years. They threw him out when he killed a man he was only supposed to lean on. Apparently he's very bitter about that, too. One of von Krankin's contacts in the United Nations recommended him to us."

"He sounds promising," said Oberon. "But are we continuing to recruit, with Morningstar so near?"

"There'll be plenty to do after Morningstar," said St. Maur. "It's a ten year programme, and The Watchmen will be needed."

"I don't think I quite realised . . ."

"Our sights have been set on Morningstar, but clearly that's only a beginning."

Again Oberon recalled the voice of Golitsyn, talking in that chuckling growl one evening after dusk, with the sea throwing spume from below as they strolled the steel deck. "The shooting war is out of date, soldier boy. Today it is different. Twenty men, properly directed, doing the correct thing in the correct place at the correct time, can be more potent than an army. More men have been killed by the proboscis of the mosquito than by bombs. So we sting, sting, sting, hey? Until now we sting only to distract and confuse, but there will be other objectives. It is a good thing the Americans have not grasped this principle. They would put it into execution more efficiently than we do. When I say 'we', I don't mean us, soldier boy. I mean our sponsors." A shrug of heavy shoulders. "You would not believe the struggles I had to set up an operation so cheap yet so fruitful as this. I tell you, there are some stupid pricks in Moscow."

St. Maur plucked the shaft from the big rotting tree trunk that lay in the shade of the tall chestnuts and said, "Besides, we've lost one or two in manoeuvres lately. Recruitment will continue."

"Should we stop the First Blood exercises and the Individual Duels now?"

"Absolutely not. The men *must* put their lives at risk in training, otherwise they have an entirely new factor to cope with when in action."

"That's true. Which reminds me, can I have Romaine and his section for San Francisco? I think they're best fitted for it."

St. Maur examined the arrow, frowned slightly, then put it in his quiver and drew out another. "Romaine's dead," he said.

Oberon stared. "What happened?" he asked.

The beaky nose flared slightly as St. Maur sniffed. "I killed him," he said. "He challenged me to an Individual."

"Challenged *you*?"

A shrug. "I can't exclude myself from the system, and obviously I couldn't decline."

"Of course not. But why in God's name did he do it?" Even as he spoke Oberon knew the answer. Romaine was one of their three best men, and highly experienced, but there was a powerful streak of vanity in him. It was not out of character for him to have challenged the combat supremo himself.

St. Maur said, "I'm not interested in why he did it, Hugh. I know Golitsyn was none too pleased. Thought he might lose me, I suppose. Could make things rather tricky. Romaine chose an area of shore terrain, by night, no weapons. Took me three hours to pinpoint the blighter and work close enough for the kill. Regrettable, of course. Don't like losing a capable chap. But it's had a good effect on morale. Romaine wasn't popular, you know. Neither am I for that matter, but the men like to feel that the chap who's teaching them knows what he's about. I shall only suspend First Blood patrol actions and Individual Duels for the six weeks run-up to Morningstar."

Oberon said, "I think that's wise. Who can I have for San Francisco?"

"Szabo and his section. They've started special training for it."

"I'd like to be with them for that, Major. When do I return to base?"

"You're booked to fly out with me in three days' time. Can you lay on the Tarrant killing before then?"

"I can arrange the contract, certainly."

"That's all right, then."

"Will Golitsyn be staying on in London?"

"For a few days. He has a meeting with the Head Buyer early next week about equipment for the Baystrike operation."

Twenty minutes later the two men emerged from a footpath through woods and crossed a wide lawn to reach the drive at the back of the small manor house. St. Maur's wife waved to them from the terrace as they approached. She was a tall, buxom young woman of narrow intelligence and lusty appetites. Since her husband was rarely at home, she sublimated these appetites to some extent by riding horses, but not entirely. As usual she was dressed in breeches that were well stretched to contain her bottom, and a sweater that yielded to the thrust of her large breasts.

"Ronnie," she called, and waved again. "Co-eee, darling."

Her husband acknowledged the greeting with a lift of the long chin and hooked nose, not bothering to answer. This did not distress Victoria, the Countess St. Maur. Ronnie had never been much of a one for talking to her, and she quite understood that his mind was occupied by more important matters. She always enjoyed the time when he was at home because he serviced her quite marvellously, though she was vaguely surprised, whenever she happened to think of it, that in five years he hadn't got her pregnant. The doctor said that all her works were all right and that Ronnie ought to have a check-up, but that was absurd. You couldn't imagine that Ronnie of all men might be firing blanks.

"Hello, Vicky old girl," he said. They were coming up the six broad steps to the terrace. "Going for a ride?"

"In just a minute. Hallo, Mr. Oberon, how are you?"

"Well, thank you, your ladyship."

"That's good. I expect you're going to take Ronnie back to Lisbon with you soon."

"Well, this is an important time of the year in our business, I'm afraid. It's a pity there isn't enough sun for serious viticulture here in England."

"What?"

St. Maur said, "Growing grapes," and Oberon cursed himself inwardly for stupidity. You didn't use long words with Victoria, Countess St. Maur, unless they had something to do with horses.

She said, "Your Mr. thingy arrived about ten minutes ago, Ronnie. You know, from Lisbon."

"Rocha." That was the name on the Portuguese passport Golitsyn carried.

"Yes, that's right. I told Johnson to put him in the drawing room and give him *The Times*. Not *The Guardian*, there's another fearfully rude letter in it about the one you wrote the other day."

St. Maur put down his bow and quiver on the long table. "That's nothing new, old girl."

"No, but they're such pigs, these people, talking about you being a latter day Cromwell, or politically to the right of Mussolini. I mean, you're not even *in* politics, and really they just jeer and do caricatures and poke fun. Couldn't you stop writing letters and giving interviews, Ronnie?"

"Not on, Vicky. Must make it quite clear where I stand."

Too true, thought Oberon. The noble earl hadn't spent several years building a particular image for nothing. The countess patted a muscular thigh with the crop she carried. "Well, you know best, darling. I'll see you at lunch."

"Jolly good."

When they reached the drawing room *The Times* lay unopened on the table and Golitsyn was standing by the window smoking one of his powerful cigarettes, wearing a dark business suit with a quiet tie. He turned towards them, a thickset man with a broad, heavily creased face, and deepset humorous eyes. Golitsyn knew his smoking was sure to annoy St. Maur, who would conceal his annoyance. This did not trouble Golitsyn. It was desirable to have an element of animosity within the top leadership, for this produced a measure of critical appraisal that was invaluable.

St. Maur closed the door and said, "Good morning. This room is secure."

Golitsyn nodded, and the creases that ran from his nose to the corners of his mouth became still deeper as he smiled. "Good morning, Major." The eyes twinkled at Oberon. "How did the Belgian candidate's test work out, soldier boy?"

Oberon told him in a few words. He did not mind Golitsyn's amiably mocking manner, for he was aware that the Russian thought well of his abilities, and this was good, for Golitsyn was a big man, a man entrusted with the creation of an instrument that would change the face of the world.

"Congratulations," said Golitsyn, and moved to an armchair. "Are there any matters arising from this?"

At the sideboard, pouring a brandy, St. Maur said, "Oberon will tell you that Modesty Blaise is totally unsuitable as a recruit, and should be deterred from thinking the attack was directed at her. The best way to do this would be to have Tarrant put down. By a hired hand, of course."

Golitsyn accepted the brandy and sat thinking. "I like it in principle," he said. "But it must be placed in reliable hands."

"I suggest the Polish twins," said Oberon. "They'll cost twenty thousand, but they're bankable killers. I can use my bearded persona and put the contract out through the Chan organisation."

Golitsyn considered. The two men known as the Polish twins had a surname that only another Pole could pronounce. Most of the world's intelligence organisations had them on file as providing an assassination service. Many of those organisations had used them. The thing about the Polish twins was that they had never been known to fail. This was because their commercial probity would not allow them ever to give up. If you paid to have a man killed, and the first attempt was thwarted, or the second, or third, then regardless of difficulty or expense the Polish twins would pursue their target until they had discharged their obligation.

"What currency will you need?" said Golitsyn.

"I'll have to check with Chan, but I imagine gold."

"When?"

"Chan will know where to find the twins, and he should have an answer in a few hours. Then I have to deposit the payment with him. Could it be ready by noon the day after tomorrow?"

"Yes. Come to my hotel. The usual place." Golitsyn sipped his brandy. Very satisfactory, he thought. A clever suggestion from the beak-nosed English aristocrat, and one with a long-term benefit. It would be a distinct advantage not to have the experienced old warhouse Tarrant around at the time of Morningstar.

Five

"SHE'S madly in love with me," said Willie Garvin. He patted Ethel's thigh fondly. "Aren't you, me old sweetheart?"

Ethel shifted coyly, and blew in his ear. Willie recoiled, plunged the mop in the bucket, and began to wash her belly. Tarrant said, "What do you think is the secret of this irresistible attraction you have for elephants?"

"Not all elephants, Sir G. Just Ethel."

"I'd still like to know your secret."

"You 'ave to pull a thorn out of their feet, then they remember you."

"Surely you're thinking of lions?"

"Don't talk dirty in front of Ethel. She can't stand cats."

"I beg her pardon."

Tarrant sat on an upturned tub in a marquee which was part of Gogol's Circus, now set up on Blackheath. It was a Sunday, and there was no performance. He had not known the circus was here until he had seen the big top and the surrounding tents and caravans. When he had stopped his car and asked at the office for Willie Garvin he had only half expected to find him here.

"What brings you down this way then?" said Willie.

Tarrant made a wry grimace. "Pirie has a flat just off the heath. I come out to see him occasionally."

"How's he making out?"

Tarrant shrugged. "He manages all right as long as the door and the windows are open, and there are no loud noises or sudden movements."

Pirie was thirty-six and had been one of Tarrant's field agents. Betrayal had led to his capture in Budapest, followed by transfer to Moscow. There, in Lubyanka, he had held out for six weeks against brutal interrogation. In the end, inevitably, he had been broken, but by then his contacts had been pulled out to safety. Later Tarrant had exchanged a Hungarian agent for the husk that had been Pirie.

With an effort Tarrant switched his thoughts away from the man he had just left. Idly stabbing the hard-trodden turf with the ferrule of his umbrella he said, "Why on earth did you buy it, Willie?"

"Ethel's not mine, we're just good friends. She's part of the Solino act."

"I meant the circus. Modesty once told me you own it jointly with Georgi Gogol. What made you take a half share in a tenting circus?"

Willie ducked under Ethel and began scrubbing her other side. "It was impulse buying," he said. "I worked for a spell in a circus way back, when I was in me teens. Then I came across this one in the South of France not long before we wound up *The Network*. Georgi was short of cash, and I was 'appy to be a sleeping partner and let 'im run things, so I bought in."

"That doesn't tell me why."

"Well . . . I spend a few weeks a year with it, sometimes popping in when it's on tour, sometimes when it's in winter quarters, and I lend a hand wherever I fancy. It's fun, that's all. Well, maybe not all. Have you ever been to bed with a lady trapezist, Sir G.?"

Tarrant pondered, then shook his head slowly. "Not that I can recall."

"You ought to give it a whirl. Lady trapezists 'ave unusual talents."

"I'll certainly bear the thought in mind."

Tarrant sat feeling rather sad, idly watching the scrubbing of the elephant. It was a good few years now since he had possessed a family, and his options for the evening lay between being alone in his flat or seeking company at his club. Since neither appealed, he was reluctant to leave. After a while he said, "Have you heard from Modesty?"

"I 'ad a card a few days ago. She sent it from Bryce Canyon."

"Does she really walk barefoot in the wilds, Willie?"

"Sure. That's the way she walked from God-knows-where in the Balkans to Morocco and back when she was a kid, so it comes natural for 'er."

After a little silence Tarrant said, "I'm coming round to the view that the crossbow man was in fact after me, not Modesty."

Willie looked up sharply. "Why's that?"

"I'm sure I've been under surveillance since then." Tarrant lifted a shoulder. "I've never been in the field, so I haven't an agent's skills in spotting these things, but I don't think it's my imagination."

Willie relaxed. "It wasn't," he said. "The Princess fixed for you to be kept tabs on by the Rossiter agency for a couple of weeks, just in case. They were to spot anyone showing interest in you, and let me know."

Tarrant stared. "Why the hell did she arrange that?"

"She 'appens to be a bit fond of you, you crusty old sod. That's why."

Tarrant looked away with a smile. "I withdraw my protest."

"Rossiter put a good team on it. You were smart to spot 'em. What've you done about it?"

"Done?"

"Counter measures. You didn't know they were doing an escort job."

"I've taken no counter measures, Willie. I can't have people put in prison or deported for watching me. I might have them questioned, warned off, but what's the point? That won't stop serious people. I'm afraid that in this country we have to wait till an offence has been committed before we can do much about it."

"You could be dead by then. Why 'aven't you got a bodyguard?"

"Because serious people will kill him first, if he gets in their way. There simply isn't an answer to this sort of thing. Anyway, you can call off Rossiter's team now."

Willie patted Ethel's trunk and moved away with his bucket and mop. "No sweat. I called 'em off a week ago, when they said there was no sign of surveillance."

Tarrant scraped a small circle in the turf. "Are you sure?"

"Yes." Willie stood still, eyes suddenly narrowed. "Why?"

"I felt that the presence had departed a few days ago. But it was back yesterday, and today I'm almost sure I spotted the tail for the first time. A grey Cortina. I was behind it coming through Greenwich. Perhaps they were doing a front tail for a while. The registration letters were GST, which happen to be my initials. I'd not have noticed it otherwise. When I left Pirie it was parked a little way down the road. Two men in it. I didn't see them sufficiently well for a description. I joined the A2 for London and saw your circus on the heath, so I pulled off with the vague idea that I might find you here. When I came out of the office I saw a grey Cortina parked about fifty yards from mine, on the edge of the heath. I'm sure it's the same one."

"Two men in it?"

"I think so. I didn't stare."

Willie went to the open door of the marquee and whistled. An olive skinned boy of about fourteen with curly black hair appeared. Willie said, "I'm leaving you in charge of Ethel, so make sure she gets 'er supper, Pedro."

"Si, señor." The boy swelled with pride.

Willie led the way between tents and trailers to where several caravans were drawn up. "Where's their car now?" he said.

"Directly to our right, about a hundred yards away."

"Good. We can take a look from Georgi's caravan."

Georgi Gogol was a Hungarian with a thin face and a waxed moustache. He greeted Tarrant courteously when introduced, and at Willie's request produced field glasses from a drawer in the well furnished and comfortable caravan. "Is trouble, Villee?" he said.

"Not for us, Georgi." Willie knelt by one of the windows, holding the glasses just above the lower edge, and adjusted the focus. Ten seconds later he became utterly still, and Tarrant heard him breathe, "Oh, Christ . . ." Another few seconds passed, and Willie got to his feet, handed Georgi the glasses, and sat down on one of the cushioned seats.

Georgi said, "Your face don't tell me there is no trouble, Villee."

"It's not a circus problem. Is the phone cable plugged in?"

"Sure." Georgi rose from his desk and fingered an end of his waxed moustache. "I don't care to know, Villee. I take a valk now, see some rehearsal." He bowed stiffly to Tarrant. "A pleasure to make the acquaintance, sir."

When the door had closed Willie said quietly, "You ever 'eard of the Polish twins?"

"In what connection?"

"Never mind. If you knew about 'em you wouldn't ask."

"Tell me."

"They'll be on your files somewhere. Zygmunt and Mikolaj Zdrzalkywicz. Twins. Probably the best professional hit-men in the world. They can pass Customs on any frontier without their murder weapons being found because they're in full view, attached to their arms. Their hands, Sir G. That's all they ever use. They charge fifteen to twenty thousand pounds a contract, they work about seven or eight times a year, and they never fail. They get paid in full in advance, and once they lock on to a target they never quit. Five years ago they spent more than six months on a job. When the Polish twins accept a contract, the target's dead."

Tarrant took out his cigar case. "You're not very encouraging," he said. "Would Mr. Gogol mind if I smoke?"

"Go ahead."

Tarrant selected a cigar, took out his cutter, clipped the end carefully, and spent the time a Punch-Punch claro merited for lighting. Willie Garvin sat rather slumped in a corner of the bench seat, his rough-hewn face blank, his blue eyes empty.

Tarrant said, "It may seem absurd, but there's nothing I can do —"

"Shut up." The words were spoken without emphasis, but Tarrant was instantly silent. He drew on his cigar and studied Willie Garvin more carefully. Abruptly it seemed that he was looking at a stranger, for this was not a Willie Garvin he had ever seen before, this was a man so totally withdrawn as to be virtually absent from the shell of his body. Yet for Tarrant there was a curious echo of familiarity in the aura that encompassed Willie, and after a few moments he recognised it. This was a phenomenon he had witnessed once before, in Modesty Blaise, under the stalactites that roofed the great underground cave of Lancieux. Unarmed, naked, greased so that she glinted like a silver statue in the reflected lamplight, she had stood between Tarrant and the smiling killer whose monstrous strength and skill had already defeated her once.

In the caravan the silence continued. Reluctantly Tarrant considered his own situation. Full protection would require a team of eight men working shifts over twenty-four hours. That was out of the question. In the long run, the utterly determined killer must always succeed. The nerves of his scalp crawled, and coldness touched his stomach. He could have the Polish twins picked up, perhaps deported as undesirable aliens, but there was no way of sealing the country against their return. In the end, the result would be the same.

He looked at Willie Garvin again, and for a moment had the fanciful notion that the big man was actually communing with Modesty Blaise, not by any paranormal means but simply by his profound knowledge of how she would react to any combination of circumstances. After a little while Willie sighed and stirred. "I'll 'ave to 'ave a little talk with the twins," he said with bleak resignation.

Tarrant frowned. "Will that be effective?"

"If I don't make any mistakes it might work out. You ready to play it my way to set up a meeting on me own terms, Sir G.?"

Tarrant smiled grimly. "I don't know what you can achieve in view of what you tell me about them, but by all means try."

"Right. Get those field glasses and 'ave a look at 'em through the window. They're parked facing this way."

"Might they also be watching through glasses?"

"No. They'll just be keeping an eye on your car. What they're doing is tailing you till they find a nice chance to sign you off quick and easy with no interference. They'll do it for weeks if need be. Obviously they don't fancy the circus as a killing ground. Too many people wandering about."

Keeping low, Tarrant adjusted the glasses to bring the Cortina into sharp focus. Two men in the front, both with straight fair hair and broad identical faces, one in a grey sweater, the other in dark blue. The latter was reading a newspaper.

As he watched, Tarrant heard the sound of the telephone dial. After a pause, Willie spoke. "'Allo Liz, it's Willie. Can I 'ave a word with Dave?" Another pause. "Yes, fine thanks. What about you? And the kids? Good. All right, love, I'll 'ang on."

Tarrant lowered the glasses, moved to one side of the window, and sat up straight. After half a minute Willie said into the phone, "Not bad. Look Dave, 'ave you been working on the site today? Ah, I thought you might. Locked up now? Good. I want to fix a little meeting there. Can you slip down the road and open the gates? Yes, now. I'll give you a buzz when I'm finished there. Thanks, Dave. See you." He put down the phone.

Tarrant said, "Don't your friends ever ask questions."

Willie shrugged. "Some do. Dave Selby doesn't. I stopped some people who were aiming to stripe 'is wife's face with a razor a year or two back." He went to the desk, picked out an A to Z from the bookshelf above it, and riffled through the pages. "Look, Sir G." He waited for Tarrant to join him, and pointed with a pencil. "When you leave 'ere, drive north through Blackwall tunnel and turn left so you double back round the Isle of Dogs, then up past Millwall to Lime'ouse. You'll pass a pub on this corner, Dave Selby's pub. Carry on —"

"What's it called, Willie?"

"Sorry. *The Stag*. Carry on for a couple of 'undred yards." The pencil moved from side to side. "It's a derelict area, disused wharves, 'alf demolished ware'ouses and suchlike. Going to be redeveloped one fine day, maybe. Anyway, Dave's got permission to set up a small landing stage by the river and build a carpark just 'ere." The pencil made a cross. "He does a bit of tourist trade in summer, and can make a bob or two running trips up to The Tower. There's a bloody great corrugated iron fence all along 'ere, but you'll see double doors, same corrugated iron, just round this bend. They'll be open. All right so far?"

It was a route Tarrant had driven a year ago when showing American friends the site of Execution Dock and the *Bunch of Grapes* in Limehouse Causeway, where Dickens was said to have been a regular customer. Tarrant's visual memory was good, and he said, "Yes. Go on, Willie."

"Don't stop on the way, especially once you're running through old dockland. There are some places you could 'ave a minor war and nobody would 'ear. So keep going, and if the Polish twins try to pass, don't let 'em. There's not much chance they'll try, but watch it anyway."

"Yes."

"Turn in through the gates. If you look half right you'll see a derelict four-storey factory with no windows or doors, nothing inside either. Whatever machinery was in there 'as been ripped out and sold for scrap long ago. The place is due for demolition soon, and Dave Selby is setting up 'is carpark and landing stage be'ind it. Doing it 'imself, with hired equipment and a couple of labourers. You drive along a tarmac track full of pot-'oles to the factory, 'ere. Look . . ."

Willie drew a pad towards him and began to sketch. "Park on the west side, there. Get out of your car quick, and go in through the big doorway. Stone steps leading up in the far left corner. Up you go to the top floor, nice and steady. Straight to the middle window on the east side, and look out. There's a zig-zag iron fire-escape running down the wall. Wait till you see one of the twins coming up it, then turn round and walk back down all the steps till you're at ground level again. I'll see you there."

Tarrant lifted his eyes from the pad, puzzled. "How do you know what will happen?"

"I'm guessing."

"I see. And then what? Why split the twins if you want to talk to them?"

"Just a hunch. We'll see 'ow it works out."

Tarrant said thoughtfully, "Suppose they don't wish to talk? We could be in a bad situation. I'm not armed myself. Will you be?"

"I always carry a set of knives in the car." Willie laid down the pencil. "Give me thirty minutes start, Sir G. A bit more won't matter, but don't make it less. Then play it just the way I said." He moved briskly to the door, which was on the blind side of the caravan from the men in the grey Cortina.

Tarrant said, "But I can't for the life of me see what —" He stopped. The door had closed, and Willie Garvin was gone.

*   *   *   *   *

It was not long after six on a Sunday afternoon, and it seemed to Tarrant that the world was empty as he drove through the skeletal wastes of what had once been dockland. He had seen a van and a car parked beside *The Stag*, but in the last half mile he had passed no other vehicle and seen no pedestrian.

The grey Cortina was somewhere behind him. It had fallen back to leave several cars in between going through Blackwall Tunnel, then it had closed, only to drop back again once his riverside route was established. He had last seen it in the mirror less than a minute ago, emerging from a bend.

There had been little time for Tarrant to speculate on what Willie hoped to do. Georgi Gogol had returned to the caravan within a minute of Willie's departure, and had engaged Tarrant in polite conversation about the Royal Family during the time of waiting. Driving away from Blackheath he had been too occupied in watching the road and his mirror to have room for any other thought. On his left now was the long tall fence of corrugated iron, green painted, scored with rust. On the curve of the road ahead, the gates stood open, and Tarrant felt his nerves grow taut.

He slowed, turned through the gates, and eased his Rover along the broken tarmac drive that led to the gaunt building of soot-blackened brick a hundred yards away. Beyond it, to one side, he saw a shovel-loader, another caterpillar tracked machine, and part of a storage shed. He turned the corner, as instructed, saw the wide gap of the doorway, and braked to a halt. Beyond the next corner lay the seeming chaos of a building site, the piles of sand and stacks of brick, the torn earth, the great puddles, the timber for shuttering.

As he left the car and walked across a muddy track to the building he thought he heard the distant sound of another car from the direction of the gate. Inside, there was nothing left to show what the factory had once manufactured. The floor was of

concrete, with shallow rectangular pits where machinery had once
been set. Square concrete pillars supported the floor above. There
was more light than he had expected for the windows were tall.
Tarrant walked across dank stone to the corner where the steps led
up. He found himself moving stiffly, hands clenched, shoulders
taut, and he made an effort to relax.

There were three flights of steps between this floor and the next,
but after the first flight his view of the ground floor was cut off.
Here, on the steps, it was much darker than before, the only light
coming from a small window on the middle landing, and Tarrant
was ashamed to feel sweat on his brow as he emerged briefly into
the light of the first floor.

∗   ∗   ∗   ∗   ∗

On the broken drive, Zygmunt Zdrzalkywicz waited until his
brother had turned round the corner of the building, then moved
away from the Cortina and walked through the main doorway. A
big man, he moved lightly, his body networked with muscle and
sinew that combined the strength of teak with the flexibility of
whalebone. He carried no weapon, but his hands could break
brick or bone with equal ease, and the toe-caps of his pointed
shoes were lined with steel.

He and his brother had considered the possibility of a trap when
the Rover driven by the Englishman had turned into this deserted
place, but a trap seemed barely possible. If the Englishman had
spotted the tail it could only have been this afternoon, and there
had been no time to take counter action, not the way the English
worked. As Mikolaj had pointed out, suppose this Tarrant did
have some policemen waiting, what could they do? He and his
brother were breaking no law — not until the moment when they
killed, and that would not happen today if the police were there.
More likely the Englishman had a rendezvous with some
undercover agent in this place, in which case the agent would also
have to die.

Zygmunt paused to study his surroundings, then walked
towards the steps he could see in the far corner, weaving to sight

round pillars where the Englishman might be lurking. He was ten paces from the foot of the steps when a man in dark trousers and shirt stepped out from the shadows beside the bulkhead wall of the steps, a big man with fair hair, quiet eyes, and empty hands. There was no apparent menace about him, but Zygmunt felt the back of his neck bristle, and knew he faced an enemy.

The man said in a flat voice, "Which one are you? Zyg or Mik?"

Zygmunt slid easily into an unobtrusive ready-posture. "Who asks?" he said.

"Garvin. Name's Willie Garvin."

Zygmunt felt a throb of pleasure. He and his brother had heard many stories of this man who was supposed to be so dangerous yet who walked doglike at the heels of the woman Modesty Blaise. It was said that he was formidable in combat, and that he was incomparable with the throwing knife. The first claim did not disturb Zygmunt, the second posed the need for caution.

"Garvin," said Zygmunt. "Ah, yes. The man with the knives."

"Not today. I just came to say, if you want Tarrant, you 'ave to go through me."

"I understand."

Zygmunt sprang from his standing position, without warning or initial recoil, coming in at a perfect height for the toe-strike to the heart that would bring instant unconsciousness followed by death within two minutes. Surprisingly, the strike made only partial connection, and that off-target, but he heard Garvin grunt. Landing on one foot he spun clear of a scything hand and countered with a paralysing hand-axe to the bicep. Again there was no full connection, and Zygmunt knew shock as Garvin's elbow tested the muscle-armour of his ribs with the vicious power of a hard-swung hammer.

He drew back a step, summoned total force and concentration, then became a machine of execution, striking at blinding speed and in a dozen different ways with feet and hands that served as spear, axe, or mace, and were no less lethal. His opponent's speed and defence were such that there could be no chance of conscious calculation. Instinct alone ruled, formed and sharpened by endless practice and experience.

After twenty seconds Zygmunt knew he had drawn blood, and without taking any serious punishment himself. Garvin was weakening, and with the next attack he stumbled and went down backwards. Zygmunt leapt in, swerving, wary of the feet, poised for the kick to the temple which would end the matter. But abruptly, bewilderingly, with a speed that was impossible and therefore shattering to confidence, Zygmunt was stopped short, his neck in a ferocious ankle-clamp.

For a moment the battle was frozen. Zygmunt was braced in a half crouch, staring down the length of his opponent's crossed legs, neck clamped between the ankles. Willie Garvin, shoulders on the floor, arms spread, blood running down the side of his face, was looking up at him. Zygmunt tried a hand-axe to the side of the knee, but a jerk of the legs that held him destroyed the power of the strike. He drew in a long breath and gripped the ankles, tensing to send a burst of power into his fingertips that would bring agony and paralysis.

In that moment his opponent twisted, turning on the pivot of a rounded back so that his body was bent almost double and the top of his head was close to Zygmunt's spread feet. It was a move from nowhere, unnamed, unclassified, to be found in no system of martial arts, and with all Zygmunt's experience he was unable to guess what it presaged, but saw only that he could drive a heel into Garvin's face.

Even as he lifted a foot the ankle was seized, then the other ankle, and he was in a three-point hoist, being lifted by the two feet and by his neck in a high parabola over Garvin's body. His hands started the powerful finger-probe into the ankles clamping his neck, but too late; for somehow there had been a small change of direction, so that he was being swung with increasing speed and head first and with all the weight of his two hundred pound body at one of the sixteen-inch concrete pillars, not at the face of it, but at the V of its edge, and his mind screamed at him to get his hands forward as a shield, but time had run out, and he was dead before his senses could register the crushing impact.

✻   ✻   ✻   ✻   ✻

Tarrant stood by the rectangular hole where a window had been on the top floor, looking down. A minute ago the Polish twin had mounted the iron fire escape to the first floor and disappeared through a door or window there, presumably to check that the target, Tarrant, was not there. This one and his brother were operating a simple pincer tactic to prevent escape, as Willie had no doubt foreseen. Tarrant wondered what Willie was saying to the other twin now, and wondered again at his purpose in splitting them in order to "'ave a little talk" with them.

The man reappeared on the fire escape and began to climb again. Tarrant waited. It was essential to wait until the man was mounting from the third to the fourth floor before starting down the stone steps, otherwise there might be an encounter. Willie should have mentioned that when giving instructions, Tarrant thought. Or perhaps he had felt it was too obvious.

The moment came, and Tarrant moved away from the window and began to walk down the first flight of steps, trying to make no noise. It was when he reached the second floor, ears pricked and straining, that he thought he could pick up the whispering sound of feet starting down the steps from above. Twenty seconds later he emerged on the ground floor and stopped short. Willie Garvin was leaning against a pillar, a hand pressed to his ribs, breathing hard, one side of his face red with blood. At his feet a man lay still and crumpled against the base of the pillar.

"Christ Almighty!" Tarrant said in a whisper. "What happened?"

Willie Garvin looked at him with a cold eye. "The other one coming?" he said.

"Yes. Right behind me. But for God's sake —"

"Out." The voice was quiet but the word cut like a knife and was accompanied by a thumb jerked in the direction of the doorway. "Get motoring. I'll ring you later. Maybe."

"But —"

"*Out! Don't bitch me up now!*" The harsh whisper rode on ragged breathing.

With an enormous effort Tarrant walked forward, past Willie Garvin and the dead thing at his feet, on towards the doorless exit.

His mind was numb, except for one small place where it was as if a brilliant light had been switched on in his head, showing him what Willie Garvin must have seen with dreadful clarity as he looked through field glasses and recognised the Polish twins. The logic was inexorable. When these men had been paid for a contract killing, the target was dead. They had been paid to kill Tarrant, and so, within a measurable time, he would die. No protection, no negotiation, no defensive measures would save him. One thing only could stop the Polish twins, and that was the fearful task to which Willie Garvin had set his hand.

Tarrant stopped by the last pillar and turned, half hidden by it, but with a line of sight that gave him a clear view of the area where the steps debouched. He would not bitch Willie Garvin up now, but he could not walk to his car and drive away. That was impossible. Impossible.

He saw the figure come from the shadows of the final flight of stairs and stop short. Willie had moved a pace or two away from the pillar. His back was to Tarrant but his voice came clearly and was steady now as he said without emphasis, "Who paid you for the Tarrant contract, Zyg? Or is it Mik?"

The man's stance altered. His eyes were fixed on Willie, and Tarrant realised that he had not yet seen the figure slumped by the pillar as he said, "Where is Zygmunt? Who are you?"

"I'm Willie Garvin." The tone was almost conversational. "Brother Ziggie tried to kill me so he could get to Tarrant. Now he's dead. That's 'im, there. So if you want to earn your contract money, you're on your own, Mik."

The head turned slightly. For seconds the man was frozen, then a thin and terrible sound broke from his throat and he exploded into movement. Tarrant sucked in his breath, flinching, for it was as if Willie Garvin faced an attack by a mechanical flail. It needed only one strike to land correctly, and the battle would be over, for when timing was exact the hands and feet of the Polish twin held the power of an axe. Against such weapons there could be no simple blocking in defence. The parry must either be a deflection or a disturbance of balance by pre-emptive strike.

In the poor light Tarrant was unable to tell what damage was

being done during that first long engagement, or to whom. The
two men were evenly matched for size and weight, and both were
masters of hand combat. Willie would have expended precious
energy in dealing with the other twin, but for the moment this one
was fighting in a blind fury, which would reduce his efficiency. It
was hard to tell where the balance of advantage lay.

The two men broke the engagement and were suddenly still,
poised, assessing each other. Then a new phase began. In his
younger days Tarrant had been a fencer of international standard,
and now he was eerily reminded of a bout with the épée. There
would be long moments of stillness, of minimal movement,
change of stance, and small feints; then a sudden flurry of action
almost too fast even for his trained eye to follow, ending with a
disengagement and another phase of stillness.

It was after the third disengagement, and as Mikolaj moved in
abruptly with a fresh attack, that Willie Garvin broke and ran. The
other came after him like a cheetah. Tarrant stopped breathing.
Willie ran six paces, seemingly blinded by panic, for he was
running straight at a pillar. And he did not swerve. With the
impetus of his speed he ran *up* the pillar for two full strides, crepe
soles gripping the rough concrete. The back somersault was quick
and smooth.

A circus trick, Tarrant thought dazedly. A trick for a clown, an
acrobatic clown. Mikolaj had no hope of stopping. He began a
swerve, thrusting desperately with one foot, throwing up a
protective arm above his head, but Willie Garvin was dropping
behind him, close behind, one hand slashing obliquely down in a
shuto strike to the side of the neck just below the ear, with all the
added power of his hundred and eighty pound body dropping
from a height of six feet.

Tarrant saw the man in the blue sweater go down as if hit by a
thunderbolt. Willie landed in the same instant, feet spread, hands
poised. For a moment he remained crouched, ready, then slowly
he straightened, turned away, leaned one shoulder against the
pillar, and stood sucking air into his lungs. After a moment or two
he pulled a handkerchief from his pocket and began to mop blood
from the side of his face.

Tarrant's foot disturbed a stone as he moved across the concrete floor, and Willie's head came round sharply. Tarrant said, "Only me," and moved on. Mikolaj lay face down, the angle of his neck leaving no doubt that it was broken.

Willie drew in a harsh breath and croaked, "I told you to piss off."

Tarrant found that he was trembling slightly with reaction. He said, "Let's have a look at you," and took the handkerchief from Willie. When he had wiped some more blood away he found a two-inch cut running horizontally across the top of the cheekbone, just below the hair line. "It's not deep but you'll need a plaster," he said. "I've got some in my car first-aid kit. Is anyone likely to wander in here?"

"No. If they do they'll be trespassing, and we can see 'em off." Willie's voice was steadier now.

"Just as well." Tarrant went out to his car. When he returned a minute later, Willie was gone and so had one of the bodies. A narrow door in the back wall stood open now. Tarrant had not noticed it before. As he walked towards it, Willie came through, the heel of a hand pressed to his cheekbone. Tarrant stripped the backing from a plaster and pressed it over the cut.

"Thanks." Willie crouched, hoisted the other twin to his shoulders with a practised heave, and made for the narrow door, turning sideways to edge out with his burden. Tarrant followed. He had questions to ask and comments to make, but this was not the moment. Beyond the rear of the building was a cleared area where hardcore had been laid and a start made on running in a nine-inch surface of concrete for a car park. A brick wall was half built along two sides. Nearby stood some construction machinery, and with it a Land Rover that Tarrant recognised as Willie's. Close to the shuttered edge of the most recent run of concrete, a section of hardcore had been ripped up to leave a trench ten feet long. Willie walked across to it and dropped the body in. Tarrant saw that it was some five feet deep, and the other body already lay there.

Tarrant said, "How did — ?" He stopped.

"I scooped it out with the trench digger just before you got 'ere," said Willie. He turned a bruised face to Tarrant, one eye swollen and half closed. "I reckoned it'd save someone a bit of time. Them or me," he added with grim humour. He moved away, climbed into the seat of a small dumper truck, started the engine, and drove it to the pile of hardcore and gravel excavated from the trench. Tilting the great iron bucket, he shovelled the debris back into the trench in two brief operations, then he ran the machine back and forth over the mound to flatten it.

He returned the dumper truck to its position, switched off, beckoned Tarrant, and moved to the Land Rover. Tarrant felt his aching nerves relax, and found it suddenly easier to breathe. He walked over to join Willie and said brusquely, "Why the hell didn't you *tell* me what you were going to do?"

"You'd have argued." Willie winced, and massaged his ribs. "There wasn't any argument, not with the Polish twins accepting a contract on you, but you'd have argued."

Tarrant sighed. "Perhaps," he conceded. Then, with sudden anger, "But in that case what were you bloody well doing without your knives?"

Willie nodded, and his swollen mouth twisted in something that might have been a grin, but his eyes were bleak. "Silly me. I could've taken 'em both at twenty feet with me knives, no problem. In the back, even."

Tarrant looked down, closing his eyes for a moment, seeing what Willie had seen long before, in the caravan. The Polish twins had been professional hit-men. Assassins. Murderers. But Willie Garvin was not, and so he had no choice but to place himself between the killers and their target on terms which ensured that they launched an attack on him intended to be lethal. Then he could react.

Tarrant recalled the terrifying power and speed of the twin he had seen in combat with Willie, and felt a sudden chill in his blood. It had been a very close run thing, as no doubt the first battle must have been, probably with the outcome of both hinging on Willie's gift for innovation. After a moment or two Tarrant opened his eyes and said, "I'm very much obliged to you."

"Don't mention it." Willie gave him an amiable pat on the shoulder. "Let's go and see if they left the key in the Cortina, plus some other goodies maybe. They were just wearing sweaters and tight pants, and I didn't find a thing on them, so they must've left some bits an' pieces in the car."

As they moved over the broken ground Tarrant said, "There's no chance of our late friends being disturbed?"

"No. Dave Selby's doing a run of concrete every day, and by noon tomorrow they'll 'ave a permanent two-ton coffin lid."

Tarrant wiped sweat from his face with a handkerchief and said, "Which might have been ours. Were they very, very good?"

Willie considered. Then he said, "As good as I've ever seen. They didn't 'ave any weaknesses, except their mental posture was a bit too orthodox. Bit of luck for me. And for you, Sir G. I mean, you're probably in the clear now. Someone wanted you knocked off and put in the crossbow man, who failed. Then they went for broke and put the Polish twins in. That's top weight, and these things get around among the real pros. When it comes out that the twins took the job and they've never been seen since, that's a real stopper. I can't see anyone else taking on the contract."

They were approaching the two cars now, and Tarrant said, "Modesty has occasionally referred with some conviction to your efficiency, Willie. I begin to understand the depth of her feeling.'

Willie shook his head. "I got the important bit wrong," he said disconsolately. "If she'd been doing it she'd 'ave found out who hired 'em, some way or another, but I couldn't figure it in time."

Tarrant gave a shaky laugh. "You'll just have to try harder," he said.

The key of the Cortina was in the ignition. Willie did not touch the door but said, "Got a duster in your car, Sir G? We don't want to leave any dabs."

"I have a roll of clean rag, or a pair of heavy duty rubber gloves I carry for dirty work."

"This is dirty work all right. They'll do fine."

Tarrant fetched the gloves. Willie pulled them on, opened the door, and felt in the glove compartment and along the shelf under the fascia. He gave a grunt of satisfaction and stood up, holding two small leather wrist bags. "The twins were stripped down for action, like we reckoned." He handed the two bags to Tarrant.

"There just might be something to 'elp finger whoever put the contract out. Get your backroom boys to 'ave a look."

Tarrant took the bags. Willie walked to the boot, opened it, closed it, and returned. "There's nothing else. It's pretty certain to be a hired car. I'll drive it up to the carpark near The Tower and leave it there. You follow in your car, then bring me back so I can pick up the Land Rover. We'll be 'ere again in twenty-five minutes, but we'll shut the gates while we're gone. All right?"

"More to the point, are *you* all right?"

"It was a bit like being run through a rock-crusher, but I didn't cop anything serious." Willie slid behind the wheel of the Cortina. "Let's go. And you can do the gate-shutting. I'm feeling a bit stiff."

Six

"I'M sorry, old thing."

"Oh, come on Ferdie, you mustn't refuse at the first fence." Victoria, Countess St. Maur, looked up at the man lying on top of her and spoke with stern encouragement.

Ferdie Clarkson lowered his face to the pillow and spoke plaintively close to her ear. "It's not the first fence, Vicky, it's the second time round, and I'm just having a bit of a rest."

"All right, but if you fall asleep on me like you did last time — "

"I definitely won't, old thing."

"Good."

"You know, I think another reason why I get blown a bit quickly is because of old Ronnie."

"You needn't worry about Ronnie, he's in Lisbon."

"I know, but I sort of *imagine* him appearing."

"Good lord. I don't know how anyone can imagine things like that."

"Then you're lucky. I think he's a frightfully fearsome sort of chap."

"Well, I suppose he is, rather. But the point is, my riding always goes much better when I'm getting covered regularly, and if Ronnie's not here to do it, that's his fault. You *are* here, Ferdie, so come on."

"It's funny, him spending so much time abroad, making wine and so on."

"I hope you're gathering yourself for a gallop, Ferdie."

"Can't say I took to those partners of his when I met them last year. Oberon and what's-his-name. Seemed a bit rum to me. Ronnie says they're first class types, but I must say I was surprised to see old Ronnie going into business with foreigners."

Victoria nibbled his ear and said coaxingly, "Ready, steady, go?"

"Just a tick, old love. You know, I was talking to a chap the other day, and he reckoned old Ronnie was a sort of young de Gaulle, except he's not French, of course. Not a bad notion, eh?"

"We really ought to get started, Ferdie. It's quite safe here in the cottage up till four, but old Biggs comes by on his rounds soon after that, and if he sees Brandy tethered in the garden he might look for me."

"Only just gone three. Lots of time, Vicky."

"Well, if you're only up to one more fence."

"I know the papers often talk as if old Ronnie was batty, but they used to talk about de Gaulle in much the same way."

"You're going to retire from the race if you don't liven up a bit, Ferdie. Look, roll over and let me get on top before it's too late."

"I think there are quite a lot of pretty hard-headed chaps who think Ronnie might be on the right lines — steady, old thing. Hang on a jiffy. Ah, there we are." Ferdie Clarkson relaxed on his back, with the countess kneeling astride him. "I mean, with the way things are going," he said, "and if it comes to the crunch, I'd rather have people like old Ronnie running things than a bunch of loony commies. Wouldn't you?"

Victoria, Countess St. Maur, neither heard nor answered. Her entire mind, such as it was, had become focused on the heat in the pit of her stomach. She settled herself in the saddle, barely conscious of Ferdie's gasp as she clamped him crushingly between her thighs. Her headscarf lay within reach. She took it by the corners, leaned forward to slide it behind Ferdie's neck, and doubled an end round each hand. Then, with a short rein and firm control of her mount, the earl's wife clicked her tongue and began to ride.

*   *   *   *   *

In another county, in the big kitchen of a sprawling farmhouse, Sir Gerald Tarrant faced another earl's daughter and said, "I called at *The Treadmill* and they told me Willie was up here at your place. I do hope you don't mind me dropping in."

Lady Janet, in corduroy slacks and a khaki shirt, eyed him suspiciously as she poured tea from a blue and white striped teapot into blue and white striped cups. "I don't mind as long as you're not going to get him into some sort of trouble," she said.

"Trouble? Oh no, not at all," Tarrant said warily. He did not know how much Lady Janet knew, and was anxious not to put a foot wrong. "I just hoped he might help me with a piece of information."

"Well, all right. I'll give him a call. Sorry to be aggressive, but he's in no shape for one of your . . . your affairs. Not after the accident yesterday."

"Ah. The accident," Tarrant said in a neutral tone.

"I thought you were there."

"Oh, I was. Yes. I — um — " Tarrant felt a wave of relief as Willie came into the room. One side of his face carried a huge bruise, but he looked cheerful. "'Allo, Sir G. What brings you to the wilds?" He slipped an arm about Janet's waist, kissed her cheek, then moved to sit down, limping slightly.

Tarrant said, "Oh, nothing important. It can wait till I've had a cup of that excellent tea."

Janet said, "He's such an awfu' liar, Sir Gerald. First he tells me he hurt himself falling off Ethel, can you imagine? Then it turns out she's an elephant, but you don't get bruised like that falling off an elephant. Not Willie, at least, he can fall off a roof and land just so. Will you look at this." She caught Willie's wrist, flicked open the buttoned cuff of the tartan shirt he wore, and pushed the sleeve back. Tarrant saw that from wrist to bicep the arm was yellow and brown with bruising, and he remembered the sounds of the battle he had witnessed. This was the cost of deflecting those killer strikes of hand and foot.

"It wasn't just falling off Ethel," Willie said with a patient air. "I fell among the liberty 'orses and got trampled. I told you, Jan."

"Aye. You told me." She looked at Tarrant. "You should see his thighs."

"Thighs are rude," said Willie reproachfully. "You're ruining my reputation."

Tarrant said, "Have you seen a doctor?"

Willie smiled and waved a dismissive hand. "I'm all right, honest. Jan spent hours last night soaking me in witch 'azel and going over me with an ultrasonic whatsit."

Lady Janet passed the cups of tea, sitting at the head of the scrubbed table between the two men. "You never fell off an elephant into liberty horses in your life, Willie Garvin," she said dourly. "You two are up to something, I bloody well know it. I wish to God we knew just where Modesty is. I'd get in touch and tell her of you."

Willie patted her hand. "Jan was the school sneak," he said proudly to Tarrant.

She did not smile, but said a little shakily. "I should be used to it by now, but it still frightens me when I know something's going on."

Willie lifted her hand and touched it to his lips. "There's nothing going on," he said gently. "Nothing at all, as far as I know. Whatever was going on is finished now. I can't put it 'igher than that, Jan, because it might be different tomorrow. You know 'ow things just sort of . . . crop up with me."

She sighed and managed a smile. "I know, Willie. I mind well how I cropped up with you myself, when those awfu' men were trying to run me off the farm." She picked up her cup of tea. "I've one or two phone calls to make, so I'll leave you to talk over old times. Be sure he looks after you well, Sir Gerald."

"I shall insist, my dear."

When she had gone, Tarrant said softly, "My backroom boys have been through the contents of those two wrist-bags. Mainly personal items — keys, money, ballpoint pen, no cigarettes, a packet of mints, that sort of thing."

"No letter? Diary?"

"No, but there was a folded page torn from an A to Z street map, with an address scribbled in the margin. Off Eaton Square. The man who lives there is a wealthy jeweller named Chan. My police colleagues suspect he runs a very large operation in fencing stolen jewels, but they've never been able to prove it."

Willie nodded. "That's right. The Princess never used 'im because we didn't like some of 'is little ways. He's a fixer. A middleman. A finder. If you want something done, he'll find the people to do it, for a rake-off."

"So he might have arranged the contract with the Polish twins, on behalf of another party?"

"More than likely. But that doesn't mean he can finger the third party. There could be a double or triple cut-out."

"Of course." Tarrant passed his cup to be refilled. "But I'd quite like to discover who put out the contract on me."

Willie shook his head. "I pass. These days I only do what I 'ave to."

Tarrant blinked, startled. "I didn't mean you. Good God, I'd never dare to face Janet again. But I might have my own people see what they can find out."

"Waste of time. You're not allowed to do the sort of things you'd need to do to make Bernie Chan talk."

Tarrant shrugged. "Long may it continue so, Willie. I just do the best I can within that framework."

"Sure. By the way, I rang Liz Selby this morning and she said Dave was out on the site, running in another section of concrete."

"I know," Tarrant said dryly. "I drove past at noon to have a look for myself."

Ten minutes later, when Lady Janet returned, Tarrant rose to leave, declining an invitation to stay for a pot-luck dinner. "Thank you, but I've been away from my desk far too long today, and I must spend this evening catching up."

"Then I'll come and see you away. No, you stay where you are, Willie."

As they crossed the yard to where Tarrant's car stood by the gate she said, "I'm still worried. Willie usually gives me at least a rough outline of what goes on."

"I'm sure you needn't worry, Janet."

She bit her lip and looked down. "Last night I was thinking I might ring Weng. I know Modesty's very strong on communications," she gave a little backward nod of her head, "they both are, so she'll probably be calling Weng every few days from wherever she finds herself. I was going to have Weng ask her to call me, so I could tell her how anxious I am." She gave Tarrant a rather forced smile. "If Willie's in danger, I'd be glad to have Her Highness back here with him. You know?"

"Yes." Tarrant rested a hand on the car door, hesitating. Then he said, "At the risk of annoying Willie, I feel bound to tell you this. Yesterday I was under sentence of death. Today I'm not, because Willie . . . intervened. You wouldn't wish to know the details, I assure you. That's why he tells that ridiculous elephant story."

After a little silence she nodded. "No, I wouldn't wish to know the details. I was cured of curiosity about that area of Willie's life when I learned for myself how dark it is in there. Are you safe now, Sir Gerald?"

"Yes."

"And whatever it was, is it truly over?"

"Yes. I give you my word."

She exhaled a short fervent sigh of relief. "Well, thank God for that."

"Amen. And not forgetting Willie."

That night, lying in bed with Willie's head cushioned on the softness between her shoulder and breast she said, "Are you all right?"

"Sure. You want proof?"

"Another night. Willie, nobody's tried to find out where Modesty is, have they? I mean, as you thought might happen?"

"No. There's been no approach to Weng. No enquiries."

"So maybe the crossbow man was aiming at Tarrant that night."

"Could be."

"And whoever sent him might try again. Might try to have Tarrant killed. Yet he goes around with no protection."

"You can't protect against an assassin, Jan, but I wouldn't worry about it any more if I were you."

"If you say so, Willie. It's just I have fondness for Tarrant after what we went through together that time in France." She lifted a hand to touch his cheek. "I'm glad now you fell off Ethel."

A silence. Then: "Right into those liberty 'orses."

"Aye. That's the way it goes, sometimes." After a long companionable silence she said, "Who's Kim Crozier?"

"He's a doctor, love. Why?"

"No special reason. I was thinking about that evening at the penthouse, and remembered Modesty saying she was going to San Francisco to see Kim Crozier. I think I'd heard the name before, but couldn't place it."

"I mentioned 'im when I told you about that slave plantation called Limbo, in the middle of the jungle in Guatemala."

"Ah, he was the black doctor they kidnapped to look after all the millionaire slaves?"

"That's 'im. Lovely bloke. Helped set things up so Modesty was able to lead a break-out and stop the last-day massacre. He's got a practice in San Francisco now, and that's 'er favourite town in the States, so she's seen 'im a couple of times since." Willie lifted his head slightly. "You'd like it there, Jan. Why don't you come out with me later this year for a week or two, when things are quiet on the farm? We've got a nice little studio apartment at Sausalito. That's the posh bit, a few miles north across the Golden Gate Bridge."

"I think I'd really love to do that, Willie. But will Her Highness not mind?"

"Christ, no. We've got these places 'ere and there, some I bought, some she bought, and some we bought together, like Sausalito. But we don't keep count anyway."

"Capitalist pigs."

Willie kissed her neck. "Never mind about another night. What about now?"

"You surely can't feel lecherous when you're so stiff?"

"They go together, Jan."

"I meant — " she broke off, laughed, and turned towards him. "You'll not fall off me like you did off Ethel, I'll see to that."

✻   ✻   ✻   ✻   ✻

It was late afternoon when Modesty Blaise came off the ferry from Sausalito and angled her way across the city on foot, through Chinatown to Columbus Avenue, then down Mason to Fisherman's Wharf. The mist over the bay had cleared at last, and the sun had broken through white cloud to give a gentle warmth.

She strolled for an hour, bought a seafood cocktail and a pretzel from sidewalk stalls, sat watching the fishing boats tied up along the Embarcadero, found herself in conversation with other strollers from time to time, discouraged two pick-up attempts without giving offence, and listened to a three-man group playing in Ghirardelli Square.

At noon she boarded a Powell Line cable car and stood jammed among the passengers, hearing the gripman sing out the stations as the car clanked its way up and down the San Francisco hills to Union Square. There she went into the Francis Drake Hotel, drank a glass of fresh orange juice in the coffee shop, freshened up in the powder room, then left for the ten minute walk to the Chinese restaurant on Grant where she was to meet Kim Crozier.

It was a Friday. She had enjoyed the leisurely morning in Sausalito, the afternoon in San Francisco, and was looking forward to the rest of the day and the weekend ahead. Her capacity for enjoyment was large, and her likes were uncomplicated. On arrival the day before, she had rung Willie Garvin and learned that the crossbow man's target must have been Tarrant, not herself; that another attempt had been unsuccessful, and that Willie felt certain there would be no more. He had spoken in free cryptic and given no details over the open line, but this did not trouble her. If Willie said Tarrant was safe, then she could forget the matter.

Near the corner of Grant and Sacramento, as she paused to look in a shop window, a taxi with two men in the back passed her. Both would have recognised her at once if they had seen her face. As it was, the bearded man happened to be glancing at his watch. The other thought fleetingly that the girl they had just passed looked rather like Modesty Blaise from behind, but the impression lasted no longer than a millisecond, for Ben Christie was on CIA business and had more important things on his mind than a chance likeness.

The taxi reached The Grasshopper five minutes before Modesty Blaise arrived, and by the time she entered the restaurant the two men were seated in one of the booths, so she did not see them.

＊   ＊   ＊   ＊   ＊

Kim Crozier was watching the door when she came in at two minutes to six, and at once his pleasure at seeing her wiped away the unease he had been feeling as the time of this meeting drew near. She wore flat shoes, and a shirt in very fine blue and white check tucked into a plain grey skirt. Her purse — her handbag as she would call it — hung at her side from a shoulder strap. Her black hair gleamed, her eyes were bright and ready to smile, and it was a joy to watch her move. When she had been brought to the slave plantation called Limbo, it had been Dr. Kimberly Crozier's duty to give her a full physical examination. It was still his opinion that she was the healthiest human specimen he had ever known.

It was good to see her again, very good, despite the niggling anxiety that troubled him. Her face lit up as he walked towards her, and again he felt vague surprise that in his imagination she was always bigger than in reality.

"Kim. You're looking as lovely as ever."

"You've just stolen my line." He kissed her, nodded to the hovering head waiter, and took her arm as they moved to the booth. "Perrier water?"

"Please."

They sat looking at each other across the table, half smiling, renewing visual contact, amending tiny distortions of memory. After a little while she said. "How's the work going, Kim?"

"Pretty good. I work two days a week at the hospital, and the rest at my practice. Today's a hospital day, but somebody's standing in for me."

"I'm glad all's well. Do you ever hear from any of your Limbo patients?"

"Quite a few. The Schultzes send a card now and again. Stavros writes occasionally. Valdez likewise, plus he sent me a present at Christmas. An Aston Martin." The handsome black face creased in a smile of mock despair. "That's on top of Stavros and Valdez and Marker all chipping in to buy me a good practice. What does a guy say?"

"You kept them alive, Kim. It's for them to say, and they're saying it."

The waiter came, and they spent time on their order. When he had left, Kim said, "Do you hear from any of them yourself?"

"Yes, I've had cards and invitations, but only from the ones you mentioned."

"And you're the girl who got them all out."

"I was only there a month, Kim. To most of them I was just another new slave. You were there seven years."

"I haven't forgotten how it ended. You've had no trouble from the bullet wound?"

There was a hint of puzzlement in her look. "You saw for yourself last time I was here. There's not even a scar to be seen."

"Sure. I was forgetting." He fidgeted with his table napkin. "How's Willie Garvin?"

"Fine. He sent his regards."

"Take him mine, honey. What have you been doing with yourself lately?"

"Oh, keeping reasonably busy. Willie and I got caught up in a little trouble in Morocco, but it came out all right in the end. I'm building a long dwarf wall with mellow second-hand bricks in the flower garden at the back of my cottage in Wiltshire. It's my first effort at laying bricks, and I'm painfully slow at it, but if you want a great sense of satisfaction, Kim, build a wall."

"I'll bear it in mind."

"No, don't. I'm stupid. A doctor doesn't need walls, he's got people to build."

"It's a lot more chancy with people. Satisfying sometimes, but other times you're either just not smart enough or there's nothing you can do. But go on."

"Go on what?"

"Go on talking. Tell me what else you've been doing. Describe your place in Wiltshire. What happened in Morocco? Entertain me."

"Well . . . I've been amusing myself carving semi-precious stones. I'm quite a good lapidary, and I used to do a lot of work with precious stones when I was a wicked criminal. Wait a minute, I can't remember if you ever knew there was a time when I wasn't completely virtuous."

"My fellow slave and best buddy in Limbo was Danny Chavasse, late of *The Network*. Remember?"

"Of course. Danny told you. Well, an American I happened across in those days is a rock hound, and through him I've cottoned on to the idea of carving more everyday gemstones. You can go at it with more panache when you haven't got something worth a fortune on your dopstick. Therapeutic, like building a wall. And if you want to know what Wiltshire's like, you could come to England on your next vacation and stay at the cottage with me."

"Sounds fine," said Dr. Kimberly Crozier, not quite convincingly.

Two waiters appeared with a trolley and began to set out the dishes on the table. When they had finished and left, she picked up her chopsticks and said, "Are you free for the weekend, Kim? I'm staying at the apartment in Sausalito, like before, and you're very welcome."

He sighed and rubbed the middle of his brow with a finger. "Modesty . . . that was great. I mean, last time. But my news is, I'm getting married in the fall."

She lowered a morsel of chicken to her plate and gazed at him with eyes full of laughter. "So *that's* what's been worrying you? Having to say no to a lady?"

He sat back with relief. "Some ladies might take it amiss."

"Ah, you should know me better than that. Tell me about her."

"She's a nurse, a very pretty and very intelligent black girl named Beryl. We met a couple of months ago, and kind of clicked."

"That's marvellous, Kim, just what you need. Why didn't you bring her to lunch?"

"She's on duty right now. But she knows we're old friends from Limbo, and what you did there, and she's kind of excited about meeting you."

"Call me when you're both free, and we'll make a date."

"You're a very nice lady."

She laughed and shook her head. "Never that, Kim. But if I tell a man, 'no thanks and here's why,' I don't expect him to feel aggrieved. Same thing vice versa. So now you've got it off your chest, and there's nothing to feel awkward about, and you can relax. Right?"

"I'll do that ma'am," he said thankfully.

It was an hour and half later when he called for the bill. She had thought earlier that they might take in a theatre before going back to Sausalito together. Now she felt it would be better to leave Kim the option of ending the evening at this point.

"I'm going to the powder room," she said, "can you find out for me what's on at the Curran Theatre tonight?"

"Sure, honey."

When she returned a few minutes later Kim Crozier was by the small bar, studying a newspaper presumably borrowed from the barman. She was about to go across to him when a man stood up and moved out from a booth table just in front of her, his back towards her. As he turned towards the door they came face to face, and her eyes widened with the same surprise that she saw in his.

"Ben!" she said. "Ben Christie, the rock hound himself. Who's going to say it's a small world first?"

His eyes went beyond her for an instant, then came back, and now they were suspicious, without recognition. "Wrong guy, lady." His voice was soft, wary. "Sorry about that."

She held down a wave of self-directed fury and looked startled, embarrased, half turning, aware of a figure standing a pace or two to her left rear, watching. "Oh my God, it's for me to apologise," she said contritely. "Just for a moment there I thought you were my cousin Ben, but you're taller, and not that much of a look-alike. I'm sorry . . ." she backed away a little, gesturing apologetically, and glanced at the dark young man with the beard watching her, watching Ben Christie.

Ben ignored her and looked at the man. "You ready?"

The other nodded. "Sure. Let's go." His eyes rested on Modesty a moment longer, then he turned. Ben Christie moved past her and together they made their way to the door. Beneath the anger and distress hidden by her rueful smile of embarrassment she was distantly aware of a small element in her subconcious scratching for attention, but there was no time to give thought to it now.

She moved quickly to Kim Crozier, gripped his arm hard, still smiling, and breathed, "Never mind the theatre. Quick, Kim." He gave her a startled glance, then put down the newspaper and moved to the door with her. She made him halt as soon as they were in the doorway and said, "Two men just went out, one in a brown suit, one in grey. Step out and check which way they've gone, Kim. Don't be obvious."

He stared, began to speak, changed his mind, and took a step or two out on to the pavement. After a moment he patted his jacket pocket and turned back impatiently as if having forgotten something. "They're on the corner, waiting for a cab I think. The one in grey looked back this way."

"He would. He's checking on me, and he mustn't see me."

"Modesty, what the hell — ?"

"The other one is a CIA man working under cover and I just blew him." Her face was impassive but the intensity of her distress was almost tangible. "Is your car the grey Aston Martin a little way up the hill?"

"Yes."

"Will you follow them? I tried to cover up when I realised he wasn't alone, but if the other man spots me he'll know I was faking, so I daren't come with you."

"Follow them? Modesty, I've no experience in this kind of thing."

"For God's sake, Kim, I've *blown* him, and that could mean he's a dying man. It's an easy city for tailing. If they're using a cab they can't be going too far, and I just want to know their destination." She was speaking very quickly now. "Don't get too close, and just do the best you can. I'll go and wait in reception at the St. Francis. Phone there and have me paged as Miss Johnson."

He found himself crossing the road, glancing at the corner and seeing the two men still there, then walking slowly up the hill to where his car was parked, wondering whether to get in and wait or try to lurk out of sight, feeling sweat on his brow, and relief as an empty cab came down the hill to save him the decision, muttering to himself, "Jesus, there's never any *peace* around once you show up, Modesty girl!"

He withdrew the thought as he got behind the wheel, deciding it was unfair. She could be extraordinarily peaceful to be with. Then the cab ahead pulled away with its passengers, and he had no time to think of anything but the task in hand.

Modesty watched the Aston Martin go by, waited thirty seconds, then moved out from the doorway and walked quickly south towards Union Square. A small but sufficient part of her being was focused upon her movements and surroundings, the rest was wholly absorbed in a mental exercise to dissolve all tension, anxiety and guilt, leaving her mind quiet and poised for whatever she might have to demand of it.

In Stockton Street she spent seven minutes buying an overnight case, jeans, a shirt, sweater, headscarf, and a packet of cotton wool. There was no message for her when she reached the St. Francis. She booked a room in the name of Johnson, told the reception clerk she was expecting a phone-call, hired a car at the desk, and was shown up by a bell-boy. The jeans were not a good fit, for her legs were long in proportion to the size of her waist, but she was not concerned with looking smart. She put on the new shirt, laid the sweater to hand, peeled off a layer of cotton wool and put it in her handbag, then went to the mirror, loosened her chignon and tied her hair back at the nape of her neck.

She was lying on the bed when the phone rang twenty minutes later. Kim's voice said, a little breathlessly, "Can I talk?"

She listened for the hollow sound of the switchboard remaining on the line, then said, "Yes, all clear."

"I'm on the Embarcadero. They came here and went into a bar for a while. I was scared I'd lose them while I was getting parked, but I didn't, and then I was scared of leaving them while I phoned you in case they moved on. So I kind of lurked, and after half an hour a fishing boat came in, and they both went aboard and it pulled out again. It was heading west out of the bay."

She accepted the bad news without heaviness, holding her mental balance steadily. "Wait there for me please, Kim. I've hired a car, so I'll be with you in a few minutes."

"You'll find me on the corner of Powell."

She put down the phone, blocked off the momentary and futile longing to have Willie Garvin within call, picked up the sweater and her handbag, and went out. The car keys were ready at the desk. Traffic was heavy, but ten minutes later she found a place to park the Scirocco in Beach Street and walked to the corner where Kim waited. She had not used the cottonwool to alter the shape of her face, for as yet there was no point, but with her new clothes and her altered hair style she was close to Kim before he spotted her among the other strollers. Taking his arm, she crossed the road and began to walk along Fisherman's Wharf.

"The fishing boat's called *Old Hickory,*" he said. "Are you figuring they might come back?"

"It's the only way to re-establish contact, so I'm hoping. And hoping it's not too late."

He glanced down sideways at her. "Can you tell me some more about it now, honey?"

They stood a little way from the row of fishing boats lining the wharf, and gazed out across the bay as she told him briefly of the time when she had led *The Network* raid on Bora's ship, and found Ben Christie with a broken head, tied in a sack ready for drowning.

"I had him nursed at my house for while till he was on the mend," she said, "and I met him again last year when he was over in London. When he suddenly appeared in front of me at the Grasshopper, I spoke his name. That was criminal stupidity, Kim. If I'd seen that he was with somebody else I expect I'd have held off and waited for him to speak, but the other man came up behind me . . ." Her voice faded, she made a mental picture of the bearded face she had glimpsed, and again felt the twitch of some small deep memory trying to stir within her.

Kim said, "You weren't mistaken? I mean, you're sure it was Ben Christie?"

"I'm sure. And I'm sure he's on CIA work. He knew me, I could see it, but he had to give me the brush because I named him, and it wasn't the name his bearded friend knew him by."

"Okay, but you tried to cover, so maybe you didn't blow him. If you did, that's bad but it doesn't necessarily mean he's in danger. He could be on some routine job."

"He could. On the other hand I could have killed him. I can't just walk away and leave it."

After a few moments Kim said, "What do you aim to do?"

"I was hoping to do a shield job on Ben until he could assess whether or not he's blown. If yes, he could pull out fast. If no, then his mission's still on, and I fade. But now they've taken him out to sea on a fishing boat." She turned remote eyes to Kim for a moment. "That's a good place for serious interrogation."

People were strolling, talking, gazing, eating fresh crab or shrimp at Tarantino's Crab Stand, buying, selling, gossiping, and Kim Crozier had a sense of unreality that made his mouth go dry. "So what can you do?" he said. "Tell the police? FBI?"

She shook her head. "It's CIA business. I'd like to tell them Ben could be blown, but the problem is to get anyone to listen. A woman phoning their H.Q. at Langley with a story like this could take days to reach anyone high enough to know who Ben Christie is and what mission he's on. They probably get five hoax calls for every genuine one."

"You have some powerful contacts here. Limbo people."

"Too slow, Kim." She took her eyes from the bay to look at him. "Can you wait here for an hour, or maybe ninety minutes? I doubt if the boat will come back in that time, but if it does I want to know who comes off, and where they go — if you can manage it."

"I'll try. Where will you be?"

"I can be at the Sausalito studio in half an hour, and I'll ring a man in London who's a chief of intelligence. It'll be early morning for him there, and I'll reach him at his flat. He has direct access to the CIA top brass, and more than enough credibility to make them listen. I know it's a long way round, but there's no other way that Langley can know the situation within the next hour."

He was deeply apprehensive that he might fail her, and said, "Wouldn't it be quicker to phone this man in London from a booth? Or if that's too public, from the St. Francis?"

She looked out over the bay again. "No. It wouldn't make that much difference, Kim. It'll soon be dusk, and there's nothing the CIA can do till that ship comes back. If then. Besides, I want to pick up a few things from the studio. Some sort of opportunity might crop up before the CIA are ready."

"Opportunity?"

"Don't ask me for what, Kim. I don't know, I haven't the faintest goddam idea what comes next or what I'm going to do about it, but Ben Christie is my friend, and a good man, and I'll just do the best I can."

She turned and walked away, heading across Jefferson to the place where she had left the hired Scirocco.

Seven

"WE are using twenty-four kilos of explosive in shaped charges," said the voice in the gathering dusk.

Ben Christie nodded, leaning with his elbows on the rail of the little ship, watching the moving lights of the traffic passing across the Golden Gate Bridge a long mile away. His companion was a lean wiry man of middling build, who spoke precise English with a slight Middle European accent. Christie thought he was probably German. His name had been given as Hans, but that was unlikely to be his real name, any more than John was the real name of the bearded young man who was now on the bridge of the herring boat, aft of where they stood.

Hans was very ready to talk, and Christie was anxious to listen, but it was difficult to concentrate when half his mind was occupied with trying to guess whether John suspected him, and what was being discussed on the bridge now between John and the Scotsman called Sandy, and Szabo, from somewhere in the Balkans, whose name just might be genuine and who appeared to be in executive charge of the operation under John.

It had been the cruellest kind of bad luck, moving out of the booth and coming face to face with Modesty Blaise. She had been very quick, very smooth in recovery. Quick and smooth enough to convince almost anyone that she had made a mistake. But John was undoubtedly a big wheel in The Watchmen, and suspicion would be second nature to its members, otherwise the organisation could never have resisted penetration for so long.

With an effort Christie forced his mind to focus on what Hans was saying. ". . . you do not handle explosives, Mr. Lang?" That was Christie's cover name.

He had adopted a laconic persona, and now he said briefly, "Only in cartridges."

"Ah, yes. For shooting."

"Right. You use a big team for this job?"

"Szabo leads a section of seven. John directs. The others are ashore now, providing back-up and emergency getaway."

"Hell of a big job for a small team."

"The planning is good, you understand. Has John told you about this operation?"

"He gave me the bones of it soon after we came aboard. No details. Sounds pretty crazy."

"Not crazy. Most interesting." Hans pointed to the distant bridge. "The span is more than twelve hundred metres. The cables from which the bridge is suspended are almost one metre in diameter, and consist of more than twenty-seven thousand separate wires encased by a steel tube."

Christie said, "Not easy to break."

"But not impossible, Mr. Lang. A steel collar of shaped charges, bolted into position where the cable reaches the top of the tower, will explode with a shearing effect."

Christie turned his head to stare. "The *top* of the tower? How high's that?"

"Two hundred and twenty-seven metres. A medium hard climb in darkness, for it was of course necessary to use the dark of the moon. Last night a dinghy takes us from this ship to the base of the tower on the Marin County side of the bay. For the first eighty metres there are cross braces to assist my ascent. After the bridge level it is more hard, for I must ascend by an outside corner of the tower, but in one hour and a half I am at the top."

"With a steel collar and twenty-four kilos of explosive?" Christie wanted desperately to disbelieve what he was hearing, but Hans's unemphatic voice was very precise and sure.

"I take a nylon cord, Mr. Lang. The most danger, after I reach the top, is from the cold and the wind, but in my pack I have special clothing to put on, and a rope cradle. With the cord, I draw up a light metal hoist, a pulley wheel which can be clamped to the tower, and with it a stronger line. My colleagues in the boat below then hoist up to me the explosive. This is penta-erythol-tetra-nitrate in blocks of three kilos, each in a curved steel trough with connecting lugs so that the troughs can be linked together round the upper half of the cable's circumference, and each trough with an adhesive base protected by a tear-off silicone coating to make my work more easy. The hoist and the cord bring up to me two blocks of PETN at a time, and each haul requires between fifteen and twenty minutes to complete."

Christie moistened dry lips and tried to put grudging admiration into his tone as he said, "You were through in less than ninety minutes?"

"Considerably less, Mr. Lang, for I had rehearsed several times under simulated conditions."

"This was last night?"

"Yes. We waited for an evening with mist to give additional cover."

"And you reckon nobody's spotted it all through today?"

Hans smiled in the darkness. "If you look at the main cable, you will see that it is encircled by a heavy steel ring at intervals of only a metre, perhaps. The troughs carrying the explosive have the same red-brown colour as the whole bridge assembly, so now there is one extra half-ring, close to the top of the tower. I think it would be difficult to detect, even with field glasses."

There was a silence, and when Christie spoke he had no need to force the note of awe in his voice. "What happens when it blows, Hans?"

"Expert opinion has no doubt that the cable will break."

"What experts?"

"The experts upon whose advice The Watchmen can draw," Hans said gently. "In this case, engineers of course. The cable on the seaward side of the tower, at the northern end of the bridge, will be sheared through sufficiently to break under the weight it carries. I must tell you that the weight of each cable between the two towers is more than seven thousand tons. The broken cable will remain anchored at the southern end, but at the northern end there will be close to three and one half thousand tons falling from a mean height of seventy metres upon a bridge which has lost half its support. Concensus of expert opinion is that the northern end will break completely and fall into the bay, taking with it all traffic on the bridge at that time."

Christie said automatically, "Not bad. Maybe that'll teach those government ass-holes a lesson. When do you blow it, Hans?"

"Tomorrow, during the morning rush hour when the bridge is full. We could have detonated today, but John decided this would cause less damage."

"Radio beam trigger?"

"Yes. A detonator in each section of the collar, activated simultaneously from a transmitter we have aboard, using the ship's aerial. I was concerned that in an area of much activity across the whole radio-frequency spectrum there could be accidental detonation by other sources, but the experts have provided John with a device which emits power at two different frequencies in rapid alternation, and this uniquely will trigger the detonators."

The experts have provided . . ?

Christie sought for an incurious question to coax Hans into being more specific about the experts, but could find no satisfactory way of framing it. To know who backed The Watchmen was important, but there was a more urgent priority now. In little more than twelve hours the Golden Gate Bridge would collapse. God alone knew how many cars and trucks would go down into the bay if that happened. His over-riding task was to give warning. Even so, at the first hint of any precautions being taken, that scything collar of explosive could be blown at the touch of a button.

Ben Christie felt a rivulet of icy sweat trickle down his chest, and with it came the realisation that he had been silent for too long. He laughed softly and said: "It's beautiful, Hans. Beautiful. Who we doing it for? Vietnam Veterans, huh? Ex-service? Poor bastard POWs?"

Behind him John's voice said, "The Watchmen will claim responsibility for the event, Mr. Lang, and we shall say that it is an operation on behalf of the Armenian Freedom Fighters."

Christie turned, peering through the gloom. There was something chilling about the way they all kept calling him 'Mr.' Lang. After a moment he nodded and said, "Armenians? Oh, sure John. Sure."

John said, "Let's get down to business." He led the way aft to the dining cabin behind the wheelhouse. "Sorry to keep you, but I've been busy on the radio with one or two administrative matters." The light was on in the cabin, the windows curtained. The engine throbbed easily as the little ship cruised slowly at five knots, steered from the bridge wheel by the man called Sandy, coming about now to maintain its distance from the Golden Gate Bridge.

Christie followed John into the cabin and was about to close the door when he found Szabo behind him, a big dark man with a massive chin, muscles that moved under his tight shirt like snakes in a bag, and a Colt .45 Commander in a holster at the back of his belt. He gave Christie a grin and a pat on the shoulder, then moved across to sit down on a bench, drew the Colt, and began to check it over.

John leaned against the table and waved Christie to a chair. "Our superiors are rather choosy about accepting recruits for The Watchmen," he said with a pleasant smile, "so we tend to do some intensive vetting."

Christie shrugged. "Sure. Makes sense."

"I'm glad you agree. We had a very pleasant general chat over dinner at The Grasshopper, and everything checks out with the recommendation we had for you, but as I hinted, rather guardedly since we were in a public place, we do put recruits through one or two tests."

Christie nodded. He was careful not to watch Szabo, but he had heard the sound of the magazine being removed and replaced, and the click of the slide as the automatic was cocked. He was trying very hard to stay cool, both inwardly and outwardly, but had a growing sense of being in a bottleneck situation with little hope of backing out.

John fingered his beard and said with an engaging smile, "For security reasons, if a man fails the tests we are bound to ensure that he isn't in a position to talk about us afterwards."

Christie said, "I'm not so stupid I can't add up, John."

"Let's be plain. The Watchmen do quite a lot of killing."

"I know that."

"So why do you want in, Mr. Lang?"

It was a question Christie expected, and one which had occupied much of his concentration during the past few hours. His assessment, based on John's attitude, was that to claim commitment to a cause, any cause, would be fatal. Whatever the Watchmen did, it was never for any of the widely varied causes for which they claimed to be acting. Their true purpose was deeply hidden, and probably known only to a handful of top men. The front agents of The Watchmen were simply mercenaries, very special mercenaries. Christie had made up his mind while he was talking with Hans, and now he did not let the bearded man's question hang in the air, but said coolly, "I want to get rich, John. And quick. I spent years killing for Uncle Sam and getting paid peanuts. I figure I can do a lot better killing for The Watchmen."

John laughed. "You can indeed, Mr. Lang. We have unlimited financial backing. How many hits have you made?"

"Outside the war, just five. One was a double."

"Using a gun?"

"One time it was a knife, because there had to be no noise."

"Let me see the gun, please."

Christie hesitated only fractionally before lifting the flap of his jacket, and made himself remain quite still when John stepped forward and slid the Smith & Wesson .44 Magnum from the shoulder holster. The forward end of the trigger guard had been cut away and the hammer had been dehorned. It was the gun of a professional, with a four inch barrel, a silk-smooth action and a punch like a miniature cannon.

"That is one hell of a weapon," said John admiringly, and laid it on the table behind him, "but you won't be needing it for the test. You've no objection to using this, I take it?" He opened a drawer and took out a machete in a sheath.

Christie grinned. "I chopped up some gook prisoners pretty good with one of them."

"We'd like you to do a test killing with it."

"Here in San Francisco?"

"Yes."

"Okay. When."

"Tonight."

Christie felt relief surge through him. They would be letting him off the boat, and once he was ashore The Watchmen could not monitor him through every move of locating his target and making the kill. Given three minutes on a phone to Casey, he could have all traffic approaching the bridge halted, and a flight of helicopter gunships homing in with searchlights on *Old Hickory*. Casey, his controller for this mission, carried that kind of muscle.

He made his grin become eager, wolfish, and said, "Just give me a name and a picture of the guy, then set me down where I can pick him up. He's dead."

John beamed. "That's what I like to hear. But it isn't a guy, Mr. Lang."

Christie shrugged. "It was a dame I used the knife on, that hit I said about just now."

"No problem, then." John went to the door and opened it. Christie started to rise, but was waved down. Hans backed into the cabin dragging a big whicker laundry basket. John closed the door. Hans gave the lid of the basket a pat, winked at Christie, and moved to stand by the starboard window.

"This is for the corpse," said John briskly, and looked at the CIA man.

A cold wave of unease rippled through Christie. He said, "Okay, let's go."

"Go where?" said John, and threw open the lid of the basket. "Come and look, Mr. Lang."

He stood up, inwardly bracing himself to show no emotion. A black girl, thin, huddled, wearing a cheap cotton dress, lay in the basket. She looked about nineteen or twenty, but might have been younger, for the needle punctures on her bare arm marked her for a junkie. Her eyes were open, gazing past him with vague euphoria, and she seemed completely unaware of her situation. Christie felt his stomach churn and sickness rise in his throat as he saw that the basket had an inner lining of heavy duty plastic. When he looked up, John was smiling at him, offering the now naked machete hilt first.

Christie kept his eyes expressionless, his voice flat, as he said, "Who's she?"

John's eyebrows came a little closer together in the ghost of a frown. "My dear chap, we have no idea. What does it matter? Just kill the creature, will you?"

Christie tried to infuse a tinge of contempt into his voice as he said, "You call that a test, for Christ's sake? Look, just give me a moving target, the tougher the better. I got no time for kid stuff."

Hans shook his head sorrowfully. Szabo sighed. John said patiently, "You miss the point, Mr. Lang. We are only interested in recruits who understand that the act of killing is of no importance. They must not need a difficult target, or a worthy opponent, or the heat of combat. They must be willing to take a life, or hundreds of lives as we shall be doing tomorrow morning, for no other reason than that The Watchmen have so ordered." He smiled encouragingly. "Rest assured that we shall certainly test your skill and ability against a worthwhile target later, but our first test is designed to find out the degree of readiness to kill. Do you follow me?"

Christie stared at the shining blade of the machete. He knew that Szabo's gun was on him now, and that at the first hint of a wrong move a soft-nosed bullet would shatter part of his spine and spread the fragments through his body like shrapnel. He would fall dead into the open basket, on top of the pathetic black junkie, and they would both end up in their weighted coffin at the bottom of the sea. Then, when morning came, the steel girdle of shaped charges would shear through the yard-thick cable, the bridge would collapse, and six lanes of traffic would tumble into the waters of the bay more than two hundred and fifty feet below.

If he died now, all this would happen. Of this he was coldly certain. If he lived, if they ran a second test tonight, with a target somewhere ashore, if he could reach Casey by phone for no more than a minute, then the monstrous mass killing might yet be prevented.

But he would not live if he did not take the machete now.

❧   ❧   ❧   ❧   ❧

Kim Crozier stood in the shadows watching for her, and felt his muscles jump when she spoke in a soft voice from just behind him. "I'm back, Kim."

He turned, and saw that she had changed into slacks and a loose tunic, both dark, either black or navy, he could not tell, and she carried a small handbag on her arm. A flash of white caught his eye, and he peered at the bandage swathing the palm and wrist of her left hand.

"What's that? Have you hurt your hand?"

"It's nothing, Kim. What about the fishing boat?"

"She hasn't come back."

"I see. Thanks." There was a relaxed composure about her now, a quietness of demeanour that seemed to set her at a distance from him.

He said, "I slipped into a bar across the road and rang Beryl. Said I couldn't pick her up tonight and didn't know how long I'd be kept. So what now?"

"Nothing." She put a hand on his arm. "You go and pick up Beryl, do whatever you were planning."

"I can't just walk out on you."

"You won't be. It doesn't look as if anything's going to happen, but if it does I might need a free hand, and I won't have that if you're involved."

"Look, Beryl and I had no plans, Modesty. I was to pick her up when she came off duty, and we were just going to drive back to my place for the night, that's all. By now she'll be on her way there by cab, and she'll expect me when she sees me. No problem."

Modesty said, "I've got your number. I'll ring you if there's any way you can help."

"Easier if I stay around."

She looked at him with remote affection. "Kim, I'm deeply fond of you, but at this moment I have to tell you to get out from under my feet."

After a long silence he said reluctantly, "Okay. I guess this is your kind of business, but just take care, Modesty. I hope to God you're ready for trouble."

"I keep a few bits and pieces at my various pads, it's a habit from my wicked past." She touched the tunic just below her right hip. "I'm wearing a gun, so be comforted. I'm sorry I've spoiled your evening, and I'll ring you some time tomorrow. Now we'll say goodnight, Kim." She rose a little on her toes to kiss his cheek. Her lips were soft, and he caught a hint of her perfume, but when she stepped back he saw in her eyes a look he had seen before, in another time and another place, and he knew there was no more to be said.

Anxiety wrenched at him as he walked away, oppressed by a sense of helplessness. After a while he looked back, but she was no longer in sight.

In London it was six a.m., and Tarrant sat on the edge of his bed in a dressing gown, speaking into his bedside phone. "I thought you'd wish to know," he said. "I passed the information through Robson, at their London office, because he can talk direct to CIA Langley by scrambler. He's just rung me back with an acknowledgment from Bernard Mason, so it's evidently gone straight to the top."

Willie Garvin stood by his bedroom window looking out across a meadow to a line of poplars marking the bank of the Thames. He was wearing slacks, a sweater and trainers, and had been about to go for an hour's run when Tarrant's call had come through.

"Willie? Are you there?"

"I'm thinking."

"Sorry."

A few seconds later Willie said, "Did Modesty tell you what she aims to do?"

"Try to re-establish contact, then keep tabs on the Christie group, but she's hoping a CIA team will make contact with her and take over soon."

"If Ben Christie doesn't show up when the boat comes back, she'll do something."

"I know. And it could be a hell of a time before CIA get a team into action. They don't have men on call in all areas."

"That's the bit I was thinking about, Sir G. Why's CIA doing a penetration job in an internal matter? FBI handles internal stuff."

"In the main, yes. But this may be a matter with foreign origins, which makes it a CIA job."

"All the same, there'll surely be an FBI office in San Francisco, and they could take over from Modesty in 'alf an hour if she's still on the wharf and if the Company ask 'em to."

"The Company and the Bureau don't love each other, Willie. You know that as well as I do."

"They don't 'ave to love each other. You don't love Boulter and his Section Nine, but if one of Boulter's agents was at risk and you were asked for 'elp, you'd give all the backing you could raise."

"We're little people with little organisations, Willie. I doubt whether there's any channel between CIA and FBI that could get back-up to Modesty within twenty-four hours. We'll just have to hope that Ben Christie's field director has some sort of team on the spot."

"Did you ask Robson?"

"Yes. He said he didn't know, which means Langley wouldn't tell him."

There was another silence. Tarrant waited. After a while Willie Garvin said, "I'll be at Heathrow by seven-thirty. If she comes through again, tell 'er I'm on my way and with any luck I'll be at the studio in Sausalito by around fifteen 'undred hours Pacific Time."

❋   ❋   ❋   ❋   ❋

There were few strollers on the wharf, for at this hour the restaurants were busy with diners, but two men had appeared from along the Embarcadero three times in the past half hour. Both were casually dressed, one in a loose sweater and a well worn yachting cap, the other bare-headed and wearing a sports jacket with leather patches at the elbows.

She thought it unlikely that the CIA could have got a team to the spot in less than two hours from the time she had called Tarrant, but when the men appeared for the third time she walked across Jefferson and turned east so that she would pass them on a well lit stretch. They appeared to eye her without interest, but when she halted and turned on the water's edge by the closely packed fishing boats she saw that they had followed her.

The man in the sweater touched his cap, smiled, and said, "Miss Blaise? Modesty Blaise?" When she nodded he held out something in his hand and said quietly, "I'm Jake Perry, CIA. This is my partner, Herb Ashton."

She looked at the identity card in the window of the rectangular leather case and saw the photograph and signature. Perry said, "About Ben Christie."

A feather of relief touched her, and she said, "Somebody moved fast, I didn't think Langley would be able to send anyone in for hours."

Perry put the card away in a hip pocket and said, "Langley?"

She stared. "Where else? They couldn't have got my message until an hour ago, so I take it you were already here and in touch."

The two men exchanged a glance, then Perry said, "We got word about you from Ben."

"*Ben?*"

"Sure. He's carrying a matchbox radio, and he must have managed to get by himself for a couple of minutes, maybe in the john. Told us about what happened in the restaurant, and that you'd probably tailed him. If so you'd be here waiting for the boat to come back, he figured."

"You mean he's not blown?"

"Seems not. Anyway, our team chief had us come across to find you." Perry glanced about him, then looked at her again with undisguised interest. "Herb and I know about you from Ben Christie. You're a very active lady, Miss Blaise, and our team chief here says there's a real interesting file on you at Langley, so he got worried you might do something kind of positive, which could foul up this very sensitive operation we have running. Might be bad for Ben if any alarms get tripped by accident."

She said, "I've been worried about that myself, but it doesn't arise now you're taking over."

Perry said, "Our chief would like a word with you, ma'am. He's interested in a description of this guy who was with Ben when you spoke to him in that Chinatown restaurant."

She nodded agreement. "Where and when?"

"Right now, Miss Blaise." He pointed north across the water, to where the grim hump of the island was hidden by darkness now. "We set up base on Alcatraz for this phase of the operation, and we have a boat waiting just past pier 39."

"All right, Mr. Perry. Let's go."

As they began to walk, Perry said, "I guess your message will have come through from Langley by now. We're in direct radio communication with them."

Ten minutes later she was sitting on a cushioned locker which ran along the port side of a small cruiser's combined deck saloon and wheelhouse. Herb Ashton sat opposite her, arms folded. He was a man with hair en brosse above a quiet face and placid brown eyes, and so far he had uttered no word. Jake Perry stood at the wheel, taking the boat out at an easy fifteen knots.

She sat relaxing, thankful that her fears had been groundless, asking no questions, knowing that she would be given no answers. This was CIA business, and she was a stranger who had blundered into the field.

Herb Ashton unfolded his arms and rested his right fist on his knee, with the four inch barrel of the Smith & Wesson .41 Magnum pointing directly between her breasts at a range of five feet. His voice held an accent that in no way matched a name as Anglo-Saxon as Herb Ashton. "I haf soft-point bullets in the gun," he said. "They make hole big as grapefruit."

On the last word, the man who had called himself Jake Perry glanced round at her. "Don't move a finger, babe," he said quietly. "Don't even quiver. He's not kidding, and he's just itching for an excuse. Gets a real kick out of making big holes in people."

She sat frozen, fighting for control against the new shock battering at her nerves, not understanding how this could have happened, but knowing that these men were not CIA agents, and that if there had been any doubt about Ben Christie's cover story before, she had now blown it utterly.

Perry was bringing the cruiser round towards the west, heading for the jaws of the bay. He said, "Here's what you do, but do it very slowly, because we've been warned about you, sugar. First you let the strap of that shoulder bag slip off your shoulder, then you lift both hands slowly till they're high over your head, clasped tight, fingers interlocked. Got it?" She looked at the gun barrel, then at the eyes of the man facing her, and assessed her chances of successful action at zero.

The fingers of her bandaged hand were curled loosely, and when her arms were stretched above her head she said, "I can't clasp them. The left hand's gashed, and I shot some novocaine in only an hour ago. It's numb."

Perry looked over his shoulder and said, "Cross the wrists. Right, keep 'em like that. Now lift your feet up and lie face down on that seat, keeping your arms stretched ahead just like they are now. And slowly, lady, slowly."

She obeyed. The other man stood up, and a moment later she felt the muzzle of his gun pressed against the nape of her neck. A loop of nylon cord was slipped over her hands and jerked tight. The free end was passed round the rail at the end of the seat and secured one-handed with a clove hitch. She heard Perry speaking, presumably on the radio, saying, "We collected the client okay. She'd managed to get in touch with the Company, so she figured we were Company people."

Perry was efficient. The Company was service slang for the CIA, and Perry was telling his masters that Modesty Blaise had made contact somehow. The gun moved from her neck and she felt it on her thigh, pressed against the massive femoral artery. Moments later a noose was drawn tight about one ankle, then about the other, so that her feet were held in a twelve-inch hobble.

With her head pointing aft she could no longer see either man, but she heard Perry say, "Take over here, Nico. I'll frisk her myself. Oberon said she could be full of surprises."

Oberon!

She saw again the face of the man who had been with Ben Christie in the Chinatown restaurant, and recalled the nagging sense of fugitive unease that would not be pinned down. Now the cause was coldly and ominously clear. Take away the beard and you would have the barely remembered face of the pushing and arrogant young recruit she had thrown out of *The Network* during the winding up phase. Hugh Oberon. The full name came back to her now. A recruit of immense potential, but with a deep flaw that left him totally unable to comprehend or accept *The Network* ways and patterns of operation.

Perry's hands were examining her body and clothing inch by inch. He had found the kongo, the little wooden mushroom which made such a potent striking weapon, hidden in the club of hair that hung at the nape of her neck. He had removed the Colt .32 from the hip holster belted beneath her tunic, and had found the flat ten-ounce Sterling .25 automatic taped to her thigh, with access through a Velcro slit in the seam of the trouser leg.

Hugh Oberon. She remembered how Garcia had said later that she had been wise to deport him for six months, because he would make a dangerous enemy, and by the time he returned she would be gone, *The Network* closed. She had not recognised Oberon in the restaurant a few hours ago, but he must have recognised her at once, and so her attempt to pretend she had mistaken Ben Christie for someone else could never have begun to succeed.

Perry took her by the feet and twisted so that she had to turn on to her back. He pushed up her tunic, unhooked the front-fastening bra, broke the shoulder straps and drew the bra away to examine it closely, smiling as he found two small lock-picks in the seams of the cups. "We'll have to double-check you, sugar," he said. "You're real sneaky."

She lay still, not resisting, not allowing herself to hope he would miss anything, for that hope could bring tension which might point the way. Her mind was focused on filling the gaps in her appraisal of the situation. Oberon was here with a team. Some of his team would surely be on *Old Hickory*. These two, calling themselves Perry and Ashton, had either come from the fishing boat or had been on stand-by ashore, but they were well equipped for emergencies, even to the extent of holding forged CIA identity cards. That kind of provision, she thought with remote irony, had been *Network* practice. Evidently Oberon had been quick to learn.

Perry had unfastened her belt, groped her thoroughly, and was now checking the soles and heels of her shoes. They were genuine, for she had no pair of her special combat boots at the Sausalito studio. He picked up her handbag, sat down on the other seat, and began to go through the contents carefully.

"A spare clip for the automatic, spare cartridges for the colt, a short coil of rope with a small folding grapnel, and what's in here? Ah, a miniature first aid kit. You certainly came well prepared, babe. Here's a box with a hypo and some ampoules. Barbiturate sleep-shots, maybe?" He grinned. "We have easier ways of keeping people out of action, ma'am. A lipstick? Now why would she want to freshen up at a time like this, Nico? A little jet of tear gas or mace if you twist the base, you reckon? We'll try it outside later . . ."

She closed her ears to his monologue, and emptied her mind, knowing there was nothing useful for it to feed on. Ben Christie might be dead or alive. Whatever had happened to him was unalterable. As for herself, they would not kill her yet. They would take her to Oberon, and then her situation would be different from what it was at this moment, either better or worse, but different. Until then it would be a drain on her mental energy to make any speculative appraisal of that future situation, for it was unknowable.

Eight

GOLITSYN was giving half his mind to consideration of the messages coming through about Modesty Blaise as he leaned back in his chair and surveyed the chessboard, but he did not want to lose to von Krankin, so a distraction was called for. When he had relit his pipe and shaken the match out, Golitsyn said, "It is my firm belief that Stalin was a stupid prick."

Von Krankin looked up, blue eyes questioning in the square and curiously concave face beneath the short fair hair. "A what?" he said.

Golitsyn shook his head. "Your colloquial English is not so good, Siegfried."

"It is sufficient," von Krankin said stiffly. "We use English as a common language only because St. Maur is too bloody arrogant to speak anything else. What was that you said about Stalin?"

Golitsyn explained, moving his bishop as he did so. Von Krankin said, "On what grounds do you say he was a stupid prick?"

"There are plenty, but I will tell you one. In 1945 he could have had Greece like that." The dead match snapped between Golitsyn's fingers. "I was a very young man at the time, but I was a protégé of Mikoyan, the cleverest of them all, and that was his view. We could have had total control of the whole of the Balkans within ten years if the opportunity had been taken."

Von Krankin shrugged and moved his rook. "And of all Europe by now," he said, "but then there would have been nothing of interest for people like us to do, Golitsyn."

The Russian grinned. "A good point," he acknowledged. "Though we might then have offered our services to the Americans, as counter-revolutionaries in the cause of freedom from the yoke of Communism." He saw that von Krankin had failed to note the trap, and would now be mated in six moves.

It was early afternoon, and the two men were sitting in the command hut of the small base established a little way inshore on the island of Deserta Grande. Both wore dull green trousers and a jacket in battledress style. This clothing served as a uniform for The Watchmen in training, but also made plausible working gear for them in their secondary roles as drillers, rig mechanics, floormen, roustabouts and other categories of occupation aboard the drillship half a mile off-shore.

A First Blood patrol action had been scheduled for this afternoon, an action in which two patrols of The Watchmen would be matched against each other in the inland valley where the mock-up street had been built. It was a test of leadership, individual skill and team co-operation, the competition ending when the first man on one side or the other was killed or wounded. These affairs usually ended with a minor wound since plastic body armour was worn over vital parts, but there had been two killings in the past year. Today's exercise had been cancelled by the field commanders, St. Maur and von Krankin, when signals had started to come through from Oberon on the Baystrike operation.

The first signal out of the cipher room had reported an encounter with Modesty Blaise in which she had not recognised Oberon but had by chance revealed that the proposed new recruit, Lang, was an undercover man. Real name Ben Christie. Query FBI? Query CIA?

The name was among several thousand in Golitsyn's files, and he had not had to refer back to Moscow for identification. Orders had been sent to Oberon telling him to delay elimination of Christie and take appropriate measures against possible covert action by Modesty Blaise. This was a hunch on Golitsyn's part, but based on a measure of deduction. He had a deep respect for the ability of this woman, whose files he had studied with interest, and he was distinctly uneasy about her presence in the area of Operation Baystrike. If she could be picked up and eliminated with Christie, so much the better. Golitsyn had the distinct impression that she was a spoiler, though perhaps rarely by choice. If he had believed in god or devil he would have felt that one or the other used her as an instrument of disruption, a stumbling block, a trip wire. Far too often she seemed to be tossed into a scene in which she had no part, there to cause chaos and disaster. The sooner she was dead, thought Golitsyn, the better.

Three minutes later the door to the signals room opened and St. Maur came in, a pink message slip in his hand. "They've picked up Modesty Blaise and have her aboard the fishing boat," he said, stalking across the room to stand gazing down his beak of a nose at Golitsyn and von Krankin.

Golitsyn looked up with a raised eyebrow. "So easily?"

"It appears she accepted two of Szabo's team as CIA men without question because she had somehow contrived to get a message through to CIA headquarters at Langley, and was expecting contact to be made."

Von Krankin said, "That is not so good. CIA will soon be looking for the fishing boat if she told them Christie is on it."

Golitsyn nodded. There was a silence in the room. The relationship between the three leaders of The Watchmen contained elements of hostility, but this was superficial. They were men devoid of the capacity to like or dislike, to feel affection for a friend or hatred for an enemy. Each was governed by a purpose which allowed for no such natural emotions. They worked together with great efficiency and with cold respect for one another, but no shred of friendship.

One day, in ten years time or less, and after a period of civil disorder, St. Maur knew that he would govern the United Kingdom, as von Krankin knew he would govern West Germany. Both had strong extremist support in their respective countries, and that support would spread rapidly to the middle ground as people craved for an ending to strikes, racial conflict, political sterility, civil unrest, and all the inevitable problems of democracies.

Golitsyn sometimes amused himself by speculating privately on how long his two colleagues would last as Presidents-for-Life of their respective territories. They were both too strong to be puppets, and of course they were ideologically unsound, for neither was a Marxist. They were quite simply authoritarian. The long-term Moscow plan was that St. Maur and von Krankin would in time be replaced by more biddable presidents, but Golitsyn was quite certain his colleagues knew this, and he doubted that they would be easily disposed of once they had been put in power.

Himself he had no ambition for overt power, preferring the role of the king-maker in the shadows. Of covert power he probably had more than any other man in the world even now. He had devised the idea of The Watchmen, and it had found such favour with the men in the Kremlin that he had been given unlimited backing and a free hand. Even the KGB had no authority over him, yet were required to provide him with a communications system and all equipment and information available to them.

Golitsyn believed that one day, when the old men in the Kremlin were to be replaced by new men, he would have a very big voice in deciding who those new men should be, but he had no feeling of destiny about this, as St. Maur and von Krankin had about their future, for of the three he was alone in having a sense of humour, and this had prevented the development of a dictatorial ego. At heart he was a games player, and his purpose was to use the whole world as his field of play, but there was no element of sport in his approach. If Golitsyn had a sense of humour, it merely meant that he would cut your throat with a chuckle instead of getting intense about it.

Now he took his pipe from his mouth and said, "Oberon must be instructed to bring forward the Baystrike operation. What time is it there now?"

"Approximately twenty-two thirty hours," said St. Maur.

"Then let us tell Oberon to destroy the bridge at any time within the next ninety minutes, at his discretion, at a moment of optimum traffic."

Von Krankin said, "It will not be like the rush hour, but there should be a good amount of cars going home between eleven and midnight."

"Sufficient," said the Earl St. Maur. "In fact I prefer it. Fifty cars, perhaps, instead of five hundred. I've always felt that a too massive loss of life on Baystrike might spark the Americans into launching a total effort to uncover us."

"It is the last operation of The Watchmen until September," said Golitsyn, "so it had to be big. But this will be big enough. How long to get the message to Oberon?"

"Seven minutes." St. Maur turned to the door. "It's a simple instruction so we can use code instead of cipher."

Golitsyn said, "And he is to kill Christie and Blaise, of course."

"Of course."

The door closed behind St. Maur. Von Krankin said, "I would not like the Americans to make a total effort. They can be very good."

"A military distraction has already begun," said Golitsyn. "A limited move through the Chagai Hills into Baluchistan. It will distract the Americans from Baystrike, and Baystrike will distract them from Baluchistan. That is how it works, Siegfried." He looked down at the table and moved his knight. "Check, and mate in four," he said.

*   *   *   *   *

She sat in the dining cabin with her bound hands between her knees. There was blood on the cushions, and Ben Christie was slumped beside her, eyes closed, a blood-soaked towel roughly knotted about his right shoulder. His face was the colour of dirty milk, and she did not know if he was sufficiently conscious to understand what was happening. Szabo stood beside the door, arms folded, gun holstered, studying her with amused curiosity. Oberon sat hitched on one corner of the table, watching her with intent green eyes in which a pinpoint flame of hatred glowed.

". . . so we played a little joke on Ben," he was saying in a mild voice. "We pretended he hadn't been blown and we put him through the first stage of a Mohs test. That's a test for hardness, Mam'selle." There was sarcasm in the tone of the last word. "And Ben certainly did his best to save all those poor people on the bridge, didn't you, Ben?"

Her mind was busy calculating the interaction of a dozen factors in the situation, but her face was empty of expression and she was careful to register every word Oberon spoke. In her mental posture there was now neither hope nor despair, only appraisal and readiness. She listened carefully on principle, because in Oberon's words there might be information, and that information might be of use to her, now or in a little while, or much later if she survived.

It was ten minutes since *Old Hickory* had hove to for the cruiser to make fast alongside. She had been taken aboard with bound hands and hobbled feet, and handed over to a powerfully built man whom Perry addressed as Szabo. The two spoke briefly together while Perry's companion held her with a gun at her back. She could not hear what was said, but noticed that *Old Hickory* carried a very tall aerial, probably set up once the boat had left the bay. It suggested that she was equipped for long-distance signalling.

Perry and the man calling himself Herb Ashton went down the ladder and cast off the line. The cruiser drifted clear, then the sound of its engine rose and she stood with Szabo's gun against her spine, watching the white wake of the boat as it curved away at an easy pace towards the bay.

Szabo said, "Walk," and took her into the dining cabin. A fair-haired man with a meaningless smile was fixing or possibly refixing a makeshift dressing on a wound that had shattered Ben Christie's shoulder. Ben's jacket had been removed, but not the shirt. The dressing was evidently meant to plug the bleeding as a matter of convenience rather than as a measure of first aid.

Ben was in shock, and she could not tell whether or not he recognised her when his half closed eyes wandered over her, for they were unfocused, and filled with a dark torment that seemed too alien to have sprung solely from physical pain. She knew that his cover could not possibly be restored, but there was nothing to be gained by an admission, so she looked at him without recognition or greeting, and sat down beside him when ordered to do so.

The fair-haired man knotted a towel over the lumpy dressing, stepped away and leaned against the bulkhead. Neither he nor Szabo spoke. Two minutes later the door opened and Oberon came in. Mentally she stripped the beard from his face, and saw that even without this there was a substantial change in him. In three years he had lost the brashness she remembered and had grown into a different personality, mature, controlled, and with an ambience that to her was so deadly she felt the hairs on the back of her neck trying to rise like hackles.

"You've been very useful to us this evening, Mam'selle," he said in his soft, barely perceptible brogue. "Is there anything you wish to say to me?"

She glanced to one side as she answered. "This man is badly wounded. I'd like to dress his shoulder better."

Szabo chuckled. Oberon sat on the corner of the table and said, "There's no point, since you'll both be dead very soon now. And incidentally, so will your friend Tarrant, if he isn't dead already. That has been satisfactorily contracted to the Polish twins. But there's something I want you to see before you go, Mam'selle." The tiny red glow came into his eyes, and she sensed the effort he made to prevent his voice shaking with the rage that swept him. Hugh Oberon carried Spanish pride in his blood, and she realised now that what to her had been an irritating incident, soon forgotten, to him had been an ego-shattering experience on a huge scale. She had humiliated him, first by having Willie Garvin deal with him as casually as if swatting a fly, and then by dismissing him from *The Network* without bothering to punish him, warn him off, or even speak to him. The handout of a cash stake when the ship reached Perth had perhaps been the worst insult of all in his eyes.

He looked at his watch and said, "Go and check the rate of traffic, Hans." The fair-haired man went out, still with the empty smile on his lips. Oberon looked at Modesty again and said, "You're going to see the size of operation Hugh Oberon can set up. You're going to see the Golden Gate Bridge fall into the bay, Mam'selle."

She had switched off her emotions from the moment of capture, and when he began to talk about the tower, the great cable, the girdle of shaped charges, and the detonation by twin radio beams, she simply fed the data into her calculations, as she had fed in the reference to Tarrant and the presence of Ben Christie, alive but badly wounded, when she had first entered the cabin. These calculations could have no specific answer, they produced only tentative options and percentage chances, with unknown and unknowable factors entering the equations.

Now Oberon was speaking in a mocking tone of Ben Christie and some kind of hardness test. A mose test? She found the reference cryptic, and wondered briefly if it was linked with the horror she had seen in Ben's glazed eyes. Oberon was saying, "Even if you hadn't blown Ben's cover, I don't think he'd have penetrated any deeper than our outer screening. He tried hard to stay cool when we put him through the Mohs test, but it wasn't convincing. You see, we had this black kid —"

She broke in, speaking without emphasis. "You talk about 'we' and 'us'. Who are you, Oberon? Who are you blowing the bridge for?"

Information. It might die with her, but there was no point in giving weight to that consideration. Oberon studied her for a moment or two, then he said, "We are The Watchmen, and this demonstration is on behalf of the Armenian Freedom Fighters."

She looked through him, and after a moment he went on, "As I was saying, we picked up this black kid, a junkie, and —"

He broke off again as the door opened. Hans came in and said, "About twelve to fifteen cars a minute each way. I do not think it will increase."

"That's not at all bad," said Oberon. "We'll do it now." He stood up, opened a small trunk that stood in the corner, and took out a steel document case. With a nod towards Modesty he said to Szabo, "Bring them both along, and be *very* careful with the woman. Slip a noose round her neck."

Two minutes later she stood under an awning on the afterdeck, her feet still hobbled, her wrists still bound, and a running noose looped about her neck. Hans stood to one side of her, gripping the standing end of the rope, a gun in his other hand, held across his body so that the tilted barrel was aimed at her head. He had been careful to place himself so that he would have been beyond the reach of her arm even if her hands had been free.

Szabo had slapped Ben Christie hard across the face to rouse him, then hauled him out, holding him by his good arm and urging him along on rubbery legs to prop him against the cabin bulkhead. In the light of the deck lamp under the awning Modesty saw Ben's legs begin to fold when Szabo let him go, but then his good hand found support on a lifebelt hooked to the bulkhead, and with an effort he managed to stay on his feet. His head came up and he looked dazedly about him, but his eyes passed over her without recognition.

Three paces away from her was a small table. Oberon was taking something out of the document case and standing it on the table, an object in grey plastic, about a foot square and three inches deep, two dials and a single switch on its top surface, a large and a small socket set in one side. She knew this must be the transmitter Oberon had described, with the twin frequencies that would detonate the girdle of explosive.

Old Hickory was moving again, at about five knots on a northerly heading. When she looked east towards the bay she could see the loom of the bridge's great towers against a sky only marginally lighter, and lower down, spanning the jaws of the bay, were two twinkling belts of light moving in opposite directions, headlights seen through the steel struts of the parapet.

Szabo looked up and called, "Feed out the power and the aerial lead, Sandy."

Her view of the ship's bridge was cut off by the awning, but she heard a muffled acknowledgment and a few moments later two thin cables snaked down. She watched Szabo drawing down sufficient slack to reach the transmitter, and saw that one cable would supply power to the instrument, the other would feed output into the tall aerial. When the switch was thrown, one end of the western cable of the Golden Gate Bridge would be scythed through, and fifty or more cars and their occupants would go down with the bridge into the bay below. Then, after a minute or two for Oberon to relish his triumph, she and Ben would die.

She absorbed this data, looked slowly about her, and made her final calculation.

*   *   *   *   *

Awareness came slowly through the mists of pain, anguish and despair that clouded Ben Christie's mind. He was looking at two feet, and deckboards. They were his own feet, he realised, and with a great effort lifted his head. As he did so an eerie clarity filled his mind, as if some part of his being had moved away from his body and was observing the scene, untouched by all emotion.

The table stood in the middle of the afterdeck. On the right of it, the bearded man, John, was bending over a grey control box that lay there, looking towards the one called Szabo, who was moving away from the hunched figure of himself, Ben Christie, propped unsteadily against the bulkhead. Szabo was taking two lengths of cable with him. On the left of the table was Hans, the one who had climbed the tower, holding a gun to cover a girl beside him, a girl with dark hair, strangely familiar. Modesty Blaise . . . yes, he remembered now. She must have come after him, and they had been ready for her.

A pang of grief penetrated Christie's passionless survey. Not her, too. Not after the black girl . . .

Horror and pain broke through the barriers. He was within himself again, knowing what had been and what was to come, racked by the knowledge that he was helpless, drained of strength, too feeble even to stand unaided. And she was helpless too, wrists bound, feet hobbled, a halter of cord about her neck, one hand injured and bandaged. The clarity and the heightened perception were still with Christie, and it seemed to him that he was watching the scene in slow motion. Szabo alone was moving, one foot slowly completing a pace as he walked towards the table.

Christie left him to complete the long journey and turned his attention to Modesty Blaise. There was something different in her position, but he could not quite understand how it had changed. Her bound hands were in front of her chest, her head had turned a little and she was looking at Hans, a pace away on her right. Her bandaged left hand was tilted so that if it had held a gun it would have been pointing at Hans's head, just as his gun was pointing at hers.

A spark of unreasoning hope touched Christie as he saw that the curled fingers of that bandaged hand were beginning to unfold. Now they were straight, pressed stiffly together, and now starting to arch back. The report was barely audible above the boat sounds, but as if with magnified vision Christie saw a small black-rimmed hole appear in the wad of bandage swathing her hand, a hole close to the root of the middle finger, and from it issued a tiny coil of smoke. But by then Hans's head had jerked slightly, and his gun was falling, and there was a little eruption on top of his skull as the small-calibre bullet made its upward-angled exit after passing through his brain.

A point two-two pen gun under the bandage, Christie thought laboriously, a pen gun triggered by pressure with the heel of the hand, and Jesus Christ but she'd had an ace-in-the-hole after all and she was in with a chance. To him she seemed still to be moving in slow motion, but much faster than the others, as he watched her jump forward, put bound hands on the table, and make a swivel-vault to drive both feet into the face of the bearded man on the other side so that he was flung back against the rail.

Szabo had dropped the cables and was reaching for the gun at the back of his hip, lunging forward. She swivel-vaulted again before the gun was clear, but this time landed only a glancing blow with one foot to throw Szabo off balance. Christie heard a wordless sobbing cheer break from his own throat as he lurched forward. She used her bound hands like pincers to snatch up the transmitter, and a kangaroo jump took her to the starboard rail. Szabo had regained his balance and was crouched, rising, lips drawn back, eyes wide with shock, the gun coming up, and she made no attempt to reach him but spun round and hurled the transmitter out over the rail. She continued the turn, one hobbled foot lifted to maintain the speed, and faced Szabo again, but too late for attack or evasion, for his gun was at the aim and there was death in his eyes as his finger tightened on the trigger.

Ben Christie used the last of his strength, going forward, a tilt of the deck helping his stumbling run, going towards her, past Szabo, interposing himself, trying to spread his body wide to give her as much cover as possible. He felt the hammerblow of the bullet smashing into his back somewhere below the left shoulderblade, and he cried, "*Go . . . go!*" in a screaming whisper as he was flung towards her by the impact.

Her eyes were vast black pools only inches from his face as she went back with him, dropping her bound hands over his head and shoulders to hold him close and prevent him falling as she leaned back over the rail and heaved with ferocious strength to lift him, then twisting, carrying him with her over the side, a bullet splitting the air above his head as they cleared the rail and fell.

There was bruising impact, shock, agony, water choking him. She was twisting round, getting her body beneath him. He felt the softness of her breasts thrusting against his back as she lifted him, then his face broke the surface and he sucked in air.

The boat was already thirty yards away, and in the light from the afterdeck he saw the silhouette of Szabo leaning over the rail, foreshortened, aiming his gun. He heard two shots, perhaps three. They were not very loud, for the sound was whipped away by the wind, and he felt no impact. Her voice spoke close to his ear, a gasping whisper. "Ben . . . can you hear me?"

He made an affirmative sound. The boat was sixty yards away now and starting to turn to port, the superstructure cutting off Szabo's line of sight. Christie heard her suck in breath, then say quickly: "If they come close I'll have to take you under, Ben. Try not to struggle. Understand?"

This time he managed to croak, "Yes." His mind was very clear, as if the immersion in cold water had roused him. The pain was fading rapidly, and he felt a kind of drunken laughter starting to bubble within him from relief and exhilaration at the miracle she had contrived. He hoped she had snapped the neck of that bearded bastard when she dropped him with the head kick. The Scotsman at the wheel, the one they called Sandy, would bring the boat round and start a search. There would be only Szabo to man the spotlight — if they had one. Hans was dead, she had made sure

of that, and the bearded bastard, John, he would be out of action
for a few minutes at least. If Modesty knew the bay she would
know that the tide was now carrying them west, and they would
have covered quite a little distance before the boat could double
back . . . but oh Jesus, they were allowing for that and the boat was
coming at them now, only thirty yards to his right as he lay half
floating, half supported by her body beneath him.

He felt her hands at his face. She said, "Deep breath, Ben." A
bandaged palm covered his mouth, two fingers clamped his nose,
and she took him quietly under. He felt sudden fear that when the
need to breath became too strong he might lose control and start to
struggle, but as they drifted below the surface his chest felt cool and
easy, and after a little while he slid gladly down into a dark sleep.

*   *   *   *   *

Her inner clock, which never failed her, told her that it was an
hour past midnight. There were gaps in the cloud cover now. She
could see a thin moon and a few stars. They were nearer to the
bridge than they had been two hours ago, for the tide had turned,
but their drift had been diagonally across the approach to the bay
and she thought there was little chance of their reaching the shore
anywhere this side of the Golden Gate. It was more likely that they
would be plucked into the middle of the rip that flowed under the
bridge, but there was nothing she could do about it. Attempting to
tow Ben Christie would be a useless waste of energy.

The search had lasted for only twenty minutes, then the cruiser
had come racing out to *Old Hickory* again, summoned by radio no
doubt. By that time she had little fear of being found, for the
fishing boat was a good four hundred yards away. The cruiser did
not join the search, but came alongside for a few minutes before
moving out to sea at speed. From her position low in the water it
was hard to tell what was happening, but she had the impression
that *Old Hickory* was also making out to sea.

She assumed Oberon would have an escape route, probably by
rendezvous with another vessel. It was not a point that concerned
her now. During the early minutes of the search she had taken

Ben Christie under twice. He had passed out the first time and knew nothing of the second. As soon as she felt the danger of discovery had passed she filled her lungs to float high with his head supported on her breast and his body at right angles to hers while she eased the leather-backed razor blade from its recess under the buckle of her belt and cut the cords from her wrists and feet.

This freedom was a huge relief, and for the next fifteen minutes she worked steadily at her immediate problems, husbanding her strength for what would surely be a long ordeal to come. She pulled Ben's shoes off, then her own, and let them sink. She felt in his hip and trouser pockets for any useful item but found only a wallet and some coins. The towel was still knotted about his shoulder. She did not know whether or not the wound was bleeding, and if so, how badly. He had taken another wound at close range, in the back and probably upward angled, from Szabo's gun. She had not seen the bullet exit from his chest as he fell against her, so it was almost certainly lodged somewhere in a lung. There was nothing she could do except perhaps to prevent excessive loss of blood.

Using the blade, she cut a piece from the end of the towel, then spent long minutes groping about his back under the water, seeking the bullet's point of entry. When at last her fingers found it, she set her teeth and forced a twist of the towelling into it, thankful that Ben was unconscious. She felt his pulse. It was fast, but perhaps a little stronger than she had feared. Carefully she eased him up so that he lay with his head high on the slope of her breast, almost on her shoulder, then began to assess her situation.

She was more than a mile from the bridge, but not much more. The tide would soon be setting into the bay, but she did not know how long it would take to bring her to the bridge, or where it would then carry her. It was pointless to attempt to tow Ben Christie in any particular direction at this stage, for he was a dead weight, and even in still water she would barely make four hundred yards in an hour. All she could do was support him, and hope they would be carried to land somewhere in the bay, or perhaps spotted from a boat. If CIA Langley had responded to Tarrant's alert, there might be boats out looking for *Old Hickory* at some time during the next few hours.

The water was cold but not bitterly so. In years gone by she had once spent half a year in the Thar desert in the open, under the tutelage of the *guru* Sivaji, who had lived for six generations. Without speaking he had imparted to her those ways by which even the unconscious body processes might be subjected to the will of the mind. Tonight, she knew, she could withdraw from herself yet leave her body with a substantial measure of immunity to exposure. Certainly she could survive the night, but she could extend no protection to the man in her arms.

She lay holding him loosely, their bodies lifting and dipping to the movement of the sea, and she drained from herself all regret, sorrow and anxiety. When acceptance was complete, she began the *mantra* for induction of her mental withdrawal.

Each hour she roused from her waking sleep sufficiently to assess her situation anew, but at some time after one o'clock she came suddenly to full wakefulness at the sound of Ben speaking. The top of his head was almost touching her chin, and though his voice was weak it was very clear, for there was no wind now, and the only background noise was from the soft lapping of small wavelets. She knew she had missed none of his words, yet he spoke as if in the middle of a sentence, and in his halting voice there was a note of grief that seemed almost beyond bearing.

". . . She was a junkie they picked up. A black girl. Just a kid. I had to kill her . . . kill her with a machete to pass the test. They test their people, The Watchmen do. I couldn't see any other way to get off the boat . . . try to warn Casey about the bridge."

She felt his body heave, and he began to sob. Appalled by what his words had revealed, she moved a hand to cup her palm against his cheek and said, "There, Ben, there. I'm with you and everything's going to be all right. It's Modesty. Remember?"

He said brokenly, "And then they laughed, because they'd known all the time . . . known I was CIA. God knows how. Modesty covered fast enough, pretending 'bout me looking like some cousin . . . but somehow they knew, and still they put me through their test. As a joke. A joke."

She said, "The one with the beard is Oberon, and he knew me from years ago. That's why it didn't work when I tried to cover. I'm sorry I blew you, Ben. So sorry."

"There was this kid in the basket . . . a junkie . . ."

She broke in quickly. "They were never going to let her go, Ben. She was dead from the time they brought her aboard."

He said in a voice tight with pain, "When it was over . . . when they laughed and told me they knew who I was, I tried to kill him, the one called John . . . I still had the machete. But Szabo was ready. He drilled me." She could feel the horror and torment in him. It would have possessed her also if she had not set barriers in her mind to ward it off, not daring to risk the drain on her mental energy.

"They're going to blow the bridge," he said with sudden urgency. "Hundreds and hundreds of cars going down . . ."

"No, we stopped them. Remember? I got to the transmitter and threw it overboard. And Szabo would have killed me but you took the bullet for me."

"Szabo?" he said slowly. "Wait a minute. Ah, yes. You're . . . you're Modesty. That bandaged hand was phoney, and you killed Hans with a pen gun. Something like that. They didn't catch us, then . . .?"

"No. The cruiser came back and I think both boats went out to sea. Ben, thanks for what you did."

"You . . . don't owe me a thing. I remember . . . remember when . . ."

"Ben, you spoke of The Watchmen just now. Will you tell me all you can about this operation? Once we get ashore you're going to be busy having bullets taken out of you, so there'd better be one of us available to tell about what's happened."

"Sure . . . sure. Get on to Casey. Tom Casey. Good guy. My director. Call 535-2063. Tell him about the bridge. They fixed a ring of . . . of shaped charges round main cable . . ."

"I know that part, Ben. Oberon told me."

"Who?"

"The boss. The one with the beard."

"Ah. I only knew his cover name. John. Can you . . . find him, Modesty?"

"I'll find him." She had a fleeting vision of a black girl in a basket, and hatred burned within her. She quickly crushed the vision and the hatred. "Give me what you know, Ben. Names, contacts, everything."

"Sure, Modesty . . . sure." His voice was becoming weary. "Bit tired. Let me think . . ."

In slow sentences, sometimes with gaps of silence so long she thought he had lost consciousness again, he told her how CIA had created the character of Dave Lang, war veteran turned criminal, in preparation for another assignment. That he had been recommended to The Watchmen as a potential recruit was a totally unexpected stroke of luck, and he had at once been switched to the task of penetrating The Watchmen. His field director was Tom Casey. The man controlling the operation from Langley was called Franklyn. She heard a thin edge of anger in Ben Christie's wavering voice as he spoke of Franklyn. As a safety measure, there had been minimal contact between Ben and his director throughout the mission. Approach by The Watchmen to the potential recruit had been made through a series of cut-outs, culminating in the meeting with 'John' today.

"Don't know . . . much more," the weakening voice whispered into the darkness. "They run tests. You fail, you're dead. Must be like that. Once they'd told me . . . about the bridge, they couldn't let me live if I didn't go through with . . . you know . . . the black kid. Oh, Jesus, that skinny black junkie."

She spoke close to his ear, with all the reassurance she could muster. "It didn't happen, Ben. It was a bad dream. A bad dream. You're wounded and feverish, and you keep having this nightmare. Listen to me, Ben. Do you know what getaway they planned? Do you know where they're based? Who's behind them?"

"Sorry . . . don't know. They said . . . blowing the bridge for the Armenians. *The Armenians.* That's crazy. The black kid . . . she was just a bad dream? Truly? Tell me, honey. Tell me again."

"A bad dream. Truly, Ben."

"Ah, thank Christ. Still seems so real." His body twitched suddenly and his quavering voice sharpened. "What you staying for? Get swimming, Modesty. God's sake, you can make it easy. Hit beach an' call Tom. Ol' Ben okay, no sweat. Just float easy till you come an' pick me up. Go, honey, go."

"Yes, Ben, yes." She stroked his face and spoke soothingly "I'll be leaving in a few minutes, don't worry. Just waiting for the tide to turn." The last words were meaningless, but she thought he was too disoriented to analyse them.

"Few minutes? Promise?"

"Promise," she lied. "Now just try to rest, Ben. Everything's going to be fine."

"Sure. Sure, Modesty." His words were becoming slurred. "Glad that . . . that black kid . . . jus' a lousy dream."

The voice trailed to silence. His breathing was loud and ragged now, his pulse weaker and unsteady. She twisted her head to look for the lights of any boats in the approach to the bay, but found none. If Ben was to live she would have to get him ashore soon. Towing him would be painfully slow and exhausting, but it might repay the effort now, for to change their line of drift by as little as a hundred yards could make a difference of hours. Taking his head between her hands, she began a steady breast-stroke kick with her legs.

By three o'clock, at the darkest hour, she had passed under the bridge only a long stone's throw from the base of the southern tower but had failed to reach it, or her objective, Fort Point on the lower jaw of the bay. The drag of the current had been too strong and her strength was drained away by the long hard struggle. Now she drifted slowly with her burden into the widening waters beyond the Golden Gate, the cold creeping into her bones.

She feared Ben had died, for she was no longer able to detect a pulse in his neck; but this, she knew, could be because her fingers were too numb. There might yet be a thread of life in his body, and it was impossible for her to consider leaving him. She did not resign herself to any inevitable outcome, for she had no capacity for acceptance of ultimate defeat. There was traffic in the bay, even at night, especially towards dawn. With first light she might be spotted by a Coast Guard cutter, a crab boat, a tug, or an early morning yachtsman in a small boat.

She visualised the lie of the nearer shore. From Fort Point the cliffs curved back, the wooded ground dropping gradually to the marina, then came Fort Mason, the Maritime Museum and Fisherman's Wharf. The bay was full of shifting currents, and she thought she was probably moving at three to five knots on the flowing tide. It was impossible to know where she would be taken, and with her strength gone she could no longer exert any influence on the course of her drifting.

Easing Ben's head up on to her breast again, she rested her hands across his body to hold him securely, then withdrew into quiescence once more, slowing the life processes to hoard her remaining energies, leaving only a glimmer of awareness to keep watch on her situation.

Nine

"EXCUSE me, are you Mr. Garvin?"
She was a slim, attractive girl in her middle twenties, black, with marvellous eyes, and she was waiting for him as he cleared Customs at just before three o'clock on a cool bright afternoon.

"That's me. Willie Garvin." Blue eyes assessed her warily.

She said, "I'm Kim Crozier's girlfriend, Beryl."

"Ah. Kim." He relaxed a little, then stiffened again as the light coat she wore fell open and he saw the white apron of her nurse's uniform beneath. "Is Modesty all right?" he said quickly.

"Yes." She put a hand on his arm. "She's had one hell of a time, but she's all right."

"Hurt?"

"Just exhausted. Suffering a little from exposure. Kim says she ought to be dead from it, but she'll be fine in a day or two."

Willie exhaled a long breath of relief. "Thanks, Beryl. Where is she?"

"In a room at the Ashfield Hospital, under Kim's care. She spoke by phone to a man called Tarrant in London at about six this morning, before she went to sleep, and he told her you should be arriving on this flight, so Kim asked me to come along and pick you up. Let's go to the carpark, Mr. Garvin, it can take quite a time getting out of this airport."

"Call me Willie."

Fifteen minutes later they were joining light traffic moving north. The car was an Aston Martin belonging to Kim, and she handled it well, using the gears without flashiness. When they were clear of the airport Willie said, "D'you know anything about a man called Ben Christie?"

"Yes." She glanced at him. "I'm sorry, Willie, but he's dead.

Do you want me to tell you what I know so far, or will you wait to hear it from Modesty?"

"She's awake now?"

"Woke up half an hour before I left. Kim's allowing two CIA men to talk to her at four. Well, I suppose CIA, but they could be Secret Service or whatever."

"Give me what you've picked up so far, please Beryl. I know the bit about Modesty and Kim in the restaurant, and her maybe blowing Ben Christie's cover."

"Yes. Kim told me about that, and he thought she was worrying unduly, but he was wrong. The trouble was, this man with Ben Christie knew her from of old, but she didn't recognise him because he'd grown a beard, and anyway she didn't see much of him way back apparently. His name's Oberon."

"*Oberon?*" Willie leaned his head back and closed his eyes for moment. "Oh God, what a lousy break."

"She got Kim to tail them, and Ben Christie was taken aboard a fishing boat called *Old Hickory*. The police found out this morning that these people bought it only two weeks ago. The boat went out to sea, Modesty stayed on the wharf and sent Kim home. That was after she'd been back to her place in Sausalito to ring Tarrant and change her clothes and get a gun and so on. But then she was picked up by two of Oberon's people pretending to be CIA men."

"He'd called them by radio from the boat?"

"Yes. Anyway, they took her out, way past Golden Gate, to where this fishing boat was cruising about in the dark. She found Ben Christie had been shot in the shoulder and was in a pretty bad way, but they hadn't killed him yet because they were keeping him alive to see the bridge go up. Same with her."

"The bridge?"

"Golden Gate. They were all set to blow it up."

He turned to stare at her. "You're joking."

"No, honestly, Willie. The night before, they'd fixed some sort of iron ring round one of the main cables. A collar in sections, right up by the top of the north tower. Modesty said something about shaped explosives. Wedges, I think."

"'Ang on a minute." He sat visualising the bridge, working out sums in his head, considering logistics, materials, and means of access. She said nothing, driving smoothly, a competent girl with a special touch of serenity about her that reminded him of Modesty. "All right, it figures," he said. "Go on, Beryl."

"I don't know all the details, Willie, but Kim and I were with her while she was telling all this to a CIA man called Tom Casey. Ben's boss, I think. He didn't like her telling it all with us there, but Kim wasn't going to have us leave her, she was real weak, Willie. He threatened to kick Casey out and put her to sleep for twenty-four hours, so Casey quit arguing and we stayed. He's quite a decent guy, really, but he's worried sick and he's been hit hard by Ben Christie's death." She paused. "Sorry, where did I get to?"

"On the boat. They were going to blow the bridge."

"Yes. Well, she was tied up pretty good, and they had this radio ready to send a signal that would set off the explosive. Took her and Ben Christie out on deck to see it. I'm not sure about this bit, but she had a sort of pen gun, a tube firing one bullet, and it was hidden in a bandage she'd put on her hand. Does that make sense?"

"Sure. She was expecting trouble, and that's a gimmick she's used before."

"Well, she killed one guy with this thing before they threw the switch, and somehow she knocked down Oberon and another guy, named Szabo, and she got to the radio thing and threw it overboard. Szabo still had a gun and he shot to kill at close range, but Ben Christie came to life and got in between, so he took the shot in the back. Then Modesty grabbed him and took him over the rail with her. That was around eleven last night, about a mile the other side of Golden Gate. The boat searched for a while, but didn't find them in the dark. After that she just did what she could to stop Ben bleeding and keep him afloat. There was a time when he was pretty rational. He told her Oberon and his team were Watchmen. Or part of The Watchmen. They said this operation was in support of the Armenian Freedom Fighters. He thought that sounded crazy, and so does Modesty, but it's what they said."

"'Ow long was she in the sea with Ben before they were picked up?"

"Five or six hours, and they weren't picked up. She knocked herself out trying to get ashore, but couldn't make it. Then they just drifted, and around four or four-thirty she found herself close to the marina. A man on one of the boats there helped her out. He called the cops and an ambulance for her, then she called Kim herself, and we got there just after the ambulance. She had a number from Ben, for contacting Tom Casey, so Kim did that and Casey met us at the hospital. Ben was dead on arrival. Kim and one of our other doctors there figured he'd probably been dead a couple of hours before she got him ashore."

"What about the bridge?"

"I guess the cops didn't believe it at first, but Kim got mad as a wet hen and told them that if she said it, they'd goddam better believe it. Then they moved fast, closed the bridge to all traffic and sent for a chopper and an explosives expert. I didn't see any of this, but by now it was sun-up, and later I heard Casey say you could pick out the iron ring on the cable with your naked eye if you knew where to look. An army major was winched down from the chopper, and he dismantled the thing. It took him two hours, and the radio says in his opinion it would have sheared the cable all right. The story only broke an hour ago, because the police kept it under wraps until the major finished. There were crowds, of course, but nobody knew what it was all about until the police released a statement."

"Was Modesty mentioned?"

"No. No names."

"That's something, anyway." After a little silence he said, "You're a nurse, Beryl. Is she really okay?"

"Yes. Kim's very happy about her. And amazed. But . . ." She shook her head with a troubled air.

"But what?"

"Physically she's unaffected, but there's something in her eyes, Willie. Maybe I see it because I'm a woman. I think there's something she hasn't told us about. Something even worse than staying in the sea all night with Ben to keep him alive, and losing him in the end."

He said slowly, "That's not like Modesty. She can usually shed things. Did you tell Kim?"

"Yes, and it worried him, but he hasn't had a chance to talk with her alone yet. As soon as we got to the hospital Tom Casey arrived and she was talking to him, telling him what had happened. Kim wanted to check her over, but apart from getting into a dry robe she wouldn't allow anything until she'd got the whole story out to Casey. Then we had to tell her Ben Christie was dead. She just listened, and sat quietly, then lay down and went to sleep. It was weird, Willie. She didn't wake up even when Kim turfed Casey out and started to check her over."

Traffic lights ahead changed to red. She eased the car to a halt and turned to look at him. "I don't think there's anything else I can tell you."

He smiled at her. "You've done fine, Beryl. And thanks for everything. I didn't know Kim 'ad got 'imself a girlfriend."

"Well, it's only been a few months, but we both think it's great and we're getting married soon."

"Lucky old Kim."

She laughed. "You're a nice man, just like Kim said." The magnificent eyes were smiling, then suddenly became grave. "I figured I'd meet you and Modesty one day, but not like this, and I haven't had a chance to say thank-you to her yet for what she did in Limbo. But I can say it to you now, Willie, and I do. Kim's told me all about Limbo. Seven years as a prisoner there, and at the end he'd have been massacred with all the rest of the slaves if it hadn't been for you."

"It was a rum old business," Willie said vaguely. "We just sort of stumbled on it."

The lights changed and the Aston Martin moved sweetly away. "That's not how I heard it," she said, "but we won't argue."

Less than half an hour later she opened the door of a hospital room and stood aside for Willie to enter. She had taken off her coat now and put on her nurse's cap. The bed was empty. Kim Crozier, in a white jacket, leaned against the wall. Modesty Blaise, in a towelling robe, feet bare, stood by the window, gazing out. A broad-shouldered man in his middle forties, bespectacled, with short cropped hair, sat in a tubular chair with a small tape recorder resting on his knee. A little way from him, in a similar chair, sat a very handsome man, perhaps ten years younger. He had dark hair with a curl in it, classical features, and an athletic body clothed in a very expensive suit.

When Beryl and Willie entered he was speaking with a New England accent, but broke off to turn and gaze with frosty grey eyes. Kim pushed himself away from the wall and said, "Thanks, honey. Hi, Willie. This is Mr. Casey," he indicated the older man, "and this is Mr. Dean. Gentleman, this is Mr. Garvin, from England."

At the moment of stepping into the room Willie had felt tension in the air. He shot a single glance at Modesty, caught the movement of her eyes, and knew that the handsome Dean was the source of it. Willie smiled and said in a smooth BBC news reader's voice quite unlike his own, "Good afternoon, Kim. Mr. Casey. Mr. Dean." He walked across the room, took the hand Modesty reached out to him, touched her knuckles to his cheek, then turned beside her and said politely, "Sorry to interrupt. Please continue."

Casey said, "Pleasure to meet you, Mr. Garvin."

Dean turned to look at Kim Crozier and said with open impatience, "Get him out of here please, doctor. The nurse, too. I'm dealing with a classified matter."

Kim said softly, "Don't give me orders, Mr. Dean. This is my territory and Miss Blaise is my patient. I'm letting you talk to her because she asked me to allow it, but the nurse stays, and I stay, and Mr. Garvin stays. You want to talk classified matters, you wait till I tell you Miss Blaise is fit enough to be questioned without medical support available."

Dean stared with intense dislike. "She's fit enough now," he said in a hard voice.

Kim smiled without humour. "I'm the doctor, Mr. Dean. I'm the one who decides."

Dean turned his cold gaze on Willie. "This man isn't a doctor and his presence isn't necessary."

"I am her spiritual adviser," Willie said gravely.

Dean rose to his feet, breathing hard through his nose. Casey said, "I think we're crowding Miss Blaise a little hard, Frank. Maybe you'd like me to carry on here while you talk with Langley. I remember Ben telling me she has appreciable status there —"

"What?" Dean's voice was brusque and his eyes were still on Willie.

Casey said patiently, "After she pulled Ben out alive from that narcotics mission in the Mediterranean area a while back, he managed to have sight of the CIA's file on her part in the Sabre-Tooth operation, and later there was —"

Dean broke in again. "Just button up, will you, Tom? Yesterday she killed Ben Christie, and with me she has no status at all."

Casey stared down at the floor, and when he looked up again his face held no expression. Dean gazed slowly round the room. Some of his lofty confidence had been chipped away, and he was standing to his full height under the need to establish domination. Watching from where she stood quietly by the door, Beryl had the impression that Willie Garvin's apparently mild regard was having a disconcerting effect on him.

Dean fixed hostile eyes on Modesty and said. "Right. We'll continue."

She had been standing with hands in the pockets of the robe, head tilted a little, looking down sideways with absent eyes as if remote from the currents of animosity in the room. Now she looked at Dean with quiet courtesy, waiting.

He said, "We've established that you saw Ben Christie in the restaurant and blew his cover. You then risked compromising him further by having him tailed by Dr. Crozier here, a man totally without experience in such matters. You saw fit to send a message to CIA at Langley via the British Secret Service, who hardly know the meaning of security, and you then walked into an obvious trap and were taken aboard the fishing boat *Old Hickory*. You say you can give photofit descriptions of three of the four men aboard. The fourth was referred to as Sandy, but you didn't see him. You can also describe two more from this task force of The Watchmen, the CIA impostors who picked you up with so little difficulty. When you were taken aboard, Ben Christie had recently received a gunshot wound in the shoulder. Now we'll go on from there. Who shot him?"

"Ben told me it was Szabo." Neither in her voice or manner was there any resentment at Dean's brutal summary.

"Why hadn't they shot him before? He was blown from the moment this man Oberon saw you together."

"I can't answer for their motives, Mr. Dean. They didn't shoot me either. My guess is that they wanted us both in good shape to see the bridge fall into the bay."

"So why had Christie been shot?"

"When he knew about the bridge, Ben didn't try to hold his cover any longer. He told me he'd tried to blast the transmitter with his gun, but Szabo was already covering him, and Ben took a bullet through the shoulder at close range before he could get a shot off."

Willie Garvin was not looking at her, but of all the people in the room he was the only one who knew that the last thing she had said was a lie. She went on to repeat her conversation with Oberon and to describe the move out on to the afterdeck. Casey watched the running tape. Dean began to pace a step or two one way, then the other, head turning to keep his gaze on Modesty. Soon he stopped her and said, "So they've taken your two guns, one concealed, plus other offensive or defensive items, and you've got your hands tied and your feet hobbled. But you've still got a pen gun concealed under a hand bandage, and a blade slotted into your belt. How come you're so well equipped, Miss Blaise?"

"I've operated in risk areas for British Intelligence and I thought it sensible to use whatever protection I happened to have at hand."

"You've also operated extensively on your own account."

"Yes. That, too."

"Describe exactly what happened on the afterdeck."

She went through it slowly, in detail, stopping once for Casey to change the tape. ". . . so they had to be stopped before the power and the aerial were connected to the transmitter. That's when I used the pen gun to shoot Hans through the head. I was able to take Oberon out with a kick, using the table for support. It's possible I broke his neck, but I doubt it. I came back the other way to take Szabo out, but only knocked him down. Then I went for the transmitter and managed to throw it over the side. Szabo had his gun out and was coming up to the aim. He might have managed to kill me before I'd completed the throw. I don't know. Certainly he would have killed me an instant later, but Ben came stumbling between us. It was quite deliberate. He took the bullet in his back, then fell against me. I managed to take him over the side with me . . ."

She described the search, soon curtailed, and the return of the cruiser, presumably with the remainder of the team, then told of her impression that the cruiser had made off out to sea. Casey looked up and said, "They had a rendezvous of some kind arranged. *Old Hickory* was scuttled. Some loose stuff from her was found floating around this morning. No clues."

Dean stopped pacing and moved towards Modesty. Standing close to her he said, "Hands and feet tied, but you took care of two men with guns after using your only shot on killing Hans? I think you're lying, Miss Blaise. I don't think you could do that in a million years."

She said without heat. "I had to be quick, but I managed it, Mr. Dean."

He shook his head, looking coldly into her eyes. "No. You're not that fast."

She said with slow reluctance, "Mr. Dean, you have a gun in a shoulder holster just forward of your left armpit. I don't know what make it is."

Willie Garvin smiled. Dean said suspiciously, "So?"

He barely registered the white blur of the robe as her body moved, and had not quite interpreted the small quick tug at the left face of his jacket, rather like a miniature gust of wind plucking at it, before he found himself looking down the barrel of his own handgun six inches from his nose, held in her left hand, herself suddenly still again, dark blue eyes showing only the same patient courtesy as before.

"It's a point three five seven Combat Magnum," she said. "A good gun." It spun in her hand as she offered him the butt. He took it wordlessly, pale with anger, and she turned away to stand beside Willie Garvin again.

Off to Dean's right, Kim Crozier was grinning. "She's that fast, Mr. Dean," he said. "Only she's a little slow today after a long hard night in the sea."

Dean put his gun away. There was sweat on his handsome face and his voice was throttled by rage as he said, "Casey will complete this preliminary interrogation. But don't leave town, Miss Blaise. Don't even try, because you'll be under close surveillance. Tomorrow I'll be back with a CIA doctor, and we'll go over it all again. Then we'll do it once more next week, maybe, and again the week after that and the week after that. I'm going to hold you and question you till I'm satisfied I've wrung every last drop of information out of you, Miss Blaise, and that's going to take a long time."

He turned to make for the door, stopping short when he found Kim Crozier barring his way. Kim was no longer smiling. He stood with folded arms and said in a soft hoarse voice, "If you want to stay in your job, Dean, you'd better listen to me real hard, because all I need is an hour on a telephone and the goddam sky is going to fall on you."

"*What?*" Dean's voice cracked with anger on the word.

Casey said, "I'd listen if I were you, Frank. With a name like Kim Crozier, he's not kidding."

Bewilderment and wariness seeped into Dean's fury. "What the hell's that supposed to mean?"

"I'll tell you," said Kim. "But first I'll tell you something else. I don't know what you have against Modesty Blaise, but I've stood here listening to you do the dirtiest hatchet job on her I ever heard. If she hadn't blown Ben Christie's cover he'd still have blown it himself because when he knew they were going to wreck the bridge and dump maybe five hundred automobiles in the bay he had to stop them if he could. So he tried, and they shot him. But Modesty tried too, and made it, just. You want to imagine what the bay would be like now if she hadn't been around? You worried she'll grab some credit, Dean? Forget it. Ben Christie saved that bridge and all the people on it, that's the story you can put out, and nobody has to know Modesty Blaise was anywhere around. But maybe if you'd alerted Mr. Casey here when her message first got to you at Langley instead of wasting the night flying out here to take over, he might have got boats out keeping *Old Hickory* under surveillance, and they might have picked up Modesty Blaise and Ben Christie hours earlier, and Ben just might have been alive now."

Dean said coldly, "Stick to medicine, doctor. I'm still waiting to hear how you're going to have the sky fall on me."

Kim sighed. "Never thought I'd use the leverage," he said. "The name rings no bells with you? Dr. Kim Crozier? Black guy?"

"Should it?"

"For weeks last year all the papers were running a story about a place called Limbo. A slave camp set up in the heart of the Guatemalan jungle, with around sixty slaves working a coffee plantation." At the word Limbo, sudden understanding had come into Dean's eyes, and with it an increase of wariness. Kim went on, "Those slaves were the richest men and women in the world. But the *richest*. Multi-millionaires, male and female, whose deaths had been faked by —"

"Okay, I've got it now," Dean said brusquely. "You were a slave there too, but you were their doctor."

"I looked after them for seven years. That's how long the earliest of them spent there, until the last day came. And those millionaires and millionairesses got around to thinking of me as a pretty special guy. Look, I'll cut this short, Dean. Here's the bottom line. With a dozen telephone calls I can bring around forty *billion* bucksworth of heavy influence on Washington. Enough to crucify you. Try a few names for size. Cy Hart, with half the oil in Texas. Miriam Surridge, the diamond heiress. Schultz, the supermarket king. Senator Chard, the banker. That's just a few of the Americans, but there were foreigners in Limbo, too. Very powerful people. I reckon I could have three European and three South American ambassadors at the White House door in forty-eight hours."

Dean's face had become faintly mottled. With an effort he said, "So you've got a line to some pretty big people, doctor. What's going to make them go to bat for Modesty Blaise?"

Kim laughed. "Jesus Christ, they'll go to bat for Modesty Blaise all right, and you'd better believe it, because —"

From the window Modesty said, "No, Kim."

He stopped short, frowned at her, then gave a reluctant shrug and said, "Okay. Let's just say they'll go to bat for *me*. And in a big way. You want to try it, Dean?"

Dean stood staring at him, hating him, and said nothing. After a moment or two Kim said quietly, "Okay, you'll get all the information she can give you, and it'll be as full a debriefing as you've ever known. You can complete the preliminary today and you can check with her again in a day or two. But you start leaning on her the way you said, and sure as God made little apples I blow the whistle on you."

Dean buttoned his jacket, picked up a black leather briefcase from beside the chair where he had been sitting and said, "You finish up here, Casey."

Beryl opened the door for him as he went out of the room. After she had closed it again Kim ran a hand through his tight curly hair and said to nobody in particular, "What the hell was eating that man?"

Beryl said crisply, "Good looks and a king-size *machismo*. He couldn't bear to know what Modesty did. She's just a girl, so it was torture for him. Oh, excuse me." The last words were addressed to Casey.

"Not a bad diagnosis." The CIA man's voice was tired. "Off the record, he's a good administrator who fancies himself as a mission controller, God help us all. With a little luck my report will put him back where he belongs, but neither tears nor prayers are going to bring Ben Christie back." He looked at Modesty. "I directed Ben on three missions, and we were old friends. Thanks for trying."

"I'm sorry, Mr. Casey. Sorry I blew him, sorry I didn't get him out alive. He was my friend, too."

"I know. He told me way back." Casey shrugged. "Like the doc here says, Ben had to blow his own cover once he knew the score." He touched the recorder. "Are you feeling okay to finish this?"

"Yes. There's not a lot more. Only what Ben said while we were in the sea, and he wasn't conscious for very long."

"Right. If you'll just tell it the way you remember it, please." He switched on the recorder.

Fifteen minutes later, when Tom Casey had gone, Kim said, "Right, let's have you back in bed, Modesty. You need rest."

"No, I want to go back to the studio now. I'll rest there. Please, Kim."

He studied her worriedly. "I've seen you in some bad moments in Limbo, especially that last day. But you look different from any way I've seen you before, and I don't like it. Is there something you haven't told us, honey?"

"I'm all right, Kim. If you're worried, you and Beryl can come out to Sausalito tomorrow to see me. Any time you're free. I'll be fine by then."

He was still uneasy. "Would you like Beryl to go with you now? She could stay the night." He looked at the nurse. "Okay with you, sweetheart?"

"Fine. I'm not off duty for another couple of hours, but you can fix that."

Modesty shook her head and smiled. "You're both very kind, and thank you, but no. Willie's good at looking after me. Can you track down my clothes please, Kim?"

He sighed and picked up the phone. "You always were a stubborn broad," he said.

Her clothes had been dried and pressed, but were still salt stained. Beryl found her a pair of sneakers and she sat with Willie in the back of the Aston Martin while Kim took them to where she had left the hired car the night before. When Willie drove across the Golden Gate Bridge there were still police launches cruising around the base of each tower and clusters of people gathered to stare from vantage points, even though all activity on the tower had long since ended.

She said, "It was The Watchmen who put out that contract on Tarrant. Oberon said they hired the Polish twins."

"That's right, Princess. But it's all over now, like I said on the phone. I managed to get between them and Tarrant."

She turr ad her head to stare at him. "You coped on your own?"

"I didn't 'ave much choice. Can't say I enjoyed it much."

"There's only one way to stop the Polish twins."

"Yes." ✦

She reached out to push back the sleeve of his jacket, and saw the fading but still ugly bruising on his forearm. After a few seconds she took her hand away and rested her head against his shoulder.

At the studio Willie said, "Into bed, Princess. You promised Kim." He looked at his watch. It was six o'clock. "You 'ave a couple of hours sleep, then I'll slip out and get a take-away meal for us. Better than me setting fire to the kitchen. Would you fancy a hot drink now? Or something?"

It was warm in the studio but she shivered suddenly and shook her head. "Not yet. Hold me, Willie. I'm going to cry."

He picked her up and sat down in a corner of the big leather settee, holding her on his lap, her head on his shoulder, her face hidden against his neck. Her body began to shake and he felt the tears come, but she made little sound as she wept. With his free hand he stroked her arm, patted her thigh, touched her cheek in wordless sympathy. She would be grieving for Ben Christie, he knew, but there was more to it than that. He had seen it in her eyes, as Beryl had, and Kim also had been aware of a special distress in her.

After a while, when the shaking of her body had stopped and she lay as if asleep in his arms, he said softly, "You want to tell me, Princess?"

He felt her head nod against his shoulder. After a moment she spoke in a whisper, her lips close to his ear. "Poor Ben. They ran a test, Willie. A mose test they called it. I think that's what Oberon said. I didn't know the word."

"Mohs. Em oh aitch ess. It's a scale for the hardness of abrasives."

"Ah. Yes. He said it was a test for hardness." She drew in a long slow breath. "They had a girl there, a young black junkie doped up to the eyebrows, and they told Ben to kill her with a machete. Ben didn't know he was blown, but he knew they were going to bring the bridge down, and he thought if he could hold his cover he might get ashore and prevent it."

Willie said in a low, uneasy voice, "But there was no point in a test. They knew who he was by then."

"Just Oberon's little joke. A fun thing."

"Oh, God."

"Yes. Well, there it was. Ben had to face the cold equation, Willie. The life of a junkie they were bound to kill anyway, set against the lives of all the people who would die when the bridge came down. So he . . . he faced it. And when it was done, they told him. Told him his cover had been blown from the beginning. He said he went berserk then, and tried to kill Oberon with the machete, but Szabo was ready, and shot him. They'd taken Ben's gun earlier. He didn't have a chance."

Willie sat holding her, his spine creeping with horror. They were long inured, both of them, to the sickening elements of combat, to the reality of torn flesh and broken bones and spurting blood, in friend and foe alike, and in themselves. Both had killed, more than once, under the bleak necessity of saving their own lives or those of their friends. But no man who was not evil and a killer had died at their hands, and none had been destroyed in cold blood. What had been done to Ben Christie was something different, something worse than killing, and their imagination shrank from the dreadful concept.

She said, her words still muffled, "When we were in the sea he was like . . . like a creature in torment. He kept coming back to it, weeping with the agony of what he'd done." Her voice shook again. "God's truth, Willie, I don't know if he could have lived with it. When he was feverish, rambling, I kept telling him it was all a bad dream, and that it hadn't really happened. Maybe it helped a little, I don't know."

Willie said softly, achingly. "Oh, Jesus Christ I'm sorry, Princess, I'm sorry."

She stirred in his arms, lifted her head, kissed him on the cheek — a rare demonstration of affection between them — then stood up briskly, wiped her cheeks with her fingers, pushed back her hair with both hands, and gave him a tired, crooked smile. "Thanks, Willie love. Sorry to lumber you with a piece of it."

"As long as it 'elps."

"Oh, it does. It does. But I didn't tell Casey, and I'm not going to. I'm telling nobody, not even Kim." She held her elbows and hunched her shoulders a little, as if cold. "I'm not having that story put down in Ben's file when they close it. He probably never did a tougher or braver thing in his life, Willie. But it wouldn't come out looking that way in a report. Can you imagine?"

"He'd sound like a butcher." Willie got to his feet. "You going to 'ave a little sleep now?"

"Yes. I had to tell you first."

"Sure. Get into bed and and I'll bring you some 'ot milk with a little whisky. You need warming up inside."

"Put a spoonful of honey in for me. There's some in the larder."

"Right."

Five minutes later he sat watching her as she lay propped on an elbow in her bed, sipping the warm drink he had concocted. She was naked, and as she moved he saw a narrow plaster on the outer curve of one breast.

"What's that, Princess?"

She looked down. "Just a deep scratch. When they had me tied up on the cruiser they frisked me and took my bra away. That's when it happened. There were only a couple of lock-picks in it, and they wouldn't have helped anyway."

"Just the one scratch?"

"A bruise or two from when we went over the side, and stiff shoulders and thighs from trying to tow Ben ashore. I'll have one of your magic massages in the morning, please. Don't worry about getting me anything to eat tonight, I'll sleep right through till morning now, and by the time you've finished I'll be as good as new." She drained the beaker and handed it to him. "Thanks, Willie. And thanks for getting here so quickly."

He stood up and adjusted the blinds to darken the room. "I 'aven't 'ad anything to do so far, Princess."

"You're here. That's enough."

At the door he paused and turned. She was still sitting up, propped on one straight arm, and even in the semi-darkness he could see that the dark sapphire eyes held a question. "What did you mean by 'so far', Willie?"

"Up to you, Princess. You reckon to do anything about this? I mean, about The Watchmen?"

"I'm going after them," she said simply. "Not to avenge Ben and not out of any noble motive. It's entirely selfish and can't be justified, but I'm going after them because I hate them. Me, personally, I hate them, root, leaf and branch, for the cruel and evil bastards they are. As far as I'm concerned, it's a war now, Willie."

It was entirely like her, he thought, to go to war with an army of two against an unknown force, but it was not necessarily either reckless or ill-considered. She had done it before, and won. But she would not even count Willie Garvin in until he had declared himself, for from the day *The Network* went out of business she had never taken him for granted.

He said, "I'm in, Princess. And we've got a lead, because whoever hired the Polish twins did it through Bernie Chan. Now you tuck down like a good girl and 'ave a nice sleep."

Ten

GOLITSYN came down the ladder from the drillship and stepped into the fourteen foot dory. Major the Earl St. Maur was already aboard. The man at the wheel took the boat away at a steady speed, heading for the bleak grey shore of Deserta Grande less than a mile away.

"It would be amusing," said Golitsyn, glancing back at the drillship's towering derrick, "if we did in fact strike oil."

St. Maur closed the notebook in which he had been writing and frowned. "I hope that's not likely," he said. "It would be damned embarrassing. We've only two experienced derrick men on our strength, and I doubt if they could cope with the situation."

"It's no problem," said Golitsyn. "The weight of mud in the drill hole should be enough to prevent any uncontrolled flow, and if it isn't, then the blow-out preventer comes into operation. Two men with know-how can easily cope, Major, but I don't imagine it will arise. The original crew of the drillship went down a couple of thousand feet in the first week or so without striking oil. That was to impress the Minister for Energy of course, when he came out from Lisbon with his advisers."

"There's been more drilling since then though."

"Very little, Major. Since we paid off the genuine crew and replaced them with our own people we've only done enough drilling to keep up appearances in our reports."

St. Maur tilted his head back and stared down his beak of a nose. "So for one reason or another this is a factor not worth considering?"

"Probably. The geological surveys were faked, and in any event we can cope."

"Then I'd be obliged if you would refrain from raising issues not worth taking into account, Golitsyn. It's just a bloody nuisance. There's enough to think about without pointless distractions."

Golitsyn pursed his lips and nodded judicially. "My apologies, Major." Inwardly he was rather pleased to have annoyed St. Maur slightly without the Englishman realising that it was deliberate. This called for nice judgment. Satisfied, Golitsyn leaned back and contemplated the small coastal settlement they were now approaching.

Deserta Grande showed the sea a forbidding coast. Here and there the steep rock of the shore fell back a little to leave a half-moon of stony beach, a few of these with a dry valley offering access to the rugged interior of the island. Together with the two smaller of the Ilhas Desertas, the island was uninhabited except by birds, rabbits, wild goats and seals.

Until recently tourist agencies in Madeira, twelve miles away, had run occasional boat trips out to the islands. These had ceased at the request of the Drioga Corporation when the concession for drilling in the area had been negotiated with the Portuguese government. All in all, Golitsyn reflected, the arrangement was working very well. The Drioga Corporation was registered in the Bahamas, and any attempt to identify actual persons controlling it would fail. The drillship was leased through Libya under an agreement whereby Drioga would supply all technical and support personnel, and there were ample cut-outs in the arrangements. If everybody vanished overnight from the drillship and from Deserta Grande it would be impossible to trace them. The two supposed corporation officials who had acted as hosts to the Portuguese minister during his visits were in fact English-speaking KGB men flown in via Lisbon as and when required.

A short but substantial jetty, prefabricated, jutted from the northern tip of the rocky beach where the Drioga Corporation huts were laid out. Permission had been secured from the Portuguese to establish this temporary land base by claiming that it would simplify matters of accommodation and the landing of stores. This claim was untrue, but not sufficiently unreasonable as to make the Portuguese minister wonder about it. From his point of view the deal was a good one, and he was content to let Drioga handle their own logistic problems. After all, they had paid an up-front sum of four million dollars for the privilege of spending around a hundred and fifty thousand dollars a day for the running and hiring costs of the drillship in the hope of finding oil or gas, and it would probably cost them between twenty and twenty-five million dollars to drill one hole, so it was reasonable to let them do things their own way.

Cheap at the price, thought Golitsyn as the dory turned to come alongside the jetty. Dirt cheap when you reckoned the immense profit to be earned by The Watchmen from a sum that would buy no more than one flight of modern fighter aircraft.

Von Krankin was waiting for them on the jetty. He watched them climb the short ladder from the dory and said, "Good morning." It was usual for two of the three leaders to sleep aboard the rig now since the signals and cipher section had been transferred there when it was found that the rig aerials gave more reliable communication with Moscow than the necessarily covert aerials of the shore base.

St. Maur said to von Krankin, "Good morning. How did the night manoeuvres go?"

The German nodded. "Very well. I have made out a report for you to read."

"Thank you. And Oberon?"

"An excellent performance."

"Not markedly affected by the Baystrike failure?"

Von Krankin considered. "Affected, yes. But to our advantage. His one fault was over-confidence, and this has now been eliminated. He is angry with himself, naturally, and has a very great hatred for this woman Modesty Blaise, but both the anger and the hatred are very cold, for he has converted them into a powerful drive for even greater efficiency in himself and in the men."

They were walking slowly along the jetty now, and St. Maur said, "Good. I don't want to get rid of him. He's a chap who'd be very difficult to replace at this stage."

Golitsyn said nothing. He agreed with St. Maur but was a little uneasy about the effect of the Baystrike failure on the morale of The Watchmen, and he wondered how the major would handle this when he began his preliminary briefing on Morningstar in the command hut a few minutes from now.

St. Maur said, "When Morningstar is over, Colonel, we shall need some plastic surgery on a few faces before their owners can move about freely again. Oberon and Szabo, Forster and Blik."

Golitsyn said, "Yes. I'm informed that the British have provided Interpol and all western intelligence services with good photofit pictures of the four faces that were seen by Modesty Blaise during Baystrike. Oberon can assure the others that first class plastic surgery will be arranged after Morningstar and before their next period of leave." He paused, then went on, "It has just occurred to me that either Forster or Blik, or both, might do us a considerable favour if they were killed during Morningstar. Identification of their bodies as the two CIA impostors in the Baystrike affair would tie The Watchmen into Morningstar admirably."

After a moment von Krankin said, "It would certainly be convincing proof. Far more so than our usual claim to responsibility. But I am reluctant to lose Forster, he is a very capable man." He glanced at St. Maur. "Blik, perhaps?"

The major nodded. "Yes, we could spare Blik in return for sufficient advantage. It would have to be convincingly arranged, of course." He gave a short grunting bark, which was his version of laughter. "Pity we can't leave Modesty Blaise as a fatal casualty, too. Throw the security people into chaos. Pull the head-mask off and there she is, a member of The Watchmen. Leader more likely, eh?" He made the grunting bark again.

Golitsyn stopped walking, and after a moment the other two halted to wait for him, puzzled. "That would be extraordinarily good, Major," he said, eyes half closed, gazing into the distance.

"What?"

"Your idea concerning Modesty Blaise. Except that we would have to include Garvin. It would be implausible if he were not found dead with her."

"Good lord, I wasn't serious." St. Maur frowned. "I don't mean I was joking, you know, just thinking aloud I suppose."

"It can be very useful to let the imagination wander," Golitsyn said absently. He stood with hands behind back, head bent a little, looking down at the ground, absorbed in his thoughts. After perhaps ten seconds he shrugged briskly, sighed and shook his head. "No. Not possible, I'm afraid. To get hold of Blaise and Garvin would require much reconnaissance, careful planning, and a full section for the operation, perhaps two. We can't afford so big a distraction during the run-up to Morningstar. It's a pity, though."

He moved on again, still thoughtful. "But I would suggest that after Morningstar, and when Oberon's appearance has been sufficiently altered, we should give him the opportunity to hunt down and kill that woman. For one thing it will be necessary to his ego. At present his defeat at her hands is a stimulus, but if he has to wait too long before it is redressed, the knowledge will fester in his mind and diminish his usefulness to us. Secondly she is a spoiler. Read her dossier and you will see that as if by some natural law of physics she is drawn into well planned projects as a speck of dirt is drawn into a delicate piece of machinery, and with equally damaging results. I shall feel easier when she is dead, and this man Garvin with her."

St. Maur said, "Sounds damn mystical stuff to me, coming from a chap who's only supposed to believe in dialectical materialism or whatever it is. But I'm in favour of Oberon being told today that he can have a crack at Blaise after Morningstar. You do it, Colonel. It'll give him something to look forward to. And now if you don't mind we'll forget this bloody woman while I concentrate on the briefing."

Forty-two men were assembled in the biggest of the huts that formed the shore base for the drillship. This was the common room and entertainments hut, where films were shown every evening except when night training was scheduled. This morning the men sat relaxed, listening to Oberon. He stood on a low platform at one end of the room, talking quietly and economically about an exercise the previous night. The men were of several nationalities, yet the common factor in them made them more of a kind than if they had been of the same stock. All were genuinely hard men, not of the loud-mouthed and overtly aggressive kind, but men to whom controlled violence was a necessity as well as being both art and science.

There was also a missing factor common to each man, a congenital inability to respect any life but his own. Another's death, another's wounds, another's pain, all were meaningless to them. This did not signify that The Watchmen were stupid. They had the skills of their trade, the courage to use those skills, and the confidence that these two qualities bred in them. In general their need for women was not great, for they tended to love their chosen weapons and the stimulus of using them far more than the soft playground of a female body.

They were listening attentively to Oberon now as he used a pointer and chalk to illustrate his comments on a blackboard to one side of the platform. Even among these hard men Oberon was outstanding, and if a Watchman made the same error twice in training, Oberon would mark him for rejection. This was subject to confirmation by the leaders, but on the three occasions that it had happened in the past eighteen months they had always confirmed. Rejection by The Watchmen did not mean that you were sent home. It meant that you were killed.

Oberon was saying, "On the approach to shore, only the canoes of No. Four Section came in at exactly the right place and exactly the right time. The rest weren't bad, but there's room for a lot of improvement. I scarcely need to tell you that faulty approach can ruin an action before it gets started. We are The Watchmen, and we don't make that sort of mistake."

He had shaved off his beard on the night of Baystrike before transferring to the cruiser and scuttling *Old Hickory*, but the change in him went deeper than clean-shaven cheeks. A quietness had entered into Oberon, a dangerous quietness that made even the hard men of The Watchmen tread warily with him. Now he laid the pointer across the pegs of the easel, dusted his hands and said, "That's all for the moment. You're about to have a preliminary briefing for our next operation, Morningstar, by far the biggest we've undertaken. For the next few weeks we shall be training and rehearsing for that. All sections will take part, and I'm instructed to tell you that there will be a bonus of ten thousand pounds credited to the Swiss account of every man involved."

There was a stir of satisfaction among the men. The door opened and von Krankin entered followed by Major the Earl St. Maur and Golitsyn. None of the men stood. Discipline in The Watchmen was ferocious but not in any degree regimental. St. Maur said, "Good morning, gentlemen," in his hard nasal voice and marched to the platform. There was a murmured response, and Oberon said, "Good morning, Major." In the early days some of The Watchmen had regarded St. Maur as what he appeared to be, a typical English aristocrat soldier of the old school, short on brains and competence. Time had disabused them of this notion, for St. Maur had shown himself to be a master of combat and weaponry, as hard as the hardest, and more than equal to the best of them. His killing of Romaine following an Individual Challenge had established his reputation beyond all question.

Golitsyn and von Krankin took chairs behind a table on the right of the platform. Oberon moved to one side and leaned against the wall. St. Maur moved to the back wall, pulled down a roller blind to display a large scale map of an island, took a notebook from his pocket, and gazed slowly round the ranks of the seated men with his cold blue eyes, gathering their attention.

"The island is Porto Santo," he said, picking up the pointer. "This is to be the area of operation for Morningstar, on or about the sixteenth of September. A week from now we shall have a large relief model of the island set up here for you to study, but you all have a general knowledge of the place because over the past weeks you've been there a few at a time on tourist trips from Funchal. Nine miles long, three wide, with a sandy beach extending along almost the whole of the southern shore."

St. Maur turned and ran the tip of the pointer along the yellow strip. "Porto Santo lies twenty-five miles from where we stand," he went on. "Population of about three thousand, main town Vila Baleira as marked here in the middle of the south coast. Only two main roads, one running the length of that coast then turning north to Serra de Dentro, the other crossing the island from Vila Baleira north to Camacha, passing to the east of the airfield, here, which is a reserve air base for NATO."

St. Maur glanced at his notebook for a moment or two, then resumed. "There's a new hotel been built here," the pointer touched the map between road and shore, a little to the southwest of Vila Baleira, "consisting of a complex of de luxe chalets spread around a central building with the usual public rooms and facilities. The Portuguese government has placed this Hotel Atlantis at the disposal of the four heads of government and their advisers who will be attending a summit meeting in September, the President of the United States, the Prime Ministers of the United Kingdom and West Germany, and the President of France. Security preparations have already begun. The Portuguese are in charge, since they are the host country, but they're working in consultation with specialists from the four summit countries. We have information about the preliminary plans, and we shall have detailed and up-to-date information during the coming days. The objective of Operation Morningstar is to execute the four heads of government."

St. Maur stopped speaking, laid down the pointer, slipped his notebook into his pocket, and stood with hands behind back, turning his head slowly to encompass all the listening men in his gaze. "I'm going to break off there for a minute or two to deal with a matter that may be troubling some of you. As you know, in San Francisco recently The Watchmen had their first operational failure. I want to tell you that I join with my colleagues, Colonel Golitsyn and Captain von Krankin, in being relieved that it happened at this stage of our programme."

Golitsyn thought, "By God, I do believe he means it. He's no actor." Certainly there was no breath of a cynical murmur from the listening men as there would surely have been if the major had not carried conviction.

St. Maur said, "You're all experienced chaps and you know well enough that chance sometimes plays a part in an operation. Not luck. We make our own luck. I do mean chance. Now I've been waiting for chance to cause a hitch in our plans because it was bound to happen sooner or later. In the event it happened during Baystrike and it could have been serious. Yes, the operation failed, but what pleases me is that it wasn't due to faulty planning, bad security, lack of provision for emergencies, or faulty execution. It failed through a million to one chance that nobody could have foreseen. A double chance, really, because we had a potential recruit who turned out to be a CIA man, and we had a chance intervention by this woman most of you seem to have heard of, Modesty Blaise."

Even the sound of the name made the sweat of fury break out over Oberon's body. With an effort he kept his breathing steady and willed his tensing muscles to relax. St. Maur said, "Despite this our task force leader, Hugh Oberon, came very close to pulling the job off. When that became impossible, his local planning arrangements were such that he was able to withdraw his task force from the situation and bring the men home without leaving any trail to be followed. We lost one man, killed by Modesty Blaise. The CIA man died of wounds. Now, why should we feel some relief at this failure? I'll tell you."

The major tilted back his head, stared slowly round, then suddenly grinned. His teeth were large and white. "Because it's behind us now," he said. "We've had our million-to-one chance, and the task force coped without leaving a prisoner or a shred of a clue to point to who we are or where we are. Lucky? No, just efficient. And since million-to-one chances don't come in pairs, we won't run into any similar mischance during Morningstar because we got it over and done with in Baystrike."

Golitsyn nodded soberly for the benefit of any men who might glance his way. Not bad, he thought. In fact, very good. Nobody was looking sceptical. Give the major credit, he'd put the thing over without any hint of it being a pep-talk. A remarkably able fellow, within his limits, Major the Earl St. Maur.

"Back to Operation Morningstar," said St. Maur. "You'll be given more information about Porto Santo as we go along, a great deal more. I've already told you that the intention is to execute the four heads of government, and I'm well aware that you have no interest in the reason for this. You would never have been accepted as Watchmen if you hadn't shown yourselves to be entirely free from national or political concerns. Now as to method."

The major picked up the pointer again and referred to his notebook. "Right. We don't yet know precisely where each head of government and staff will be housed, but thanks to Colonel Golitsyn's intelligence operations we've had sight of the preliminary plans for security. The conference will be taking over the whole of the Atlantis Hotel, and security will be in the hands of the Portuguese, though their men will be consulting with and supported by the security services of the countries concerned. Now Porto Santo must be regarded as a security man's dream. No strangers can hide among so small a community, and access can only be by boat or air. We believe about one hundred and fifty soldiers will be stationed there for the meeting, plus a contingent of police and a few personal bodyguards of the four leaders. Look at the map, please. The three small black circles marked here, here, and here represent prefabricated guardrooms which are being put up to house the soldiers. If you join them by lines, as shown, you'll see that we have a triangular perimeter round the hotel complex."

St. Maur moved away from the map and faced his audience, the pointer sloped over his shoulder. "Security measures are designed to counter an attack by a lunatic or perhaps by a small group of fanatics. They're not designed to counter an assault by a powerful, well-trained force with heavy fire power. After all, where could such a force come from?" The major grinned again, and there was a murmur of chuckling appreciation from his listeners.

"Right. Now, Captain von Krankin will be drawing up detailed plans and revising them as we receive fresh information. Today I'm just going to give you the basic tactics so that you'll understand what we shall be doing in our training. In broad outline, we shall be landing after dark in canoes, from a mother ship, masked against radar by the usual scattering of fishing boats that go out from Vila Baleira every night. We shall land about half a mile to the west of our target area — all except the frogman section which will be engaged in attaching radio controlled limpet mines to the three motor torpedo boats in the harbour."

St. Maur turned to the map again. "Number One Section will move direct to the airfield and their task will be to destroy whatever helicopters and planes may be there. Number Two Section will be split into three pairs and each pair will cover one of the guard rooms. Both these sections will come under the command of Captain von Krankin, and they will have bazookas as well as normal small-arms. Nobody will open fire until the first moment of alarm or until ordered to do so over the mini-radios you'll be wearing. As always we shall get as far as we possibly can in this operation in complete silence."

St. Maur ran the tip of the pointer round the perimeter triangle. "Numbers Three and Four Section will be under my personal command, and our task will be to take care of the patrolling guards, if possible without raising any alarm, so we shall be using knives, wire, and the crossbow." There was a ripple of amusement from The Watchmen, in which von Krankin joined. The major nodded and lifted a hand in acknowledgment. "Yes, you all know I hate the damn things, but you're none of you any good with the long bow and I have to admit that Three Section in particular can shoot a pretty accurate bolt, even by night. We had hoped to have a very expert crossbow chap joining us before now but he failed his Final."

St. Maur looked down at his notebook. Golitsyn registered that he had chosen not to reveal that it was Modesty Blaise who had caused the crossbow expert to fail. The omission showed good sense. Outside their particular skills the rank and file of The Watchmen were not of high intelligence, and it would be bad psychology to offer them a jinx to worry about.

The major said, "Our aim will be to clear the western side of the triangle, and to contain the eastern and southern sides. Section Five, under Hugh Oberon, will pass through from the west once we have cleared. Since Romaine challenged me and I killed him, this section has no leader, so we're going to have Hugh Oberon himself lead them in carrying out the prime objective of Morningstar. They will be the Execution Squad, and they will enter the main hotel building and execute the heads of government there. Resistance should be light, especially if we have achieved good penetration before the alarm is sounded. We shall choose an evening at the end of the conference, when the Portuguese Prime Minister will be host at a farewell dinner for those attending, so they'll all be together. At the moment of the final assault, or earlier if an alarm is raised, the motor torpedo boats and aircraft will be destroyed at once and the guardrooms bombarded by bazookas."

St. Maur flicked over a page of his notebook. "Right. During this stage, Sections Three and Four will control the perimeter. Oberon will advise by radio as soon as the executions have been carried out. Then, as we all know, comes the most difficult stage of the operation, disengagement and withdrawal. We shall rehearse this again and again, by night, on a mock-up of the terrain which will be established inland here within the next few days. From now till Morningstar, all our training will be at night. Every man will wear a headmask with eyeholes while training, every man will rehearse the operation several times wearing a gasmask, every man will carry precisely the weapons and equipment he will be carrying on the night."

The major paused, put his notebook away and laid down the pointer. "I don't expect to have any serious casualties. The combination of surprise, fire-power, and intensive training will give us an overwhelming advantage. When we start to disengage we shall make use of several ingenious items supplied by Colonel Golitsyn's backroom experts to cause confusion. At the same time the security forces will have to cope with the airfield in flames, the m.t.b.'s disabled and sinking, and the three guardrooms with probably two thirds of the soldiers involved blown to hell and gone. We shall embark in our canoes at the point where we landed and rendezvous with the mother ship by radio beam since she will show no lights. Number Six Section will have kept that embarkation point secure and they will cover our withdrawal. They will also have a motor launch for their own withdrawal. I don't think this is going to prove at all a tricky operation, but if we do have casualties then it's vital for section commanders to ensure that any wounded are brought out with us so they won't have to face interrogation."

St. Maur turned a little to glance at Golitsyn and von Krankin. "As I said, this is a preliminary briefing in broad outline. Section commanders will be provided with a typed version of this briefing later today, so they can make sure all men in their sections are fully familiar with the general plan. We expect to complete the operation and be off the island within forty minutes of landing there, and of that time only the last fifteen minutes should require overt action, including eight minutes for withdrawal to our embarkation point. I think that's all for the moment, but I'll just ask my colleagues if they have anything to add."

Von Krankin shook his head. The typescript was his, and would say all he wished to say. Golitsyn made a small apologetic gesture and said, "Perhaps it would be worth explaining that after withdrawal our whole force will be brought back here, Major."

"Ah, yes. Thank you." The major faced his audience again. "We shall disembark one shift on the drillship and the other two here at base. Then the mother ship will leave, and within an hour of our return you'll be a team of oil riggers. A rig manager, rig superintendent, and three or four marine personnel will be flown in a few days before, and they will deal with whoever eventually comes along to ask if we've seen any Watchmen around lately. The rest of you just have to look convincing."

He looked at Golitsyn again. The Russian shook his head. St. Maur said, "Right, that's all. We'll deal with questions when you've studied your preliminary orders. I recommend you to get some sleep in during today, because we'll be on night ops again tonight. Thank you, gentlemen. Off you go."

Hugh Oberon watched as the men slowly filed out of the big hut to a buzz of conversation. He had heard a murmur of approval from the men of Number Five Section when St. Maur had told them who their leader would be, and this had given him as much satisfaction as the major's brief comment on Baystrike.

Golitsyn got up from the table and called, "A word with you, Hugh."

Oberon went across. St. Maur and von Krankin were standing at the map, discussing some element of the operation. Golitsyn tapped a finger on Oberon's chest and grinned. "Relax, soldier boy. When God throws a spanner in the works, don't blame yourself."

Oberon managed a laugh, and rubbed the back of his neck. "Thanks, Colonel. I didn't think you believed in God."

"I don't, soldier boy. But I believe in spanners. They happen. Be glad this one happened when it did, as the major said. And think forward, because we have a very special job for you once Morningstar is over and we have changed your appearance sufficiently."

"A new operation for The Watchmen?"

"A job for you. Personally. We want you to get rid of somebody for us."

"Well, I'll be glad to see to that, Colonel. Anybody I know?"

"Modesty Blaise." Golitsyn thumped him on the chest, grinned again, and turned away. "Relax and enjoy yourself, soldier boy."

Eleven

THE red-head with green eyes was standing by the pier glass as she stepped out of her skirt, moving with a dancer's grace, and hung it neatly over the chair beside her blouse. From where Bernie Chan sat on his big circular bed, slowly undoing his bow tie, he had a perfect all-round view of her, and it was his opinion that her legs were the best he had ever seen. The very thought of them in action sent a quiver of delightful anticipation down his spine. He could see them extremely well because she was now wearing only very sexy pants and a bra to match. Bernie Chan transferred his gaze to the splendid contents of the bra, and quivered again.

Her complexion was not of the kind normally found with red hair, but that would be the Spanish blood in her Bernie decided, taking off his shoes. It went with her name, Teresa. *Hot* Spanish blood, probably. Certainly she liked him a lot, he could tell by the quiet but absorbed way she had looked at him and listened to him down at the dance studio earlier that evening. She had sat near him when she took a break from the exacting routine under rehearsal, and she had only hesitated for a moment or two when he asked her to have dinner with him.

Bernie Chan, jeweller, fence, fixer, middleman, a quarter Chinese, three-quarters Liverpool, owned the dance studio and rehearsal room off Charing Cross Road. This was only one of several properties he owned, but in a way it was his most treasured because it brought him into contact with the theatrical profession and provided a fertile hunting ground for picking up girls. Bernie was within a year of forty but looked younger, a plump, smooth, well-manicured, sweet-smelling man whose bathroom was stacked with male toiletries.

He said in the adenoidal accent of his home town, "I like yer her, T'resa."

"My — ? Oh, my hair." She gave him a warm smile. "Well thank you, Mr. Chan. I can tell you're a gentleman."

"Where d'you come from, love?" he asked. "You sound a bit Scottish."

Her eyes widened. "That's clever. I thought I'd lost any accent I had when I was a kid."

"I got a good ear." He got up and began to wander about the big bedroom in his stockinged feet, hands in trouser pockets. She watched him a shade curiously, her hands resting on her hips, and after a moment or two she said, "Is there anything wrong, Mr. Chan?"

"Eh? No." He made a dismissive gesture. "Just there's no rush. I like to take things easy. Get to know each other a bit."

"Oh, that's what I like, too." She glanced at the door. "Are we waiting for those two men in the sitting room to go?"

"No, they stay, T'resa, Dick an' Rodney are my minders."

She looked intrigued rather than surprised. "You mean like bodyguards? But why, Mr. Chan?"

"Call me Bernie. I keep 'em around because I'm in business, see? They do negotiations for me. Don't worry about 'em."

"All right, Mr. — I mean Bernie." She indicated the door to his dressing room. "Can I pop through to your bathroom, please."

"Help yourself, love. Then I'll tell you the sort of thing I like."

She giggled and picked up her handbag. "That ought to be interesting. I won't be a minute."

The bathroom window was at the back of the house. She opened the slats of the blind, switched the light off and on again three times with slow regularity, closed the blinds, and turned on the taps of the wash-basin. She passed a few moments marvelling at Bernie Chan's collection of aftershave lotions, then picked up her handbag and went back into the bedroom.

It was five minutes later when the phone rang. In the bedroom, Bernie ignored it, wholly occupied with other interests. In the sitting room a chunky dark-jowled man in an armchair said, "Get it, Dick," without looking away from the horror film running on the big television set. Dick, a tall man with a crew-cut and a vicious mouth, had barely started to moved when the phone stopped ringing. He shrugged and slumped back on the settee. Exactly three minutes later the bedroom door opened and the red-head appeared. She was still in her pants and bra, and looked nervous.

"Would you come and take a look at Mr. Chan, please?" she said, and her Scottish accent was more pronounced now. "He seems to have fainted and I can't rouse him."

Rodney, the chunky man, said, "Christ!" and came springily to his feet. She stood aside as he reached the bedroom door. Dick was following. She pointed to where the phone stood on a side table in the sitting room and said uncertainly, "Do you have his doctor's number in the personal book there?"

Dick paused, anxious and clearly shaken. Then he gave a grunt of assent and turned towards the phone. He was picking up the book when everything stopped. A few seconds later she came into the bedroom. Bernie Chan lay unconscious on the bed, still in shirt, socks and trousers. Rodney stood looking down at him with a baffled air, clearly having no idea what to do. The red-head said, "I don't know what caused it. I mean, he hadn't really started to get excited."

Rodney said, "He's breathing. You can see his chest moving."

"Yes, but have you noticed that bruise coming up just behind his ear?"

"Bruise?" Rodney bent low to peer at the far side of Bernie's head. That was the last thing he remembered for quite a long time.

The doorbell chimed softly. With the kongo still in her hand, Modesty Blaise walked from the bedroom, past the unconscious figure of Dick, and out into the hall. All three men now had bruises behind the ear. She went downstairs and opened the front door, standing back behind it as two men in overalls and caps entered carrying a rolled Chinese rug on their shoulders. She closed the door and said, "Upstairs, then left, Willie."

Half a minute later the two men put down the rug in the sitting room. Professor Stephen Collier, carrying the rear end, straightened up and surveyed Modesty Blaise with stunned astonishment. "My God, you've dyed your eyes green!" he said.

"They're green contact lenses, Steve," she said. "Keep your gloves on and don't touch anything." Willie had produced a slim box containing a hypodermic, and was preparing to give Dick an injection. Collier's lips were dry, and the perspiration on his forehead was not all due to carrying the rug. He glanced at Dick, winced at the sight of the red swelling behind his ear, and followed Modesty through into the bedroom. Rodney was sprawled on the floor, Bernie Chan still lay unconscious on the bed.

Collier leaned against the wall by the door and eyed Modesty morosely as she thumbed back one of Bernie's eyelids to examine the pupil. "You look vulgar in those tarty knickers," he said. "I'm not enjoying this at all."

She straightened up and stared at him indignantly. "You're the limit, Steve! Who complained he'd had enough of being accidentally caught up with us in situations where only a lunatic would have bet a brass button on our chances of coming out alive? Who said he'd like to volunteer for some nice safe bit of caper, when we were actually in control of the situation just for once, however briefly?" She was stepping into her skirt and zipping it up as she spoke. "Who said we'd always failed him miserably, because the first he ever knew about being embroiled in one of our tangles with the ungodly was when someone started hitting him over the head, so he wanted to sample an alternative approach before he died? Who threatened to sulk for a week and tie himself to the railings at Number Ten if we didn't – ?"

"Me, me, me," Collier broke in, raising his hands in a placating gesture. "And I've been enjoying it up to now, my beauty. You know. The signal from the window, and having the phone ring three times to tell you we're ready, all that stuff. I don't doubt I shall enjoy the next bit, too." Willie had appeared and was injecting Bernie Chan, sitting on the edge of the circular bed with his hypodermic. Collier gazed at the unconscious man with distaste. "I'm only pointing out that I'm not enjoying this bit much," he ended austerely.

Modesty grinned and patted his cheek. "I know what's bothering *you*, buttercup," she said. "You don't like the notion of that slob on the bed having his wicked way with me. Right?"

Willie caught her eye as he moved to deal with Rodney, and flickered a wink at her. Collier said defiantly, "Yes. Yes, it bloody well offends me on your behalf."

"Well thanks, but I haven't got a behalf. Anyway, we didn't get that far because —" she controlled a choke of laughter and shook her head. "Sorry. We didn't get that far because Bernie has to wind up slowly. But it wouldn't have been the first time I've let myself be laid in a good cause, and you know it. What the hell?" She was buttoning her blouse, looking at him with amused sympathy. "I'm not waiting for Mr. Right, and I could forget something like Bernie Chan in five minutes. Now, are you going to start enjoying yourself, Steve?"

Collier touched a finger to the peak of his cap. "Yes, ma'am. I am. I'm certainly going to do that, ma'am."

"Good." She turned to check her wig in the pier glass. "Then I might not tell Dinah about your moaning and complaining."

Willie, kneeling beside the chunky man as he put his hypodermic away, said, "What was the joke, Princess? I mean about Bernie winding up slowly."

"Ah, that." She moved round to the far side of the bed, struggling to control her expression, and bent to pick up something from the floor. It was a policeman's helmet. She held it up and said, "Bernie has to walk about wearing this for a while before he can make it."

Willie Garvin had started to rise, but sank back on his knees with a sound between a hoot and a hiccup. Collier gazed with open mouth, then his legs buckled and he slid slowly down the wall, convulsed with silent laughter.

Minutes later two men in overalls and caps carried the rolled Chinese rug downstairs. The rug was heavier now, for Bernie Chan was asleep within it. A red-head with green eyes and long legs, dressed in a grey suit, was waiting for them by the front door. She opened it for them and watched them carry their burden to a van parked outside. When they had put the rug in the back and driven off, she closed the front door behind her and walked away in the direction of Hyde Park.

⁕   ⁕   ⁕   ⁕   ⁕

Bernie Chan came slowly to consciousness. He could hear somebody whimpering, and several seconds passed before he realised the sounds were coming from himself. His head throbbed. He felt cold and sick and frightened. As he stirred, he became aware of something hard encircling his right wrist, and he heard the metallic sound of a chain moving. Warily he opened his eyes without lifting his head. He was lying on the dusty floor of an old-fashioned cellar. The walls were of brick, and the part in which he lay was the size of a large room. In one wall a square arch opened on to what was presumably another part of the cellar, and through this arch came light from a low wattage lamp set in the ceiling.

A cellar? Bernie Chan groped back into the fog that wreathed his memory. He had been at home. Dick and Rodney had been there. He had been in the bedroom with . . .? Yes, with Teresa. The red-head. And . . .

He could recall no more, but sweat broke out on him as he realised that she must have set him up. He wondered only briefly what had happened to his minders. Serve the stupid bastards right if they'd ended up in the river. But who was behind it? Who had hired the bitch to set him up for the snatch? Who? Who?

His stomach twisted with renewed fear as he heard the sound of an ill-fitting door being pushed open with a squeak of wood on wood, then feet descending stairs into the cellar. More than one pair of feet. Bernie Chan closed his eyes and let his head sag to one side. Sooner or later he would have to know what his captors intended, but at the moment he preferred to find out later, when he had had time to collect his wits.

Through his eyelids he was aware of a light being flashed on his face, then it was gone, and the feet moved on. Two pairs of feet. He half opened one eye. The two men wore what appeared to be dark boiler suits, with stockings over their heads. They stood in the far corner, one man shining a torch down on a huddled shape there, and Bernie realised with a curious sense of comfort that he was not the only prisoner.

A man sat slumped against the wall in the far corner, and in the light of the torch Bernie could see the chain running from handcuffs on his wrists to a massive staple set in the wall. He could also see that the man had been savagely beaten. His jaw was monstrously swollen, and the whole of one side of his face was a mass of bruises and abrasions. From the way he sat, with arms hugged to his ribs, Bernie gained the strong impression that the man's body beneath the light grey windcheater had suffered no less than his face.

The taller of the two men who had just entered ran the torch beam over their victim and bent to peer at him, then spoke in a voice with a thick mid-European accent that might have sounded comical if it had not been so chilling. "So you vake up again, Garvin? Zat iss most goot, for now my frien' and me ve haf made a liddle rest since ve haf some nize chat mit you an hour ago."

Bernie Chan's thoughts spun. *Garvin?* Willie Garvin? Modesty Blaise's man?

The taller captor gave a sudden rather high-pitched laugh and drove a boot into the prisoner's ribs. Bernie Chan shivered at the impact, and at the wheezing grunt from Garvin as he tried to twist away. Next moment the other man had joined in, kicking and stamping. Bernie Chan closed his half open eye and lay very still, listening to the sounds and trying not to imagine what Willie Garvin must be going through. He was not in fact distressed by Willie Garvin's troubles as such, except to the extent that he might become a victim of the same troubles himself very shortly.

After a while he heard the taller man say, panting a little, "Enough, Armand. Our orders do not zay to be killink zese men, only to make such softenink-up mit zem for beink ready ven our brincibal vill redurn in the mornink."

The shorter man spoke rapidly in very broken English interspersed with several words Bernie vaguely recognised as French. He did not understand what was said, but evidently the taller man did, for he replied with a touch of irritation, "Zertainly ve haf to do some nize jumpinks on Mr. Chan also, but it is vaste of time before he vake up."

The one called Armand mumbled something and Bernie heard their footsteps approach. The light shone on his face again. He lay utterly still, mouth open to give loud catarrhal breathing. A foot pushed him, but he did not stir. The voice said, "Our friend mit the beard gif him too much drug I zink, but he must vake soon. Ve comink back in vun hour to make some more kickinks and jumpinks."

The light moved from Bernie's face. Footsteps moved away across the floor, up stone steps, then came the squeak of the door being slammed shut. A minute of silence passed, and Bernie Chan sat up very slowly. His wrists were handcuffed, and a strong chain held him stapled to the wall in the same way as his fellow prisoner.

Across the cellar Willie Garvin said in a low voice, distorted by his swollen jaw and lips. "You did all right lying doggo, mate, but it won't work next time. Got any idea who they are?"

Bernie peered at him in the feeble light, heart pounding with fear. "Me? Christ, no! Don't *you* know?"

Willie Garvin shook his head, then gave a shrug. "I got enemies. Could be any one of 'alf a dozen be'ind it. They set me up with a bird, and I woke up 'ere."

"Same with me," Bernie whispered frantically, "but I got no enemies. Well, not this bad. You Willie Garvin?"

One good eye and one half closed eye surveyed him from the bruised face. "That's right. Who're you?"

"I'm Bernie Chan."

"I know the name. Who hates you this much, Bernie? I mean enough to 'ave you beaten up every hour all night before he comes along 'imself tomorrow to finish you off. That's what they said. I want to know 'is name, Bernie, because if I can get out of this I'm going to find the bastard and do the same for 'im."

"Get out?" Bernie clutched at the words. "How?"

"I got a lock-pick in the 'eel of me shoe, but the bloody thing's jammed and I 'aven't been able to get it off yet."

"Well keep *trying* for Christ's sake!"

"What d'you think I'm doing? Listen, I just asked you a question. Who hates you this much, Bernie?"

"I don't know! Nobody!" Bernie's whisper was shrill. "It's all a mistake, it *must* be."

"Don't kid yourself." Willie Garvin had his shoe off and was wrestling with the heel. "Look, when they come back and start putting the boot in on you, curl up as much as you can and try to spot the kicks coming so you can ride 'em a bit. Makes a big difference. And another thing, act like you're 'urt worse than you really are. They reckon they've bust 'alf my ribs, but I doubt if they've done more than just crack one or two of 'em. You want to give 'em the rough breathing so they start worrying they might kill you too soon."

"Oh, Jesus!" Bernie clutched his head in his hands. Closing his eyes, he made an immense effort to be calm and told himself firmly that this must undoubtedly be a bad dream, a nightmare. He pinched his shackled wrists a few times, then opened his eyes. It was happening to him in reality. He moaned with terror.

Still struggling with the shoe, Willie Garvin said, "The bearded bloke, he's in charge of these two, but he's not Mr. Big. Not the one that foreign clown calls their principal."

Bernie said emptily, "Bearded bloke?"

"He's gone now. Finished 'is part of it, I suppose. Youngish with dark 'air and a beard. Bit of an Irish accent." Willie Garvin paused in his efforts and pondered for a moment. "He said something about you to the others. I wasn't too interested, but I think it was something about you copping out on a contract with the Polish twins."

"What?" Bernie Chan's voice rose to a squeak with hysterical indignation. "I never! I bleeding *never!* I know the one you mean now! He came to me to fix a contract with the Polish twins for knocking off some big intelligence bloke, so I fixed it. He knew the twins had to be paid in advance, and he came up with the gelt and I took my commission and paid 'em. All right, so it was six weeks ago and the twins haven't done it yet. I've seen nothing in the papers and they haven't reported back, but Jesus I *told* him there was no guarantee on time. You know how the twins work, don't you?"

Willie said, "I've heard. But this bugger you're talking about doesn't seem to know. He must reckon you've welshed on 'im, Bernie, and he don't like it. Or his boss don't like it."

"I'll explain," Bernie croaked eagerly. "I'll explain to 'im, see? Tell 'im how the twins are sure as God, but they'll do it in their own time."

Willie nodded grudgingly. "I 'ope he listens," he said. "But it won't 'elp you tonight. Those two goons are going to kick 'ell out of you every hour. Remember what I said, Bernie. Curl up so your knackers don't get 'ammered, and try to —"

"Will you shuddup for God's sake!" Bernie yelped.

"Just trying to 'elp," Willie said off-handedly. "We're both in the same boat, but I'll tell you one thing. Maybe neither of us is going to come out of this alive, but if you don't and I do, then you can rest easy in your grave, Bernie, because I'm going to find that bearded bastard *and* 'is boss, and cut their stinkin' livers out."

"And what bleeding good will that do me?" Bernie demanded in a whispering scream. "I'll be dead, won't I?"

"Well, yes. But you just 'ave to take the rough with the smooth, Bernie. Look, you must know *something* about this bloke you fixed the contract for. You couldn't do it over the phone."

Bernie Chan slumped against the wall, suddenly drained by despair. "Just called himself John," he said without interest. "That's all. John. Came to my office in Hatton Garden with two grand in krugerrands as good faith."

Willie gave a grunt of satisfaction as the heel of his shoe finally yielded. Bernie sat up straight and said with dawning hope. "You got the lock-pick? Can you open the cuffs?"

"That's what I'm going to find out," said Willie. "What 'appened next?"

"Next?"

"With John, you stupid gitt. Can't you get it through your 'ead that I'm going after these buggers? I want everything you've got on 'em?"

Bernie sat up straight, dry-mouthed as he watched the dimly seen figure across the cellar hunching over the handcuffs. It occurred to him that at this moment the last thing he wanted was to upset Willie Garvin. He said, "Well, we talked about the contract. He wanted the Polish twins, nobody else, and he was offering twenty grand in krugerrands. I said with this high-up intelligence bloke as the target I couldn't go to the twins with less than twenty-five." Bernie scrambled to his knees in sudden excitement. "Hey, you're right. There's a boss behind him, because he had to make a phone-call from my office to get an okay for the extra."

Willie turned a bruised face towards him and said coldly, "Of course I'm bloody right. Did he get the number himself? Did he get your switchboard girl to get it? What did he say?"

Bernie shrugged, crestfallen. "Just a couple of words, like, 'Can I go to twenty-five thousand?' Then he put the phone down and agreed the price. He was using the phone on my desk and he got the number himself. He didn't say any names, Willie. I thought I got the number, but I must've slipped up somewhere."

Willie Garvin opened the cuff on his left wrist. "What d'you mean, you thought you'd got the number?"

"Well, I'm musical. It's natural with me. I play piano by ear and all that."

One and a half chilly blue eyes stared at him across the cellar, and Willie Garvin said, "What the hell are you talking about?"

"It's to do with the phone number," Bernie said hastily. "I got one of those press-button phones, and the different numbers make different musical notes when you press 'em. You can play little tunes on 'em if you want. I mean, you press 951 and you got the first three notes of Three Blind Mice. I don't know proper music but I can put any tune into do, re, mi, fa, easy. Tonic sulphur they call it, don't ask me why. So this John, he dialled the numbers holding the phone away from his ear, and I made a little do-re-mi tune of it in my head. Are you getting that other cuff off, Willie?"

"I'm trying, aren't I? Where did you slip up?"

"Can't figure it." Bernie shook his head. "He left two minutes later and I wrote the number down. Tried ringing it next day but got no answer about three times. Then the last time a man answered, but it was a taxi-rank phone somewhere out in the sticks, so I must've got the number wrong."

After a while Willie Garvin said, "Maybe. You remember what it was?"

Bernie stared. "No. It was weeks ago."

"Can't remember the do-re-mi?"

"I never even tried. What's the point anyway?"

"I might be interested. You said you wrote it down. Where did you write it?"

Bernie struggled to hide his exasperation. More than anything in the world he wanted to be delivered from this nightmare, and Willie Garvin was his only hope. In Bernie's view he should stop asking bloody useless questions and concentrate on the cuffs, but you didn't say that to the only man who might save you from being kicked to a pulp during the next few hours. Bernie said, "I was looking in my diary while he was getting the number, and I jotted it down as I heard the notes."

"Desk diary?"

Bernie gritted his teeth. "No, pocket diary."

"Where is it now?"

"My place off Eaton Square, in my jacket. I wasn't wearing it when they picked me up tonight."

There was a silence lasting for a full minute. Bernie heard his companion exhale a long breath of satisfaction and saw him stand up, massaging his wrists. Then he moved forward, past Bernie, making for the door beyond the arch. Bernie said in a frantic whisper, "Willie, for Christ's sake, don't leave me like this! Wait! Listen, I'll pay! Willie, *please!*"

The big figure in the archway paused, and Bernie glimpsed the bruised and bloodied face as it turned towards him. Willie Garvin said, "No 'ard feelings, Bernie, but I could waste ten minutes getting you out of them cuffs, and then I got a passenger to worry about."

Bernie moaned with terror and scrambled to his stockinged feet, held in a crouched position by the chain. "For the love of God get me out of here," he said through chattering teeth. "I'll pay. Jesus, just name it and you got it."

Willie had started to turn away, but now he paused, and after a moment moved slowly towards the chained man. "All right," he said reluctantly, "I'll risk a long shot. We'll settle for that phone number, Bernie, the one our bearded friend rang, even if you did get it a bit wrong."

Bernie made a wordless sound of gratitude, pressing his thighs together as he almost lost control of his bladder in the sudden huge access of relief. "You're a prince Willie, a prince," he babbled. "The number, sure. Anything, *anything*."

"Kneel down and lift your 'ands so I can get a bit of light on the cuffs," said Willie. Bernie obeyed thankfully. His companion moved behind him and began to work on one of the cuffs with a lock-pick. "Don't throw your 'at in the air yet," he said grimly. "There's them two rib-kickers upstairs. We'll try going round 'em, but we might 'ave to go through 'em."

"You'll fix the bastards," Bernie said prayerfully. "You're the best there is for a rumble, Willie. Everyone says so."

"Let's 'ope they're right. Having a couple of cracked ribs won't be a lot of 'elp. Neither will you, Bernie boy. Now shut up and let me concentrate."

Five minutes later the second cuff opened and Bernie Chan stood up, free. His clothes were drenched with sweat from fear and anxiety. Willie said, "Stick close be'ind me and do whatever I say. Exactly what I say."

Bernie croaked, "Yes. Yes, Willie." Even in the poor light he could see the bloodstains on the big man's windcheater, and he wondered how badly Willie Garvin was hurt. Not too badly please God, he prayed, thereby making his first attempt for thirty-two years to communicate with the Almighty. Willie moved away, and Bernie followed him up stone steps running beside the wall to a door at the top. There was a light switch beside the door. Willie reached out and clicked it off. The door squeaked as he opened it, and Bernie shuddered with new fear. For two full minutes Willie remained completely still, gripping Bernie's arm hard, then he relaxed a little and moved warily forward.

Somewhere in the house a radio was playing, or perhaps it was a television. Bernie could see very little, for the only light came from a crack under a door facing them, and even this was feeble. He had the impression that they were in a big kitchen, or perhaps a scullery, with a stone floor. As his eyes adjusted he saw a tiny blue flame, the pilot light from a gas water heater. Willie drew him forward a few paces. He heard the scrape of a chair, and then was pressed down on to a wooden seat. Close to his ear Willie whispered. "Stay there and don't move."

Briefly there was a long vertical panel of light as Willie opened the door, but in a moment all was dark again as he presumably found the switch immediately outside. Bernie did not hear his return, and his nerves jumped at a touch on his shoulder and more whispering: "There's a long passage with doors off. I think it leads to a back door. Wait till I check whether it's locked."

"You'll come back for me, Willie?"

A hand patted his cheek, "Don't sweat."

Willie Garvin was gone again, soundlessly. He must have left the door open, for now the sound of a familiar television advertising jingle came clearly to Bernie. It told him that the two vicious men he had seen putting the boot in on Willie were not far away, and he felt spiders with icy feet crawling up his spine. Doubts beset him. If Garvin could get an outside door of the house open, surely he would run for it, and that would leave Bernie sitting, waiting, until . . .

His toes curled under the stress of nebulous but horrible imaginings, and he almost screamed aloud when a hand touched his shoulder again. Willie Garvin's voice breathed in his ear, "It's locked, but there's a side window open. Leads out to a back garden. Come on." Again Bernie's arm was taken in that comforting grip and he was urged slowly along the passage, his blood chilling as they passed the door of the room from which came sounds of a television programme, a late night western film to judge by the shooting.

They came to a small window that stood open. Bernie felt cool night air on his sweating face, and saw dimly under a thin moon the silhouette of a hedge, a small shed, and part of a fence. Willie whispered, "Out you go. Wait for me just round the corner of that shed."

"Wait? What for?" To Bernie any delay seemed lunacy.

Willie said, "I'm going to turn the gas cooker full on in the kitchen. There's a pilot light to set it off, and with any luck it'll blow the whole bloody 'ouse down on those bastards." He vanished into the darkness of the passage. Bernie Chan hesitated, then began to clamber awkwardly out of the window, trying to make no sound. His relief when his feet touched the ground was vast, but he was still so fearful of making any noise that he went down on hands and knees to crawl slowly across some rough grass to the corner of the shed. There he rested on all fours, panting, debating with himself as to whether he should wait or run. The obvious thing to do was run, but this was a garden greatly overgrown by tall shrubs, and in the darkness he could see no clear way out. It might be safer, he decided, to wait at least half a minute or so for Willie Garvin.

The decision gave him a feeling of virtue. He got slowly to his feet, and in that moment heard a sound behind him. His head jerked round and he saw a great dark figure appear from beyond the far corner of the shed an instant before a powerful flashlight was shone in his face, dazzling him. Bernie Chan's blood turned to water, and with a wail of despair he turned to run.

Twelve

PROFESSOR Stephen Collier surveyed his cards. Across the table from him his partner sat relaxed, sipping a glass of Montrachet. She had removed her very fine red wig and green contact lenses, taken a shower, and put on a silk shirt and slacks. Her face was without make-up.

It was just after midnight, and they were in the sitting room of the penthouse. Dinah sat on Collier's left, thoughtfully fingering the corners of the braille cards she held. Weng was on his right, partnering Dinah. They had been playing for an hour now. Weng and Collier had won the first rubber, thanks mainly to Weng who was the best of the four players. Now, with the change of partners, Weng and Dinah were a game up in the second rubber.

Modesty had held poorish cards throughout, but had found enough support on this hand for Collier to bid game in no-trumps. He had gained the lead on the third trick, and was now considering his best line. "It would be of some help," he said severely, "if you could manage to be a little more scrutable, Weng. This wily oriental attitude can be carried too far."

Dinah said, "Careful, Weng. He's fishing."

"I know, Mrs. Collier," the houseboy said. "And I am smiling an inscrutable smile."

Dinah wore a housecoat and was ready for bed. She and Steve were staying the night, but she had no intention of going to bed until Willie Garvin returned. Neither had anybody else. Collier said, "Very well, mes enfants. I now lead the heart eight towards Modesty's ace queen jack ten five two."

Dinah felt along her cards and laid down the heart six. Collier said, "The heart queen from dummy please, partner."

His wife said, "Why don't you reach for it yourself, buster? You're not supposed to be waited on."

"I know, my darling, and it's not that I'm lazy, it's just that women simply adore to fetch and carry for me, and I like Modesty to enjoy herself. I claim no credit for this immense attraction, of course, it's a natural gift I've always had."

"I've noticed your power over women myself," Dinah said pensively. She turned her head to Modesty. "You should be with him when there's a scrummage to get drinks at a theatre bar during the interval, with a couple of girls serving. I think he must have a cloak of invisibility he puts on."

"I got us drinks at The Globe last month," Collier protested.

Dinah nodded. "That was at the end of the show when everyone else was scrummaging for coats at the cloakroom. Could I have a recap, please?"

"I could do with one myself," Collier acknowledged. "Now let's see. I led the eight, you played the six, and Modesty is now putting on the queen for me with her own dainty hand, which I hope will be an example to you."

Weng said, "And I am playing the five, Mrs. Collier."

"God's in his heaven," said Collier fervently, and picked up the trick. His finesse had succeeded, and Dinah must therefore hold the heart king. He returned to his own hand with the club ace and led another small heart, announcing it for Dinah and finessing again by calling for dummy's jack. He would now be able to fell Dinah's bare king with his ace and then enjoy three more heart tricks from Modesty's long suit.

Weng laid the king on Collier's jack and picked up the trick. "I have taken it with the king, Mrs. Collier," he said.

Dinah laughed, and groped for her husband's hand to pat it. "Oh lordy, lordy, you walked into that one, tiger."

Collier turned an indignant gaze on Weng. "*You* had the king! I demand to know why you didn't put it on my queen first time round."

"Because that would have established the suit for you while you still had an entry to Miss Blaise's hand, Mr. Collier," Weng said patiently. "My partner played high-low which told me she had two hearts, and I had three, so I know you have none left, and clearly there is no other entry to your partner's hand. I fear you will be two tricks light."

"I blame my partner entirely," said Collier bitterly. "All it required was an unobtrusive shake of the head or a light kick under the table."

The hand was played out and the penalty entered on the score cards. Collier said, "On second thoughts perhaps it wasn't entirely Modesty's fault. I'm playing under the handicap of being in titanic agony from my toe. Even for a man of my stoic courage it's pretty distracting."

Modesty said, "What's wrong with your toe?"

"I think it's broken in three places."

"No, have you really hurt it, Steve? Do you want me to have a look at it?"

"My sweet, you think only of your own pleasure. I really mustn't indulge you."

Dinah said, "How did you hurt it, anyway?"

"Kicking Willie Garvin," Collier said resentfully. "He'd got a bit of battleship armour round his ribs, hadn't he, Weng?"

"I think it was only a piece of thick leather, Mr. Collier." Weng finished dealing and picked up his cards. "I wish Mrs. Collier and Miss Blaise could have heard your foreign accent," he added.

"So do I," Collier agreed. "Their admiration for me would know even fewer bounds. I was quite marvellous."

Dinah said, "You didn't really use that voice you were practising here earlier, Steve?"

"The very one. Laurence Olivier would have eaten his heart out to hear me." Collier pitched his voice half an octave higher and said, "I zink berhabs ve vill to be comink back zoon to make some nize wertical jumpinks op unt down on warious parts of Mr. Chan."

Dinah put fingers to her lips and turned her head towards him. "Steve, you didn't!"

"My darling, you all know I can't act, I can only ham. And Willie said Bernie would be in such a state that I could ham to my heart's content. He was, too."

Dinah giggled. "I bet you loved every minute."

Collier, sorting his cards, said slowly, "As a matter of fact, no. Not every minute. It was all faked, but when Weng and I started putting the boot in on Willie, I suddenly felt nauseated. I suppose by the concept of what we were doing."

Modesty said, "I warned you, Steve."

"You did indeed, mon vieux. I wonder how you knew? I seem to remember you getting us out of one or two corners so tight that the Grim Reaper's scythe was more or less touching our necks, and on those occasions I've rejoiced in watching you smite the ungodly hip and thigh. But when I took on the mantle of the ungodly myself, I found that merely pretending to kick a helpless victim revolted me."

"That's because you're a nice man," said Modesty, surveying her cards. "Simple, but nice. It's why all we women adore you and want to fetch and carry for you."

Collier laughed. "I fantasise," he said. "It's Willie who has the magic with the dollies. And by the way, do you know exactly what he proposed to do with the distraught Mr. Chan once Weng and I had left?"

Modesty shook her head. "We worked out the general idea together, but the rest is up to Willie."

Dinah was feeling each card in her hand carefully. "I worry about him," she said. "I hope he'll be back soon. Okay Weng, I'm ready."

Weng said, "No bid."

Collier said impressively, "*Three* clubs."

Dinah said, "Double."

Collier said, "In that case I withdraw my bid of three clubs."

"You can't do that!"

"My darling, it was not I who made that bid. I was momentarily possessed by a demon who spake through my mouth. You know how they do."

"Sure. So you and your demon are in three clubs doubled."

"Very well. I'm confident my partner will rescue us."

Modesty said, "No bid."

Collier looked across at her with wounded eyes. "Betrayed," he said reproachfully. "And me with my bad toe, too."

*   *   *   *   *

For the second time in a few hours Bernie Chan emerged slowly from unconsciousness. The back of his neck ached and he was crumpled awkwardly in what at first seemed to be a small, partly upholstered cupboard that vibrated slightly and was moving. After a few moments it dawned on him that he was huddled in the front seat of a car, half sitting on the floor.

Memory rushed back, but it was fragmentary and blurred. The cellar . . . the two men working Willie Garvin over with their feet. Then the escape. He had been waiting in the dark garden, by the shed, and . . . something terrifying had happened, but he could not remember what it was. Fearfully he lifted his head and half opened an eye, to find himself looking up at a steering wheel and the swollen face of Willie Garvin beyond. A sob of relief broke from Bernie and he began to struggle into a sitting position.

Willie Garvin, driving carefully, slowed for a corner, then glanced down. "You all right, Bernie?" he said.

"Uhh . . . yeah. Okay." Bernie held his aching head in his hands. "What . . . what happened?"

"They 'ad someone prowling the garden, and he jumped you. With a cosh, I reckon."

"Oh, Jesus, yes. I just saw this big light." Bernie blinked to clear his vision and stared out of the window. They seemed to be passing through an inner London suburb, and Willie was driving an old Ford Zephyr, keeping to the speed limit. Bernie said dazedly, "How did we get here?"

"Blimey, 'ow d'you think? I came out just in time. Kicked 'im in the goolies, then picked you up and got out through a side gate." Willie had a hand pressed to his chest. "No joke carrying you with me ribs cracked. I think I tore a muscle. Lucky there was this old banger on the corner only about fifty yards away, unlocked. I dumped you in, shorted the ignition, an' took off."

A great wave of emotion swept through Bernie Chan. Tears of gratitude streamed down his face. In spite of everything, Willie Garvin had saved him from severe injury and probable death. It was a miracle. Willie Garvin was the most wonderful man in the world.

When he could speak again Bernie said brokenly, "You're a prince, Willie. Oh God, you're a bleeding archangel, honest. I'll never forget this. Anyone else would've left me, but you got me out. You're a prince, Willie, a Christian prince. On my mother's grave —"

"You're welcome," Willie broke in, wincing a little, a hand to his ribs. "But I reckon we'll both 'ave to lie low for a bit. We don't know who 'ad us snatched, so they might come at us again."

"Right. Right." Bernie looked about him anxiously. "Where was the house, Willie? Where are we now?"

"Don't know about the 'ouse, I never stopped to look. After I started the car I drove through backstreets for about a mile, then found meself in Islington. We're in Euston Road now. Where's your place?"

"Off Eaton Square."

"I'll drop you there before I ditch this 'eap. If I was you I'd get meself new minders, Bernie. Better still, go away for a long 'oliday. A long way away. I've got to get meself fit before I try sorting out these bastards, so it'll take a bit of time."

Bernie shivered and nodded. "I got a bit of business in Hong Kong."

"That's a nice long way."

"You said about sorting them out, Willie. You reckon you can get a line on them?"

"I don't know. You just give me that phone number and I'll take it from there."

"Phone number? Oh, yeah. Sure."

"Tonight, Bernie. I'll 'ave disappeared by tomorrow."

"Anything, Willie. Anything you say. Christ, you're the best friend I ever had." Bernie choked on his words, overcome by emotion again.

Willie said, "Any time. Now lean back and take it easy."

Ten minutes later the car pulled up outside the door of Bernie Chan's house. Willie said, "Get the diary and make it quick, Bernie. I don't want to 'ang around your place with a hot car."

"Too bloody true," Bernie said fervently, and hurried on unsteady legs up the steps. Before he could reach the door it was opened by Rodney, who stared with astonishment and relief.

Rodney said, "Bernie! What happened, for God's sake? We been worried sick!"

Bernie hit him across the face and yapped, "I'll talk to you later, you useless gitt!"

Rodney followed him up the stairs. Dick met them at the sitting room door, and Bernie hit him across the face before he could speak, then hurried into the bedroom and closed the door. He came out two minutes later, moving more steadily, snarled at his minders, and went on downstairs.

Willie Garvin wound down the car window and leaned across. Bernie crouched and handed him a page torn from a pocket diary. "That's the number, Willie, but like I said, I think it's wrong. Maybe just one figure wrong, I don't know."

"Thanks, Bernie. I know it's a long shot. You okay now? Your minders on the job?"

"Sure. I'll have 'em watching over me with shooters till I'm out of the country. Here, take this, Willie." He reached in and put down two small leather drawstring bags on the passenger seat.

"What is it, Bernie?"

"Krugerrands. My commission on the Polish twins job." Bernie reached in and put a hand on Willie's shoulder. "You saved my life, Willie. You're the best. A Christian prince, a real human being. I got to say thank you somehow, so don't turn me down."

Willie Garvin switched on the engine. "All right, Bernie," he said. "I won't."

※   ※   ※   ※   ※

It was one a.m.

Collier said, "You can't be serious." He was partnering Weng now. Modesty and Dinah had just bid and made a small slam to give them rubber in only two hands.

Modesty said, "What do you mean, I can't be serious? You pay me one pound sixty-four pence and Weng pays Dinah the same."

"But Dinah can't extort money from your staff."

"Oh, rubbish. Weng's loaded. He gets an enormous salary from me, and he usually plays bridge three afternoons a week at one of the top London clubs and makes a good seven thousand a year free of tax. I think he must be one of the few millionaire houseboy-chauffeurs in the country, aren't you, Weng?"

The young Indo-Chinese smiled. He owed his life and his education to Modesty Blaise, and there was no job in the world he would have exchanged for the one he had, which he found infinitely interesting and rewarding. "Not quite a millionaire, Miss Blaise," he said, "but I am happy to pay Mrs. Collier one pound and sixty-four pence."

Collier said, "Don't speak, anybody. Total silence, please. I've just thought of something I want to ask. It's the third time I've thought of it, but somebody always butts in before I can get it out, and then the thought slips down one of the small but deep craters in my mind and is lost for a while."

After a silence Dinah said, "Well?"

Collier rested his elbows on the table and gripped his head in his hands. "It's gone," he said resentfully. "While I was explaining and exhorting you to silence it slipped quietly away. No, wait. It's coming back. Yes. Ah, yes." He lifted his head and looked at Modesty. "This is the question, my beauty. How did you manage to pass yourself off as a dancer at that practice studio in order to pick up the lecherous Bernie Chan?"

Weng grinned and rose to top up the glasses of chilled white wine. Modesty said, "I don't need to pass myself off. When I'm in London I usually spend two afternoons a week there. As myself, I mean, not with red hair, green eyes and naughty knickers."

He stared. "As yourself doing what?"

"The whole bit. Barre work, exercises, routines, chorus work. I know a couple of choreographers, and they let me join in with any group they're rehearsing."

"Good God. You actually do this top-hat, tights and silver-knobbed cane stuff?"

"Why not? There's nothing better for balance and timing, and nobody in the world more generally fit than your professional dancer."

Collier nodded, remembering more than one occasion when he had seen those long, shapely but steely legs flash into action. "Yes," he said reminiscently, "I must say you perform a devastating pas de deux. Or even trois. Why didn't you say that it also helps muscle control?"

She looked puzzled, "Why should I?"

Dinah said, "He insists that muscle control is your fetish, honey. He says whenever he's persuaded you to utter a few reluctant words on the subject of how to win a punch-up, you always mention muscle control. Well, actually he says you always *mumble* something about muscle control."

Collier said, "Supergrass. I wasn't for a moment implying that Modesty mumbles, heaven forbid. I don't want a thick ear, do I? No doubt her diction is excellent, but I *hear* it as a mumble because I don't know what she means. I'm confused by these vague terms. After all, what is muscle control?"

There was a brief pause, then Dinah heard him say, "Good God. Do that again." Another pause, then he began to chuckle on an incredulous note.

Dinah said, "Let me in on it."

"I will, my darling. Your raven-haired friend is sitting with her hands resting on the table, arms bare. She made no apparent movement, but suddenly it was if . . . well, as if a small mouse appeared under the skin of her left forearm. It ran swiftly up the arm, vanished under the sleeve, appeared on her shoulder under the shirt, presumably shot across her back, then down the other arm, where it promptly went into reverse, travelling up, across, and down again, except that this time it went across — close your ears, Weng lad — across her upper bosom. Oh, my God, she's done it again, but this time it was a snake rather than a mouse."

Dinah winked a sightless eye at Modesty and said, "You must do it for him in a leotard one day, so he can watch the mouse and snake do a full circuit. I'll have him on a choke chain for that."

Collier said, surprised, "Full circuit? Legs, body and everything? How do you know she can do that?"

"Willie told me," Dinah said patiently, "one day when I asked him about it because you kept on saying Modesty always mumbles something about muscle control. He figures she's unique."

"Then why didn't you report back?" Collier demanded. "Why are these priceless bits of information withheld from me? All these years I could have lunched out on the cachet of knowing a girl who can imitate mice with her muscles. And snakes too. How lucky you are that I have a forgiving nature."

Dinah spread one of the packs face down and said, "Let's see who gets you for a partner this time, Professor. If it's me, I want a written guarantee that you won't do any of your psychic bids."

"As a matter of fact I've abandoned them," said Collier confidingly. "It may have stemmed from when I got Modesty into five spades with only four small trumps between us."

They cut for partners, and Weng moved round to face Modesty, Collier to face his wife. A hand was dealt, and as the bidding ended there came the faint hum of the private lift serving the penthouse. The tiled foyer was in view from the sitting room, and Collier turned in his chair as the lift doors slid open. A man in Arab robes stepped out, then threw back the burnous to reveal a face that looked as if it had been kicked by a horse. "Evening all," said Willie Garvin.

"Hallo, Willie love."

"Good to have you back, honey." From Dinah.

Collier said, "For vich reason iss he to be vearink zuch brebosterous clothinks?"

"I didn't want to be seen walking from the garage with a face like this." Willie shrugged off the robe. "I'll just 'ave a quick shower, Princess. Apart from anything else, I've picked up a good bit of Bernie's aftershave."

"So did I."

He grinned and moved off along the passage. Willie had his own bedroom in the penthouse, with a bathroom en suite. Six minutes later he reappeared, his face scrubbed clean of the make-up, hair still damp, wearing a shirt, slacks and sneakers, carrying a small leather bag in his hand. Modesty laid down her cards. "Bacon, eggs and suchlike, Willie?"

"Lovely, thanks."

She stood up. "Play my hand for me. We're in three spades. Ask Dinah or Weng for the bidding, Steve will only lie his head off."

"Foiled," said Collier. "What happened after I broke my toe on your ribs, Willie?"

"I saved Bernie from a cruel and 'orrible fate, and made a friend for life. Well, at least for 'alf an hour, which was long enough. Put your cards face down, Dinah."

She smiled in his direction and obeyed. "Okay. Why?"

"Present for you." He moved behind her, put the heavy little bag in her lap, and bent to kiss her cheek. "Thanks for lending me Steve."

She touched the bag. "What is it?"

"A bit over a thousand quid in krugerrands, courtesy of Bernie Chan. He wouldn't take no for an answer, so buy yourself a nice dress or something."

"Oh, my God, Willie, no!" Her sightless eyes were wide. Collier leaned back in his chair, laughing silently.

Willie said, "It's tainted money, so I can't touch it, neither can Modesty. We'd be chucked out of the Band of Hope. Besides, we always pay our accomplices well in case they squeal, and I've got another bag for Weng. Daren't give this one direct to Steve, he'll only spend it on debauchery, so that's it. There's no argument, Dinah love."

Weng said, "Thank you very much, Mr. Garvin. I shall invest it wisely."

"I bet you will." Willie sat down and picked up Modesty's cards. "All right, what was the bidding, my little yellow peril?"

Dinah said, "Just a minute. Give a girl time to say thank you, Willie. Thank you from both of us. You're a lovely man."

"I'm a Christian prince," said Willie. "Bernie Chan says so."

Collier laughed aloud, joyously, then leaned forward. "Before we start, a question. We have no idea what you were trying to get out of Bernie Chan tonight, or why, and we wouldn't dream of asking. But did you get it?"

"I 'ope so." Willie studied his cards. "Can't say for sure yet."

Dinah felt across the corner of the table, found Willie's wrist, and held it tightly with her small hand. Not long ago she had heard the radio report of the attempt by The Watchmen on the Golden Gate Bridge at a time when she knew Modesty was in San Francisco. Also at that time Willie Garvin had flown out there at a few hours' notice. Dinah now suspected that for reasons of their own they were going after The Watchmen and were seeking a lead. The thought frightened her badly, and she had not spoken of it to Steve. Tonight's performance had been one of their divertissements, or they would never have let Steve take part in it. A move against The Watchmen would be entirely different, and she dreaded what might lie ahead for these two friends to whom she and Steve were bound by so many ties. But there was nothing she could say to change their intention, and she would not try.

After a moment she took her hand away and said, "You just take care now, Willie."

*   *   *   *   *

Forty minutes later Modesty pulled on a dressing gown and walked barefoot along the passage to Willie's room, tapped on the door and went in. He sat in an armchair waiting for her, wearing a bathrobe and pondering *The Times* crossword. She said, "Stay put, Willie," and sat on the bed. "How did it work out?"

"Bernie didn't know who hired him, Princess, but it was a bloke with a beard, so let's settle for Oberon. All I got was a telephone number." He passed her the page torn from the diary and told her Bernie's story.

She stared at him, amused and almost disbelieving. "It's true? Bernie Chan can hear those press-button phone notes and translate them?"

Willie smiled. "He was in no shape to be kidding."

"Well . . ." She shook her head. "There can't be many crooked jewellers with that kind of talent. But he says he got it wrong. How wrong, would you think?"

"Maybe not at all. Suppose that's an ex-directory number used only by the top Watchmen if they want to talk to . . . well, let's say their Supremo."

"Based in this country?"

"No reason why not, Princess."

"All right, go on."

"Well, they can 'ardly run a fully staffed H.Q., or they'd have sprung a leak long ago. So it's likely the phone isn't manned for much of the time unless a call's expected. That could explain why Bernie kept getting no answer. And since anyone other than a Watchman coming through on it must be an accident, the bloke who answers always says something like Johnson & Son, Florists, or Mr. Bunn the Baker, or station taxi rank. So that makes it a wrong number, except to a Watchman."

She thought for a while, then nodded. "Could be, Willie. Let's start by having the number checked out as it stands. If we get no joy, we'll assume one number wrong and start playing with a phone and a tame musician. No, better still, Dinah. She has a fantastic ear."

Willie said, "The phone people won't check it out for us. will you do it through Tarrant?"

"No, I don't want to involve him. With any luck we're going to be playing well outside the rules, and I don't want to make problems for him. I think we'll be sneaky and ask Fraser."

Fraser was Tarrant's assistant, an ex-agent with a timid manner that hid the nature of a wolf when it came to dealing with his country's enemies. He would break all rules in a good cause, and for him Modesty Blaise was a good cause.

Willie grinned. "Jack Fraser won't ask any questions."

"I'll call him tomorrow and arrange to meet him." She stood up, slipping the scrap of paper into her pocket. "I'd never considered that The Watchmen might be based somewhere in England."

"Neither 'ad I, till now. But even if I'm right, it still doesn't tell us what they're aiming at with these seemingly pointless attacks." He got out of the chair.

"We've been over that," she said. "Number one, the actions *can't* be pointless, they're too expensive. Number two, The Watchmen must have the kind of financial backing that could only come from a government or a multinational or an oil company. Nobody else is rich enough. We can't see how the last two can get any advantage out of what's been done, so that leaves a government."

"And only Moscow fits for size and style." Willie wandered across the room. "We know The Watchmen pulled a couple of anti-Russian actions, but that's standard. It would look fishy if Russia had been odd man out." He sighed and rubbed the back of his neck. "Which still leaves us wondering what the hell they get out of it."

She said slowly, "I've been thinking about that. It just might be an enormous cut-out, to distance themselves from something they plan to happen. All operations so far have supposedly been in support of various lunatic-fringe protest groups, which doesn't make sense."

Willie stood very still. "You mean they were just feints?"

"That would make sense, at least. It lets them hide the real sucker-punch among all the phoney ones, with the blame going to The Watchmen."

Willie whistled softly. "Blimey. If you allow only six months for recruitment and training, that means they started setting up this whole caper nearly three years ago as camouflage for something that's still to come."

"What's three years, Willie? Moscow thinks long-term, you know that."

"Sure." He stood with hands in the pockets of his robe, staring down at the floor. After a while he lifted his head to look at her, suddenly quite sure that in principle at least she was right. "Ockham's Razor," he said. "It's the simplest assumption to make sense of the facts. You're a clever lady, Princess."

She shook her head. "I sometimes make a good guess."

"Well, that'll do till you get clever. The thing is, what's the sucker-punch going to be? And when is it coming?"

"God knows." She took the scrap of paper with the telephone number from her pocket, looked at it, and put it back again. "But He's not the only one who knows. Let's see if this leads us to the Supremo."

"And if we get a name or names?"

"We tail the most likely, and more carefully than we've ever done before. There's an operational base somewhere, there must be, and we need a top Watchman to lead us to it. I doubt if it's in this country and I'm damn sure it's not behind the Iron Curtain because they want to keep their noses clean. I fancy Libya myself. But wherever it is, that's what we want to find, because that's where we'll find Oberon."

There was silence for a while, then Willie said, "Dinah knows we're going after The Watchmen."

She looked up quickly, dismayed. "She does? Oh, goddam it. I hate for her to fret. Did she tell you?"

"No." He remembered her fingers holding his wrist. "But she knows all right."

"Well . . ." Modesty made a wry grimace. "So it goes. Let's hope we can get it over with quickly, though I doubt it." She turned to the door. "Goodnight, Willie love. Sleep well."

"You too, Princess."

When she had gone he lay on the bed for a while, thinking. To take on the powerful and brilliantly organised Watchmen was a formidable prospect. Perhaps too formidable. Not that he disapproved of her intention. There could be no success without the possibility of failure, and if this was to be the time when their luck ran out or their skills proved insufficient, then that was the way it was written. His only regret stemmed from the feeling that this caper offered no sparkle. Despite the high risk it was a grim and downbeat chore, a dirty job, rather like Hercules cleaning out the Augean Stables as opposed to the more interesting problem Perseus solved by using his shield as a mirror in order to cut Medusa's head off without being turned to stone.

Willie smiled briefly at his odd fancy, then slid into bed and turned out the light. Five minutes later he was asleep.

It was next day at four o'clock that Fraser phoned The Treadmill. He was evidently alone in his office, for he was not projecting his usual ingratiating timidity but spoke with laconic briskness. "Hallo, Willie. Weng tells me Modesty's with you. Put her on, will you?"

"Sure. Hang on a tick."

They were in the big combat room at the rear of The Treadmill, and for the last two hours had been doing intensive training with weapons and on the dojo. Modesty wore a tee-shirt and shorts, and was working on a punchbag in the shape of a lifesize human figure. It had been so skilfully crafted that the leather exterior seemed to have been sculpted, and on it were marked all main nerve centres and pressure points. At Willie's call she turned away, picked up a towel and crossed the dojo to join him, mopping sweat from her neck and face.

She said, "Thanks, Willie," and took the phone. "Yes, Jack?"

Fraser said, "That phone number you asked about. I have a name for you. Don't know whether it's the one you want, but it's an interesting name."

"Yes?"

Watching her, Willie Garvin saw no change of expression as she listened, except that for perhaps two seconds her eyes went out of focus and he knew her mind was racing. She wiped her mouth and nose with the towel and said, "Many thanks, Jack. No, I don't know either, we'll just have to see. I'll tell you about it one of these days. Thanks again. Take care."

She hung up the phone on the wall fitment and sat down on a locker beside the gun rack. Draping the towel round her neck she looked up at Willie and said. "The subscriber on the ex-directory number I gave Jack Fraser is Major the Earl St. Maur of Woodlands Manor, Sussex."

There was a long silence. After a while she stood up, slipped an arm round Willie's waist and walked with him down the long room to the twin shower cubicles in the corner. They stripped, showered, put on white towelling bathrobes and sat together on the wall bench.

Willie said, "Could be, Princess."

She leaned forward to wring water from her hair, then pushed it back as she sat up again. "I think so, too," she said. "It just could be."

Thirteen

IT was two hours before sunset, and Oberon sat with von Krankin at a small table in a corner of the command hut, eating breakfast. Both men had recently risen and swum for ten minutes in the clear fresh sea. Since final training had begun, The Watchmen lived by night and slept by day.

Oberon said, "The major flies in today?"

Von Krankin nodded. "He had to put in an appearance in Lisbon for a day or two, but he will return this evening, so we shall have five full dress rehearsals on successive nights before the night of Morningstar."

The summit conference was assembling in Porto Santo. Presidents and Prime Ministers would arrive in two days' time and their meetings would begin the following morning. After three more days, when the conference ended, the Portuguese Prime Minister was to be host at a dinner for the principals and their aides.

Oberon said, "Five full dress rehearsals? No day of rest before the big night?"

"We have decided against that," said von Krankin. "If the men sleep the previous night instead of rehearsing, they will be restless during the daylight hours before the operation begins. Better to maintain our routine."

Oberon poured himself more coffee. After a little while he said, "It's a good decision. Are there any logistical problems remaining?"

"No. All weapons and equipment have been delivered and tested. The small vessel which will be the mother ship is cruising off Morocco. It will come here by night on the fifteenth, two days from now, for practice in taking men, canoes, and equipment aboard, and in disembarking them at sea. It will be out of sight before first light and will return at sunset on the night of Morningstar to carry out its part in the operation. It is registered in Liberia, has a Greek crew of five, and will be sunk with its crew after it has brought our task force back here following the operation."

Oberon nodded approvingly. "Has a decision been taken to have Blik die during the action?"

"Yes." Von Krankin pushed aside his plate with the empty shells of the two boiled eggs he had eaten, and reached for another piece of toast. "Blik dies. You must see to this with much discretion, of course, and abandon the intention if there is any possibility that the event might be observed or suspected by our people. The Portuguese guards will be armed with their Model 48 FBP submachine guns, and Colonel Golitsyn has obtained one of these for you so that Blik will be found with the correct 9mm Parabellum bullets in him, fired from a Portuguese gun."

The door opened and Golitsyn entered, a broad grin on his face as he moved with his rolling gait to the table and sat down. "Gas," he said, and drew the coffee pot and a china mug towards him, chuckling. "Kukiel says we have found gas." Kukiel was the engineer in charge, and one of the two genuine technicians.

Oberon said softly, "Well, I'll be damned."

Von Krankin went on buttering his piece of toast and said, frowning, "I should have included this contingency in my analysis of the situation."

"Moscow isn't listening, so we needn't worry about self-criticism, Captain," said Golitsyn.

"I do not worry about any such communist techniques, Colonel," said von Krankin coldly. "I would certainly have taken this event into account if I had not been told it was most unlikely. I should now like your view as to whether it is good or bad for us."

"Good, my dear fellow, good," said Golitsyn, eyes twinkling. "Consider how genuine it makes us appear. We have found natural gas for the Portuguese, and they will be delighted. I suggest we radio a message via our Lisbon office to the Prime Minister today. It will mean a ministerial visit with journalists and press photographers tomorrow, but so much the better. It will only last an hour or so, and they can take pictures of our happy crew hoisting a few thousand feet of drill-string up through the riser." He looked at Oberon. "We shall need an assortment of bit-players for that, soldier boy, but make sure that neither you nor any of Szabo's section go near the rig at this time. We don't want your photographs taken."

"I'll pick half a dozen suitable men for it, Colonel," said Oberon. "They can wear helmets and goggles to make them fairly anonymous." He stood up suddenly, pushing hands deep in his pockets then taking them out again as if realising that this was a nervous action. "Have you had any news about Tarrant?"

"No advertisement in *The Times*," said Golitsyn sympathetically. "Which is not surprising since this morning's situation report tells me among other things that Tarrant flew into Funchal himself yesterday with the advance party from London. And in answer to your earlier inquiry, we have had people trying to track down the Polish twins in London for the last two weeks, but they're not to be found."

An ugly glitter touched Oberon's eyes, and he placed his chair under the table with careful restraint. "I can't conceive that the Polish twins could fail," he said. "Tarrant has no bodyguard, so he's an easy target. It seems Bernie Chan took the money but neglected to make the contract. He'll have to be killed for that."

"Perhaps," Golitsyn nodded, cradling his mug of coffee in his hands and gazing down into it. "But the Tarrant contract was a side issue. If this were a crystal ball, the people I would most like to locate at this moment are Modesty Blaise and Willie Garvin." He looked up, and suddenly there was no humour in the deep brown eyes, only a cold wariness. "I made an inquiry about them three days ago, and our London people report that they also are nowhere to be found."

     ✳   ✳   ✳   ✳   ✳

"An oil rig?"

"Yes, señorita. The English lord flew out last night on the helicopter which belongs to the Drioga Corporation. Fortunately we were watching the back of his apartment as well as the front. It was after dark when the car came for him, and he left very quietly, in the way of a man who does not wish to attract attention."

Seated under the awning on the afterdeck of *The Sandpiper,* a fifty-five foot motor sailer moored in the Cascais marina, Modesty Blaise said, "You followed him to the heliport?"

The Spaniard put down his coffee cup and nodded agreement. "Both Pepe and I, on our motor cycles and in communication by small radios in the helmets, in case of difficulty."

Willie Garvin lounged by the rail, gazing idly about him, ready to give warning if anyone came within earshot. Like Modesty, he wore a shirt and denim shorts. They had been in Cascais for a week now, living on the boat which they had sailed from Falmouth in six days. They could have flown to Lisbon in fewer hours but had no reason for haste in following up the lead they had decided to pursue. Besides, there was a substantial advantage in using *The Sandpiper.* She carried equipment they could never have taken safely across borders.

Claudio said, "The Lord St. Maur went only to the heliport. I tried to follow him into the place of departure, pretending to be a stupid tourist, but it was not permitted. Pepe found a position on the perimeter where he could watch with night binoculars. The lord remained in the place of departure for a short while, then came the helicopter and we saw him go into it, for I had joined Pepe now. I went to telephone Ramon and his brother, and they relieved us at two. At eight the lord had not returned. I sent Pepe to keep watch on the apartment, Ramon on the office, and came at once to tell you what I have now told."

Willie said quietly, "How did you know it was the Drioga helicopter, Claudio?"

"Ramon spoke to one of the mechanics there in the morning. Not in a way to make him have suspicion."

Modesty said, "I'm sure of it." When she had hired a team to keep tabs on the Earl St. Maur in Lisbon she had picked the best. Claudio and his three colleagues came from a detective agency in Madrid. She had used them in *The Network* days and knew of nobody more skilled in keeping a subject under observation unnoticed.

She said, "Do you know where this oil rig is, Claudio?"

He spread a hand. "I have not yet inquired, señorita. Do you wish me to do so? It must be within the range of the helicopter."

Willie said, "It's a drillship about twelve miles southeast of Madeira, off the Ilhas Desertas." Modesty lifted an eyebrow at him and he went on, "I know a Portuguese air hostess, and I read about Drioga in a Lisbon paper she brought in with 'er, one morning a few months back when we were 'aving breakfast. It's a fairly new exploration company, and a bit of a mystery to the rest of the trade."

"Did the newspaper say that?"

"No, but I've been fancying oil exploration shares lately, and I've got a mate who's the top energy bloke in a bank that does a lot of the financing. He told me none of the big oil companies are be'ind Drioga. It's a consortium of some kind, and they're playing it close to the chest."

Modesty nodded. Willie Garvin had a remarkably wide range of knowledgable friends, quite apart from his international harem of air hostesses who, as he claimed, kept his mind broadened by vicarious travel. She stood up and said to Claudio, "I think you've done all we wanted of you now, thank you very much."

He rose with her, a small unobtrusive man with deceptively vague eyes. "It has been a pleasure, as always, to do work for you."

"Send your bill to my London lawyer, please. You have his address. I've instructed him to settle with you immediately."

Claudio smiled. "You are most thoughtful, señorita."

When he had gone she took the coffee-cups into the galley, put them in the sink, then came out to stand beside Willie at the rail.

"Didn't expect this," he said thoughtfully.

"No."

"Might not mean anything, I suppose. Could be he's selling 'em a few dozen crates of port."

"I doubt if that's the drink of choice on an oil rig. Perhaps we should go and take a look, but very quietly."

He looked pleased. "We can be away in an hour, Princess, the tanks are full. Take us about five days, I suppose. Less if there's a good wind be'ind us like there ought to be at this time of year, so we can run under sail at least part of the time."

"Yes. Do you know how close the drillship is to the Ilhas Desertas, or how it bears from any one of them?"

"Sorry. I got the impression it's not far offshore, that's all. But we wouldn't show ourselves by daylight anyway, and after dark we'll see the derrick light. Then we can approach from the blind side of one of the islands."

"I hope it's east of Deserta Grande. I once spent a night there, out from Madeira in a small boat, and I know a little cove on the west coast. We could use the canoe from there to the drillship." She stood with arms crossed, hands holding her elbows, looking out across the Tagus estuary with a slight frown, her hair stirring in the wind. After a while she turned to look at Willie and said, "There's that summit meeting about to start in Madeira, isn't there?"

He stared, then drew in a slow breath through pursed lips. "You mean *they* could be a Watchman target?" he said doubtfully.

She gave an apologetic shrug. "No, it was just a fleeting thought, rather stupid. Let's not get carried away. All we know so far is that Oberon most certainly is a Watchman, and he may have telephoned a number which may belong to St. Maur, which means that St. Maur may be connected with The Watchmen. We know the noble lord has gone to the Drioga oil rig, and it's true that a rig offshore from an uninhabited island would make a hell of a good base for The Watchmen. But a whole string of maybe's don't amount to a shred of solid confirmation. Besides, The Watchmen always strike at unguarded targets, and that summit meeting is going to be guarded by air, sea and land. Moreover and further-more, the rig was there long before the summit was announced, so it can't have been planned. If we sent Tarrant a warning, he'd think we'd flipped."

Willie nodded, a little gloomily. "Is it worth taking a look, you reckon?"

She smiled and punched his arm gently. "It's the only game in town, Willie love." He understood her. This was the old joke of the gambler. The game might be crooked, but it was the only game in town. St. Maur might be a false lead, but he was the only one they had.

The prospect of activity, of sailing several hundred miles in the company of Modesty Blaise, was cheering to Willie Garvin. He looked at his watch, and turned his cheek to feel the wind. "Shouldn't take long to find out whether they're running something a bit more than an oil rig out there," he said. "But if they are . . . I mean, just suppose it turned out to be a base for The Watchmen, with Oberon there, and the others you saw in San Francisco. Then what, Princess?"

She said slowly, "Then I have to forget that I want to deal with Oberon myself, and we do what Ben Christie would have wanted us to do Willie. We take no chances. We pull out, sail twelve miles to Madeira, and tell Tarrant."

※　　※　　※　　※　　※

It was less than four days later when they came to Deserta Grande from the west, with the setting sun behind them, sighting the tall derrick between the southern tip of the island and its smaller companion, Bugio, from several miles out. Their hopes that the expedition might prove fruitful had dwindled, for on the second day out they had heard on the radio that the Portuguese Minister for Energy was paying a visit to the exploration rig south of Madeira, where natural gas had been found. This news item gave the Drioga Corporation a solidly authentic look, but they did not consider cancelling their plans.

Deserta Grande was long and thin from north to south, rising to fifteen hundred feet, and no more than a mile and a half in breadth. They brought the motor sailer into a small inlet that ran obliquely into the steep rocky coast, and dropped anchor twenty yards from a thin ribbon of stony beach. Here *The Sandpiper* was virtually out of sight except from the air. A single goat-track slanted up from the scrubby ground beyond the beach and soon vanished among folds of rock.

They ate a light meal, spent an hour making careful preparations for the night's work, then slept for two hours. At ten o'clock they rose, put on dark slacks, shirts, and woolly caps, blacked their faces, and launched the seventeen-foot folding canoe with its frame of ash and its rubberised canvas skin. Ten minutes later they cleared the southern point of Deserta Grande by a hundred yards and turned the nose of the canoe towards the drillship. The sea was calm with a gentle swell, the night dark, with high cloud hiding stars and moon. The red light of the derrick seemed to hang unsupported in the sky, but there were deck lights and cabin lights throwing a misty glow around the vessel.

As stern paddle in the canoe, Willie controlled its direction. Leaning forward on a stroke he said softly, "Straight in?"

She lifted her paddle, and he followed suit. Turning her head she said in a whisper, "Yes, but ease up before we touch that ring of light. We'll circle her for a while to look for the best approach."

"Right, Princess."

She turned and dipped her paddle smoothly into the water. Willie picked up her long easy stroke, and the canoe slid forward. They had covered little more than two hundred yards when a mirror image came out of the darkness at them, a two-seater canoe, on a course to pass within thirty feet to starboard, two black figures paddling in practised unison. But it was not a mirror image, for the other was an open Canadian canoe, longer, of broader beam, and riding lower in the water as if carrying more weight. For brief seconds two pairs of eyes stared at them from black-hooded heads as the other craft passed on an opposite course, then it was gone, invisible in the darkness.

Willie Garvin thought, "Christ! What the hell goes on?" He saw Modesty point to port, and dug in his paddle to turn the canoe that way, but at once swung the paddle urgently across to thwart the movement, for it would have brought them into the side of yet another Canadian two-man canoe gliding out of the night on their port bow. Beyond it was a third, closer, turning sharply to avoid them, and ten seconds later they were alone again, not paddling now, rocking slightly in the wake caused by the other canoes. Modesty turned her head to look at Willie, eyes huge and questioning in her blackened face.

He lifted his shoulders in an exaggerated shrug of incomprehension. She breathed, "Let's get the hell out of here. Wide sweep to starboard." But even as he dug his paddle in hard, a bright light sprang from the blackness, encompassing them in its powerful beam, and a hard nasal voice said without pause, "Keep quite still. Ne bougez pas. Stehenbleiben! Naõ se mecha."

The beam moved briefly to left and right, illumining two canoes which now bracketed them. In each, one man was keeping the craft steady with touches of the paddle. The other held a submachine-gun aimed. Again the light moved, to touch a third submachine-gun held by the speaker, and the voice from the darkness said. "Nationality?"

It repeated the word in several languages, and in that short time Modesty Blaise assessed the situation and made her decision. She knew that penetrating voice, for she had more than once watched Major the Earl St. Maur being interviewed on television. She knew they had found The Watchmen — and by some freak of chance had been found by them. She carried a Star PD .45 automatic in a shoulder holster under her shirt, and Willie carried the twin knives he could throw with such pinpoint accuracy, but under the glare of the light there could be no hope of using a weapon. They would die at the first hint of an attempt.

She said, "English." There was no reaction from the men in the canoes to port and starboard, no comment or sound of surprise. They were highly trained professionals waiting for orders. Or perhaps they already had them, for by the way she and Willie had been so neatly surrounded following the surprise encounter she felt there must be communication between the men in the canoes, silent communication, probably by single earplug receivers and throat-mike transmission.

"English? And a woman?" The metallic voice from behind the light was dispassionate, unperturbed. "Then I rather think we know who you are."

* * * * *

Golitsyn stubbed out his cigarette and lit another. St. Maur, von Krankin and Oberon sat round the wardroom table with him. It was five minutes since Modesty Blaise and Willie Garvin had been brought aboard. The nightly rehearsal for Morningstar was continuing, but with each of three sections working under a second-in-command.

"It would take them perhaps ninety minutes from Madeira by canoe in this sea?" said von Krankin. Oberon nodded, tight-lipped, eyes almost feverishly bright.

"We have been lucky," said Golitsyn. He was recovering now, but he had been genuinely shaken by the event. "Very lucky," he repeated. "They were carrying no radio, so it seems clear they intended to reconnoitre the drillship and shore base tonight, then return to Madeira before first light to report their findings. The weapons and ammunition laid out ready for loading practice would have been all they needed to find."

"There's no point in debating what might have happened if Blaise and Garvin hadn't run into one of our sections moving in for landing practice," St. Maur said coldly. "We have captured these two people and we should kill them as soon as possible. I only brought them aboard so that we could find out what they know and who else knows it."

Von Krankin said, "There is no time for prolonged interrogation to establish the truth of what they may say."

St. Maur shrugged. "No time to be subtle, but we have people who can rip it out of them in double-quick time."

Golitsyn shook his head. "No," he said slowly. "I want them in prime condition tomorrow night. You will take them in with the assault party, unconscious, and you will kill them at the point of embarkation, during withdrawal. We want no signs of capture or torture to be found on them."

St. Maur said, "I must protest. The woman's a spoiler, you've said so yourself, and as long as those two are left alive they'll be a danger to us. Ask Oberon."

Golitsyn smiled a little grimly. "I will, Major, I will," he said. "But I still propose to plant Blaise and Garvin as dead Watchmen, together with Blik. You are in charge of military matters, but the rest is for me to decide, and I don't intend to miss what is a golden opportunity for putting over disinformation that will cause confusion on a massive scale in the aftermath of Morningstar."

St. Maur stared down his beaky nose and said curtly, "Very well, I accept your decision."

"Thank you. May I know what is happening with our visitors at the moment?"

"They've been stripped, made to shower, and are in the sick bay being clinically searched by Dr. Djakovo. Three of our men are present, keeping intensive guard. Blaise and Garvin are being dealt with separately. By this I mean that while one is being searched the other is prone and under threat from two guns. I've given orders that when Dr. Djakovo is satisfied they have no concealed items of any kind they may be allowed to put on their underwear only, a psychological weakener, and that their thumbs be wired together behind their backs, and their feet restrained by wire hobbles. They can then be brought to us for interrogation."

Golitsyn said, "I should be obliged if you would phone down and cancel the wire, Major. Since we've agreed to use their dead bodies for disinformation, we don't want them marked."

St. Maur nodded, went to the wall-phone, spoke into it briefly, and returned to the table. Von Krankin said, "They must be kept under total restraint until they are killed. That will be your responsibility now, Colonel."

"Which I shall accept from the moment you withdraw your men from guarding them, Siegfried," said Golitsyn amiably. He turned to Oberon, who sat looking down at his linked hands resting on the table, his face taut and rather pale. "Well, soldier boy? You are the expert on Modesty Blaise. How much do you think she knows, and how much of it has she told before coming here?"

Oberon said in a controlled voice, "She and Garvin will pretend they know a great deal more than they do. They will also give the impression that their friend Tarrant, now in Madeira, knew they were making this reconnaissance and will act at once when they fail to return before morning." He lifted his head and looked round slowly at his three companions. "It won't be true. If they had told Tarrant or anyone concerned that the Drioga drilling operation was suspect we would have had half the Nato navies here by now. And if Tarrant knew they were making this jaunt they would have been carrying a radio for communication with him. I'll stake my life they're acting independently."

Von Krankin said, "How did they even suspect Drioga?"

Oberon shook his head. "I've no idea, and it isn't important for the moment, Captain. I've given my opinion, and if there are no destroyers or aircraft around this rig by first light tomorrow morning, you'll know I'm right."

Golitsyn leaned back in his chair, and something of his usual joviality touched the rugged face. "You've spoken my thoughts, soldier boy," he said. "Morningstar isn't blown, and we've been presented with two very useful bodies to leave behind. It's not a bad night for us after all."

Oberon's voice cracked with tension as he said, "I want to be the one to kill her, Colonel. I want to take her in an Individual."

Golitsyn chuckled and wagged his head. "No. They must both be in prime condition."

"But it could be set up here, on the rig, half an hour before we leave," Oberon said, his body rigid, jaw muscles locked with the urgency of his need. "I swear I won't leave any suspicious external marks."

Golitsyn's amusement vanished. He lowered his head, looking up from under heavy eyebrows, and said, "No, I repeat no, Mr. Oberon. The subject is closed." A thick finger lifted to point between the green eyes. "You can kill her during withdrawal from Morningstar by submachine-gun. That's all. And don't disobey me, Mr. Oberon. Moscow would be mortally displeased with you if you ruined this remarkable opportunity for the sake of personal revenge. You understand me?"

Oberon inhaled deeply, compelled his body to relax, then nodded. "Understood, Colonel."

St. Maur said without animosity, "I endorse what the Colonel just said to you, Hugh. Disobedience at any level in The Watchmen won't require action from Moscow. It will be dealt with on the spot." He stood up. "I suggest we rejoin our sections now. Good practice in improvisation, finding them and taking over command again.''

Von Krankin said as he rose, "You can retain the three men at present guarding the prisoners until midnight, Colonel. After that we shall require every man for a full-scale rehearsal until O-three-hundred, and when that is completed the whole task force will be sleeping till noon, so they will be rested for tomorrow's operation. One or two of the auxiliary personnel will be available for guard duty if you wish to use them.''

Oberon said sharply, "I wouldn't advise that.''

Golitsyn grinned. "I don't suppose you would," he said with avuncular good humour, "remembering what she managed to do when you had her prisoner on that boat off San Francisco. But don't worry, soldier boy. Nor you, Siegfried. I intend that the good Dr. Djakovo shall provide means of restraint, once I've had a little chat with them. Soviet pharmacologists have produced a versatile range of narcotics for use in our psychiatric hospitals, and today the safest handcuffs come out of a bottle.''

St. Maur stood looking out of the wardroom window towards the dark bulk of Deserta Grande. He said, "Since your plan won't allow intensive interrogation of Blaise and Garvin, why waste time having a little chat with them, Colonel? Not much point, is there?''

"None at all," agreed Golitsyn. He took out his pipe and began to fill it thoughtfully. "Simple curiosity, that's all. These two are something of a legend, and I'd rather like to see them and exchange a few words before they die.''

Major the Earl St. Maur turned from the window with a shrug. "Extraordinary," he said, half to himself. "Still, entirely up to you, of course.''

Oberon said with suppressed urgency, "I'd be very grateful for a few minutes with them myself, Major. Just to say one or two things I'd like them to hear before they go.''

Pale blue eyes flanking the thin hook of a nose studied Oberon without expression. St. Maur's towering ambition was as coldly relentless as a glacier, and he was a man unable to comprehend hatred, but he had a leader's understanding of men, and he knew that this man's ego had been badly mauled by Modesty Blaise. Oberon had been refused the chance to kill her on equal terms, and it was not enough for him that she should simply die at his hands while unconscious. He had a huge need to make her feel the totality of her defeat; to pronounce the death sentence, watching her eyes; to parade before her his immense success as a task force leader in operations of The Watchmen, and in every possible way to shatter her ego while boosting his own.

Give Oberon that, and he would do a better job tomorrow, St. Maur decided. He glanced at Golitsyn, gave a small nod, and lifted an eyebow in inquiry. The Russian leaned back in his chair, amused. Here it was again, he thought, the unexpected reaction. Anybody knowing St. Maur would have banked on his automatic refusal of Oberon's request, but that simply meant they didn't know him well enough. In some respects the English lord had a touch of genius.

Golitsyn gave Oberon one of his warm smiles. "Enjoy yourself, soldier boy," he said. "Take ten minutes on your own with them. But you just talk. You don't touch, hey? And you remember all the time, I want them in prime condition."

＊   ＊   ＊   ＊   ＊

The ship's hospital consisted of a very well equipped surgery and operating theatre, with dental facilities, adjoining a ward furnished with eight beds. There were no patients at this time, but two of the beds were occupied. Modesty Blaise lay on one, in the plain black bra and panties she wore for working purposes. Willie Garvin lay on the next bed in his boxer shorts. Both had their arms tied to the framework of the bed with strips torn from a sheet. The bonds were not tight, but they could not have been slipped in less than a few seconds, and two men with submachine-guns stood watching. A middle-aged Czech in a long white coat leaned against the bulkhead beside the door to the surgery. This was Dr. Djakovo, and he stood with folded arms, contemplating the captives with interest.

Both the man and the woman seemed to be fully relaxed and untroubled by their plight. There could be no doubt that they were aware of it and could cherish no hope of escape, for the search had uncovered every weapon and device concealed in their clothes and on their bodies. Yet there was an air of remoteness about them as if they had mentally removed themselves from the situation. It was most curious, thought Dr. Djakovo. He had never before encountered quite such phenomenal control, and if he had been anything but a materialist he might have felt there was some element of the mystical about it. How interesting it would be, he reflected, to experiment on these two with some of the more recent mind-bending drugs.

The ward door to the passage opened and Oberon came in. He had put on a shoulder holster containing a Colt Commander .45 automatic, and his green eyes held little flames of profound excitement. He said to the two guards, "All right, wait outside till I call you in again." As they moved past him he said to Dr. Djakovo, "I have clearance to talk with the prisoners alone."

Djakovo nodded and moved away from the bulkhead. "Yes. Colonel Golitsyn rang down. Is she the one who made Baystrike go wrong?"

"She's the one." Oberon's voice sounded thick and furry with hatred.

At the door Djakovo paused and looked back, adjusting his spectacles. "They are a most interesting pair," he said. "Most interesting."

Fourteen

OBERON moved to stand between the ends of the two beds, and as he looked down at Modesty Blaise and Willie Garvin the passion that swept him made his head swim. They observed him with a remote gaze, but neither of them spoke. He fetched a chair and sat down, looking from one to the other, remembering.

"You're going to be dead by this time tomorrow," he said with soft ferocity. "Dog-meat. Finished. Destroyed. Are you listening, you arrogant bitch? The whole world is going to believe that you were among the leaders of The Watchmen, and that you got killed during tomorrow's action. Not that it will matter to you then, because I'll have put a dozen holes in your guts with an s.m.g."

When he paused they remained looking at him without interest. Rage spurted within him, but he controlled the wild urge to smash his foot into her face. Golitsyn's warning was not to be taken lightly. He leaned forward and said. "*The Network* was nothing. A pissy little bunch of smalltime sneak-thieves. Do you have any idea of just how big The Watchmen are? How they're actually going to change the face of the world? And I'm right there among their top men, Miss Modesty bloody Blaise. I'm a very key man. Not good enough for you and your piddling *Network*, of course. Christ, I could have re-shaped that whole organisation to make the Mafia look like a bunch of cheap pickpockets, but you turned me down, you stupid cow."

Oberon sat back, breathing deeply. His voice had become unsteady, and he did not want that. He was the winner, and could afford to be cool in savouring his triumph. "I'm somewhat disappointed," he said more lightly. "We occasionally have Individual Contests between Watchmen, and I wanted to take you in a set piece like that. You and Garvin both. I could, you know . . ." rage suddenly hit him again and he said through set teeth, "I bloody *could*, by God! Twice you've caught me on the blind side, you tricky bitch, but you'd never do it again. It's a pity I won't have the chance to show you, but we just happen to be running our biggest ever operation tomorrow, and I have to keep you in prime condition so we can use you for disinformation."

He took out the Colt and checked it, using the movements to gather control of himself again. When he slipped the gun back in its holster and looked up he was smiling, and it was very nearly a genuine smile.

"I'm going to be bigger than you ever were," he said almost dreamily. "I'm with people who know all about power, and I'm going right to the top with them. I'm a professional among professionals now, and compared with my kind you're just amateurs. Soon you'll be dead amateurs. Finish. No more Modesty Blaise, the tinpot Mam'selle. No more Willie Garvin with his overblown reputation." He laughed suddenly. "You're pathetic. Here you are, beaten, and you don't even know who The Watchmen are or what we're all about."

She gave a little sigh and looked bored, knowing that the less encouragement she gave Oberon the more she would feed his need to talk. Information gave strength to any hand, no matter how poor, and already they had learned that she and Willie were to be kept for killing tomorrow. That was invaluable knowledge. Under immediate threat of death, Willie might have been able to break the strips binding his arms and get into action faster than anyone anticipated, but it meant taking a thousand-to-one chance of last resort.

She lay listening, as Willie would be listening, while Oberon spoke, not paying close attention, but storing up his words for mental playback later, to be sifted for further useful information. Their capture had been a brutal shock, stunning and confusing in its unexpectedness, but they had absorbed it now. They had used well-tried mental techniques to eliminate strength-sapping anxiety, leaving them free to find the inner balance that would offer their best chance of perceiving an opportunity and using their skills to make use of it.

Because Oberon was alternating between fury at past remembrance and euphoria at the present situation, he was occasionally hard to follow in his mixture of abuse and gloating, but it was not for this reason that she was giving him only part of her attention. The rest was engaged in the priority need of assessing the nature of their captivity during the coming hours. Their transfer from canoe to drillship had been supervised by the Earl St. Maur, who was addressed as Major, and a man called von Krankin, who appeared to be of equal authority. In the sick bay she and Willie had been made to strip and shower before Dr. Djakovo searched them. The guards had been about to use wire to bind them when a phone call had come from the major. After taking it, the doctor had given revised orders and a sheet had been torn to provide less severe bonds than the wire. Now Oberon had revealed that she and Willie were to be planted as dead Watchmen in an operation next day, and it seemed clear that they were to be kept unmarked by signs of captivity for this purpose.

So they would be closely guarded by armed men, the professional killers of The Watchmen. But was that all? Or even . . . was it so? They had been told they were to die, so anyone knowing their reputation would also know that at some point they would attempt to escape, no matter how hopeless the situation, because they simply would not wait tamely to be killed. But a failed attempt would leave them either dead or wounded, and this would not fit The Watchmen's opportunist plan. They were to be kept in 'prime condition' until left for dead after the coming operation, Oberon had said. Which meant restraint without damage, or even the chance of self-damage.

So . . .

The door opened and a burly man with a heavily creased face and deepset eyes came into the ward. He wore a drab green tunic and trousers, with calf-length boots in soft black leather. The face was vaguely familiar, but she could not place it. Oberon stopped speaking and stood up. The newcomer looked at him with twinkling eyes and said gruffly, "Time's up, soldier boy. Enjoy yourself?"

Oberon smiled back, and this time his smile was entirely natural. He seemed relaxed and a little sleepy, pleasantly so, almost as if he had just had a woman. "I got a lot off my chest, thank you Colonel," he said, and moved to the door.

Colonel. The word triggered memory, and she knew she had seen the face in the old *Network* files, the section concerning Intelligence. The man was Russian, a KGB man, they had dealt with him once, though not face to face . . .

Willie breathed a word only she could hear, "Golitsyn."

The man was saying, "Leave the gun with me, soldier boy. We'll take no chances with these two, hey?"

The Colt changed hands. Oberon went out. Golitsyn moved to stand between the beds and looked down at the prisoners with unconcealed interest. She studied him quietly, deciding that to get anything useful out of this man called for a different approach. Oberon's outpourings had been encouraged by lack of reaction. This one was not driven by emotion, and too experienced to be easily tricked, but he wanted information himself, and might well bargain.

He sat down on the chair at a safe distance, the automatic resting on his knee, and said with cheerful sympathy, "Pretty bad luck you had, running into our full dress rehearsal like that."

Her voice was light and easy as she said, "Oh, that's all right. These things happen, and we never fret about them. What's that thing you often say about fretting, Willie?"

His mind meshed with hers and he knew how the game was to be played. "You mean, '*Fret not thyself because of the ungodly*'?" he said, turning his head towards her.

"Ah yes, that's the one."

"Psalm thirty-seven, verse one."

She gave a small laugh. "Don't expect me to remember." They were looking at each other as if Golitsyn had been forgotten, and he found himself making an effort not to show that he was disconcerted. He decided that silence was his best counter for the moment, but almost at once Willie lifted his head from the bed to look at him and said, "I've often wondered. Was it you who gave Rykov the chop?"

Golitsyn felt in his pocket, took out his pipe and tobacco pouch. Now he was startled. Rykov had been his greatest rival in the GRU at one time, and it was in fact perfectly true that Golitsyn had arranged for him to be disgraced by failure in a major project, but Garvin could not possibly know that. *The Network* files had been remarkably good, no doubt, but it was extraordinary that Garvin could have remembered faces from photographs, and mentally cross-indexed facts to provide grounds for the inspired guess he had just made.

Filling his pipe while keeping the automatic to hand in his lap was awkward, but Golitsyn found he needed the occupation to give himself a few moments for thought. Thumbing tobacco into the bowl with an air of patient equanimity he looked up and said, "You know who I am?"

Modesty said with the manner of one stating the obvious, "Colonel Golitsyn." She left Willie to amplify. He was the one with the gift of total recall.

"Colonel Mikhail Golitsyn," said Willie earnestly, "of the Glavnoye Razvedyvatelnoye Upravleniye, formerly of the Komitet Gosudarstvennoi Bezopasnosti, but if you don't want us to say anything, Colonel, we won't."

Modesty said admiringly, "I don't know how you manage to pronounce all that, Willie. Do you practise with tapes?"

"I 'ad them stolen," Willie said disconsolately. "It's ridiculous, I reckon. What could you get for 'em? But you know what people are these days."

Golitsyn put his pouch away. His face still bore a look of placid good humour, but this hid increasing bafflement. These two could not be fools, so they were playing a game, yet there was no hint of this in their manner, and even if it was a game, what was its purpose? Their reaction to capture and the absolute certainty of death, which Oberon would surely have made clear to them, was like nothing Golitsyn had ever known before, and he was a man with much experience in such matters.

He said with a chuckle, "You're very well informed, Mr. Garvin.

I'm mildly interested to learn how you know so much about me."

Willie looked away, seeming to lose interest, his eyes wandering absently round the ward as far as his position would allow. "It's psychic," he said vaguely. "You can't really describe it."

Modesty smiled apologetically. "He always says that," she told Golitsyn, "but I don't believe it myself. I think he has other means."

Other means? Golitysn put a lighter to his pipe, the gun in his hand again. He found himself not quite comprehending, but feeling the fault was his rather than theirs. It was very odd. Blaise and Garvin lay half naked, helpless, and under sentence of death, yet somehow during this encounter so far they had achieved a curious psychological initiative. He decided on a direct approach, and said, "Does anybody know you've come here, Miss Blaise?"

Willie chuckled, his eyes closed now. She glanced at him reprovingly and said, "Behave yourself, Willie." Then, to Golitsyn, and again apologetically, "There's not much point in our saying yes or no, because how could you be certain we're telling the truth, Colonel? All you can do is just wait and see, really."

So Oberon's prediction as to what she would say had been completely wrong, thought Golitsyn grimly, and his asking of the question just now had made him look a fool. "We'll leave that," he said with leisurely unconcern. "How would you feel about telling me what led you to this drillship? It's not important, but I'm curious."

Willie opened his eyes. "Not important?" he said wonderingly.

Modesty said, "Willie, he's only *pretending*. Of course the Colonel knows it's important. After all, what led *us* to The Watchmen might lead somebody else, once we've gone."

"Gone? Gone where?"

"Passed on. Called to Higher Service. You heard what Oberon said."

"He said he was going to kill us."

"That's what I meant, but let's not get morbid about it, Willie."

Golitsyn felt as he might have felt if watching a game of tennis that was going too fast for him to follow. They both lay looking at him now, amiable and unresentful. He took his pipe from his mouth and said, "Leaving the question of importance aside, I'm still curious."

Modesty eyed him pensively. "Well, so are we," she said with mild reproof. "We'd quite like to know more about The Watchmen, wouldn't we, Willie?"

He shrugged. "Can't see much point, Princess."

"Of course there isn't much point, but we mustn't go through life only doing things that have a point. It's bad for dilettantism, don't you agree, Colonel?"

They looked at him again with polite interest, awaiting his opinion. "Probably," said Golitsyn. He paused, making a swift appraisal and coming to a decision. Then: "I'm quite willing to tell you about The Watchmen."

She gave a little nod, pleased but not delighted. "All right. Then I'll tell you how we found you."

Golitsyn felt suddenly that he had gained control of the situation, and was glad. "So I have to trust you?" he said genially.

"Yes." She left it there, the flat affirmative.

"Very well. How much did Oberon tell you?"

"He spent most of his time in an ego-boosting exercise, so he only told us that you have your biggest operation on tomorrow night, and that you intend to put across the disinformation that we two are Watchmen who happen to get killed in the shooting. Since we all know there's a summit meeting on Porto Santo, we can guess the operation is connected with that."

"It is." Golitsyn's confidence had returned now. He could not recall having lost it, even briefly, for at least fifteen years. "We're going to kill the Heads of State and Prime Ministers," he said. "All of them."

"Not a bad idea." She turned her head to Willie. "What do you think?"

"Not bad," he agreed judicially. "But not easy."

For the first time Golitsyn was able to feel a touch of contempt. "Perhaps you don't quite appreciate," he said, "what can be achieved by a small group of well trained, well equipped and well led men. You must have grasped by now that The Watchmen are an instrument of my own country's government, but since you want to know more about them I'll tell you exactly how we plan to carry out Operation Morningstar."

"Morningstar as one word?" she inquired. "Meaning the medieval spiked mace?"

"So I understand from Major the Earl St Maur, who chose the name."

"It sounds interesting. Please go on."

He spoke for two minutes, very concisely, outlining the plan for the assault on Porto Santo, and was only slightly bothered by the occasional admiring nod or murmur of approval from his two listeners. When he finished and was re-lighting his pipe, Modesty Blaise said, "It's very nice indeed, Colonel. Much bigger than anything else The Watchmen have done for Free Armenia, and Quebec Liberation, and all the other phoney causes. But, please don't think me rude if I ask, where does it *get* you? Or rather what does it do for the GRU and the KGB and Mother Russia? For one thing it's going to be a bit suspicious if only western leaders get knocked off, and for another they'll be replaced immediately by their Vice Presidents and Deputy Prime Ministers or whatever."

Golitsyn grinned. "It's an exercise in misdirection," he said. "As soon as we've signalled success, two groups purporting to be Watchmen will assault and take over the Soviet Embassies in Bucharest and Belgrade." He waved a hand to clear the smoke wreathing his head. "They'll kill both our ambassadors and a few selected staff – we've established some expendable sacrificial goats there for the purpose. There will also be an unsuccessful attack on some of our beloved leaders in Moscow, so The Watchmen won't appear to be anti-west. But by sheer chance, the freedom-loving leaders of Mother Russia will be luckier than the equally freedom-loving leaders of the west."

Modesty said with an air of interest. "What about your embassies?"

"Ah. Well, they're really the whole point, Miss Blaise. We have a couple of native puppets in those countries ready to stand up and shout that destroying The Watchmen transcends the question of national boundaries. Then we, that is the USSR, will say that we can't expect those two countries to take a hard line with the terrorists when the lives of foreign embassy people, *our* people, are at stake, so we'll deal with the matter ourselves. No compromise. No negotiation. A parachute battalion dropped without warning on each capital at dawn to attack and destroy the terrorists. Within a week we shall have our local puppet in charge, and our own armour in the city — to help him keep the peace, of course."

"The Yugoslavs will fight," said Willie. "They're a tough people."

"Some will," agreed Golitsyn, "but we shall be rather unsympathetic with urban guerillas. It might take a while before we have the same kind of control we have in Poland and Czechoslovakia, but it will come. Once we're there we'll stay. We're long-term thinkers, you know."

Modesty said, "And you're banking on the notion that you'll have several weeks to get through phase one with no real decision-making in the west — in America particularly. By which time it's going to be too late for threats or countermoves to alter the situation?"

Golitsyn smiled at her. "Of course. And we have some influential opinion-makers in the west to guide matters our way. After what happens in Porto Santo tomorrow, it's going to be quite a while before the western world wakes up to the fact that the Warsaw Pact bloc has expanded to reach the Adriatic. But who's going to start a war about it then?"

He sucked his pipe for a moment, then said absently, "We'll have Greece in another two years. It's a nibbling process, you see, always concealed by what conjurers call misdirection. And the more we expand, the more the European countries are going to lose the will to resist." He cocked a humourous eye at Modesty. "Britain in eight years, but we'll do that from inside of course."

She lifted her head. "With Major the Earl St. Maur as our new Cromwell?"

"Naturally. I think he will make an excellent Lord Protector for you."

She stared at him, her head still lifted a little from the bed, and at last she said, "But he's extreme right wing. Why do your people want him in power?"

Golitsyn sighed and shook his head. "My dear young lady, if you haven't understood that the extreme left and the extreme right are one and the same thing, you have understood nothing of the power game. St. Maur is an authoritarian. A Big Brother. That's all we need. When national power is concentrated in one pair of hands it simplifies matters greatly, because then we have only one person to support or bring down — whichever suits us best."

After a brief silence Willie Garvin said, "Where do *you* end up, Colonel?"

Golitsyn shrugged. "If it all works, I believe I shall have overall control of both the KGB and GRU. That will be a unique position, and I want no other." The creases in his heavy face deepened in a smile. "I'm not a politician, Mr. Garvin. I'm a games player."

Modesty said, "And if it doesn't all work?"

He looked at her, still smiling. "Then I lose the game, Miss Blaise. As Rykov did. And now perhaps we could conclude our agreement by your telling me how you came to suspect that The Watchmen were located here."

Part of her mind had been left to work on this question while she listened to Golitsyn, and now she answered with neither haste nor hesitation. "Oh, that was fairly straightforward. Oberon put out a contract on Tarrant with the Polish twins. After Willie killed the twins —" she saw Golitsyn's eyes widen a little, but continued without pause, "we found Bernie Chan's address on one of them, so we worked out a scenario to get Bernie talking, and we were lucky. Apparently Bernie asked more than Oberon was authorised to pay for the Tarrant contract, and Oberon had to phone St. Maur for clearance. He gave Bernie's switchboard operator the number to get, and it was noted in her book."

Golitsyn said softly, "He gave the number?"

"Yes, otherwise we couldn't have got it from Bernie. Then we traced the number to the Earl St. Maur's country seat, thought he might be a likely candidate, and kept tabs on him till he led us first to Lisbon, then here."

And very nice too, thought Willie Garvin. The whole thing rang true because it *was* true — except for the tiny point about Oberon revealing the telephone number. That supposed lapse in security had shaken Golitsyn and would surely stir up trouble sooner or later. It didn't solve the present problems he and Modesty faced, but at least it was an arrow shot in the air in the direction of the enemy.

Golitsyn got to his feet and said, "I'm much obliged." His pipe had gone out and he put it in his pocket. Gun in hand he moved to the telephone, watching the prisoners, and spoke into it. "Call Dr. Djakovo in his cabin and say I want him to come to the hospital right away." He put the telephone down and said, "You'll be placed under sedation now."

Willie Garvin had distanced his emotions from his thought processes, and felt only a faint chill of alarm, a faraway blend of fear, anger and disappointment. With head turned he watched Modesty's hand. It lay against the bedframe, held there by a torn strip of sheet securing the wrist. If she kept her first two fingers stiff and straight, doubling the other two in at the knuckles, then he would instantly cast aside all mental restraints to let loose the strength that extreme fear, the ultimate fear of death, could unleash. He did not allow himself to doubt that he could break the ties holding his wrists to the bedframe, nor that he could get to Golitsyn in two seconds and kill him in three. He would almost certainly have been hit by at least one bullet by then, but perhaps not in a vital place. The Princess could wriggle free in four or five seconds, and they would then have Golitsyn's gun and any other item in the ward or surgery that might make a useful weapon. A scalpel or two, perhaps, as replacements for his throwing-knives.

It was not a hopeful scenario, but if Modesty decided that a thousand-to-one chance was the best they were likely to get, then . . .

He saw her fingers straighten, all four of them together. After a moment they separated, two and two. Negative action.

Willie maintained his mental posture. The door opened and Dr. Djakovo came in. Golitsyn said, "I want these two fully sedated from now until the expected completion of tomorrow's operation, but with no obvious indications of the treatment."

"They must not die before then, Colonel?"

"No."

"Then I will give a sufficient dosage of a long-acting hypnotic to ensure unconsciousness for eight hours, and renew that dosage one hour before earliest possible recovery."

Golitsyn did not waste a question asking if the doctor was sure this would be satisfactory. Djakovo knew his job, and he also knew the penalties of failure. Golitsyn moved to stand at the head of Modesty's bed, and held the gun within a few inches of her temple. "Go ahead," he said. "The woman first."

Djakovo disappeared into the surgery and returned a few seconds later with a hypodermic syringe, two needles in sealed packs, and a small, dark brown bottle. A bottle, she noted, not an ampoule. It was typical of the curious blend of ancient and modern in Russian medicine, like using leeches on Stalin when he was dying. Djakovo moved between Modesty and Willie, set the bottle down on the locker between the beds, broke open one of the sealed packs and fitted the needle to the syringe. He unscrewed the cap from the bottle, pierced the inner rubber seal with the needle, and drew a colourless liquid into the syringe.

Modesty had her head turned to watch him, and Golitsyn said, "Please don't resist, Miss Blaise. It will serve no purpose." She scarcely heard him, for the whole of her perception was focused on the bottle containing the hypnotic, encompassing it, knowing it, remembering it.

Djakovo took a pinch of flesh on the side of her thigh and slid the needle in, pressing the plunger. Golitsyn said dryly, "There's no need to change the needle, doctor. The possibility of cross infection won't be troubling them."

"Very well." Dr. Djakovo picked up the bottle again and drew a larger dose into the syringe. Golitsyn moved to the head of Willie's bed, holding the gun close to his temple, watching him warily. As Djakovo held the syringe up and cleared the needle of air, Willie saw a little knot of muscle appear suddenly on Modesty's thigh. It moved down like a mouse scuttling under the flesh, past the needle puncture, stopping, moving back, vanishing, appearing to one side and rippling swiftly down and back again, becoming snakelike, pulsing along the leg. Her eyes were closed in total concentration, and Willie saw a pale pink droplet appear on the thigh where the needle had gone in. Then came another, followed by a thin trickle as her muscles squeezed blood and liquid from the tiny aperture.

Willie found that he was talking, had been talking from the instant he realised what she was doing. ". . . so tell Oberon he can 'ave my knives, Colonel. It's not that I like 'im, you understand, but I know he fancies 'imself better at anything than anyone else, so he's bound to strap 'em on and try 'em out. That's if he ever gets back from Porto Santo. And the way I reckon 'im, he's more cocky than good, so when he goes for a quick draw he might do a bit of open 'eart surgery on 'imself. You can 'ave me boots, Colonel, and the major can 'ave me surgical truss . . ."

He felt the needle in his thigh and kept talking. Through half closed eyes he saw that she had ceased her muscular contractions around the area of the puncture and had moved her leg slightly to hide the small damp patch. Impossible for her to have expelled more than part of the dosage, he knew, but if she had got rid of as much as a quarter of it . . . if she recovered in six hours instead of the expected eight . . .

Willie felt himself going. He had made no attempt to do as she had done. Both men were watching him, and even if they had not been he lacked Modesty's extraordinary ability in muscle control. Each had skills to which the other could not aspire, and this was one of hers. Whether it would suffice to offer them a fighting chance was impossible to judge. If it did, then the task of seizing that chance would be up to her alone, for he could be no more than a burden to her for a full eight hours.

So there it was. The question of whether they were to live or to die rested with Modesty now. A sense of contentment touched him, and his last thought before darkness came upon him was to be thankful that the issue lay where it did.

Fifteen

THE night exercise ended soon after two in the morning. It had gone well. Von Krankin was pleased, St. Maur satisfied. As the men returned to their shore-base huts to clean and check their equipment before settling down to sleep, Golitsyn said, "Can you spare one good man to guard the prisoners from noon onwards tomorrow, Major?" He wore a topcoat and stood not far from the jetty, hunched a little against the chill night wind.

St. Maur said with vague irritation. "You've changed your mind, Colonel. I understood you to say you preferred drugs to guards."

"I do. But I am in a belt and braces mood at this stage." Golitsyn lifted a hand to forestall argument. "I know the prisoners are unconscious and will remain so, and I know I can use auxiliary personnel as guards, but I want one top-class man for the final hours, if you please."

St. Maur shrugged. "Inside the ward with them?"

"No." Golitsyn paused, trying to clarify his motives for himself. "The hospital area has no windows or ports. The only access door is at the end of a short passage. It has a bolt on the inside. I will have the bolt removed and screwed on the outside. With the door locked and bolted, and your man stationed at the point where the passage turns, no attempt to break out can succeed."

Von Krankin said, "Break out? When they are under heavy sedation?"

Golitsyn smiled in the darkness. It was not an easy smile. Ever since his brief exchange with Blaise and Garvin he had felt a curious sense of disquiet such as he had never known before. "Humour a foolish old Russian colonel, Siegfried," he said patiently. "All your people will be well rested by noon. Give me a man from then on, and I'll make do with auxiliaries until he takes over."

"It is a decision for the major," said von Krankin, a touch of stiffness in his manner.

Unexpectedly St. Maur said, "By all means. I've no time for hunches myself, but I'm damned if I want you feeling unnecessarily nervous, Colonel. Our chaps can scent that sort of thing, and it wouldn't be good for morale. You can have Szabo for the job until his section is called for embarkation. They're the last. All right?"

"Szabo will do very well, thank you, Major. Goodnight."

Golitsyn turned to the jetty, where the dory waited to take him to the drillship. The other two watched him go. After a few moments St. Maur said, "Bloody man's got the jitters. Can't have him twitching about all over the place during the run-up."

"Agreed," said von Krankin. "It was right to give him Szabo, even though the idea is pointless in all other respects. It is my opinion that this Blaise and Garvin pair have been much over-rated."

Major the Earl St. Maur looked at the illuminated dial of his watch and yawned. "Perhaps. But it's of no consequence anyway now," he said indifferently. "They're doped up to the eyebrows, and Djakovo will keep them that way till Oberon kills them tonight."

   * * * * *

Awareness of danger came to Willie Garvin with the first ghostly tendrils of returning consciousness. He lay still, breathing slowly, deeply, letting memory return, feeling the ties that held his arms to the side of the bed, listening.

There was the faint sound of the sea, the slight movement of the drillship, and the nearer sound of Modesty's breathing from the bed beside him. Nothing else. After a little while he allowed his eyelids to open no more than a fraction. One light in the ward was on, the other two off. There was nothing to indicate time of day or night. His internal clock, usually reliable, suggested that day had broken.

She must have been watching for the slightest movement of his eyelids, for now he heard her voice, a whisper. "It's all right, Willie. Nobody here but us."

He opened his eyes and turned his head. She lay looking at him, a touch of relief in her dark blue eyes as she gave him a brief smile and said, "It's within a few minutes of nine in the morning, and there's nothing we have to do for a while yet, so take your time."

He gave a small nod and lay relaxed, feeling a touch of nausea from the narcotic but untroubled by it, marvelling as he looked at her. It wasn't bad, he thought. Nine hours ago they'd both been drugged to await death. But she'd come up with a counter-stroke the ungodly had never dreamt of, and followed it up in a way he hadn't yet figured himself. He should still have been unconscious from a second injection, but they were both alive now, and awake, and although they were still prisoners their chances had moved from a big zero to something like evens.

He said in a whisper, "What 'appened?"

"I got rid of some of the dope by muscular contractions while they were injecting you, and woke about five." She paused, listening, then went on. "Wriggled out of these arm ties and had a look round the surgery. Found that bottle of dope, worked the rubber cap off and emptied the stuff down the sink. Refilled the bottle with distilled water and fixed the rubber cap back on again. Took time, because I was a bit muzzy. Didn't dare hurry, but sweating cobs in case someone came in. No trouble, though. I got back on the bed and worked my arms under the ties again. Nobody came till just on seven. Then it was Djakovo with a guard, to give us our next injection."

Of distilled water. So that was how she had worked it. A glow of pleasure touched Willie as he relished the simplicity of it. He mouthed, "Now what? Weapons?"

"No. Our clothes and weapons not here." She turned her head to look towards the door. "See the vent in the door?"

He twisted his head and saw the metal circle set in the door, a vent with six thin petal-shaped apertures which could be opened or closed by moving a steel disc. She said, "I've taken a look through it. The door's locked and there's a man with an s.m.g.

The Night of Morningstar

sitting ten paces away at the turn of the passage. What's more, they've unscrewed the bolt on the inside, and I wouldn't be surprised if it's on the outside now."

Willie considered what she had told him. They could surely find something among the surgical instruments to improvise a lockpick for the door, and a scalpel would do duty for a throwing knife to deal with the guard. But with the door bolted outside, several seconds would be needed for a breakout, and the submachine-gun would cut him to pieces long before he could get in a throw. He looked at Modesty and lifted an eyebrow.

"We wait," she breathed. "If they're going to leave us for dead on Porto Santo, they'll have to dress us first, and they're almost certain to use our own clothes, plus the face-mask hoods they wear and our own weapons. Wouldn't look right if we were found unarmed. Golitsyn said the mother ship would come in at dusk for the task force to embark. That's the most likely time for them to give us a final jab and get us dressed for the job."

Willie nodded. And that was when their best chance of a breakout would come. She whispered, "Next jab due around one o'clock. We'll put ourselves into a light coma before they come, Willie, so we look right."

"Sure, Princess." He was silent for a while, then: "If the bloke along the passage with the s.m.g. is still there when we take out the blokes who come to dress us . . ." There was no need to complete the question.

She said, "I know. He's only got to get a single shot off, and we'll have the whole ship gunning for us. Try to figure how we might work a quiet breakout, Willie. It's not just getting ourselves away. We have to stop Operation Morningstar, and a quiet breakout is our only hope for that."

Twenty minutes later he whispered, "All right for me to 'ave a look round?"

Her bare shoulders moved in a small shrug, and she began to wriggle her arms from under the ties holding them. "It's a risk, but what isn't? I'll watch the door. The vent's slightly open, and with the overhead light in the passage he can't see my eye there. I'll hiss for a warning — it could pass for a ship noise if it's heard."

Willie worked his arms free, checked that he could slip them back under the ties in four seconds, then stood up, moved across the ward, and began to prowl slowly through the surgery and operating theatre, quietly opening drawers and cupboards, studying shelves, registering all he saw in the photographic memory that was his gift. There were instruments in plenty. He tested the balance of a scalpel. A little light for deep penetration, but at only thirty feet it would do well enough. A pity, he thought ruefully, that there was no way of making a throw through one of the small vent apertures. That might have solved a major problem.

After five minutes he moved back into the ward, settled himself on the bed in his bonds, and gave a soft hiss to draw Modesty's attention. She turned from the door, passed quickly across the surgery on bare feet, and was lying on her bed in the secured position in just under five seconds. Her head turned towards him and she whispered, "Anything, Willie?"

"Not yet, but I know what we've got available now. I'll sleep on it."

"All right, so will I. Let's go."

He closed his eyes and rolled them upwards, then gently moved the focus of his mind through every part of his body to relax muscle, sinew and tissue. When the body was quiet he called up in his mind's eye the image of a small round black stone. This was the token upon which he had meditated for many days in the desert under the guidance of Sivaji. He had never seen it since, and it was just a stone, but he would have recognised it among a million by its essence. In the ear of his mind he heard the rhythmic syllables of the word he had been given, and in a very little while both the image and the sound faded as he slept.

A degree of awareness remained, as if some part of his being had moved away from his body to remain watchful. It did not hover in space or have any three-dimensional location, neither was this awareness visual. He had achieved that condition only once, after some days of mental preparation. Modesty had achieved it several times, and had once extended that visual awareness beyond the bounds of the room in which she lay, a power Sivaji could exercise at will. But despite two or three further attempts, she had never achieved it again. "I guess I'm just not pure enough, Willie love," she had said with amusement later. "But I prefer to be that way."

✻   ✻   ✻   ✻   ✻

During the morning Dr. Djakovo spent half an hour in the surgery at his desk, tidying up his medical records, and another ten minutes later cleaning and stitching the hand of a kitchen auxiliary who had cut himself. On both occasions he made a cursory examination of the two captives. Their pulses were slow, their breathing slow, their pupils large. It was hardly likely to occur to Dr. Djakovo that the symptoms of drugged sleep might be closely imitated by those of self-induced trance.

At one o'clock he returned to give a further injection. This time Colonel Golitsyn and the Earl St. Maur were with him. "Sedation satisfactory, doctor?" said St. Maur.

Djakovo withdrew the needle from Modesty's thigh and pushed it through the rubber seal of the bottle again. "Completely," he said. "There was never any question about it."

"Good." The major glanced at Golitsyn. "Make you feel happier, Colonel?"

The Russian nodded. His brief faltering of confidence had passed now, and he regretted having let it show. "We should all be happy to have these two safely immobilised," he said. "You know Garvin killed the Polish twins?"

"Did he, by God?" For once the earl was impressed. "That's really rather good. Damn shame we couldn't recruit him, but there you are."

Golitsyn said, "When do you want them dressed ready to be carried on to the mother ship?"

"I'll send a couple of Szabo's chaps along just before departure. Allow fifteen minutes to get them dressed — tricky with limp bodies. I'd be obliged if you'd have their clothes here ready for dressing by nineteen hundred hours."

"I'll see to it, Major. Presumably they must also be equipped with the weapons they were carrying?"

"Yes, but just Garvin's knives and her gun. Oh, and that kongo thing she uses. Forget the lockpicks and other gadgets. They wouldn't be carrying those on an operation like Morningstar."

"Very well."

Dr. Djakovo set down the hypodermic and bottle on the locker. "Is there anything else, comrades?" he inquired.

Golitsyn shook his head. St. Maur said coldly, "Don't call me comrade, you bloody man." Golitsyn chuckled and moved towards the door. He felt himself again now, but he did not intend to suggest that Szabo might be taken off guard duty in the passage. That would only point up his earlier needless anxiety.

"Remember to check the shore-base first aid facilities, doctor," he said. "Minor casualties will be dealt with there."

"I have arranged to do so this afternoon, Colonel."

A few moments later there came the click of a key turning in the lock, and the snick of a bolt being pushed home. From their remote elsewhere/nowhere, Modesty Blaise and Willie Garvin registered the departure and the significant sounds, and slept on.

At six o'clock the doctor returned and gave the final injection. This time Szabo accompanied him, gazing down at Modesty's body with a blend of hate and lust. As they were about to leave an auxiliary came in carrying the clothes, boots and weapons Modesty and Willie had been wearing. He put them down on one of the empty beds, and the three men went out. Szabo locked and bolted the door behind him.

Two minutes later Modesty said softly, "Willie." Thirty seconds passed while he roused himself quietly to normal consciousness. As he opened his eyes she whispered, "They've brought our clothes and weapons back well ahead of time. With any luck we'll have a clear hour before they come to dress us. If we have to we'll just go for broke with a bust-out, but I don't much fancy our chances of fighting our way off the ship. And if we go down, they can run Morningstar. I'd be a lot happier if we could work something soft-shoe style."

Willie slowly closed one eye. "I've 'ad a little idea about that bloke guarding the passage," he said.

They slipped their arms from the strips of torn sheet and pulled on trousers and boots. Willie strapped on his twin knives in the light leather harness so that they lay in echelon on his left breast. Modesty checked the Star .45 automatic and slipped it into the semi-shoulder holster Willie had designed and made for her. They put on their black button-through shirts, and when Willie disappeared into the surgery she moved to the door to keep watch, wondering what he had in mind, but wasting no time in questions. Standing with her eye close to one of the small apertures in the vent, she saw that the man on guard at the end of the passage was now Szabo. He faced the door, his chair tilted back against the bulkhead behind him, both hands holding the submachine-gun across his knees. She could not see whether it was cocked, but knew that it would be.

In the surgery Willie forced sideways one of the spherical brackets holding a towel rail, a slender tube four feet long of rigid black plastic. He removed the tube, laid it on a bench, and began to assemble the surgical and dental instruments he could use as tools. For the next twenty minutes he was lost in concentration as he drew the plunger out of a disposable hypodermic and with infinite care began to trim the disc on the end, constantly checking it against the bore of the long tube. When he was satisfied he cut two very narrow triangles of plastic from the lid of a small container and slit each so that they could be fitted together at right angles to each other. He cut a five inch length of stiff wire from the guard of an electric fan, and shaped one end to a chisel edge with dental cutters.

Using a surgical needle he made a hole a half inch deep in the centre of the plunger's face, and forced the blunt end of his sharpened piece of wire fully into the hole. Finally, using a dental fretsaw, he made two lengthwise cuts in the stem of the plunger to receive his slender plastic vanes.

Modesty turned her head as he came up behind her. In one hand he held the long black tube, on the palm of the other was a flighted dart with a steel shaft four and a half inches long and almost a sixteenth of an inch thick. She looked from his hands to his face in smiling acknowledgment, and reached out to rest her fingers briefly against his cheek.

It was almost a year ago now that they had been wandering round a fête in the village near her cottage in Wiltshire, and had come upon a stall where there were prizes for hitting a target with a toy blow-pipe, a half inch tube some three feet long. The darts were of plastic, with thin flights and a rubber suction cup instead of a point. Willie had been intrigued by the accuracy he found possible in what seemed such a clumsy projector of missiles.

Two weeks later, when Modesty visited him at The Treadmill, he took her to his workshop at the end of the long combat room to show her a thin brass tube with a nicely turned wooden mouthpiece and a dart made from steel wire with a bead heat-sealed on one end of it. The bead fitted exactly the bore of the tube. In the combat room, using one of his knife targets, he demonstrated not only the accuracy of the weapon, which he found quite remarkable, but also the even more surprising power of it.

In seven seconds he put three darts in a four inch circle at thirty feet. One was of unsharpened wire and penetrated the deal target to a depth of more than half an inch. The two with needle-points penetrated almost one inch.

"I'm narked because I can't figure it out, Princess," he said with a baffled air as he lowered the brass tube. "There's no sight on the thing, so you just aim by instinct, but it works miles better than you'd reckon possible, and you don't even need a flight, just the bead. Then there's the penetration. I 'ung up a joint of beef and put one right up to the bead in it at this range. I've been trying to figure how you can measure the ratio of lung power to velocity, but it's a bit tricky. Maybe pygmies use poison darts because they've got little lungs, but this thing's a killer at up to fifty feet without poison, if you're accurate."

She examined the tube and the darts. Weaponry was one of Willie's subjects, but her own interest was considerable. She would have been dead long since if it had not been so. "May I try it, Willie?"

"Sure."

"You say the aim is instinctive, but so it is when you throw one of your knives, or anything else for that matter. You're in a class of your own there. But I've no talent for throwing, so maybe I won't be accurate with this."

"Maybe. Let's give it a try."

Within ten minutes, and much to her surprise, it was clearly established that where Willie could group the darts in a four-inch circle, she could group them in a circle half that diameter. Over the following weeks and months, when they practised their combat skills both armed and unarmed, they invariably spent some time in rather light-hearted competition with the blowpipe, and her accuracy increased.

Now, in the ward on the lower deck of the drillship, she looked at the tube and the dart again, then at the slim, petal shaped apertures of the vent in the door. Willie said in a whisper, "The tube's thin enough to slip through. Couldn't improvise a bead, but I fixed flights on the dart to stop any wobble and I chamfered the face of the plunger a bit to make it more aerodynamic. Reckon you can manage without a mouthpiece?"

She nodded. That was no problem. The only question was whether the dart would fly true. She took the tube and dart from him, and moved away from the door to one end of the ward. Willie walked quietly to the far end, lifted a dark grey mattress from the nearest bed, and stood it against the wall. With a red fibre-tipped pen from Djakovo's desk he marked a two-inch circle and put a quarter-inch dot in the middle.

She slipped the dart into the tube, raised the end to her lips, holding it with both hands, filled her lungs, and almost at once exhaled with a sharp, fierce puff. There came the soft impact of the dart hitting the mattress, burying itself until only the plastic flights were showing, white against grey, and less than half an inch from the red spot in the middle of the circle.

Willie eased the dart from the mattress and came towards her, a sparkle in his eyes. "Lovely," he whispered and put the dart in her hand. "I made a probe of the same wire." He held up a few inches of wire with a very short portion at one end bent to form two opposed right angles.

She nodded. "Go ahead."

He moved to kneel by the door. It took him forty seconds to

locate and lift the wards of the simple lock, and as he worked he registered that for the past half hour, while he had been concentrating on other things, there had been sounds of increasing activity above. No doubt The Watchmen had been ferried from their shore base to the drillship and were now loading the mother ship that would carry them with their canoes and equipment to within easy reach of Porto Santo.

As he straightened up Modesty whispered, "I'll need more height to get the right angle. On your back, I think."

"Right."

She handed him the tube. He turned his back and she mounted him. He passed the tube up to her, then locked his forearms under her thighs and moved to stand a long pace from the door. She inserted the dart and reached forward to rest the tip of the blowpipe in the lowest aperture of the vent, ducking her head to sight on Szabo through the eliptical aperture immediately above. He was in the same position as before, semi-reclining on the tilted chair, the Sterling submachine-gun held ready across his knees.

"Down a little," she breathed. Willie spread his feet. "Hold it there. Now edge forward."

She could see that Szabo was looking towards the door, but unless he focused on the vent he would be unlikely to notice the small circle that was all his foreshortened view of the tube would allow. She moistened her lips and set them to the end of the pipe, maintaining her sighting on Szabo, taking the slight weight of the pipe on her forward hand to prevent it squeaking as a foot or more of it slid slowly through the vent. She squeezed hard with her legs, and Willie stopped. The positon was good. Because of Szabo's posture the dart would strike at a slight upward angle and be unlikely to suffer deflection from a rib. As she drew breath, Szabo's chin lifted and he stared directly at the vent. She blew with a sudden explosive emptying of her lungs.

Szabo had just registered that something was happening at the vent when he heard a brief soft sound, and in the same instant felt a minor but bewildering blow, as if an invisible fist had punched him sharply in the chest. He looked down and saw something white and slender protruding from his shirt just below the third button. Pieces of . . . of plastic? Set in . . . something . . ?

He tried to lift his head, but could not find the strength. Within him he felt a curious draining sensation. He did not know that the right ventricle of his heart had been torn open by the chisel edge of a steel dart, but the beginnings of fear and panic were starting to rise up in him when vision faded, then consciousness, and he died without another movement, slumped on his chair in the corner, the gun still held across his knees.

In the ward, Modesty tapped Willie's shoulder, slipped down from his back, and said quietly, "That was Szabo, the one who killed Ben Christie."

Willie nodded, relieved at her use of the past tense, thankful for her icy control. With only one shot, win or lose, she had shown no more tension than if she had been at target practice. Later, much later, if they survived, she might shiver a little from delayed reaction, but her control while action lasted would be total.

He gripped the door handle and pulled hard, noting the point of main resistance which indicated where the bolt must lie on the outside, then marked the place with a wet thumb and moved back along the ward. Modesty stood by the door, automatic in her hand now, and said quietly, "When you're ready, Willie." He focused his entire being on the action required, pre-setting in nerve and muscle the essential timing and co-ordination. The moment came, and he ran five long strides before jumping high, turning, smashing one heel in a sledge-hammer blow against the door panel a few inches from the mark he had made, then landing crouched on his other leg, and spinning away so that she could instantly get to the six-inch hole in the splintered panel and cover the passage.

There had inevitably been noise, but it had been short, sharp, and once only. After ten seconds Modesty slid an arm through the hole, found the bolt, and drew it. Willie had a knife in his hand as she opened the door. They listened, then moved along the passage. She detached the Sterling from Szabo's hands and passed it to Willie. Beyond the corner where the dead man sat, another passage ran between cabins to some stairs leading up. They were half way along it when a man came quickly down the stairs.

Willie's knife took him in the throat from nine paces. He staggered, half turned, then crumpled to the deck.

They ran forward. Modesty said, "Get him out of sight," and opened a cabin door at random. Willie took the dead man by the shoulders and dragged him inside. A small lamp beside the bunk had been left on. In its light they could see that the cabin had an adjoining shower room. Modesty pointed. Willie hauled the man into the shower room, propped him in a corner, pulled the knife free, wiped and re-sheathed it, then came out and closed the door.

Modesty was at the window, peering between the curtains. She whispered, "This is a better way out for us, Willie. It gives on to a kind of promenade deck. From there we can move aft and climb up to see what's happening on the upper deck."

"Sounds a good bet, Princess."

She began to slide the window open, her mind racing ahead. Golitsyn had spoken of one section of The Watchmen using limpet mines to sink the motor torpedo boats guarding Porto Santo. If those mines could be located, she and Willie just might contrive to blow a hole in the mother ship. It was a slender hope. Dusk had come, and loading of weapons and equipment for Operation Morningstar had been going on for some time now. To find the limpet mines without being seen, to prime one, set the timer, and get it stuck to a vulnerable part of the hull was to hope for something like a miracle.

Willie said, "Princess . . ."

There was an odd note in his voice. She turned, vaguely aware that he had been prowling the cabin while she stood at the window. He was holding something in his hands, a long stick, tapering at the ends, with a string twisted loosely round it. A fraction of a second later she recognised it as a long-bow, a centre-shot bow made of fibre-glass reinforced resin sheets, five and a half feet long, with a linen bowstring, but unstrung at this moment.

Willie said, "It was in the cupboard, with a dozen hunting arrows in a quiver. I think we're in the noble earl's cabin."

"St. Maur?" A memory came to her. "Yes, that's right, he's an archer. I've seen newspaper pictures of him, with send-up captions."

"Any use?" She was good with a long-bow. This one, he thought, would have a weight of over 30 pounds. A man's pull, and heavy for a woman, but she was very strong, especially in the way that she could focus her energies to produce a sudden concentration of power.

She took the bow, eyeing it thoughtfully as she weighed it, assessing its balance. "Not too convenient for carrying around, but it might just be worth the trouble. Let's have the quiver, Willie."

*   *   *   *   *

Major the Earl St. Maur stood by the rail of the mother ship, checking the men as they began to come aboard by sections. All equipment had now been loaded. The canoes were ranged along the deck, ready for lowering. Radio communication had been tested, weapons checked and watches synchronised. There had been no final briefing, for none was necessary.

Von Krankin was on the deck of the drillship, where he had been supervising the movement of weaponry and equipment from the larger to the smaller ship. There were fewer deck-lights on than usual, and these were so screened as to leave the mother ship in darkness against the remote chance that a fishing boat from Madeira might pass within visual range.

St. Maur called in his sharp nasal voice. "Thirty minutes to departure. We'll get the last three sections aboard, Siegfried, then I'll come over and get kitted out myself while Blaise and Garvin are being brought up."

"Very well, Major."

Sixty yards away Modesty Blaise stood in the deep shadow between the base of an auxiliary pedestal crane and the raised helicopter pad. It was a point from which she could watch the process of embarkation. Willie had been gone ten minutes now. The bow was strung and she held an arrow ready to nock on the string. Szabo's submachine-gun lay at her feet.

St. Maur's words had reached her clearly, and she regretted he was so placed that she could not get a shot at him without moving from cover. If she and Willie were reduced to action of last resort, the most damaging blow to the success of Morningstar would be to kill St. Maur, but she doubted that anything they might do with what weapons they now possessed would suffice to stop the operation. The single magazine of the submachine-gun would not last long, and once shooting started The Watchmen's fire-power would be overwhelming.

She heard no sound of approach, but Willie's voice behind her breathed, "No luck, Princess. They must've taken the limpet mines aboard earlier. I got to the loading area, but it was mostly empty crates and containers. I 'ad to knock off a bloke who came to fetch a box while I was there, one of the frogmen it was. Couldn't find any small arms, bazookas or grenades, just a bit of machine gun ammo that won't fit the Sterling, a few assorted detonators, and the box this frogman was fetching, with about thirty one-pound packets of RDX."

She sensed his frustration. RDX was a very powerful plastic explosive. Given time and free access to the mother ship, Willie could have wrought havoc with it, but these two vital elements were denied him. She whispered, "Any way you can make good use of it?"

"There's a guard boat aft," he said, "so we can't get at the screw or the rudder. Can't make a bomb out of the 'ole lot to do any damage from outside. I can try getting to the mother ship's engine room with it. Wreck that, or the steering gear, and we stop Morningstar."

Possibly. But Willie Garvin would be dead. She had already given thought to the idea of getting aboard the mother ship, and rejected it. The deck of the smaller ship lay much lower than the drillship deck. Thick fenders hung between them, and a single broad gangway ran down the drillship's side from a break in the rail. She said softly, "No chance, Willie. Not even if I start a diversion. And in a few minutes St. Maur's going to find Szabo dead and us gone, or somebody else is going to find a missing frogman, so we haven't much longer to work under cover. But I've had a thought. Remember when Jock Miller came down to spend a few days at The Treadmill last year? He'd been doing some contract work for one of the North Sea oil companies operating from Aberdeen, and he told us that weird story."

After ten seconds of silence Willie Garvin said, "And we know they struck gas 'ere only a few days ago."

"Yes. Do you think we could manage something on those lines?"

She heard a ghostly chuckle from him. "Princess, you're lovely," he whispered.

"It's going to be hellish difficult."

"Could be worse. I know where there's a dead frogman stuffed in a crate with all 'is gear. That's going to 'elp a lot. I just 'ope things work the way Jock said."

"If they don't we've lost nothing. I'll start using the bow in five minutes, or before if somebody raises the alarm, and I'll carry on with the s.m.g. Whichever way it goes, when you've done the job rendezvous with me two hundred yards out on a direct line between here and the southern end of Deserta Grande. The southern end, not the shore base. If the idea hasn't worked, we'll swim for where we left the yacht hidden. Say an hour for that. Get on the radio and call Weng. He's not due on listening out schedule till half an hour or so later, but he might start early. If we get through, Weng can phone Fraser, who can get an emergency call to Tarrant. It's a two hour run to Porto Santo for the mother ship, so if we can only delay things here for an hour maybe the message will get through in time."

"Right."

"And Willie . . . don't wait more than five minutes for me at the rendezvous area. I might be busy. After that time, start swimming."

"Right."

He was gone. She watched as men dressed in the battle order of The Watchmen were marshalled in sections to make their way down the gangway from the drillship. Briefly she wondered how Willie proposed to work the mechanics of the task she had set him, but then put the question from her mind and concentrated on trying to pick out Golitsyn or Oberon from the figures moving about between the base of the towering derrick that rose amidships and the break in the rail at the top of the gangway.

She could see the man St. Maur had addressed as Siegfried when she and Willie had first been taken aboard the drillship. He was certainly one of the key men in Morningstar. If she could put four or five such men out of action — St. Maur, Oberon, Golitsyn, and anyone who appeared to be a section leader, then the feasibility of the operation might be destroyed.

Almost five minutes had passed when she saw a man come running from a companionway, calling out as he made for the one called Siegfried. She took up her stance, drew the bow, and loosed. The figure of Siegfried tottered a pace sideways and fell to the deck. All movement froze, and there was silence. She put her next arrow into the man who had run from below, to silence him, then nocked another on the string and waited.

It was a beautiful bow, and the arrows were perfectly matched to it, with good stiff spines to give better cast and accuracy. The Watchmen, professionals all, had scattered from the area by the gangway, seeking cover. The two men who had fallen did not stir. St. Maur's voice came from the mother ship, hard and penetrating: "What's the delay up there?"

Several men started to answer, but were silenced by an authoritative shout. A lone voice continued in accented English: "Bad trouble, Major! Somebody shooting arrows. Long-bow arrows. Captain von Krankin and one man down. Probably dead."

For two seconds there was silence, then St. Maur's voice came again, cold and precise. "Blaise and Garvin must have broken out. Douse those decklights. Douse *all* lights."

She gave a grim nod of acknowledgment. St. Maur was devoid of nerves, and thought fast. She had hoped to see him come racing up the gangway into view, so that she could pick him off, but he had foreseen that. The men on the drillship had not been able to detect the direction from which the arrows had come, and several were still in sight, crouched against a bulkhead or a corner of the derrick base. She was able to loose three more arrows, hitting two men for certain, before the lights went out.

She looped the sling of the submachine-gun over one shoulder and moved to the rail, nocking an arrow on the string, hoping to get sight of St. Maur on the deck below, but there too all lights had been put out. The silence now was eerie, and she guessed that The Watchmen had switched to using their earplug and throat-mike intercoms.

As her eyes adjusted to the darkness she picked out the long slope of the gangway. St. Maur would be sending some men back on to the drillship to deal with her — *no*! Shock touched her as she realised that men were moving *down* the gangway still, and in the same instant understanding came. St. Maur's prime aim was to get the mother ship loaded and away so that Operation Morningstar could begin. Two enemies loose on the drillship were not to be allowed to divert him from that. They could be dealt with later by the skeleton crew and reserves remaining aboard.

She leaned out over the rail. Aiming was awkward but the range was short, and she put an arrow into a man near the top of the gangway, who fell causing confusion among the men immediately below him. As she loosed another arrow a strong beam of light sprang from the foredeck of the mother ship and swept along the rail, picking her out before she could duck into cover. She threw herself back, dropping to the deck as two submachine-guns chattered and bullets whined above her head, some hitting the rail and becoming ricochets.

The light swept back and forth, then was joined by another, making the rail a death trap. She left the bow and quiver where they had fallen, ran across the deck bent almost double, climbed the ladder to the empty helicopter pad, and ran back to the starboard side again. She was above the traversing beams of light now. Lying prone on the edge of the pad, she had sight of the gangway and the mother ship deck where the men were moving aboard. She switched the change lever on the Sterling to the single shot position and fired twice. Two men fell from the gangway, but before she drew back she gained the impression that these two had been the last.

The lights ranged back and forth, up and down, but she was lying out of sight now. After waiting a few seconds she wriggled forward again, peering over the edge of the pad, catching her lower lip in her teeth as she realised that the bow of the mother ship had started to swing out a little. The forward line had been cast off and the ship was about to sail. In the darkness it was impossible to discern any detail on the deck below, but even if the men had taken cover their canoes would surely be lying on the deck in readiness for launching, and if she could spray some or any of them with the remaining thirty-two bullets in the magazine . . .

She switched the lever to automatic fire and propped herself on her elbows. Even as she did so there came a burst of fire from the foredeck of the smaller ship. No light had touched her, but perhaps a man had caught the glint of her gun at the edge of the pad. However it had come about, his aim was good. Several bullets caught the edge of the pad to her right, and as she jerked back two more hit the Sterling's barrel sleeve, tearing the gun from her grasp with a hammerblow effect that left her hands numb, the right palm bleeding, the gun unusable.

She rolled away from the edge and scrambled across the pad, angry, her mouth bitter with the taste of defeat, working her fingers to get feeling back into her hand so that she could draw the .45 automatic in the holster under her shirt. There was silence again now, except for the soft shuffle of feet moving on the drillship deck immediately below, a voice calling a whispered order, a clink of metal as a gun muzzle touched some steel part of the superstructure. The men left aboard the drillship were hunting her now.

Then came a new sound, not loud, not threatening, a gurgling, bubbling sound that seemed to be spreading out all around the two ships, as if a horde of jolly Disney whales were gargling together. Lying on her back, still trying to make her hand grip the gun butt, she froze. Her stomach registered a faint sensation as of the deck beneath her moving down, slowly but positively, like a well regulated lift, although she knew the helicopter pad was a fixed structure. Far above her, the red light on the derrick moved to port, moved further than could be accounted for by any natural swell, and kept moving. She felt the pad tilting beneath her back, still sinking down, and instinctively reached out a hand to grip the edge of it, catching her breath as she saw the derrick light swing steadily across the sky.

There were shouts of alarm from the deck below, from forward on the drillship, and from the smaller ship alongside as discipline gave way under the menace of disaster. The whole rig was both foundering and turning over. Exhilaration swept her, sparkling through her veins. The unique Willie Garvin had been at work, and to mighty purpose. "Jesus . . ." she whispered with awe to the red light far above her, heeling more swiftly now. "That's my boy."

She rolled over quickly, gripping the edge of the pad as the tilt increased under the ever growing leverage of the two hundred foot derrick, then drew herself up and over the edge to crouch on one of the broad supporting stanchions that rose from the deck below. From the corner of her eye she saw to her right the upper half of the great derrick breaking away as it reached a thirty degree angle, to crash down on the afterdeck of the mother ship with a monstrous shrieking of torn metal.

Arms spread for balance, she ran down the stanchion, jumped to catch the rail, and hauled herself over it on to the ship's side which now sloped gently down to the sea. Glancing back, she saw the barely visible shapes of men and debris sliding helplessly from the deck. There were screams from the darkness, and an involuntary burst of fire from a man directly behind and below her as his sliding fall was stopped by the far rail, at sea level now. From everywhere came the noise of objects large and small breaking loose and falling.

She ran down the ship's side to the edge of the water and threw herself forward in a long flat dive, swimming hard. From thirty yards away she glanced back to see the drillship on its beam ends, no longer turning, but sinking steadily, and in the surrounding darkness all was chaos, with the sound of rending timber and steel, and the desperate cries of men. Swimming was a great effort, for the sea has been made gaseous by an infinity of tiny bubbles which had reduced its buoyancy, and she found it a struggle to keep her head above water, but when she drew farther from the ship the difficulty eased as the effervescence decreased. From a hundred yards away she floated on her back and got rid of her boots, watching the dark bulk of the two ships flatten out and vanish as they sank beneath the surface.

The Star .45 was still in its holster and she decided against jettisoning it. The thirty-four ounce weight was not too onerous, and certainly there would be a number of Watchmen afloat, either swimming or clinging to lifebelts or Carley floats. She turned to face west, away from the area where the ships had sunk. A long swell lifted her, and she saw against the dark sky the still darker silhouette of Deserta Grande, with a small prickling of lights showing the shore base. Using a steady breast stroke so that she could keep watch as she swam, she set off for the rendezvous area arranged with Willie Garvin.

At a point some two hundred yards from where the ships had been she rested, treading water, using the lift of each passing swell to scan the surrounding sea for signs of Willie. Once she heard faintly two men calling to each other somewhere north of where she waited, and once, surprisingly, she heard the sound of an engine and saw the phosphorescent wake of a small boat curving towards the shore base. Somebody had been lucky enough to find a runabout floating free. Apart from these two sounds of life she heard nothing but soft noises of sea and wind.

After five minutes she found it hard to hold down her anxiety, and after ten she began to swim slowly back towards the area of floating debris, giving a brief three-note whistle in a minor key every few seconds, a long established recognition signal.

*   *   *   *   *

Golitsyn clung to a life jacket. He had not yet gathered himself sufficiently to put it on. A few bits of flotsam drifted about within the thirty yard range of vision that the darkness allowed. He kept trying to think, to decide on some positive action, but could not make his mind work. Vague images floated in his head.

A man had come running to say something about Szabo being dead . . . then von Krankin and the man had both been killed . . . by arrows. There had been some small arms fire, and then . . . then the drillship had quietly sunk beneath their feet. Sunk. It was impossible.

He heard a noise and looked about him. A figure was swimming towards him, gasping, distressed. The man reached him and clutched at the life jacket. It was one of The Watchmen from

Dachtera's section, but Golitsyn could not recall his name. With the diminished buoyancy of the water, the life jacket began to sink under their combined weight, and in panic Golitsyn thrust at the other's face, trying to push him away. The man let go with one hand. A moment later the same hand emerged from the water holding a knife with a seven-inch spearpoint blade. With a swing of his arm he drove it almost to the hilt in the side of Golitsyn's neck.

The Russian's body drifted away, the knife still in him, and the man clutched the life jacket to his chest, trying to think what he should do next. Then his general fear turned to sharp terror as he heard and saw another figure splashing towards him in the darkness, gasping, distressed, and he remembered that he no longer had a knife . . .

Sixteen

SHE struggled to hold off despair. The two floating bodies she had so far found had both been Watchmen, to her intense relief, but there was still no sign of Willie Garvin. Now she was on the edge of the area where gas dispersing from the broken riser far below was causing loss of buoyancy.

This was what Jock Miller had spoken about. The riser was the steel pipe through which the drill was lowered to reach the sea bed. If gas was found, a period of testing followed, and this was the stage the Drioga exploration rig had reached. Wee Jock had said that the fracture of a riser containing gas was a critical danger which could sink a drillship in minutes if the fracture occurred at the mud-line. He had not been able to explain the phenomenon in scientific terms, but knew that it was brought about by a large area of water becoming effervescent. A break above the mud-line was less serious because the blowout preventer would come into operation and seal off the escape.

The sea here off Deserta Grande was charted as being three hundred feet deep, and Willie must have used the dead frogman's scuba gear to follow the riser down to the mud-line and set a charge to shatter it. There was no danger of his suffering from the bends following his ascent, since he would have been below for only a few minutes, but the shock effect of the explosion, transmitted through water, would be severe if he failed to get clear fast enough. It worried her that he might have been slowed down by the vicious cold of the sea at such a depth, for she knew he could not have found time to put on a wet-suit before the dive. And even a safe ascent would not have taken him out of danger, for by the time he surfaced the drillship would have been starting to sink, then to heel over, and the safety of anyone in the sea nearby at that time was in the lap of the gods.

She whistled again, and from somewhere to her right the same notes came back to her, feeble and breathy, as if made with difficulty. Relief swept her and she struck out in that direction for thirty yards or so, then trod water and whistled again. This time there was no response, and she felt her stomach clench with fear. An upturned canoe, one of the Canadian type canoes used by The Watchmen, drifted out of the darkness. She swam towards it. If paddles were strapped inside, and they might well be, this would hasten her search. As she threw an arm over the canoe's bottom she saw something white within inches of her face. It was a hand, a big hand, attached to an arm which curved over the bottom to the far side of the canoe, and on the back of the hand she could faintly make out an S-shaped scar.

She said, "Willie!" and ducked under the canoe to come up beside him. His shirt was gone but his knives were still in their harness. At first she thought he was unconscious, but when she slipped an arm about him and lifted his chin he peered through half closed eyes and muttered, "Couldn't get to you Princess . . . shoulder's bust and I'm . . . bit concussed . . . I – I think something fell on me."

Her anxiety was great, but her relief greater. He was alive, and she had found him. She said, "Hang on to me, Willie love. Hang on to my shoulders from behind while I get this canoe the right way up. Big lungful of air to keep you nice and buoyant while I'm doing it. Come on, now. Deep breath."

She managed the righting of the craft quickly, for she had done a lot of white-water canoeing and was experienced in the task. Getting Willie into it was another matter, for she could give little direct help. She slapped his face till he roused from his stupor, then for a long agonising minute she clung to one side of the canoe, providing a counterweight to his efforts to heave himself up over the bow on the far side, coaxing, urging, encouraging him. He managed it at last, and slumped in a face-down huddle. Very cautiously she eased herself over the stern and swivelled to take up her position, feeling new relief as she groped for a paddle and found two strapped below the gunnels.

Soon she had the canoe under way, using a C stroke to keep it moving in a straight line without having to change the paddle from side to side. Five minutes later Willie Garvin stirred and croaked, "Princess . . ?"

"I'm here, Willie. Soon have you aboard *The Sandpiper*. Are you cold?"

"A bit." His teeth were chattering. She stopped paddling, took off her shirt and leaned forward to spread it over his back and shoulders. It was thin and wet, but it would help retain a little of his body heat. He said, "Thanks, Princess. I could . . . try paddling one 'anded."

"Just lie still." She set the canoe moving again with a few long strokes. "Is it the collarbone?"

"Feels like it." His voice wavered. "Lucky, though. Didn't really know what would 'appen when the riser broke . . . or if anything would. Came up starboard side, astern that mother ship. Heard the shooting, so I swam west. Thought I might pick you up on the way to the rendezvous . . . but the ship started wallowing . . . then rolling over. Seemed like the whole bloody thing was falling on me. Not sure what 'appened next."

"Both ships went down." She kept her eyes on the dark silhouette of Deserta Grande, speaking softly, alert for any floating object that might damage the canoe. "The drillship's derrick fell right on top of the mother ship, and down they went. It was quite a spectacle, Willie. I was very impressed."

She heard a feeble chuckle, but his voice was a little steadier as he said, "You don't feel maybe I went over the top a bit?"

"No, I enjoyed the Cecil B. deMille touch myself." She thought it wise to keep him talking until he had gathered himself sufficiently to exert some measure of control over his body. It would do him no good to fall into the wrong kind of sleep now. She said, "How did you manage it?"

"Borrowed that dead frogman's scuba tank and gear . . . headlamp, too. I needed that. Used the box of RDX as extra weight to get me down. Found the riser easy enough. Spent a couple of minutes packing the stuff in under the protective 'ardware of the blowout preventer. Used me shirt to secure some of it. No problem about tamping. That pipe's under pressure of anything from eight to fifteen thousand pounds a square inch, so you've only got to crack her an' she'll do the rest herself. I 'ad three fused clock detonators and I used 'em all, just to make sure. Set them for two minutes, shoved them in, then took off like a shark was after me . . . but moving up at an angle so I wouldn't surface too fast."

When he paused she said, "I was worried about the shock effect."

"M'mm. With RDX you've got nearly three times the brisance of tetrol. Shock effect when she blew was pretty rough. Don't remember the last bit of the ascent. Must've surfaced and dumped the tank and mask. Found meself swimming 'ard just to stay afloat. No buoyancy. I wondered if the gas might ignite, or maybe put me to sleep, but I suppose it disperses too quick for that. Nothing 'appened till the ship started rolling over . . . and something fell on me. You all right, Princess?"

He had made it sound simple, but she knew that his underwater task in the utter blackness and crippling cold of those depths must have taxed even Willie Garvin's strength and will to their limits. She said, "All I got was a scratch on one hand. There's no justice." She looked about her. Apart from the prickle of lights ahead and to her right, marking the shore base, there was no sign of life anywhere. The small, self-contained world that had been the Drioga rig might never have existed.

Willie drew the shirt up over his cheek and said, "I think I'll 'ave a little rest now."

"All right. But don't go too deep, Willie. We'll be alongside *The Sandpiper* in another half hour."

"I'll take care, Princess."

She paddled steadily on, glad to have the wind at her back so that the swell helped rather than hindered her, for the two-man canoe was not easy to handle with one paddle. Her eyes moved constantly from the southern end of the dark hump of land to the sea immediately ahead and about her, then to the still figure of Willie Garvin, lying with knees drawn up, huddled at her feet in the little craft, almost invisible with her black shirt covering him.

Fifteen minutes later she rounded the point of the island, and another fifteen brought her to the small inlet where *The Sandpiper* lay hidden. Willie's breathing had become quiet and regular, and he no longer shivered as he slept. Here, close against the steeply rising shore, it was very dark, and only the faint gleam from furled sails told of *The Sandpiper's* presence. She slowed the canoe, allowing it to coast gently alongside, and was only a boat-hook's length from the yacht when a strong beam of light hit her in the face and a penetrating voice said calmly. "Hold the paddle above your head, Miss Blaise. With both hands. And please don't attempt to touch that automatic you're wearing. I hold a submachine-gun, and Hugh Oberon a point four-five automatic."

Oberon's voice said, "Do it, you bitch! But *slowly.*" She had never heard a voice inject so much hatred into six words.

For an endless moment she fought a tooth-and-claw inner battle against shock, fear, and panic, but even as she did so a part of her mind was assessing the new situation. She remembered the motor boat pulling away from the area where the ships had gone down. St. Maur and Oberon . . . yes, if any were more likely than others to come out of that alive, it would be these two. And she knew they were not bluffing. One hint of a wrong move and they would riddle her. She felt surprise that they had not done so already.

She held the paddle above her head in both hands, eyes half closed against the dazzle of the flashlamp, and felt the bow of the canoe bump gently against the yacht's side. As her pupils began to adjust, she dimly saw a boat-hook reach out to catch the gunnel and draw the canoe close alongside. The flashlamp went out and the deck-lamps were turned on. The Earl St. Maur stood looking down at her, a Sterling with the stock folded aimed in one hand, boat-hook in the other. A moment later Oberon was standing beside him, holding the Colt Commander she had seen in his hand many hours before, in the drillship's hospital ward.

St. Maur said, "Where's Garvin?"

She kept all expression from her eyes, looking up at him steadily, and said in a tired flat voice, "I couldn't find him."

"What do you mean?"

"What I say. We split up, and when the ships went down I swam to a rendezvous point we'd arranged. He wasn't there. After a while I found this canoe and searched for him. I couldn't find him. I was hoping he'd made it back here somehow."

They didn't know. The canoe had been moving obliquely up to the yacht when the light hit her, then the beam had focused more closely on her as the canoe was drawn alongside, and neither man had seen Willie curled up at her feet, her shirt covering him from waist almost to brow. Now, with only the deck lights on, the canoe lay in the shadow of the yacht's side. *And they still didn't know.*

St. Maur said, "Turn so you can place the paddle slowly on the yacht's deck. Good. Now release it and place your hands flat. No quick movements please. Good. Now crawl aboard, remaining on hands and knees."

She obeyed. The Star automatic was still in its holster under her left breast, and St. Maur must have seen it plainly. As she crawled on to the yacht's deck the two men separated so that they covered her from both sides. She wondered why they had made no move to take her gun or make her lay it down, and realised that there could be only one answer. What had happened tonight must have given her a reputation of such dimensions that they were handling her as if she had been radio-active. Death to touch. Don't get within reach and don't allow her hands anywhere near her gun, that was the policy. St. Maur's policy.

He said, "Crawl forward. Turn towards us. Now remain kneeling, but upright, with hands on your head. Very slowly."

Again she obeyed. They wore Watchmen battledress, but without head masks. Their clothes were as wet as hers. They stood a couple of paces apart, automatic and submachine-gun aimed, their backs to the rail. Willie Garvin had not stirred at the startling moment of first encounter, and she did not yet know if he had woken or still slept.

Oberon stood wordless, eyes burning as he looked at her. St. Maur said, "You've been rather unfortunate. We used this inlet during our manoeuvres, so one of our sections discovered your yacht here last night, after we'd caught you."

She looked him steadily in the eyes and said sharply, "You want to wake up. Wake up and listen to me."

He frowned slightly. "What?"

Her words had been intended for Willie Garvin. She hoped they had reached him. With a small shrug she said, "Be realistic. You're finished, unless you make a deal with me."

Oberon made a wordless sound of protest. His lust to destroy her was so intense she could almost feel it radiating from him. St. Maur said coldly, "Get hold of yourself, Hugh." Then, to Modesty: "We're far from finished, Miss Blaise. It's a great pity that my advice was over-ruled earlier. I knew very well that the correct thing to do was to kill you and Garvin right away, but some of these chaps like Golitsyn are too clever by half. Bloody man wanted you kept alive for disinformation, and this is the result."

For the first time a hint of passion crept into his hard metallic voice. "You have ruined Operation Morningstar and destroyed most of The Watchmen. In so doing you have delayed the coming of stability and prosperity to our country by as much as five years, to your eternal shame, Miss Blaise. But it's not the end of the story, I assure you. With you and Garvin dead, there will be nobody left to connect me with The Watchmen. The foundering of the Drioga drillship will be a maritime tragedy, no more. And I shall re-establish contact with the people behind Golitsyn. I shall rebuild The Watchmen."

She prayed that Willie Garvin was alert now. That he had grasped what was happening. That the canoe had not drifted away. That he was not too badly injured to take action. She said quietly, "I spoke of a deal just now." Her eyes moved to Oberon, and her voice became strong, forceful. "Would *you* deal with the noble lord, when convenient?"

Oberon gazed at her with murderous eyes, so consumed by passion that he seemed not to hear her words. She hoped Willie Garvin had heard them, and had realised they were meant for him. St. Maur said brusquely, "I don't know what you're talking about, and I don't much care. There will be no deal. I didn't kill you at once because I want to know how you and Garvin managed to sink the drillship. That's a very important piece of information, and if you give it immediately you'll have a quick death. If you don't, you'll die very slowly and painfully. You understand?"

Oberon said in a thick voice. "I'll make her talk, Major. I'll do it with my hands . . . just my hands." He began to holster his gun, taking a half pace forward.

St. Maur's voice was not loud, but it cut like a knife. "Stand *still*. And keep her covered."

Oberon froze. St. Maur said, "You will *not* approach her until I tell you to do so, Hugh. If she fails to talk, then on my word of command you will shoot her in both elbows from where you stand. Then you may approach her to carry out intensive interrogation."

There was a little silence. She acknowledged to herself that Willie Garvin must still be unconscious, and with part of her mind she prepared herself for the action of drawing her gun, mentally shutting out the knowledge that there could be no hope of dropping both men before they killed her. Neither her body nor her expression gave the slightest forewarning of her intention.

She said, "I'll take the quick way, thanks. But explaining how we sank the drillship is a little complicated, so —"

There came a sound, a soft impact, and suddenly a slim black object a few inches long was clinging to the side of St. Maur's neck, just under the jaw-bone and a little to the rear, downward angled, and she knew it was the hilt of Willie Garvin's knife, thrown from the canoe she could not see, thrown to kill instantly, with the blade slicing through the carotid artery, and she was falling to her left as the gun sagged, a short burst of fire hitting the deck timbers close to St. Maur's feet with the tightening of his finger by reflex on the trigger as he died. For less than half a second Oberon's eyes had left her, and in that time she drew and fired, once before her left shoulder hit the deck, his own shot passing inches above her, and again an instant later. Her first bullet hit him somewhere in the chest, and her second in the head. Both men had been standing close to the rail. St. Maur was still crumpling forward when the double impact of the .45 bullets threw Oberon back. His legs caught the low rail behind him and he was gone.

From below the gunnel a voice croaked, "Princess . . . ?"

She got to her feet and moved to the side, stepping over St. Maur's body. The canoe was a little further forrard than it had been, and a yard from the yacht's side. In it, Willie Garvin lay on his back, a second knife poised in his hand. He exhaled a long breath of relief as he saw her, and lowered the knife. "Christ," he said hoarsely, "that was a bit close."

"Close enough." She holstered the gun, picked up the boat-hook and drew the canoe alongside, her hands not quite steady now. "Nice throw, Willie."

"Sorry I was so long about it." He pulled himself slowly to his knees. "Took me 'alf an hour to turn over and get the knife out, then I 'ad to push the canoe out a bit, just to get sight of the bastard's 'ead."

She knelt to help him as he crawled aboard, and said, "I don't think it was quite half an hour."

"Honest?"

She smiled, and steered him to sit on a deck locker. "I want to get that shoulder strapped up, but can you hang on for ten minutes?"

"No sweat." His face was pale under the deck lights. "Going to start the engine and get clear of 'ere?"

"Yes. I doubt if anyone else is going to trouble us, but we might as well make sure. Anyway, we want to be out in the open for radio communication." She glanced at the body of St. Maur. "Better keep him for Tarrant to deal with. Once we're under way I'll see to that shoulder and get you to bed." She consulted her inner clock. "By then it'll be about time for Weng's listening out schedule."

When she had lifted the anchor and started the engine Willie said, "Weng can ring Jack Fraser, and Fraser's bound to 'ave short-wave radio contact with Tarrant, either on Madeira or Porto Santo. They might even manage to patch you through radio-phone-radio so you can talk direct to Tarrant."

She was at the wheel now, taking the motor sailer slowly out of the inlet. "I hadn't thought of that," she said. "But wouldn't it be simpler for Fraser to give Tarrant our frequency? Then we'll only be talking across twelve miles or so."

Willie Garvin began to laugh, winced, supported his right arm carefully with his left, and shook his head apologetically. "Sorry. I'm getting slow."

"No. Just tired, Willie love. But we'll soon do something about that."

He did not argue. In another few minutes she would set the yacht's automatic steering, take him into the cabin, strap his shoulder, patch any other hurts, undress him and get him into his bunk with a mug of coffee laced with rum. Then she would contact Weng, and through him, Tarrant. Certainly she would not approach Madeira with the dead St. Maur aboard until she had spoken with Tarrant. Over the air she would have to use free cryptic to give him the essence of the situation, but that would be easy enough, for they had points of reference which would be unknown to any chance listeners. *"We've found the place the rockhound was looking for. The people here were going to join your party tonight but they met with too much trouble."* Rockhound equals Ben Christie. That would be enough for Tarrant.

The motor sailer moved slowly away from the dark upthrust of land that was Deserta Grande. Willie Garvin looked about him. The night was dark, but still young. On Porto Santo the farewell dinner for the western world's Presidents and Prime Ministers would not yet have begun.

It was probable that Tarrant would use one of the security craft to rendezvous with *The Sandpiper* at sea, off Deserta Grande, so that he could get the full picture from Modesty before deciding what action to take. And then . . .

Then, thought Willie Garvin sleepily, there was going to be a right old mess for someone to sort out.

Seventeen

"IT was a frightful shock, of course," said Victoria, Countess St. Maur sorrowfully. "When they rang from Lisbon to say poor old Ronnie had drowned in a boating accident, I was really quite thrown for a while. Still, life must go on, and when you take a fall you simply have to get mounted again and carry on, don't you?"

"Yes," Ferdie Clarkson said, wincing a little. "Would you mind easing the grip a bit, old thing?"

"Eh? Oh, sorry." She relaxed her powerful thighs, and the man she was kneeling astride heaved a breath of relief. "But don't you go dozing off, Ferdie," she admonished him.

"Of course not, Vicky. But there's no rush, is there? I mean, with poor old Ronnie not around any more we don't have to be out of the cottage by four, do we?"

"Oh no, we can go on for simply ages. You know, a nice man came to see me about Ronnie a week later. Professor Collins, or something like that. No, Collier. That's right. A very nice man. He was sort of involved, you see, because he'd been out early-morning fishing off Cascais, and he saw poor old Ronnie's sailing boat suddenly sort of turn over and go down, just like that. He was the only witness, Professor Collier I mean, and he tried to find Ronnie, but he was too late. I thought it was very kind of him to call and tell me what had happened." Victoria, Countess St. Maur rotated her ample buttocks. "I asked him to stay for lunch, but he had to get back to town," she added regretfully.

Ferdie Clarkson said, "I didn't know old Ronnie went in for early-morning boating."

"Neither did I. But when I come to think of it I realise I never really knew much about him anyway. He was always very busy, popping off and doing things, you know."

She dismounted from Ferdie and knelt beside him on the bed, eyeing him with a purposeful smile. "Your turn for a gallop, Ferdie, and I must say you look in jolly good fettle." She reached out to the chair where her clothes lay, and picked up the black headscarf she had worn for riding since her husband's death. "Come on, old thing, get mounted. Tight seat, loose rein, and off we go."

❖   ❖   ❖   ❖   ❖

"How's the shoulder now?"

"Agonising. I'll need any amount of cosseting. Hang on a tick, 'ere's the next stile." Willie Garvin picked the blind girl up by her slender waist and lifted her over.

"Show off," said Collier.

They were following the footpath across the fields that lay between Modesty's cottage and the village of Benildon, in Wiltshire, returning from the White Hart where they had gone for a Sunday morning drink at Modesty's urging while she prepared lunch.

"Dinah's lost weight, you're not looking after 'er properly," said Willie as he climbed the stile.

"Ha! And whose fault's that?" Collier demanded aggressively. "From the moment you and Modesty vanished into the blue and Weng couldn't say where, she started worrying herself sick about the pair of you. So what happens? You both come back more or less in one piece, or two pieces I suppose, but I end up with an emaciated wife."

"You were just as bad," said Dinah, "going through the papers with a toothcomb every morning, spilling your cornflakes, being bad tempered, forgetting where you'd parked the car."

"Oh rubbish, that's just senility, sweetheart. I gave up worrying about the pair of them long ago. Besides, what were their dangers compared to mine? Yet are they emaciated? Did any of you fret away so much as one poor scruple of flesh on my account?"

Dinah said, "What were your dangers, tiger?"

"My darling, how can you ask? I walked unarmed into a room occupied by the countess, widow of the late Earl St. Maur, didn't I? I should have been provided with a whip and a chair, and had men on hand with pistols ready to fire blanks. God knows why Tarrant picked on *me* for that charade, anyway."

Willie took Dinah's arm and they moved on along the footpath. "It 'ad to be somebody in the know, Steve," he said, "and there aren't many about. Tarrant didn't want to use one of 'is professionals. He wanted someone with an impeccable background, to give the story artistic verisimilitude." Willie pressed Dinah's arm. "Someone intelligent, suave, reliable, and well known in academic circles."

"Ah, I can see his point," Collier acknowledged graciously. "But I wasn't warned of the danger, was I?"

Dinah said, "Oh, come on. Are you sticking to this story that you nearly got raped by a countess?"

"You weren't there," said her husband with feeling. "She'd just returned from a ride, and she received me in the stables. I tell you, if old Collier hadn't put in a bit of very nifty footwork she'd have had her wicked way with him there and then in the straw. She wears tight riding breeches, which means you can see what her thighs are like, and they're . . . well, daunting to say the least. Even her horse looked a bit compressed in the middle to me."

Dinah said, "Sounds like you passed up the experience of a lifetime, honey."

"It would have been my last experience. We moved into the house for sherry, and with it came an invitation to lunch, declined, followed by an extraordinary peripatetic conversation in which we covered quite a distance, including three occasions when I only just got out of a corner before she trapped me. I was petrified." Collier shook his head solemnly. "If that woman had managed to get me between her legs I'd have ended up like an empty toothpaste tube. Next time Tarrant wants a job like that done he can send Willie. I'll do the easy bits, like sinking drillships."

Willie looked down the grassy hill to the cottage. "You can tell Tarrant now," he said. "That's his car down there."

❖   ❖   ❖   ❖   ❖

"I didn't know you made bread," said Tarrant. He sat on a tall stool in the kitchen, a tankard of beer at his elbow, watching her.

She lifted a big lump of dough from her mixing bowl, set it down on a board, and began to knead. "I bake okay wholemeal bread," she said, "not marvellous bread, just okay. But that doesn't matter. What matters is that bread's the oldest and most primitive of foods made by man, and there's a sort of earth magic about making it. You get your soul cleansed a bit." She glanced at him with laughter in her eyes. "Mine can do with it."

"Of course." He drank some of his beer, watching the play of her forearms as she turned and knuckled the dough. It wasn't easy to accept that this was the same woman he had met on a dark sea north of Deserta Grande three weeks ago, to hear from her lips a story so horrifying that he had actually felt his scalp creep as he imagined what might have happened. After a while he said, "You haven't asked how we're playing this Watchmen business."

She paused to rub the tip of her nose with the back of a wrist. "I can guess some of it from reading the papers. You kept Willie's name and mine right out of it, as we asked, and beyond that I'm not particularly interested. You'll stay to lunch?"

"I was banking on you inviting me to do so," Tarrant said honestly.

"Good. I gather the whole of The Watchmen involvement has been hushed up, and the noble earl died in a boating accident. Steve Collier is very amusing about his visit to the grieving widow when you used him to give the story conviction. And the Drioga sinking was just one of those accidents that sometimes happen at sea."

"Yes. At a very hasty conference on Porto Santo next morning, when the heads of state and of government postponed their departure, it was agreed to keep the matter under wraps until an investigation showed whether it could be pinned on the Russians. In the event we were fortunate." Tarrant paused to drink from his tankard. "We carried out a large clearing up operation on and around Deserta Grande," he went on, "and quite a few bodies were picked up from the sea. About a dozen Watchmen had found their way back to Deserta Grande, and these were rounded up and handed over to the Portuguese. I don't think they'll be seen again. The Portuguese were almost foaming at the mouth over what had very nearly happened on their territory."

"I'm not surprised. That plan would have worked, you know."

"I do indeed know. We had the good fortune to find, in a hut on the island, a complete typescript of the operational plan. We also picked up Golitsyn among the floating bodies, and in general collected more than enough evidence to lay responsibility where it belongs."

"But you haven't broken the story."

"No. The Americans opined, and we agreed, that a colossal open row would be what they call counterproductive. But Moscow knows that we know the truth, and although they would deny it, they're terrified of it being revealed. So the policy is to use it as leverage in the arms limitation talks. We think it could give the west an edge at the negotiating table for as long as five years. In fact I've had word from my CIA colleague at Langley that the SALT negotiators are over the moon about it. He asked me to give his warmest regards to Modesty Blaise and Willie Garvin."

She looked up sharply. "You said you'd keep us out of it."

He spread a hand. "My dear, I've done so. But I had to pass on what Golitsyn told you about the ancillary assaults in Bucharest and Belgrade, which made it plain that I had contact with some person or persons who had penetrated right to the heart of the affair. It was also fairly obvious that the drillship sinking had been contrived by the same person or persons. With the *Baystrike* operation so recent, CIA would have in mind and also on file your own part in that, including your reaction to Ben Christie's murder. They had only to run through their computer what they know about you and Willie and me, and the answer would come out with something like ninety-five percent probability."

"But you made no admission that they'd guessed right?"

"Of course not. The French guessed right, too. René Vaubois said he recognised the style. I don't know about other countries, but in any event the whole thing is being handled at very top level and with very tight security. Which reminds me . . ." He drew a long envelope from his pocket and took from it two pieces of paper. "I'm afraid you're going to be angry about this."

She paused in her kneading to look at him with mild surprise. "Angry?"

He nodded sombrely. "I fear so. You see —"

"No wait." She gestured with a floury hand and gave him a small, self-mocking smile. "Please wait till I've finished. I don't want to be angry while I'm making bread."

"Of course. I wouldn't wish to spoil your earth magic."

He watched in silence for a few minutes. When the kneading was done she cut the dough into four pieces, put each in a baking tin, and set them to prove under a damp cloth. As she put the mixing bowl in the sink and began to wash her hands she said thoughtfully, "I don't think I get angry very easily. What is it, Sir Gerald?"

"Well . . . you understand that it wasn't possible for me to withhold your identity from the government minister to whom I'm responsible?"

She grimaced. "I suppose not. But I detest that man Foley. He's so bumptious."

"I share your opinion." Tarrant laid the two papers on the kitchen table. "But he has instructed me to ensure that you and Willie sign acknowledgments that you are subject to the Official Secrets Act and will not divulge any information you may have obtained concerning The Watchmen and Operation Morningstar."

She froze in the act of drying her hands and said, "*What?*"

Tarrant shrugged apologetically. "He's that sort of person, my dear."

Her eyes were dark with anger. "Willie and I aren't civil servants or in the forces, and your minister has no right to tell us to keep our mouths shut. The last thing we want is to talk about what happened, but that's not the point. Why didn't you tell him to get lost? Politely, of course."

"I rather hoped for better things," Tarrant said vaguely and somewhat obscurely. "He'll be vastly annoyed if you don't sign, my dear."

"Will he?" She drew in a long breath, lips tight. "We could have swum quietly away from that drillship with no trouble, and let

Morningstar go ahead, but Willie Garvin damn near got himself killed to save those people on Porto Santo. All right, we want to be anonymous, so Willie doesn't expect a thank you, but we also don't expect a peremptory demand of this kind from that arrogant sod of a minister."

"I'm afraid Foley is that sort of person," Tarrant said again, regretfully.

She opened the oven door to check the roast. "He's the sort of person who brings out the worst in me," she said angrily, "so just go back and tell him he can take his wretched bits of paper, unsigned, and stuff them up his ministerial arse."

Tarrant looked shocked. "You surely don't mean that, Modesty?"

"No, I'll amend it." She began to baste the potatoes. "Tell him to roll them up tightly, set fire to them, and *then* stuff them up."

Tarrant gave a long sigh, beamed with pleasure, and took a notebook from his pocket. "I must write that down to make sure I have it quite correct," he said happily. "I was hoping I might goad you to a little rare vulgarity."

She closed the oven door and stared. "What are you up to?"

He was writing carefully. "This is so much better than any protest of mine could have been. Now let me see . . . roll them up tightly, wasn't it? The point is, I have to meet with Foley and the P.M. tomorrow to make a final report on this matter. Now, when you give an account of a conversation to Foley he won't accept a paraphrase, but has a habit of interrupting with the words, 'Yes, but what *exactly* did he say?'" Tarrant paused and looked up. "Was it stick it up or stuff it up, Modesty?"

She was beginning to laugh. "Stuff, I think."

"Thank you. I simply love the adjective 'ministerial'. I told Foley I would see you today, so at some point during the meeting tomorrow he'll ask what happened, and I shall tell him you refused to sign, and he'll be very cross and say, 'Yes, but what *exactly* did she say?'" Tarrant finished writing and gave a sigh of anticipatory pleasure. "And then I shall take out my notebook and read him your very words, my dear. It's going to be a splendid moment. I rather think the P.M. will enjoy it, too."

She took off her apron. "You're a thoroughly wicked old gentleman, you know." Through the window she saw three figures approaching across the field. "Here comes Willie with the Colliers. You should have tried your goading on Steve. He'd have given you a masterly bit of vituperation."

"Yours will do."

She smiled. "Better not try it on Willie. He won't say much, but he's a genius at devising the most apt retribution."

Tarrant winced, recalling a particular occasion. "I can bear witness to that," he said with feeling. A sudden gleam came into his eyes, and he went to stand beside Modesty at the window. Collier was holding open the wrought iron gate in the low wall, bowing as Willie and Dinah passed through arm in arm.

"What a splendid idea," Tarrant said softly, but with immense relish. "The Garvin boy is indeed a master in such matters. Oh, what a truly splendid idea."